Even through the thin shirt he could feel the heat of her skin, and his fingers tightened.

His temperature spiked as his gaze lingered on her. He justified the need rumbling through him by thinking about the adrenaline aftermath. Never mind that he'd never had the desire to kiss anyone else but her after a work takedown. Seeing those big eyes and soul-stealing face, he felt his common sense go on the fritz.

It had always been this way between them. Hot and pulsing, both desperate to get the other into bed. They could communicate between the sheets. Real life was the problem.

HelenKay
DIMON

FEARLESS

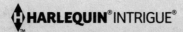

This one is dedicated to all the readers who requested another miniseries. I hope you enjoy the Corcoran Team!

Recycling programs for this product may not exist in your area.

ISBN-13: 978-0-373-74755-9

FEARLESS

Copyright © 2013 by HelenKay Dimon

Printed in U.S.A.

™ www.Harlequin.com

ABOUT THE AUTHOR

Award-winning author HelenKay Dimon spent twelve years in the most unromantic career ever—divorce lawyer. After dedicating all that effort to helping people terminate relationships, she is thrilled to deal in happy endings and write romance novels for a living. Now her days are filled with gardening, writing, reading and spending time with her family in and around San Diego. HelenKay loves hearing from readers, so stop by her website, www.helenkaydimon.com, and say hello.

Books by HelenKay Dimon

HARLEQUIN INTRIGUE

*Mystery Men
**Corcoran Team

CAST OF CHARACTERS

Davis Weeks—A former agent with the Defense Intelligence Agency and current member of the Corcoran Team.

Lara Bart—When everything goes wild and the shooting starts, Lara runs straight into the strong arms of the man who broke her heart.

Martin Coughlin—He's up for the promotion of a lifetime and a powerful position in NCIS.

Nancy Coughlin—Martin's wife. She doesn't need his money to run in D.C.'s most powerful social circles, but she does value her public image…maybe above everything else.

Clive Ebersole—Someone is paying Clive to bury very dangerous secrets. But who is really in charge?

Ronald Worth—The Deputy Director of NCIS. Old friendship and deep loyalties have the Corcoran Team investigating the stern and dedicated retired military officer's alliances.

John Gallagher—Nancy's right-hand man. He spends his days behind a desk, but is there more to him than there seems to be?

Pax Weeks—Davis's brother and fellow Corcoran team member. He is the person Davis trusts, but family secrets threaten their bond.

Connor Bowen—The leader of the Corcoran Team. He is the person everyone counts on to have a plan when the bullets start flying, but he is not sure who to trust this time.

Chapter One

Lara Bart picked up her ice water and used her palm to wipe away the puddle left behind on the coffee table. Drops slid down the side of the glass, making her hand slip. She fought the urge to dump the contents down her shirt or at least close the dull brown curtains outlining the window to the right of her chair. The sun pounded on her, filling the twelve-foot-square room with bright light and an almost unbearable heat.

It was summer in Washington, D.C. Between the soaring temperatures and bone-melting humidity she'd already lost the battle with frizz. She could feel her hair morphing from wavy to wide as she sat in the non–air-conditioned, seemingly airtight Capitol Hill brownstone belonging to Lieutenant Commander Steve Wasserman. She had to interview the man as part of a security-clearance check for Martin Coughlin, a retired navy lieutenant looking to obtain a new position with the Naval Criminal Investigative Service.

Steve and Martin had been roommates at the Naval Academy years ago, which was why she sat in the rolling heat with the backs of her thighs stuck to the leather chair and the sweat soaking through her silk blouse and seeping into her navy blazer. She had to talk with people from Martin's past and those familiar with his current life.

And because her luck was at an all-time low, this assignment qualified as a rush. Her boss at Hampton Enterprises, the private firm contracted with the Department of Defense to conduct clearance interviews, said to make this one a priority. Apparently, someone at NCIS wanted Martin hired on there and fast. That meant long hours of searching through records and asking questions, followed by a ton of paperwork.

Not that anyone cared how inconvenient a work rush was for her on top of her regular clearance caseload. That much was evident from the fact Steve had disappeared into his kitchen ten minutes ago and hadn't said a word or bothered to come out since. A wall blocked her view, but she didn't even hear him clanging around in there as expected. He'd got a message on his cell and excused himself, and she'd been stuck in the makeshift sauna alone ever since.

So much for the idea of beating the Thursday afternoon rush-hour traffic back to her condo in Alexandria, Virginia. She'd likely sit on the 14th

Street Bridge forever. Good thing she'd grabbed that granola bar before she headed out earlier today.

A loud scrape that sounded like someone dragging a chair across tile broke through her internal grumbling. She waited for another sound, for anything, but the narrow brownstone remained quiet except for the loud tick of the antique clock above the fireplace as the minutes slowly passed. Because she hated having her time wasted, she stood up, ignoring the ripping sound of her skin against the chair and the sharp sting. Despite her host's lack of social skills, this time she put her glass down on a magazine. No need to take her frustration out on his furniture.

Her shoes fell silent on the beige carpet. In two steps she was at the kitchen doorway. Her gaze went to the open back door and the small patio beyond. It took her a second longer to notice the brown shoes and khakis sticking out from behind the butcher-block island.

Guy on the floor. Her mind rushed to fill in the blanks. At fortysomething and in good shape, Steve seemed young for a heart attack. That probably meant he'd somehow fallen without making a sound.

And here she had been sitting in the other room complaining. Tiny pricks of guilt stabbed her as she switched to rescue mode. She grabbed the cell in her blazer pocket as she turned the corner and slipped farther into the kitchen, intending to perform CPR as she called for help. Her fingers fumbled on the buttons so she stopped her rush and looked down, trying to concentrate on dialing something as simple as 9-1-1.

"Who are you?"

The male voice had her head jerking up again. Her gaze bounced to her far right. There in the corner near the sink and tucked behind the oversize refrigerator stood a man. He had brown hair and a furious glare, but the real problem was the knife in his hand.

Her gaze bounced back to Steve's still form. For the first time she noticed the circle of dark red pooling beneath his body and spreading across the once off-white tiles.

"I didn't…" She cupped the phone in her palm and slipped it back in her jacket as she tried to maneuver back out of the room. "I'll just go."

Before she could turn and run, the man pounced. Just as the scream left her lungs, he grabbed from behind and around her middle, choking off all sound. The move trapped her arms to her sides and squeezed the air out of her lungs. She coughed as her gaze darted around the room for some way out of this strange nightmare.

She opened her mouth again and his beefy palm settled over her mouth. "Oh, no, princess. Not one word."

She strained and shoved her shoulders against his hold. Her neck ached from stretching and the activity exhausted her, but he didn't even move. His hand muffled her screams and her lungs burned from the effort. When she finally collapsed against him, she stiffened and moved away from him again just as fast.

Fear threatened to swamp her. She heard a roaring in her ears and her heart thumped so hard she was surprised she couldn't see it through her shirt.

"You picked the wrong day to visit your boyfriend." The attacker's hot breath blew across her cheek as he spoke.

His sick laugh rumbled through her senses and dark spots swam in front of her eyes. To keep from passing out, because that had to be the worst idea ever in this type of situation, she forced her breathing to slow. One more beat at the current speed and she'd be doubled over hyperventilating.

As she struggled to regain control of her body, words raced through her mind, blurred and garbled. She closed her eyes for a second, trying to concentrate and bring them into focus.

Stay calm. Remember what I taught you.

Like that, anxiety stopped pinging around inside of her. Her ex wasn't in the room but she could hear his voice inside her head. He was an expert at self-defense and at breaking a woman's heart. Only the former mattered right now. A brief mental review of the skills he'd taught her stopped the room from spinning.

In a span of seconds her brain rebooted. She let

her body go completely limp as she gathered her energy reserves for a big play.

The attacker tossed her around as he walked into the family room. When he finally stopped, he lifted his hand from her mouth but kept it hovering there, ready to slap against her lips again. "Are you going to be a good girl, princess?"

She nodded. Relief crashed through her a heartbeat later when the tight constriction around her chest eased. The man still held her, could crush her windpipe or any other body part if he wanted, but she could breathe without panting again. Oxygen flooded her brain as she waited for her chance.

"Thank you," she whispered, trying to sound grateful and submissive and whatever else this guy needed to feel confident in his power over her.

He spun her around. Only a foot of space separated them as his fingers dug into her upper arms. "What are you doing here?"

"Work."

He leaned in. "What kind?"

Now. She lifted her knee, putting all of her strength behind it, every ounce of will and the adrenaline flowing through her, and nailed him right between the legs. His mouth moved but nothing except a tiny squeak came out. His hands slid down her arms, all pressure from his fingertips gone, as he fell to the floor in a whoosh.

He groaned and swore as he rolled around. After

rocking a few times, he tucked into the fetal position and stayed there. Then his breath came back full force. The furious whispering started, filled with swearing and what he planned to do to her before he snapped her neck.

She blocked the words, refused to be paralyzed by them. She had to move and wouldn't get a better opportunity. She shifted around his prone body, ignoring the thrashing and threats. She'd almost stepped to freedom when his big hand clamped around her ankle.

With his body still bent over, his furious gaze stayed on her. He twisted and pulled until she hopped on one foot. She let him drag her closer as she fought for balance. It was either give in to his strength or topple over him and she knew if that happened, she was a dead woman. He'd made that clear.

"Where do you think you're going?" He almost spit as he talked.

The fury in his tone whiplashed around her. Her mind went blank except for one thing—escape. With one hand pressed against the side of the couch, she reached out, trying to grab for the lamp sitting on the table behind it. As he pulled hand over hand, bringing her closer, she stretched out to full length, ignoring his nails as they dug into her skin.

Keeping her focus on the target, she waved her hand and her fingertips brushed against the shade. The base wobbled and thudded against the wood.

Her breath caught as she waited for it to bobble then fall out of reach, but luck was on her side this one time.

With one last lunge she slapped her palm around the long stem and held on. Yanking as hard as she could, she ripped the cord from the wall and dragged the lamp over the back of the sofa toward her chest.

A ripping sound cut through the room as the top of the lamp broke through the shade. She ignored the pain shooting up her leg and the heavy weight in her hand. Pivoting, she turned and held her unexpected weapon directly over her attacker's head. And let go.

His eyes popped wide and he yelled as he moved his head on the carpet. At the last second, he let go of her and folded his arms over his face to ward off the inevitable blow.

Suddenly free, her body went flying from the momentum. She stumbled as balance completely abandoned her. Next thing she hit the floor on her knees and heard a crack. Biting through her lip to beat back the sudden thumping in her knee and scrambling on all fours, she shuffled across the carpet.

The slide against the rug burned her skin and something sharp on the floor dug into her palm. She gave a quick tug to her purse strap where it sat next to her abandoned chair a few feet away, and the contents spilled all over the floor. She grabbed for her keys and left everything else behind.

With a push, she got to her feet. One knee buckled as a sharp sting stole her breath. She ignored it all, keeping her focus on the front door. Freedom sat a few steps away, and she had to get there before her attacker showed off a new weapon. She saw the knife but he could be hiding anything anywhere.

She looked over her shoulder one last time as her hand closed over the doorknob. Her attacker had almost reached a sitting position as he felt around him for something.

Now or never.

Throwing the door open, she tripped across the threshold and down the three steps to the walkway. Every cell inside her told her to look back and see how close he was. She pushed it all away.

After a chirp, the car's locks clicked. Her hands shook as she opened the door and threw her body across the seat. From the corner of her eye she saw a shadow. The attacker stood in the doorway with his hands braced against the sides of the jamb.

When he started down the stairs her heartbeat kicked up until the hammering filled the car. The keys jangled in her hand as she tried to shove them in the ignition. Once, twice, three times she missed, clicking against the steering column. Finally one fit into the slot and she turned it hard enough to twist the metal.

Just as the attacker reached the side of the car, she slammed her elbow against the lock and jammed the gas pedal to the floor. He smacked his hand against the driver's-side window and she put all her weight on that pedal. The tires squealed and her nine-year-old car fishtailed out of the parking space and onto the one-way street, barely missing the motorcycle parked across the street.

With fingers locked around the wheel, she wrestled to keep the front end from smashing into a car right in front of her. This area of town consisted of narrow streets packed with brownstone residents who juggled on-street parking regulations on a daily basis. Her only goal at the moment was to keep from pinging through there like a pinball. And to keep moving.

She ran the stop sign and flew down the street at a speed guaranteed to get her a ticket, and right then she'd kill to see a police car. A few people standing on the sidewalks yelled at her and one shook his fist. Their neighborhood-watch outrage was the least of her worries right now.

Taking the corner too fast, she ripped around to the left at the next intersection and didn't stop while her heartbeat still clanged in her ears. Up ahead she saw a red light and traffic flow in both directions. With her eyes closed or open, no way could she pass through there and live. She needed an alternate route, but she didn't know this part of town well enough to know the best ways in and out.

Easing over, she hooked a right and flew down

another residential street. When she finally eased up on the gas, the shaking in her hands had moved to her entire body. Every cell and muscle trembled. She hadn't realized she was mumbling and gulping in breaths until the fog clouding her brain cleared a little.

She let the car slow to a stop as she pulled into a space reserved for buses. Checking the rearview mirror for the hundredth time, she scanned the street, looking for anyone who might be following. Cars passed and people walked by—a few even stared at the lady drawing in deep breaths as she sat frozen in place. But all that mattered was she didn't see the attacker.

Once the air flowed inside her at a normal rate again, she fumbled around in her jacket pocket and grabbed her cell. This time she skipped a frantic emergency call to the police. She needed the one man she'd vowed never to call again—Davis Weeks, her ex-fiancé and the same man who specialized in crazy combat skills and secretive missions.

He would know what to do. He always did.

Chapter Two

Davis Weeks rubbed his eyes as he walked out of his bathroom, fresh from a shower. Thanks to the sticky Maryland summer heat, he didn't bother changing out of the towel wrapped around his waist. He was tempted to let it fall to the hardwood floor and stand naked in front of the fan. But because he could see the narrow street one floor down from this position, he decided to keep something on. No need to scare the crap out of poor Mrs. Winston next door. The woman had to be over eighty, though from the way she winked at him all the time he wondered if she'd enjoy the show.

Sweat dripped down his back just from the ten-foot march from the bathroom to the bedroom window. Man, it was hot. That would teach him to buy a run-down town house in Annapolis then not be home long enough to fix it up or figure out some sort of air-conditioning solution.

Between the massive summer thunderstorms and the tropical storm that had blown up the coast earlier in the week, the small strip of land behind his house, listed as a backyard on the real-estate sales contract, had morphed into a muddy mess. He'd just burned off some of the extra energy rumbling around inside him by laying gravel over the driveway off the alley.

Why he'd picked a humid afternoon for the task had more to do with being limited to desk-job duties at work than anything else. He wasn't the sit-around type.

Now his muscles ached and his lower back begged for mercy. Three months shy of his thirty-fifth birthday and his bones creaked. He chalked the new pains up to too many years of chasing, shooting and diving for cover. He used to recover from jobs within a day or two. This time he neared day ten and his ribs still ached from where he'd got hit by that car. At least he'd got the bad guy.

He started to stretch his arms over his head and winced from the pull. Glancing around for a clean T-shirt, his gaze fell on the unmade bed. The blinking green light on his phone caught his attention next. With his job at the Corcoran Team he was on call all the time, and that habit gave him some comfort, but he had forgotten to bring the cell with him when he went outside earlier. He'd been unavailable for two hours, which was a record.

He swore under his breath as he reached over. A few buttons later and a voice he hadn't heard in months buzzed in his ear. Eleven months and twelve days, but who was counting?

"Davis, it's me. I'm in huge trouble. I…need you. Please be home."

Lara Bart, his former fiancée and the sole reason he went off the grid on a job that ended with busted ribs and a bruised jaw. The passing of days didn't matter. He knew that voice, could hear it every time he closed his eyes.

He also knew something was very wrong. The slight tremor. The stammer. None of that was normal for her. Husky voice, yes. Scared? Never.

The swearing this time included a few extra words and a lot of grumbling. Jamming his finger on the button, he called her back and nearly threw the phone when it went directly to voice mail.

He'd just pivoted and started stalking to his closet when the doorbell rang. He took off down the stairs with his bare feet thumping against each step.

As he hit the foyer, the rapid-fire knocking started. Breaking from protocol and his usual common sense, he entered the code on the alarm as he opened the door. Lara shoved her way inside and pressed up against him. Her arms wrapped around him as her cheek landed against his bare chest.

"You're home." She was out of breath and trembling as she mumbled the words against his skin.

The touch had his brain cells misfiring. It took a second for all the pieces to register. Her hair was lighter, with touches of blond through the rich brown waves, but still so soft. And his need for her still kicked hard enough to knock him over.

Ignoring the feel of her in his arms, he set her away from him and scanned her body, trying to remain as detached as possible as he checked for obvious injuries. "Are you hurt?"

She shook her head. "Well, except for my knee."

Looking down, he noticed the ripped hem of her skirt and red knee. That, along with the untucked and torn silk blouse, signaled trouble.

"What happened to you?" He almost dropped to the floor and checked her leg, but her next comment stopped him.

"I was attacked."

"What?"

She conducted security-clearance interviews, but there was nothing inherently dangerous about her job. He knew because he'd checked out her company and its independent contractor ties with the Department of Defense when she'd taken the position. Not that she knew that.

And it didn't matter that they'd broken up. He watched over her and always would.

"I should have called the police, but all I could think about was getting to you." Her hands were a blur of constant motion. Her gaze bounced all over the room, and she pushed her shoulder-length hair out of her eyes.

"Okay." Good, even. Being her first thought certainly didn't suck, but he needed her to calm down. "Take a deep breath."

Her chest rose and fell as she took his advice, but her hands kept shaking. "There was blood everywhere."

Dread ripped through him. Didn't sound as though this, whatever "this" was, had happened at the office. It took all his considerable control to focus the energy pinging around inside of him.

He wanted the information fast and clean, but she wasn't a field agent with the sort of delivery skills for that. Then there was the problem where her words kept jumbling together.

He cupped a hand over her cheek and lifted her head until her almond-colored eyes met his. Even terrified and twisted up, she was still the most beautiful woman he'd ever seen. Tall and trim with high cheekbones and a face that you could slap on a magazine cover without makeup.

But none of that mattered now. He needed information. Without it, he couldn't step in and fix whatever this was.

Skipping over the "blood" comment because he'd probably be hearing that one in his sleep, he went for the broader picture. "Can you tell me what happened?"

"My jacket is in the car." She looked around as panic moved into her eyes and turned her movements into uncontrolled jerks. "My briefcase." She turned to head back outside.

The last thing he wanted was her out in public until he ferreted this out. "Wait…"

A shadow moved in the open doorway behind her and the facts clicked together in Davis's head. The adrenaline started pumping through him a second later.

Jeans and a jacket, much too warm for the weather. And the gun with the convenient silencer screwed on the end. No question what that was for.

Davis assessed and acted. With a hand on Lara's arm, he tugged her around him. She practically flew as he shoved her against the wall and into the small corner at the bottom of the stairs wedged next to the coat closet. Her back hit with a thud, but he couldn't worry about that now. His concentration centered on the guy with the massive body and bald head aiming right for him.

As the attacker stepped inside, a flood of tension filled the air. Davis kicked out, trying to catch the door and knock it into the guy's head. Maybe make him drop the gun. The attacker was quicker. He caught the edge and slammed it shut behind him.

Davis reached for his weapon and touched only the cotton of his towel. No gun, not even any pants. The closest weapon was hidden across the room by the fireplace. That left few options.

He dived for the attacker's stomach. The guy

groaned as he crashed into the door and Davis smashed his hand against the knob.

Heavy breaths echoed through the room as each threw punches and aimed kicks. Davis's landed awkward because of his position and the need to keep the barrel of that gun aimed at the empty center of the room.

He slammed the guy once then twice into the hardwood, but he didn't drop the weapon. Barely looked winded.

The guy's knee came up, catching Davis in the jaw. His head snapped back and pain shot down from the base of his neck. Impressive training but Davis's was better. He rammed his elbow into the side of the guy's head and heard a sharp crack.

With the attacker off balance and reeling, Davis connected with a punch to the stomach, then one to the jaw. The guy went down hard on his knees, yelling. The gun flew across the room before spinning under the coffee table.

Davis scrambled, but the other guy wasn't going down easy. He dropped and crawled on his elbows and knees. Blood dripped on the floor from his split lip.

Knowing it was going to hurt like hell, Davis did a jumping dive, landing on the attacker and sending a knee plowing into his back. The guy howled in pain as his head tipped back and he bared his teeth.

Davis didn't wait. He threw his upper body out,

ignoring the tearing he felt along his injured ribs, and reached out his hand. The pain smacked him hard enough to close his eyes, but he forced them open again. He couldn't stop. Hesitating meant death for Lara and that was not going to happen on Davis's watch.

Just as he collected his strength and shimmied closer to the weapon, the attacker grabbed his leg. Twisting and sucker punches to the back of the knee came before Davis could brace for the attack. A shocking agony spiraled through him and his breaths came in rushed pants, but he refused to give up.

His fingers brushed against the metal. A few more inches and he'd have it. To get leverage, he balanced a hand against the floor and lifted his sore body up. Out of his peripheral vision, he saw Lara move. She sneaked up behind the men as they fought, carrying the heavy glass lamp that usually sat on the small table right near the double window at the front of the house. The same one she had bought right after they'd put an offer on the town house and he now used to hold his discarded keys each day.

Sensing something, or maybe reading the not-so-secret approach in Davis's eyes, the guy whipped around. He kicked out as he lunged for Lara. In panic, she jumped to the side and threw the lamp. It missed the attacker by a few inches but it gave Davis the diversion he needed. Stretching those last few inches, he grabbed the gun and wrenched around again.

He concentrated, blocking out everything—Lara and the pain shaking through him—to hit that target and nothing else. "Hey!"

The guy pivoted and his eyes went wide. With a roar of fury, he made a final leap for the gun.

Davis didn't hesitate. A crack split through the wrestling sounds of the room. Lara's surprised inhalation followed the guy slumping over on his side, pinning one of Davis's legs underneath.

Blood pooled, seeping into the small carpet. The room, ringing with activity a second ago, fell deadly quiet.

Davis kicked the guy off him then climbed to his knees. He pressed his free hand to the guy's neck, checking for a pulse. Next came a quick search of the attacker's pockets for some sort of identification. Davis peeked up at Lara, standing a few feet away with her hands over her mouth.

"Is he dead?" she whispered through her fingers.

The thump of a pulse grew faint then slipped away as Davis checked. "Yeah."

Her gaze searched the room, over the newspapers stacked on the edge of the couch and the four coffee mugs lined up across the coffee table. "Call an ambulance."

"Too late." With an arm wrapped around his ribs, Davis stumbled to his feet.

Out of the line of sight of the window, he crept around the family room and pulled her out of range at the same time. With his back to the door's edge, he scanned the outside for another gunman. Last thing Davis needed was another attacker blindsiding them.

When he turned back around he saw Lara watching his every move. Time to get her attention off what may be a second burst of gunfire. "Is this the guy who attacked you?"

"I don't know." She didn't even look at the downed attacker.

Davis reached out to her but it was as if she didn't even see the gesture. Her body closed in on itself as she put her hands on her shoulders, swinging her body from side to side and nibbling on her bottom lip. All while she carefully avoided looking at him or the guy on the floor.

The ache inside Davis was no longer about the death match. It was for her. For the sadness he saw pulling at her face and the tiny tremors that moved through her from the second she'd walked in the door and into his arms.

He was all too familiar with death on the job. She interviewed and wrote reports. She was normal. This was a nightmare, complete with splashes of blood and a body. "I know this is hard."

Her gaze went to the attacker then bounced back up again. "No."

"What?"

"It's not him. This is a different guy."

Now, that was a load of bad news. Davis exhaled as he tried to juggle all the questions in his mind. Rapid firing them at her would only shut her down. They had enough history for him to know she didn't react well to the interrogation thing, even if it was well-meaning. "Have you ever seen him before?"

"Definitely not."

Because she still avoided looking at the man in question, Davis tried again. "Are you sure?"

Her hands dropped to her sides as her cheeks flushed. "How can you stay so calm?"

The look was not a mystery. Just like always, anger slowly replaced the other emotions clashing inside her. Lashing out was her natural reaction.

If they had ten extra minutes to do this dance, he'd probably welcome anything that took her away from being scared, but right now he needed her to focus so he could get her out of there.

"Practice." He glanced through the house and out the back door right before he did another visual sweep of the front. Next he turned to the clock above his fireplace and calculated the lead time they'd need if this guy had a partner.

"That's your response?" Her voice dripped with sarcasm.

Good. He could handle that reaction. "I was being honest."

She snorted as she stepped around the downed attacker and came closer to Davis. "Right."

Yeah, she'd definitely shifted to the anger phase. He'd seen it coming. He welcomed it but he also knew he'd have to sit down soon.

He had taken a huge body blow and all that scrambling had knocked something loose inside him. His breathing hovered at the wheezing point. Fearing the damaged rib had slipped from aching to broken, he walked, partly doubled over, to the edge of the couch.

The color left her cheeks as quickly as it had come. "Davis?"

"I need a second." He had to think. Somehow his work life had once again intruded on her safety. She didn't even know about the guy who'd threatened her a few months ago and ended up in the morgue. That guy learned the hard way not to come after the woman of a former Defense Intelligence Agency agent turned private-security expert.

Before Davis could blink, she was at his side. Her hand went to his hair and her eyes filled with concern. "Oh, my…your stomach is black-and-blue. We need to get you to a hospital."

He hissed a sharp breath through his teeth when she tried to wedge her shoulder under his armpit and get him to his feet. "Whoa, honey."

"I'll call 9-1-1."

He caught her around the waist before she could

race through the room looking for a phone. Even through the thin shirt, he could feel the heat of her skin and his fingers tightened.

His temperature spiked as his gaze lingered over her breasts. He justified the need rumbling through him by thinking about the adrenaline aftermath. Never mind that he'd never had the desire to kiss anyone else but her after a work takedown. Seeing those big eyes and soul-stealing face, he felt his common sense go on the fritz.

It had always been this way between them. Hot and pulsing, both desperate to get the other into bed. They could communicate between the sheets. Real life was the problem.

"The ribs are from my last job." And Davis doubted they'd heal anytime soon.

"You got jostled."

He slipped his hand over hers, trapping it against his stomach. The dull ache caused by the touch was totally worth it. "Jostled?"

This time it looked as if she wanted to roll her eyes. She refrained but likely not by much. "Davis, don't do that thing where you grab on to words I say and then repeat them back to me in order to ignore or stall a tough discussion."

Most important to Davis, she didn't pull away. Not even when he slid his fingers through hers. "You know me too well."

"Exactly."

"Then you know what I'm going to say next." He pulled her in a little closer and her eyes sparkled with that compelling shade of light brown. "I need to call my team and we need to get out of here."

Her shoulders stiffened. "Police."

"Not until my people—"

"You have 'people' now?"

"—check for identification and scan records to see what hole out of my past the guy crawled up and out of." She glanced down at their joined hands and he thought he saw a smile tug at the corner of her mouth, though what she could possibly find amusing about the situation was beyond him.

"You've never referred to the team at the DIA that way before."

"I'm not working there now."

The smile vanished as fast it had come. "What?"

He understood the tension that suddenly appeared around her mouth and eyes. His job had been a huge wedge between them. Truth was his current position was much more dangerous than the old one, and she'd made it clear the old one had scared her to death. "I'll explain that later, but the 'people' I plan to call first is Pax. He's my brother and, like you, he could be a target, too."

"You think the attack is about you?"

"What else could it be?" With the Corcoran Team, a private group contracted out to government agencies and private companies to assist in high-priority but under-the-radar kidnap rescue missions, the bad guys were very bad.

Davis and his team worked off the grid, taking on the missions others couldn't do within legal parameters. That slapped a bull's-eye on their backs, and it looked as if someone had come looking for payback.

The only question was why they'd included Lara in the plan. Knowing who the attacker was and whom he worked for might answer that question. Until then, Davis was not letting her out of his sight, no matter how much she argued. And he was pretty sure she'd fight the protection.

"You're forgetting the guy who killed the lieutenant commander didn't even know I was in the house," she said, acting as if the out-of-context comment explained everything.

But the news crashed through Davis's mental walls. He'd just come up with a plan, and then she threw this new information at him. Kind of an important piece, too. "Go back. Someone was killed?"

"I mentioned that."

"Uh, no. That's a fact I'd remember."

"I'm not going to argue about who knew what when." Her hand left his stomach and she started pacing. When she got close to the body, she came scurrying right back to Davis's side. "For a second I forgot there was a dead guy on the floor. What does that say about me?"

The conversation threatened to veer off course

again, so he brought it back. "You were talking about the murder of a naval officer?"

"Let's just say that's the second time today I fought a guy off with a lamp."

The information nearly stopped Davis's heart. The idea of her injured and scared tore through him with the force of a hurricane, leaving behind a hollow emptiness in his gut. He could go a lifetime without seeing the look he had seen on her face a few minutes ago. But this went beyond fear. She'd been forced to defend herself, and that unleashed a fury inside him that had his head thumping.

He needed details. "Lara—"

"We'll come back to that when we discuss your new job." She put a hand under his chin and let her thumb brush over his lips, which stopped what he was going to say. "And, yes, I will follow you out of here. You're the expert."

Not sure of her game, he closed one eye and looked her over. "That's good to hear. A little surprising, but the right answer."

"I learned some things once you left..." That thumb made one more pass before her hand dropped. "And don't gloat. It's not attractive."

Words backed up in his throat. He had no idea what to say. In his head, the answer was clear—get her out of there now. The rest of his body had a different idea. "I'll call Pax and the rest of the team to deal with this guy and start investigating."

"Only you would use the word *deal,* like a dead man is a broken mug or something. He's a person, and being this close to him is creeping me out. Like, my insides are shaking so hard I might throw up."

That possibility didn't scare Davis, but he trod carefully with his answer because they'd had this argument before and he'd lost—big. "He tried to kill you. Once he crossed that line, I didn't care who or what he was."

When she continued to stare at him, he steered the conversation back where he needed it. "I need the phone."

She slipped away from him only long enough to grab it off the far table—then she was back at his side. "Here."

His hand slid around her waist to rest on the sexy dip of her lower back. "It's going to be fine."

"You should do one more thing before the cavalry comes."

He doubted anything mattered all that much except getting somewhere out of sight. "We'll be long gone by the time they arrive. That's the point."

"Well, before we go, you might want to put on some clothes." Her gaze traveled to his lap. "You're naked."

The words registered in his brain and he jumped up. A visual sweep down his body confirmed her comment…and the amusement in her voice. "What the…? When did the towel come off?"

"Very early in the battle."

"I didn't even notice."

"Impressive, by the way. I had no idea you knew how to bare-body fight." This time the back of her hand pressed against her mouth to stop what looked like a smile.

He had no problem with her looking all she wanted, so he played along. "I've told you before that my talents are endless."

Her gaze took another bounce down and up, then she smiled. "I can see that."

Chapter Three

Less than ten minutes later, they slipped through the kitchen and out the back door. Lara watched as Davis caught the screen before it could slam shut. Always thinking and rarely unprepared. That was how she thought about him, and her mind wandered there often.

They hurried across the porch, the boards creaking under her sensible pumps. His sneakers didn't make a noise. It was as if he placed each step with precision, including his run down the four steps to the muddy square of a backyard.

Her gaze focused on his butt. Not a bad focal point and certainly less scary than looking up into the eyes of another attacker. Two were enough for one day. Davis also made the staring easy. He had put on jeans and a T-shirt and carried a bag Lara wanted to believe was loaded down with clothes and essentials like shampoo but probably only contained weapons. He did love his big-boy toys, but at least he had clothes on now.

Through the haze of panic enveloping her and the sick ball of dread bouncing around in her belly, she smiled. It was not as if seeing Davis naked had ever been a hardship. He stood six foot one with long, lean muscles. If there was an ounce of fat on him, she defied anyone to find it. If anything, he was even more toned, more fit, than when she'd left all those months ago.

Looking at him now and holding his hand while they crept on boards balanced over the big puddles, she watched the muscles on his back tense and flex under his shirt. Nothing new there. The broad shoulders and military-short sandy-blond hair hadn't changed. Neither had the rough edge to his face, complete with a broken nose from years ago that had never healed quite right and a full, kissable mouth.

Put it all together and you got a man who was self-assured and strong, compelling and intriguing without being pretty. He walked by and women turned. He took a woman to bed and she didn't want to leave again for days. Lara knew that last one from experience.

"You okay?" His question, delivered in a monotone voice, almost blended into the sounds of traffic blocks away.

"Except for the whole thing where people are trying to kill me? Yes."

His fingers tightened around hers. "That's the spirit."

They walked to the six-foot fence running between his house and the next-door neighbor's then
followed it to the very back end. Unless he planned
to chew his way through it, she didn't see this as a
viable way out. "Uh, what are we doing?"

"Escaping." He trailed his hand over the wood
planks.

"Did you develop the power to walk through
walls?"

He shot her a sexy smile. "If only."

Refusing to get sidetracked by the shine in his
green eyes, she glanced around the yard. Nothing
was out of the ordinary. You'd never know a dead
man lay only a few feet away.

The strangeness of life going on, the sun shin-
ing and a lawn mower running nearby, struck her.
When a person died, the world should stop, if only
for a second. But nothing changed.

"Here we go." There was a click and a panel of
boards slipped open.

"A hidden door? Of course. Everyone has one."
She rolled her eyes, but his back was to her so he
missed it. That was a shame because it really fit
here.

Davis had a contingency for everything. Well, everything but her, which was part of the reason she'd
handed back the ring and still cried over the loss.

"It's my get-out-of-Dodge-fast plan." After ducking his head inside and taking a look around, he held

the door open and motioned for her to pass through. "After you."

It was not as if she had a choice. Her life had careened out of control hours ago. Now she just held on and hoped not to throw up. Her knee throbbed and the drum-crashing thumps in her head promised a killer headache any second now.

They stepped inside a fenced-off square consisting of a small shed and what she guessed was a car under that slipcover. When they reached the shed, Davis flipped open a black box and typed in a code. The gate at the back end of the enclosed space opened. It spilled out into the alleyway that ran behind his house, the same house he'd moved into a week after their engagement had ended.

They were supposed to have bought it together, even put in the offer together, but when the relationship fell apart he went through on his own. Funny how the original sales listing forgot to mention a secret car compartment at the back of the neighbor's property.

"Any chance you're going to tell me what's happening here? I feel like I walked into a movie a third of the way through."

A door Lara hadn't even seen on the house side of the enclosure opened and a tiny older woman walked out. "Is it time, Davis?"

Lara couldn't help but stare. The lady wore a long royal-blue robe buttoned up to her throat, dwarfing her under-five-foot frame. Her shocking white hair was long enough to tuck into her collar but thin enough for Lara to see the woman's pale scalp underneath. Slippers and cheeks rubbed pink with bright blush rounded out the look.

Whoever she was, she knew Davis and wasn't surprised to see him. She walked right up and put her hand on his forearm. Her eyes twinkled as she looked at him.

"Hi, Mrs. Winston." He lifted her hand and kissed the back. "I need the car."

"Go ahead." She patted his arm then turned to Lara. "Well, who is this pretty young thing?"

"This is Lara, my…" He shot Lara a warning glance. "Fiancée."

"Well, it's about time, young man. Come here, dear." Mrs. Winston gave him a squeeze and shuffled over to Lara.

It was her turn. Mrs. Winston hugged her, though her arms barely reached to Lara's back.

"Uh, hello." The older woman was so small and thin that Lara worried about crushing her by accident, so she kept the hold loose.

When the older woman pulled back, she took both of Lara's hands in her curved ones and her smile faded fast. "Did that boy fail to give you a ring?"

Lara glanced at Davis. He stood behind Mrs. Winston with an unreadable expression. Clearly this woman viewed Davis in a grandson sort of way.

Lara wasn't about to unload about all their past problems. It didn't hurt anything to let this woman think what she no doubt wanted to hear.

"Don't worry. He gave me a beautiful ring." And technically that wasn't a lie. He had. A perfect solitaire with baguettes on a platinum band.

It had broken her heart, actually shredded it in two, to hand it back. Not because she loved jewelry—that sort of thing never mattered to her—but because of what it symbolized. The commitment she so desperately wanted from Davis.

Mrs. Winston reached out and absently patted Davis's shoulder. "He's a nice boy."

He handed her a cell phone. "You remember what I told you, Mrs. W?"

"Stay inside, don't talk to anyone including anyone in a uniform, put the alarm on, pretend I don't know you and wait for you or Pax to come back." She peeked around Davis's muscled arm. "I guess I can add Lara to the list of people I can trust."

He kissed her on the cheek. "Nicely done, Mrs. W."

"My mind is just fine, you know."

"All of you is." He winked at her. "Now, back inside."

Mrs. Winston padded away without asking for an explanation. The snide part of Lara figured that was why Davis liked the woman so much. She didn't ask questions.

He closed the door, sealing them inside the odd parking space. When he turned back and walked to the front of the car, he whistled. The peppy tune continued as he ripped the slipcover off to uncover a pretty boring blue car.

Not Davis's usual style. He didn't go for flashy, but he usually chose trucks of some sort. This thing barely had a backseat.

With the driver's-side door open, he reached under the dashboard and pulled out a set of keys. He smiled as he jingled them in front of her. "Ready?"

The man looked far too satisfied with this little scene. "What, no helicopter?"

"Not on such short notice."

"Are you kidding me?"

He frowned. "Do you want to drive?"

"I'd prefer an explanation. You involved your neighbor in something dangerous. Since when do you do things like that?" That piece didn't make any sense. If anything, Davis was overly careful.

He used to talk about contingency plans and had even run through a safety drill with her one time. The second time he'd tried she'd threatened to dump a pot of hot coffee over his head. Not that she would have, but coffee was sacred to Davis so he'd fallen for it.

He insisted civilians were the main problem in most difficult situations. Something about them taking away his options and messing up the fluidity of the operations. People without skills were fine as long as they listened. Mrs. Winston obviously listened. Looked as if she harbored a schoolgirl crush, too, but Lara wondered about her ability to follow directions.

"She thinks she's my top secret assistant, but really she's a nice old lady who never gets even a phone call from her deadbeat kids in Delaware. Her husband died more than a decade ago and she's alone. I mow the back lawn, talk to her and, yes, play along with her active imagination, including installing a security system that rivals most high-tech office buildings."

She listened but the questions remained. "I still don't get it."

Nothing in his explanation sounded like the Davis she knew. With his messed-up background he hadn't learned much in the way of family coping skills. His bond with Pax was unbreakable, but coddling elderly women seemed outside of Davis's skill set.

He smiled. "From the time I moved in she tried to wander into the house. More than once she set off my alarm by accident. Almost got shot another time when she snuck in the back while I was out front. It was a problem until she decided I was a spy."

The word clunked in Lara's brain. "Spy?"

"International James Bond type."

They used to laugh about televisions shows and how they portrayed law-enforcement officials, especially those who worked undercover like he did. Expensive drinks and cars were so out of the realm of reality for Davis that he often swore his way through a program.

"You hate that term."

He shrugged. "I tolerate the whole spy thing for Mrs. W because it makes her happy."

The idea of Davis playing into that sort of nonsense to make an old lady happy made Lara's stomach do a little dance. "That's kind of adorable."

"It was necessary. But, yeah, Pax also thought it was hysterical."

The game came together in her head. "So, naturally, you told her Pax was a spy, too."

Davis flashed her that sexy smile that had sent more than one woman into an eye-fluttering swoon. "I wasn't about to go down alone. Point is, she loves it, and the wandering-around thing stopped. Now she watches the house for me and is much more careful because she's *helping* me."

"And she lets you keep a car here." Lara ran her hand over the roof, marveling at how clean it looked for being held outside of a garage.

"I actually bought the spot. Money was tight for her and it worked well with the spy story. Also gave me a place to store the car that I prefer to keep for emergencies."

The little dance turned into a full-fledged stomach jig. He presented this tough-guy tarnished image but underneath he was about helping people. Maybe it came from being abandoned by his mother that he never let anyone else get stuck out there all alone. Whatever the origin, it was one of those things that had made her fall in love with him in the first place.

"You rescued her," Lara said.

"Uh, no. I came up with a way to neutralize her." He walked around to the passenger's-side door and opened it. "Get in."

It was just like him to duck a compliment. He saw admitting to the existence of his bone-decent good side as some sort of weakness. She'd never been able to make him see that the size of his heart was much more impressive than the size of those biceps.

Rather than fight, because, really, there was nothing for her to win on this one, she slid into the seat. She waited until he'd climbed in before asking the obvious question. "Where are we going?"

"Pax's boat." Davis slid the key in and turned. The engine roared to life.

"Is being surrounded by water really the safest choice?" Then there was the problem that she got queasy if the boat rocked too much.

She'd never been on this one, but they'd gone boating with friends before. She'd tried that focus-on-a-spot-in-the-distance thing and ended up losing her lunch over the side of the boat. Not the best impression on his then–work friends.

"It's not registered to Pax. Only a few people know

about it and all of them have brutally high security clearances. Whoever is behind this shouldn't have a clue."

She waited until he'd pulled out of the spot and relocked the gate to talk about the point nagging at her. "I notice you didn't ask if I had a boyfriend before you added me to your spy story."

The car grew deadly quiet as she traced a pattern on the inside of the window. When the silence stretched, she glanced over. The rigid jaw and tick in his cheeks told her what she needed to know. This was not his favorite topic. Understandable, but she thought she knew his response, so she was prepared to wait all day. And she let him know that when she glanced over and lifted her eyebrows but didn't say a word.

He exhaled in that women-are-so-annoying way men often did when they were cornered. "Do you?"

He didn't even try to make it sound like an honest inquiry. "Oh, please. I know you know exactly what's going on in my life. Or at least you think you do."

A smile broke over his mouth. "Yeah, I'm single, too."

CLIVE EBERSOLE BROUGHT his car to a slow crawl and stopped behind the designated warehouse on the southwest waterfront in Washington, D.C. He didn't have to look at his watch to know he'd lost some time on this job. Took him longer to clean up Steve Wasserman's row house than expected. Clive had wiped the place down, except, of course, for the evidence he needed the police to find.

Remembering the scene brought Lara Bart to the front of his mind for about the hundredth time in the past two hours. He hadn't counted on her. That one proved to be a fighter and a significant complication.

Good thing she'd left her work case file when she'd run off. The documents inside helped him track her identity and find her apartment. She hadn't run back there, so he couldn't tie up that end, but the trip hadn't been a total waste. Not after he borrowed a few items.

And it had only taken him a few minutes to find exactly what he needed to take back and plant in Wasserman's bedroom. A few pieces of underwear and her address book, along with her laptop and a brush. With all of those pieces, one would hang her.

The move was off script but to his mind brilliant. And perfect in the execution. Not even the best lawyer would be able to dodge the reality of her property and DNA being all over the crime scene, as well as all over the house. She was supposed to have been there for a simple interview, but Clive had created something much bigger. A false past that tied her directly to the dead man.

It would only take a few fake emails to establish the rest of the secret life and a lover's spat. One well-placed hair from the brush and she'd be spending the rest of her days in prison. That would teach her to take him on, to think that she could actually win.

Idiot woman. She may have escaped, but she'd left enough behind for him to implicate her in the naval officer's murder.

His orders hadn't mentioned her. She'd been an unwelcome surprise, but he'd improvised. Wiped his fingerprints and any evidence of his presence away. Instead of framing the murder as burglary-gone-bad as planned, he had a new answer—her.

The question was whether his employer would see it this way. When he'd confirmed the Wasserman termination at check-in everything was fine. Delivering the news about Lara Bart's interference had caused a hiccup. Clive had been directed to appear at this destination at this time. That was rarely a good sign.

He heard the crunch of tires and glanced in his rearview mirror. A black sedan now idled behind him. He didn't wait for the phone to ring on this command performance. Taking the offensive always worked for him, and the two guns tucked within easy reach would even the balance of power.

Exiting the car, he scanned the area for witnesses. He'd been tripped up by one already today and refused to have it happen a second time.

The passenger's-side window rolled down and a

thin file appeared in the space. No words, just a tap of a folder.

Pompous and dripping with an overactive ego, his employer continued to act as if he could separate the things he did from who he was. A typical smarmy blowhard dressed in a too-expensive suit. From the sunglasses to the shiny watch to the annoying way he held his head an inch too high, the man's overblown sense of self begged for Clive to put him down.

His usual business philosophy faltered with this guy. Usually, as long as he was paid Clive ignored the overdose of attitude. The second an employer failed to transfer the payment on time and in the right amount, Clive would cut him down—literally. It had happened only twice, but his reputation remained intact. Both of those disloyal men were dead and Clive promised the same to anyone who tried to screw him.

He leaned down but didn't grab the papers. "What's this?"

His employer continued to stare out the front window. Didn't even bother to turn down the news on the radio or give eye contact. "Your one chance to fix your mess."

Clive decided he could do without the overwrought drama, but that was what this guy did best. "I already did."

"You left a witness. Worse, you opened the door to more trouble than you can imagine."

Clive kept his one hand behind his back, next to his weapon, and grabbed the file with the other. "Meaning?"

The employer finally faced Clive, but the dark glasses hid any reaction. "Your backup failed to tie up loose ends, so I am reluctantly trusting you to do it."

The words made the nerve in the back of Clive's neck twitch. "What backup?"

"I always have insurance."

"So do I. That's why Ms. Bart will now take the fall for the murder. Problem solved."

"She is the least of your worries now." His employer turned the radio volume up and looked forward again as if to ignore Clive's very existence on the Earth. "The man referenced in that file is your main concern. Neutralize him immediately."

The car took off before Clive could move away. Only luck and quick reflexes prevented him from becoming a victim of a hit-and-run or losing a foot.

But he would remember. When this was over, his employer might need a lesson. One at the end of a knife, and Clive did so enjoy his knife work.

There would be time for that later. Now he needed to focus. He flipped open the file and read the name at the top and the job history.

Davis Weeks.

Looked as though Ms. Bart had a built-in protector. That was fine with Clive. This Weeks guy would bleed out like any other man…slowly and with as much pain as possible.

Then Clive would pay his employer a much-needed late-night visit.

Chapter Four

Davis sat across from Lara on the back deck of his brother's twenty-six-foot cruiser. The gentle rock of the boat and slosh of water against the side had a hypnotizing effect. So did watching the guy four slips down stack enough supplies on the dock for a four-month voyage. Never mind that his boat was small enough to get tossed around in the ocean. Davis hoped the guy had the smarts to limit his trip to close-in on the Chesapeake Bay and have the coast guard on standby just in case.

But Davis had enough to worry about without adding another person to his Watch List. With his elbows balanced on his knees, Davis looked down at the rough white floor under his sneakers and listened to Lara's description of what had happened at the Capitol Hill town house.

A knife wound. A dead naval officer. An attacker with a gun. Lara wrestling free and going on the run.

It was a lot to take in.

With each word, the adrenaline increased in

speed as it raced through him. The need to find the guy and rip him apart nearly swamped Davis. He jammed his teeth together to keep from letting his rage out.

She wound down when she hit the part about leaving the city and heading for Annapolis. With an arm stretched over the top of the back bench, she stared at the locked gate separating the public area from the boat slips. Her mind clearly wandered to other concerns.

He knew where. "No one is coming in here who shouldn't be here."

"What?" She blinked as she looked at him.

He nodded in the direction of the mounted camera on the dock. "My team is watching the area through closed circuit."

"When did that happen?"

The woman could stand to have a bit more faith in his skills. "The second after I called Pax."

She shifted sideways and put her legs up on the padded seat. Thanks to a quick stop at the discount store, she'd changed clothes. Gone was the ripped and professional outfit. He preferred her this way. Relaxed and at ease. With her itinerary today, she'd earned a few minutes of peace.

She now wore jeans and one of those tops barely held on her shoulders with thin straps. It slipped past her waist but not by much. Another twist and he'd get a peek of her sexy bare skin and flat stomach. Not that he needed a reminder. He remembered every inch of her with his eyes open or closed.

She tipped her head back, and the fading sun streamed through her hair. Her husky voice echoed around them as she closed her eyes. "Are you in charge of this team?"

Damn, she was beautiful.

"No." The word caught in his throat, but he pushed it out.

Also fought the urge to make her tell the entire story again. She'd run through it three times, the last one while grumbling and frowning at him through all but the end. She didn't understand the importance of those tiny details that became clearer with each telling. He did.

"When did you take the job with Hampton and start doing security-clearance checks?" He knew her official start date, but the reasons for the change were a mystery.

"When I decided being an office manager at an intellectual-property law firm was not the most exciting career ever."

He'd left her in a safe job with benefits and no danger, other than falling into a boredom coma or getting her shirt caught in the copier. Now she walked in and out of situations with people she didn't know. Yes, she asked questions and collected data for a living, which should be relatively safe, but going into a stranger's house was a whole different level of danger. One he didn't accept for her.

"Isn't protocol to meet interviewees in public places?" he asked.

"Have you been reading my employee manual?"

"I'm serious." And about a half step away from being furious with her for taking huge chances.

"Usually, but this was a rush job and my boss asked me to fit the Wasserman interview in."

The sequence seemed clear to Davis. She broke protocol this one time and the world came crashing down around her. Either her being there was pure coincidence, or someone had set her up. If the latter was true, then the second attack of the day made less and less sense.

So did her sudden change of position on job-related risk. She'd hated that he took them, but now she was plunking that perfect butt right into the middle of some sort of war.

The realization made his hands shake with the need to yell. The growl roared up from his stomach, but he tamped it back down. "So, you switched jobs because you wanted something dangerous."

"I didn't say that."

"I'm thinking it was implied." She was making this conversation more convoluted than necessary, and they both knew it. The fact she didn't give him eye contact gave her away. "And you used to say I was the one with the communication issue."

She made a choking sound as she lifted her head and swung around to face him again. "Speaking of that, what's with all the team stuff? Last I checked, you were flying around the world conducting investigations about military intel."

The brunt of his anger smoothed away. Okay, this part promised to be difficult. He shot the other boater a look just to see if he was listening in. Davis looked in time to see the guy trip over his cooler. That was about as smooth as Davis felt at the moment.

Rather than dance around it, he said it straight. "I quit that job and went with a private firm."

"Oh, really. The same job I begged you to leave." The flat line of her mouth and dead eyes suggested she'd reached the end of her patience.

He couldn't really blame her. They'd gone around and around on this topic when they'd been together. She hated his work and the life-threatening situations it threw him in. That last DIA-related assignment broke them apart. He'd sat there in San Diego, listening on the phone while she begged him to come home. He'd almost crushed the cell under his hand in frustration because he couldn't get to her.

The crying and pleading had been new. Anger he could handle, but hearing the desperate tremble in her voice shredded him. Even thinking about it now started a hollow rumbling in his gut.

She hadn't cared that his old boss was trapped in

a nightmare because his fiancée had gone missing or that his boss's twin brother nearly had got killed in an explosion. She asked him to turn his back on everything he knew to be right, and he couldn't do it.

After the tense discussion, Davis and Pax had agreed they needed to finish the job. Just a few more days. Davis had justified it in his head until he blocked out the sound of her voice. The operation ended but Davis had come back to Lara and her packed bags and the engagement ring on the kitchen counter.

He couldn't deal with any of that now. "I see the irony."

"It's more than that, Davis. We broke up over your habit of picking your job over me." In the past, she'd deliver a line like that in a moment of pure female fury. Now she said it with all the emotion of reading a grocery list.

"We broke up over a lot of things." Her lack of support and refusal to accept who he really was being some of the points he remembered.

She opened her mouth twice but nothing came out. Without warning the tension left her shoulders. "I am going to let that go because you saved my life today."

Not sure he'd actually won that round but unwilling to get her riled, he nodded. "Much appreciated."

"I'm guessing you don't sit at a desk at this new job."

There always had been so much about his job

he couldn't explain. This was part of that. "I'm sitting now."

"You always were the best at dodging a question." She lifted her hair off her neck. If she was hoping for a breeze, none came.

The air stood still. The heat was actually wet, choking as it burned down your throat. Having her sit there, sun-kissed and hotter than he remembered, made his temperature spike into the danger zone. This heat had nothing to do with anger or the temperature outside. This was pure, unfiltered need. All the fighting and months apart hadn't crushed that.

"Ask me anything, but first answer one question." He rubbed his hands together, debating if this was the right time. "Why me?"

"What?"

"You could have called the police or a friend. You were thirty miles away and you'd had a huge scare and you got in a car and drove to me."

Amusement lit her brown eyes and a smile inched over her lips. "You're the only spy I know."

He really did hate that word and she knew it. "I'm serious."

"You weren't the best fiancé but you were great at your job. I knew I needed the best." She glanced at the radio on the deck next to his foot. "Anything on the news yet?"

"No." The answer was automatic. It wasn't as if the radio was even turned up loud enough to hear it. At this level it sounded more like static or a low mumble, but he knew how this game was played. "Wasserman was in the military. NCIS probably dropped a net over this while the experts come in to collect evidence."

A different emotion moved over her face. One that looked suspiciously like doubt. "Explain to me again why we aren't reporting the murder."

"I don't want questions from anyone, including NCIS, the FBI or the police, until we know what happened in that kitchen and why."

"I don't get it."

Of course she didn't, because he was purposely not explaining it. That plan might have worked on another woman, one not as smart or intuitive. One who let things slide and accepted things just because someone said them with authority. Nothing about that description fit Lara.

She picked and checked and he'd loved that about her from the beginning. A whiny, clingy type didn't suit him. He wanted vibrant…then he'd had it and lost her anyway.

The least he could do was let her see how this would go. "How many people knew you would be at Wasserman's house today?"

She shrugged. "A few. Why?"

"Did you touch anything?"

"I don't—"

"A table. The door. A glass." He ticked the possibilities off on her fingers.

"All of them. What is your…?" She blew out a long breath. "You think I'll be blamed for this?"

"Possibly." Definitely. The police would look at the forensics, and Davis feared those results would only point in one direction. Hers.

"But not coming forward will only make me look more guilty."

"That depends on why Wasserman was killed." A question Davis wanted answered as soon as possible.

"What are you saying?"

A bell dinged in the distance as birds squawked. "Someone took him out before he could talk with you. Who knows what information he had or why someone would want it silenced."

"Yes, so—"

"He asked specifically to speak with the investigator." Davis switched seats. Instead of sitting across from her, he slid in next to her with his arm running along the back of the bench seat. "Coughlin, the guy you're investigating, didn't put Wasserman on the list. He got there because he came forward. He had something to say and specifically asked to say it that day."

"How do you know this?"

His hand brushed against her back, right near her shoulders. When she didn't pull away or wince, he kept it there. "I know people."

"I'm serious."

His fingers touched her soft hair. The gentle waves wrapped around his thumb. "Do I look like I'm kidding?"

"I don't believe this." She bent forward with her arms wrapped around her waist. When she started rocking, he moved in closer.

"Hey, come here." That arm slid around her and pulled her in tight against his side. Seeing her confused made bile rush up the back of his throat. "It's going to be fine."

She stared at his wide eyes, and a strain pulled across her cheeks and mouth. "How can you say that?"

"As you pointed out, I'm very good at what I do." His fingers threaded through her hair as his mouth hovered just inches from hers.

"What is it you plan to do?"

Kiss her, deep and hard, and not stop while either of them could still move. He wasn't one to mix business and pleasure, but control deserted him when she was around.

Even after she'd left, he kept the memories of her alive. He wanted to be pissed and still seesawed back and forth, but he couldn't hold on to the rage. The hurt and disappointment, well, those lingered.

But she was talking about work and he forced his mind to focus on that. She needed protection, not pawing. "We'll figure out why Wasserman is dead and why, coincidentally, people tried to take both of us out on the same day."

"I'm confused. Do you think this is about my work or yours?"

He was still deciding. "Until I know, you are pinned to my side."

"I'm not sure that's a good idea." She said the words even as her hand traveled over his chest and down to his stomach.

"Then you should have called your imaginary boyfriend." He kissed the very tip of her nose, thinking the soft touch would satisfy him.

He was dead wrong.

"I had a hard enough time handling the flesh-and-blood type." Their heads bent so close together that her whispered words blew across his lips.

"From my memory you handled that quite well."

He gave in. One small press of his lips against hers. Quick and gentle, with barely any heat.

"Your ribs."

"I'll let you know if you're too close. So far, we're good."

She grabbed a fistful of his shirt. "Davis—"

"Trust me."

The second kiss blew the first away. This one sent energy arcing between them. His mouth over hers, pressing, touring, tasting. His hand in her hair and her cuddled against his chest.

He could feel her fingers slide over his shoulder

and trail down his back. Any closer and she would be on his lap. He no sooner thought it then his arm slipped under her legs and tugged them up and over his thighs.

The kiss exploded and devoured. Any idea that they were done flushed out to the bay. When her head fell back and he started to push her down on the bench, he knew his control had snapped and it would take an army to put it back together again.

He'd just decided to tease the edge of that thin shirt and tunnel up when the nerve ticked at the back of his neck. At first he felt more than saw movement on the walkway down to the dock. Then he heard the clang of the gate and thumps of footsteps. If the person wanted to sneak up, they'd failed. No way was this a professional killer. Well, not the enemy kind.

Davis lifted his head and, after a quick look over the side, stared down into Lara's cloudy eyes. "Company."

The boat shifted in the water and the footsteps fell louder. The chuckle came next. "Probably not the best timing on my part, but hello."

Davis looked away from the woman who meant everything and over to the brother he'd called for help. Pax stood on the ladder with a bag of what looked like food in one hand and a folder in the other.

After a quick mental assessment Davis decided all of that, whatever it was, could wait. "Get lost."

"Pax!" Lara jumped off the seat and straight into Pax's arms. He dropped his packages just in time and her smile beamed. "It's good to see you."

Lara had the power to lighten even Pax's darkest moods. They had a sister-brother relationship. They joked and she made fun of the way he hid his dates from her. And put either of them near a tub of raw cookie dough and it would be gone before you could get a spoon and jump in.

The stab of guilt over losing her extended to Pax. Davis had lost the love of his life. Pax had lost someone he cared about, and that list was not very long.

"You, too, though the circumstances need some work." Pax looked at Davis over the top of Lara's head and mouthed the word *sorry.* "You guys okay post guns and knives?"

"I was better five minutes ago," Davis mumbled.

Pax kept an arm around Lara. "And look at you beating up the bad guys. I hear the lamp is your weapon of choice."

"Kind of hard to hide in my pants, but yes."

Accepting the fact the kiss was over and not going to be revived anytime soon, Davis motioned for Pax to sit. "What did you find out?"

Pax guided Lara back to the bench next to Davis before grabbing his dropped belongings and dropping in the seat across from them. "NCIS is on the scene at Wasserman's house. Agents are looking for Lara."

The blip of happiness disappeared. She looked back and forth between the men. "What?"

"And the dead guy on your floor is, or I guess I should say *was,* a gun for hire. Former military with a dishonorable discharge. Apparently, your boy liked to shoot a bit too much." Pax handed the file to Davis. "So, it looks like we have some work to do."

Lara slumped back in the seat. "I almost hate to ask what all of this means."

The notes were few, but Davis read enough to be concerned. He flipped the pages but put the file down when he realized Lara's total attention was focused on him.

Prettying it up wouldn't help, so he shot right to the truth. "Pax is saying you're likely to be the number one suspect in the murder of Wasserman."

She shifted until her feet hit the floor, then she pulled them up, then they went back down again. Something seemed to be pinging around inside her and making her squirm. "But why would I kill him? I don't have a motive."

Davis switched to his game face—*all is well and easy to handle*—to try to calm her down. Her switch to panic mode would only make the job tougher. "We need to figure out who did and why."

"And then get to the bottom of Davis's attacker," Pax said.

Lara reached for the file but dropped her hand.

"The attacker could have followed me. He came in Davis's house right after."

Davis had already thought about that possibility and discarded it. "Did you see him following you?"

"No…" She bit her lower lip. "I don't know."

Pax looked out over the boat slips and exhaled loud enough to start a tidal wave. "What a mess, but at least some things never change."

"Like?"

"Ken." Pax pointed at the man still struggling with his pile of equipment, this time a net he'd accidentally stepped into and got caught around his feet. "Thinks he's a boater."

More like a menace, as far as Davis could tell. "I'm afraid he'll hurt himself or, more likely, someone else."

"The chances are limited. He never leaves the dock. He gathers stuff, sits on the boat and then goes home. It's an expensive hobby." When Ken glanced up, putting his hand over his eyes to block the sun, Pax waved. "Weird but harmless. But back to the attacker issue."

Her body fell. "So, what are you guys saying?"

"Looks like we're going to be spending a lot of time together." And that idea didn't bother Davis at all.

She gnawed on her lip again. "Oh."

He winked at her. "Welcome back."

Chapter Five

NCIS special agent Ben Tanner straightened his tie as he waited in the carpeted outer office of the deputy director's suite. Ben had been the special agent afloat on the USS *Forrestal* and stationed in field offices as far away as Bahrain. After sixteen years of navy and investigative experience, plus a stint at the War College, he'd faced danger daily. That didn't mean he liked walking into his boss's office and delivering bad news. Not to this guy.

The deputy director of NCIS wasn't known as a patient man. Ronald Worth thought nothing of grinding special agents under his shoe. When he got bad news, the person delivering it often felt the wrath.

The deputy had earned his position. His appointment was not part of the good-old-boy network that sometimes came with prime assignment. But he insisted, irrationally so, that things run smoothly and let everyone feel his displeasure when that didn't happen.

Ben had heard stories. Standing there in the outer office of the suite, he remembered every single one of them.

The deputy's assistant, Wayne Kline, knocked on the door and only pushed it open after being ordered in. Even then he didn't venture fully inside. "Sir, we have a problem."

Deputy Worth waved them on without looking up from the files spread out in front of him. "Not the words any boss wants to hear at the end of a long day."

Ben glanced around the office. These weren't the usual government digs, but NCIS Headquarters had moved to this space in Quantico, Virginia, only a few months ago. The suite was large and plush and, unlike the old offices at the Navy Yard in southeast D.C., had windows that opened and you could see out of.

Behind the huge desk loaded with two computers to match two wall-mounted screens sat Worth, the NCIS legend who had stopped an attack at Camp Pendleton years ago by taking a domestic terrorist down before anyone could get hurt. His career had gone stratospheric after that. People tolerated much because of his past.

The deputy continued to flip pages. "What is it?"

Wayne cleared his throat. Even looked a little green around the mouth as he talked. "It's about Martin Coughlin."

"Spit it out." Ronald looked up. For the first time his eyes focused on something other than paperwork. "Who are you?"

"Special Agent Ben Tanner."

"Right. I remember."

Ben had no idea if that was good or bad.

Worth looked Ben up and down with a scowl that suggested he'd sized up his opponent and found him wanting. A terrific way to start a meeting. "What is this about?"

Ben had heard the deputy appreciated facts, so he got right to them. "Steve Wasserman was murdered today."

Leaning back in his leather chair, the deputy's laserlike stare zeroed in on Ben. With an elbow on the armrest and a pen flipping between his fingers, he frowned. "Why does that name sound familiar?"

Ben stepped up and slid a file across the man's desk. When the deputy kept staring, Ben launched into an oral briefing. "You knew him at the Naval Academy in the mid-eighties."

"I'm aware of when I graduated. Get to the point."

"Wasserman was one of the witnesses on Coughlin's security-clearance interview list."

And that was the problem. Martin Coughlin was Worth's old friend and choice for appointment as the NCIS's senior intelligence officer. The deputy had pushed for Martin and insisted the security-clearance steps be fast-forwarded. Martin had been in the office as recently as two days ago to talk about the position.

The tap, tap, tapping of the pen continued. "Are you asking to investigate this matter?"

"Yes, sir." Ben shifted his weight from foot to foot because this guy's intense stare had the power to make you question everything. "There are some jurisdictional issues, but the matter is delicate. We should handle it internally."

The deputy stared for what felt like a full minute then nodded. "Do it. I'll pull the necessary strings. Is there anything else?"

"The case is unusual in that Wasserman volunteered to talk as part of Coughlin's security-clearance investigation. And, in general, there are suspicious circumstances surrounding the death."

The pen stopped waving. With careful precision, the deputy set it on top of his stack of files. "Isn't that always the case with murder? I mean, was the killer hovering over the body?"

"No, sir," Wayne said from his position just inside the office door.

The deputy never broke eye contact with Ben. "Then, while the death is sad, I'm still not seeing the problem. Investigate and report back."

Ben waited until the deputy reached for the papers in a classic we're-done-here signal. Ben couldn't back down because he needed the guy's attention and was determined to get it. "There is a bigger issue."

"Unless Coughlin is too distraught to go forward with the appointment as a result of this, and I doubt that since I've known the man forever, you've lost me." The deputy's voice changed, now monotone and more than a little bored.

"A woman was there—"

The deputy swore under his breath. "You're saying this is a sex scandal?"

"The problem is the murder occurred while the female investigator was there to talk with Wasserman about Coughlin."

"Was she hurt?" the deputy asked.

"She's gone."

His frown returned. "Gone where?"

"Disappeared."

"Now I'm starting to see the problem. We have a dead lieutenant commander, a missing investigator and a potential NCIS appointment at the center of it all." The deputy exhaled long and hard. "Is there any evidence Coughlin is involved?"

Ben couldn't answer that, and that was the problem. "I don't know anything yet."

"Get to work. Talk to everyone associated with this woman and Wasserman. And find her. I want a preliminary briefing tomorrow."

Ben had no idea how to accomplish all of that in

such a short time. He'd need manpower. "My team and I will—"

"Wrong."

"Sir?"

"Just you. You need to draw a circle around this. Keep the information contained until we know what we're dealing with. The death will be on the news, but right now it is an unfortunate death of a naval officer living in a very dangerous city. Nothing more, and Wayne will see that it stays that way." The deputy stared at Wayne until he nodded. "Everyone get to work. Time is of the essence."

After the deputy had rattled off his orders, he returned to the files on his desk. That fit with the reputation—rapid-fire action. You got his attention for a few minutes only, but when you had it, you had to use it.

Wayne motioned for Ben to leave.

In a daze, he walked across the floor. This was against protocol and common sense. He understood the political ramifications: the deputy and Martin were friends. Still, as a one-man job this task seemed doomed to fail.

Maybe that was the point.

Ben shook his head. No, this one had landed on his desk. Somehow he'd manage to get enough preliminary information to request more help, but until then, sleep would be elusive, if not impossible.

The door had barely closed when Ben heard mumbling on the other side. He thought he heard the words "watch him" but couldn't be sure. To be safe, Ben would cover his tracks. No way was he losing his career and all he'd worked for over Steve Wasserman.

Chapter Six

Lara stood at the railing on the back deck and watched the last of the sun's rays skim the water and dip into the horizon. The sky was on fire with a burst of orange and bright pink.

The sounds of the marina filled the quiet night. Boats swayed and bobbed, and metal clanked against metal on the sailboats. A few rows over people laughed as they sat out on their decks and enjoyed the summer night.

Despite the danger swirling around, being outside made her smile. It was inside that was the problem. The boat had a claustrophobic kitchenette and a bedroom that consisted of a mattress specially designed to fit under the front end of the boat. She didn't know much about sailing, but she knew about being sick, and staying down there, all closed in, almost guaranteed it.

To be safe she'd nibbled on the bread from her sandwich for dinner and skipped everything else. She wasn't hungry anyway. Her life had tilted and she was barely hanging on the side. Dead men at her feet and police buzzing around her life. It was all too much.

"You hiding from your former fiancé?" Pax came up beside her and assumed a stance that mirrored hers.

The comment was right, in part. After spending a short time with Davis, they'd morphed right back into old couple patterns. He'd stepped into the role of rescuer and didn't think twice about bossing her around using the "it's for her own good" excuse he liked so much. Oh, he didn't say it out loud this time around, which made her realize he had learned something during their time apart, but everything else felt strangely familiar.

He got near her and her heart tumbled. He kissed her and her brain spun with excitement. The attraction pulled between them as strong as ever. But loving him, wanting him, had never been the issue. Accepting everything else was.

"Thanks for bringing dinner," she said, verbally pulling Pax in another conversation direction with all her might.

He laughed. "Changing the subject?"

"Definitely."

"Well, getting here was no problem. I live nearby and was willing to use any excuse to see you."

"Aren't you the charmer?" She balanced her

head against his shoulder and felt the firm muscles underneath.

Both brothers made her feel safe. With Pax the emotions never boiled and bubbled. If he ticked her off, she just rolled her eyes. And he'd never made her heart hammer, while Davis had that effect on her just by walking into a room.

She chalked all of that up to her buddy-type relationship with Pax. Amazing how taking the sexual attraction and romantic-love parts out of a relationship simplified everything.

Pax pulled back and looked her up and down. There was no heat, just a joking familiarity. "You look good. Always do."

"Why hasn't some woman snapped you up?" She knew the answer. Because he ran as fast as possible in the opposite direction whenever they tried to tell him their last names.

"I always said women were smarter than men."

"No arguments here." She watched the last of the orange streaks fade away into the dark sky.

The water stretched out in front of her in a vast nothingness. The waves she loved so much during the day took on a dangerous edge at night. That was a familiar theme in her life. Hours ago it looked a soothing, shiny blue. Now she only saw a deep, mysterious black.

They stood, soaking up the evening as dishes rattled below. A shadow moved around down there.

She assumed Davis was cleaning up or maybe burning off some extra energy. He wasn't really the type to hang out on a boat and do nothing. That was Pax's thing.

Davis was constant motion, which was why she'd agreed to buy a fixer-upper with him. She'd figured he'd spend every extra hour making it shine. So when she had stepped inside earlier and seen boxes and blank walls, it surprised her.

She also knew from the way Pax tried hard not to say anything that something big rattled around in his head. The guy was like a little kid sometimes, nearly vibrating with excitement and the need to tell.

His determination only lasted a few more seconds. After a quick glance into the open doorway, he shifted to face her. His voice dropped to a whisper. "Anything you need to tell me?"

"About?" But she knew. Pax wanted her with Davis. He never pretended otherwise. He'd called for weeks after they broke up, asking her to come back before Davis turned more miserable than anyone could handle.

"My eyesight works just fine, and what I walked in on didn't look like two people happy not to be together."

The kiss. Yeah, she was still struggling to set that straight in her mind. She wanted to write it off as leftover attraction or a punch of adrenaline from the out-of-control day. To her soul, she feared it fore-shadowed much more.

All these months she'd been trying to get over him and failing miserably. No other man even clicked on her radar.

"The problems haven't changed," she said. "Davis wants to be free to go all over the world, even if it scares me to death. On his list of priorities I'm near the bottom."

And that was the insurmountable problem. When she'd needed him, lying in that hospital bed crying for him, he'd been across the country saving some-one else's fiancée.

"That's not true, Lara." All the amusement and laziness left Pax's voice. "I was there. I saw what losing you did to him."

"I lived it, Pax." Pain swirled around her until she thought it would suck her down. She tightened her hold on the deck railing to keep from going under.

The silence stretched longer this time. She no-ticed for the first time that the radio played in the kitchen area.

She was about to break the tension when Pax spoke again. "Did he tell you about his last job?"

The question surprised her. Her mind went to the discolored skin around Davis's middle and the way he grimaced when he lifted his arm too high. "You mean the rib injury?"

"I mean the reason for it."

This was new. Pax rarely did an end run around his big brother. They were two years apart and had lived through being abandoned and passed around to relatives who only cared when they received a check from the state for the boys' care. The dysfunctional upbringing and fighting to survive bound them together.

Their past also had forced Davis into a fatherly role before he'd hit his teens. Over time the relationship morphed to a more mutual one, likely because they'd worked together for most of their adult lives. It was a bond that grew out of respect and love, and neither brother tested it. But she sensed Pax was pushing the boundary by dropping hints about something he wanted her to know.

Picking her words carefully, she asked, "What are you trying to tell me by not telling me something?"

"That's quite a sentence."

Just like his brother. "Answer the question."

Pax's crooked smile didn't reach his eyes. "I thought I was being subtle."

"There is nothing subtle about the Weeks boys."

He winked at her. "On that note, I'm going to head out."

She grabbed his arm before he could move an inch. "Without giving me an explanation?"

"Don't give me that look. It says you are right on the edge of unloading on me, and I don't want any part of that."

"Then don't evade."

"We both know you're talking to the wrong brother." Pax called a goodbye to Davis then hit the ladder, but not before calling over his shoulder to her. "Good night."

DAVIS WAITED UNTIL Pax left...then waited another ten minutes. He wasn't a man accustomed to hanging around. Outside of work, patience wasn't any kind of virtue that he could see.

Despite the uncharacteristic pacing, Lara's head never peeked below to say hi. Even now he could look out the opening to the deck and see her sitting curled up on the back bench with her arms wrapped around her legs. Her cheek rested on her knees, and her head was turned to face the other boats in the row.

Enough with the hiding. He got the message. Hands off. If only his body would obey the order from his head.

He stepped out onto the deck, letting his sneakers thump against the floor so as not to scare her. "What are you doing out here?"

She didn't even move. "Getting some fresh air."

"It's sticky as hell." Though he doubted she felt it in that tiny shirt.

"I'm fine."

He exhaled, but the growing case of male indignation was lost on her when she continued to stare out over the water. He dropped down on the other side of the bench with his thigh touching hers. A rush of relief poured through him when she didn't pull away.

"I can control myself, you know." The words were barely true, but he wasn't an animal. He'd never forced a woman in his life, nor would he.

The idea she didn't want him as much as he wanted her was like a sucker punch to the gut, but living without her was something he had been doing for months now. He could manage that and still keep her safe.

She slowly turned to face him. "What did you say?"

"That's what this is, right? Stay away from the idiot male so he doesn't jump on top of you."

The marina light shone down next to the boat's deck, casting the water around the boat in deep shadows. It was tough to make out much, but he could see her face. The frown was hard to miss.

Her legs slipped and her feet fell to the floor. "You've got this all wrong."

"Look, I know I can be demanding in the bedroom, but I'm not a jerk." He believed in monogamy and a healthy sex life, whether the relationship lasted a few days or a few weeks. With her, it had lasted almost two years and he was all in. He thought only of her, always of her.

"Your bedroom preferences aren't relevant because we're not together."

The words sliced through him, but he refused to let the wound show. "I'm not sure that matters for us. Bed is the one place we've always communicated just fine."

"You're such a guy."

"That's what I'm saying. It's been a long, crappy day. You had two men die at your feet and are still standing. I'm really impressed. Everything about you makes me proud, but I won't pretend I don't want you."

Her eyes widened to the point of popping. "That's the first time you've ever said that."

"The wanting thing? Uh, I don't think so." He was pretty sure he'd said it several times tonight.

And there was no way she couldn't know. People who passed them on the street and had never met them knew. Hell, Mrs. Winston saw them together for two minutes, not touching, and got the point.

"Not that." Lara waved a hand in the air before putting it on his knee. "The impressed part."

He stared at her fingers. Looked at her hand where it flexed against his leg and felt his frustrations drain out of him. Without thinking about it, her inclination was to touch him. He didn't know what that meant, but it gave him hope again.

All those calls the first few weeks after the breakup had gone unanswered. The visits where she wouldn't open the door. He'd stopped because he refused to be a stalker and would not beg a woman who wanted him gone.

Now he wondered if he'd given in too soon.

"That's not true. I know I told you that before." When she shot him a nice-try look he searched for an example in his memory. Nothing came to him. "Then I am a jerk."

"Let's agree you have had a few jerklike moments."

Not good enough. He wasn't going to let her give him a way out with a joke. This was too important. She was too important.

He slipped his fingers through hers and willed her to believe. "Honey, I'm proud of you every single day. You're strong and independent, and don't get me started on how beautiful you are. Just looking at you makes me hard."

She leaned into him. "Sweet talker."

He brought their joined hands to his lips and kissed the back of hers. The soft skin drove him wild, but he needed to prove something to her. "I can sleep up here if that makes you more comfortable. You take the bed."

"Being out here really isn't about you."

"Lara—"

She squeezed his hand. "Davis, listen to me. It's not you."

He wanted to shrug but couldn't get his shoulders to move and fake the gesture. "Feels like it is."

"I'm sick."

"Wait, what?"

"Sick."

The lightbulb didn't just go on in his head, it exploded to life. He should have thought that through. She wasn't used to death. The usual bad guys in her life consisted of losers in the grocery store or those boring attorneys she used to work with, including the one partner who'd made a pass and almost had Davis's fist shoved down his throat in response. Contract killers were at a whole different level.

"It's probably a reaction," he explained.

"Yeah, to the boat."

"What?"

She tucked her face into the space between his shoulder and his neck. "I'm seasick. When you broke out the peanut butter, I thought I was going to hurl."

The information bounced around his mind. "Like that one time we went boating?"

"Exactly like that, complete with rolling stomach."

"But that was a weird circumstance. You don't usually get sick." He pulled back and cupped her chin in his hand.

"Not if I'm on dry land."

He laughed but stopped after he saw her grumbly frown. "Why didn't you say something?"

"You were in hottie-rescuer mode."

He could live with that. "As if that's ever stopped you before."

"Honestly, I was willing to do anything if it meant I was safe and strange men stopped jumping out to kill me."

"I can see that." He threw an arm around her shoulders and pulled her in as close as his bruised ribs would allow. He'd wrapped them earlier after Pax checked them out, but certain movements still had him hissing air through his teeth.

"So, I'll sit here until the world stops spinning, which I'm hoping is soon or we're going to see that bread I ate one more time."

The words vibrated against his bare skin. "I'll join you in sitting and just hope the rest calms down."

"You don't have to."

"Maybe I want to." His thumb slid into her hair. "Do you feel sick now?"

She looked up at him. "Are you about to make a pass?"

"Depends on the answer to my question."

"We need to be smart about this." The way she grabbed on to his shirt contrasted with her comments.

"Oh, definitely." Slowly, and giving her plenty of time to pull away, he lowered his head to kiss her.

She put a finger over his lips. "I am not sleeping with you."

"No. Of course not."

She lowered her hand to his chest. "That was too easy."

Oh, they would, and at some point they'd have to deal with the issues that drove them apart. It was clear to him this was more than the easy-to-ignore straggly ends of a broken relationship. These were threads that needed to be tied together again. He was never so sure as when he stared into those stunning eyes and saw nothing but welcome there.

Still… "The timing is wrong tonight," he said, only half meaning it.

"Gee, you think?"

But they could still kiss. He leaned in. Just before his eyes closed, a movement in the water grabbed his attention. At first he thought it was a buoy or dinghy that had broken loose.

Her smile faded as her head whipped around to follow his gaze. "What do you see?"

He was impressed she whispered despite the panicked tone to her voice. "Something."

Bending forward, he opened the storage cabinet under the bench. He felt around, moving over ropes and something that felt like a pulley. Then he felt it. Wrapping his fingers around the smooth plastic, he brought out a flashlight.

"Stay here." He motioned to her as he stood up and went to the railing.

The focused beam moved over the dark water. The rhythmic thunking didn't stop and he aimed for the sound. Following a line, the light landed on a small boat. The pieces fell together. It was the kind of boat you'd never take to the ocean but might spend hours loading down with unnecessary supplies.

She appeared at his side. "What is it?"

"Ken's boat." The light traveled over the craft but no one moved. The bigger concern was how close it sat to Pax's boat.

"I thought that Ken person never actually took his boat out."

Smart woman. "Exactly."

"What do—"

He put a hand over her mouth when he heard a thump at the front of the boat. "We've got company, and it's not Pax this time."

Chapter Seven

Not again.

Lara tried to stop her insides from shaking hard enough to rattle her back teeth. She grabbed on to Davis's hand with a death grip that would have broken the bones of a weaker man. Intuitively she knew she had to let go because he'd need two arms to fight off whatever new threat headed their way, but her brain refused to telegraph the message to her fingers.

After a reassuring squeeze, he did it for her. He turned his flashlight off with a snap and tucked the slim end into his back pocket. Next, he motioned for her to duck down. The textured floor was rough against her palms and bruised knee, but she didn't say a word. Couldn't.

Tucked against the seats behind the ship's wheel, she made her body as small as possible. Davis didn't have that luxury. With those shoulders, his body could only get so little.

Footsteps echoed against the bow lightly, but in the dead quiet of the night the still air carried the sound. Water lapped against the side of the boat, and all the associated clangs and dings continued, but the squeak of a step still stood out now that she was listening for it.

That put the attacker maybe ten feet away and slightly above them. The marina safety lighting hit the back of the boat and also highlighted their whereabouts. This guy had the clear advantage. And there could be more than one of him.

Davis pushed his palm against the small door under the seat in front of them and made a face when it clicked out loud. With quick and efficient movements, he drew something out. It didn't flash under the light, but she knew what it was. A gun, probably one of many hidden on the boat.

Back when they'd been together Davis had been adamant she know about weapons. Cleaning, firing, storing. He'd gone over the routines several times. He'd insisted the lessons were about more than simple self-protection. If he kept guns in the house, she needed to understand as much as possible about them or risk being a victim.

He touched a light hand to her lower back. "Get off the boat." The husky whisper blended into the sounds of the marina.

Her stomach ached as if she'd been kicked repeatedly. "You mean both of us."

"Eventually." He put a finger against his lips and

raised his head enough to see something that had him ducking again.

She loved the big protective alpha-male thing. But she hated the idea of leaving him behind. Knowing he was in danger would freeze her to the dock. The rib injuries and long day of fighting might prove too much for him to overcome.

Thinking to call in reinforcements, she slipped her hand into her pocket to grab her cell, until she remembered she'd left it on the table below deck. The only thing she had with her was a springy pink hair tie. Nothing helpful about that.

Davis signaled for her to slip over the side. "Stay low. I'll stand to draw fire."

Her breathing actually shuddered. "Terrible plan."

"Go."

Her mind raced to find another solution. He was the expert, but she couldn't let him make this sacrifice or take on this danger. Her gaze bounced around the deck until she felt his hand against her elbow. He gave her a sharp shake of his head and pointed to his right.

Nothing subtle about his orders this time. His stern frown suggested he was ready to throw her over the side.

Because his attention should be on the bad guy, she gave in. She glanced over and tried to see the dock from her position. It fell out of her line of vision. She knew a six-foot drop should put her on a stable walkway, and she could run from there. But without the ladder or anything to break her fall, it was going to hurt. Not the best solution but maybe her only one.

Crouching on the balls of her feet, she didn't have much traction. She shifted to get her balance as a thud vibrated next to her ear. She looked up just as the attacker reached down and grabbed her. Her scream cut off when he wrapped his arms around her chest, stealing her air.

In the time it took for his face to register in her brain, he'd lifted her off her feet and had her pressed against him as a shield. Heat radiated off of him and a subtle vibration moved through him. She chalked it up to some sort of sick evil energy.

He was dressed all in black with his face partially covered by a hood, but she still recognized him. He'd made the trip from Capitol Hill to finish the job.

He pressed a knife against her throat as Davis got to his feet. The gun was missing but she knew he had it nearby. "It's him."

"Back for a second try? You'll fail this time, too." Davis's voice never wavered. He didn't look at her either.

The attacker rubbed his cheek against hers. "I've already won."

She jerked when the attacker's hot breath blew across her ear. She smelled musk and sweat. The mixture filled her senses and she had to fight to keep from gagging. The slight rock of the boat and salty fish smell of the water backed up on her and her stomach heaved.

The guy tightened his hold around her chest until she was afraid to move. In panic she clawed at the arm around her but the hold didn't ease.

"You and your girlfriend are going to get in the cabin," he said.

It didn't take an expert to know going inside meant death. Her heart raced so fast that she was surprised he didn't feel it. She vowed to go out kicking.

Davis glanced at the two steps and doorway to the area below deck. "So we can have an accident of some sort? No, thanks."

"I can cut her now and let you watch."

The blade nicked her skin. The shock of pain was a promise of things to come. "Davis."

The attacker's whole body shook with a harsh laugh. "Listen to the terror in her voice, Davis. Use your head."

For the first time since their unwelcome guest had arrived, Davis glanced at her. Those intense eyes blazed, and for the briefest of seconds his gaze slid to the floor then came back up again. It was a clue. Something about hitting the floor. Desperation ate away in her stomach as she tried to figure out exactly what he wanted her to do and when.

"Hands up." The attacker barked the words more than said them.

After a flash of hesitation, Davis raised one hand and took a step. He came even with the attacker's side. Davis's stare bored through her as he moved.

She couldn't come up with a scenario in which Davis going into the galley ended with them surviving. And if she knew that endgame, he definitely knew. His mind never stopped analyzing and assessing. That meant he had a plan and even now was unrolling it.

He touched the stair railing. Instead of going below, he flipped around and yelled, "Down!"

The sudden change of direction had the attacker flinching. Without thinking, she angled her head to the side and dropped before she could worry about the knife. Her legs collapsed under her, leaving her sitting in a heap at the attacker's feet. When Davis launched his body and slammed into the other guy, she was trapped between their legs. Right in the line of fire.

Her breath thundered in her ears as she looked for a space to slip through. She crawled a few inches but couldn't break free. With one hand, Davis lifted and pushed her out of the way. She ducked as he jumped over her to get to the attacker.

Her last thought was to run but her body went airborne. Her back smashed against the doorway to the front cabin before she landed hard on her butt.

Bones rattled and a surge of dizziness had her head swimming and her vision blurring.

When her eyes focused again the urge to vomit hit her hard. She choked down the taste as she dragged her body, half falling and half stumbling, back to her feet as she looked to the other side of the deck.

The men rolled across the deck in an echoing series of grunts. Arms and legs flailed. A knife flashed in the light. Air refused to fill her lungs as she watched the attacker wrestle Davis to the deck. They landed with a thud as the fall knocked Davis's gun from his hand. The men scrambled, crawling over each other, using clothes and anything else they could grab for leverage.

Davis's hand wrapped around the weapon but the attacker pushed it away. Before Davis could make another attempt, the attacker slammed a knee into his back. Davis's body bent back. Tucking again, he rolled over and smacked the heel of his hand into the guy's face.

The attacker wailed as blood spurted from his nose. Instead of falling off Davis, the guy slammed his weight harder against Davis's stomach, doubling him over as he gasped.

With a final blood-freezing scream of rage the attacker brought the knife down in a swooping arc. Davis shifted his head to the side at the last second and the blade stabbed into the floor.

Fearing Davis couldn't win this one, not when

he was already hurt, she struggled to her feet and looked across the bow for something, anything, to aim at this guy. She saw cans stacked up at the far end and blinked. Her mind didn't grasp the importance or even understand what she saw until she inhaled and the harsh scent of gasoline ran through her.

He was going to blow them up.

She spun around in time to see Davis whip out the flashlight and deliver a bone-crunching hit to the other guy's jaw. The attacker's head actually snapped back. For a second his eyes slipped shut and Davis used the opening to shove the guy off. Up on his knees, Davis stretched out for the gun.

"Davis!" Her scream bounced off the fiberglass and had him turning to face her. "Gasoline."

She barely got the word out over the terror shaking her body and kicking life into her muscles. She wasn't even sure he'd heard or understood until his eyes went wide. His gaze traveled over the boat as all emotion vanished from his face.

Swiping the gun, she stood up, stopping only to kick the attacker in the shoulder when he struggled up for another round. Running, his arms pumping and cheeks hollow, Davis smashed into her. With a hand on her arm, he lifted and propelled her to his right. Her thigh slammed into the side of a seat as they went but she kept going. She didn't have a choice. Davis had her locked to his side.

The attacker got to his feet but Davis didn't stop moving. With a hand on her butt, he hoisted her up on the side railing. His body wrapped around hers like a blanket as he dropped them over the side. The air rushed around them. She closed her eyes and waited for the hard crack of the dock against her skull a few feet below. When they hit, she bounced against his chest and heard him groan.

Her eyes popped open in time to see him aim his gun at the side of the boat, as if waiting to see a face peek over. They were lower and couldn't see inside, but he was ready.

She heard a splash and Davis swore. He shifted and jumped to a crouch. A rumbling whoosh stopped him from going farther. One minute she sat there, trying to get her bearings, and the next a wall of heat punched her face. The bang rang out right before Davis slipped his arms around her and rolled them to the far side of the dock.

The floor beneath them fell away and they flew through the air again. She gasped as they hit the water. The smell of fish smacked her in the face as she struggled to hold her breath. Her eyes opened as a ball of red and orange exploded above the water. Even under she could hear the booms and crackle.

Something slapped the water near her head. Davis kicked and they swam, bubbles giving away their path, as chunks of wood and things she couldn't recognize through the haze of water crashed around them.

Just as her air ran out and she thought her lungs would explode if they went one more foot, they broke the surface. She hung on to his shoulders and he grabbed on to the side of the small hill leading to the road and the firm land beyond.

Flames shot up from the center of what used to be Pax's boat. "We would have been in there."

The explosion numbed every part of her. Her mind barely functioned, yet somehow her hands held on to Davis.

"That was the idea." Even through all the noise his voice sounded harsh and raw.

The water bobbed around them and sirens squealed in the distance. Men raced to the scene, screaming for help while the few people on the boats in the slips ran up the docks to safety. The fire consumed Pax's boat and the impressive sailboat next to it. Lara didn't see any sign of the attacker, but she had a trickle of a memory that made her think he got away.

She remembered Davis's promises about being safe and wondered if she'd ever feel okay again. "How did he find us?"

"I'll find out." His set jaw made his voice sound like a hard slap. "But your attacker miscalculated about one thing."

"You mean how he set the fire too soon?" Water

splashed up and into her mouth, and she spit it back out. She tried hard not to think about what swam around in there with them or the garbage she had seen floating on the top earlier.

"I mean that he's made a new enemy. Pax is not going to take losing his boat well."

For some reason that made Lara feel better.

CLIVE PUT HIS palms against the floating dock on the row of slips at the far side of the marina and lifted his body out of the water. He rolled to his back and stared up into the orange-hazed sky. Shifting his jaw, he checked for any breaks. That idiot had swiped him with a flashlight. Oh, he'd pay for that.

Fire trucks blared into the parking lot. Clive lifted his head and watched their flashing lights illuminate the area. He lay far enough away, covered by his dark clothes and unexpected presence. For the next hour or so all attention would be on getting that fire out and roping off the area. Sneaking away would not be a problem. Recovering from this before his boss got word might be harder.

Firemen and policemen filed out of vehicles and surrounded the docks across from him. It was quite a scene. But the wrong kind of scene.

This was supposed to be a quiet ending. He hadn't counted on a late-night dunk in slimy water. Knock them out, stick them in the cabin and then light the fire. When the woman had struggled and the boyfriend stepped in, everything got screwed up. Too much time had passed, and the fuel exploded instead of sparking to a low burn.

His boss wasn't going to like this. He was a powerful man who preferred easy answers. This was too loud and called too much attention.

But Clive knew he could spin it, bring the arrow of guilt to point at Lara Bart. She wanted to hide her tracks and pretend to be dead. After all, she'd killed her lover Steve Wasserman and had to get out of town.

Yes, that story would work. Clive knew he could build it. First, he had to tie this off before the loose ends got any longer.

Clive admitted he'd underestimated his enemy this time. Investigative desk types rarely had this skill level. This Lara person only asked questions for a living, after all. Looked as though his intel on her was all wrong.

Clive hadn't counted on Davis Weeks either. That guy could fight—he'd avoided a fireball and a gunfight.

Clive admired Davis's will to live, but Clive couldn't allow it to go on. Lucky for him, he knew where to squeeze next. Davis had a weakness for the girl. The file mentioned a brother and a work team. That was where Clive would go.

He sat up and reached for the phone in his pocket. Waterlogged and useless. Guess that meant his boss couldn't track him down now. Breaking the phone in two, he whipped the pieces into different spots in the water. It felt good, freeing.

He glanced back to the spot where he'd seen the couple go over the side. They were out there and likely alive. He could feel it. They would not be easy to take out, but he would finish the job.

And he'd save that last bullet for his boss. No way could information on this botched hit get out. It would ruin his reputation, which meant they all had to go.

Chapter Eight

Davis stood with Lara chest-deep in the cool water and felt his muscles go numb. Hypothermia and fire were not his biggest concerns right now. No, the emergency vehicles racing into the marina parking lot held that title.

The huge light and sound show would draw attention from every direction—gawkers, news media, first responders, neighbors. They would all come running, and a helicopter was likely to show up any second. All things he didn't need right now. Or ever, really, but especially right now.

Being caught here would mean questions. Lots of them, and many he couldn't answer. Fingers would point and all that hard work in hiding his and Pax's ownership of properties and vehicles, including the boat, would crumble. Then none of them would be safe.

The police already wanted to talk with Lara. Davis was determined not to let that happen, not until he knew who'd killed Wasserman and why. Then he'd handle tonight's attacker. He'd taken two shots at Lara, and Davis would make sure there wasn't a third. Seeing that knife prick her throat had started a revving up in Davis's body that wouldn't stop until the attacker was on a slab or in prison.

Holding her now helped calm some of the fury thrumming through Davis. Another night like this and the explosion of the boat wouldn't be anything compared to the one in his head. He rubbed a hand over her arm and felt her tremble from the cold aftermath. He tried to silence the humming need for revenge, box it and control it, but the fire slammed in his gut.

While the heat inside him matched the one ripping through his brother's boat, her skin stayed cool as she continued staring at the flames. He needed her safe, dry and as far away from violence as possible. But first they had to get by the police roping off the scene.

Maybe they'd stayed a minute too late.

Climbing up the slippery rock hill would mean crossing the main path that separated the marina building and parking lot from the dock and slips. Talk about making them a target. They'd have to wind their way unseen through crowds and cars. It was hard to imagine how that would be possible because they were soaking wet and obviously not law enforcement.

They'd be right under the lights and in the open.

And if people didn't see them, they sure would smell them. The mix of burned ash and dead fish would be tough to miss.

That left one really unpleasant option—swim under the main walkway coming down from the hill and keep moving until they could exit the marina on the far left side, away from the fire and crime-scene observers. It meant getting close to the flaming boat and passing in front of what was left of the hull. Wading, head nearly underwater through the muck that washed up on the rocks from the bay, might be the one step too much for Lara, who already looked ready to drop.

"We have to get out of here." When she nodded, he turned her face to look into her eyes. "Lara?"

"I'm okay."

With her hair stuck to her head and teeth chattering, she looked the exact opposite of okay, but their choices were limited here and the voices kept getting closer. "We're going to swim—"

"What?" Her gaze finally cleared and she frowned.

He took that as a good sign. Anger meant emotion and something still clicking inside her. He could work with that.

"We're going that way." He pointed to his left and did a double take.

Bright white lights skimmed across the water. A ship's horn sounded and an engine rumbled. As it got closer, he could make out fire hoses.

They were getting closed in from all directions now. With his arm still wrapped around her, he tried to maneuver over the rocks and drag her along with him. The ship's movements sent waves crashing harder against them. At the first smack of water, she slipped out of his grasp and went under.

She came up spitting. "This is impossible."

Wanting to shield her and limit the noise, he shifted until he stood on the outside, using his bigger body to block the floating debris and break the walls of water pushing into them. Flames shot up into the sky and floating debris brought fire closer to them until he batted them away.

Not giving her time to panic, he held her hand and brought her under the walkway. Each step felt like a Himalayan climb. The pressure of the water robbed their strength. He was bigger and just moving sucked the life out of him, so he couldn't imagine how difficult it was for her to lift her feet.

As they dipped lower, the walkway brushed against their heads. As they came out on the other side, voices rang out right above them. Diving on top of Lara, he dragged her out of the line of sight and pressed her body against his on the rocks. Sharp edges dug into his side and his aching ribs now thudded to the point where he had trouble catching his breath.

The water lapped around their still bodies as foam and charred debris brushed up against them. With her head tucked into his neck, he tried to blend their bodies into the hill separating the water from the land. When shoes hammered on the walkway down to the slips, he glanced up again.

People jogged down the floating docks. Hoses from the rescue boat in the harbor fired water into the flames. Male voices echoed around them.

They had to move.

Drawing her low in the water, he pulled her with him. Their mouths stayed closed and they moved quickly, cutting through muck and letting the dark water cover their bodies. The beeping sounds of trucks backing up and the thuds of boats knocking against the docks hid any stirring their moves might cause. Davis walked and kicked out, shoulders underwater as he ignored whatever wrapped around his legs and knocked into his ear.

All of his focus was on a less steep hill by the fishing-equipment rental shed. From there they could duck into the trees and follow the outside parking lot fence to freedom. By that time, everyone would be at the boat's side of the lot, overlooking the water. He and Lara would be at the back and on the run.

They finally reached the space he thought would work best for an escape onto land. Glancing back, he saw a line of men with their backs to them and the flames decreasing under the shooting water.

It would take hours to get the fire under control and hours after that to control the area and sweep for forensics. With most of the attention off the water and on other boats, now three of them burning from the explosion and being devoured by the lick of orange, they had a chance—as long as the other dangers lurking in the dark stayed away.

Narrowing his gaze, and wishing he had night goggles, he did a quick search for their attacker. Davis had his gun, but because it had been submerged in water he wasn't all that anxious to fire it. Sneaking away only to run into the attacker again would be Davis's luck at this point.

Lara's body collapsed against a smooth rock. Her chest heaved as she fought for breath. "Never thought that would be so hard."

"You did great." With his hands on her hips, he lifted her, sliding her body along the hill until her upper body reached the pathway.

Every time he let go to brace his hands and steady them both, her body deflated and whatever steam propelled her petered out. With her energy depleted, it was up to him to get them both up and on their feet.

Balancing his feet against the lowest set of rocks, he bolted up, careful not to cause a loud splash. The jump pressed his body against hers and she grunted in response. But he had leverage now. Pushing and pulling, he shimmied until he brought their bodies onto the path together.

Once his elbow hit pavement, he rolled off of her

to give her some air. With eyes open, he stared up at the strangely pink sky. The fire had cut through the darkness, and smoke hung on the stale air. Without a breeze, all the smoke and fire stayed relatively contained, but much more and the haze would fall and they'd start choking on the foul, gas-tainted air.

He came up on his side and looked down at her. Her pale face stood out against the dark ground. "You okay?"

She peeked up at him. "I'm ready for a few boring hours."

"I think I can give you that."

She didn't say anything as she sat up and put her feet underneath her. She tried to stand but her knees buckled. She would have hit the ground again, but he caught her around the thighs. His arms trailed up to her waist as he stood. His legs didn't feel any stronger. The muscles had turned rubbery, so he held on. Maybe they could hold each other up.

After a few seconds, two trucks pulled up and stopped in front of the far parking-lot gate. News trucks. The new visitors tore some of the attention away from the fire. That meant it was more likely someone would spot them, so it was time to leave.

With his hand in hers and their bodies crouched down, they jogged the few steps to hide behind the fishing shed. He kept his back against the wall as he tried to judge the distance to the fence and the best way to go through it.

Going over it wasn't an option. Not in their current drained state. Not with water dripping off them and weighing them down.

He hoped the sirens got someone at Corcoran checking the marina cameras and seeing the devastation. That was his exit plan, but he had to get Lara to the fence first.

She fumbled with something in her fingers. He looked down at the bright pink band and watched her try to pull her wet hair out of her face. Her fingers were shaking and the band kept twisting.

He put his hand over hers. "Later."

Those huge eyes stared at him. Finally she nodded and looked down as she tucked the hair tie into her front pocket.

He pulled away, ready to head to the trees planted a few feet in front of them. He jerked to a stop when she didn't move.

He turned around, ready to give a quick and quiet pep talk. But she wasn't paying attention. She stood with the band on the tips of her fingers and stared at the ground. Her body seemed frozen in place.

Following her gaze, he saw the shoes. Shoes attached to legs. A man facedown on the ground. None of it made sense.

"How did…?" His voice trailed off because he wasn't sure what to ask.

She pressed both of her hands to her chest. "Is it him?"

He had no idea whom she meant until he saw the duffel bag and the cooler a foot away from that. He recognized both because he'd spent so much time watching them being dragged around. "Ken."

"Did he get caught in the explosion?"

Davis dropped into a crouch and slipped his fingers on the man's neck to check for a pulse. He didn't feel anything but cold flesh. When he pulled them back again, blood stained his fingertips and the pool under his head came into focus.

"Not an accident." This was body number three and Davis wasn't one inch closer to understanding what was happening.

Lara's head whipped around, looking from one end of the marina to the other. "The attacker did this?"

Had to be. The small boat next to Pax's had been the tip-off. That likely meant Ken was a sacrifice. Maybe he'd fought back. Davis didn't know but he secretly hoped Ken had inflicted some damage.

Thinking about the newest needless death started a spiraling tightness inside Davis. The attacker was willing to take out anyone to get to his target. Now Davis had to figure out who that was.

When he looked up again, he noticed the car idling on the other side of the fence. It sat fifty feet away, blanketed by the dark night. Between the smoky haze pressing down on them and all the commotion in the parking lot, the car blended in.

A figure slipped around the front end and stood in front of the fence.

It was hard to make out the details from this distance, but Davis knew this wasn't an enemy. He'd been watching this figure his whole life, first as a pseudo babysitter then as a partner. Always as a brother.

Davis promised to refrain from saying, "I told you so," but running all those contingency plans for all those years had paid off. The DIA training and leadership at Corcoran made this all possible. Smart men who knew you had to be prepared for the worst case had taught him to be ready.

And now Pax had come to break them out.

BEN WALKED THE area around the fishing shed. Crime-scene lights bathed the entire area in brightness. After two hours of fighting the flames, the fire had died down to a smoke trail. Most of the police and fire vehicles still filled the parking lot as some of those in charge spoke with the press.

So much for keeping the investigation quiet.

He'd flashed his badge and explained the fire was related to an ongoing investigation. He walked onto the crime scene and tried to make sense of what he was seeing. Ben wouldn't even have come here if not for the emergency call from the deputy. Seemed Ronald Worth had got his hands on an unredacted file that led him from Lara Bart to a man named

Davis Weeks. The confidential financial statement he'd filled out for his security clearance and work through a place called the Corcoran Team listed this boat as an asset.

It all struck Ben as too neat. Too convenient.

Lara Bart seemed to be at the top of everyone's threat list all of a sudden. Especially odd for a woman who'd sailed through her own security-clearance investigation to land a job preparing them for others.

Ben hadn't seen the forensics on Wasserman's house yet, but Wayne had called to let him know the deputy believed they would point to Lara and she should be the main target of the investigation. Without any real evidence or motive, people were very willing to believe she'd killed a naval officer.

Now Ben had arrived at another crime scene with a link to Lara Bart. Two dead men in one day. Either this woman had gone off the edge and was engaging in a wild crime spree, or something more sinister was at work here.

Funny how it all led back to Martin Coughlin and his NCIS appointment.

Even more interesting that he seemed to be the only one making that connection and wondering if Lara was being used.

Ben came around the side of the building, widening his circle as he scanned the area. His shoe pressed against something. He looked down, expecting to see a rock. Unless rocks turned pink from fire, this was something else.

He crouched down and grabbed an evidence bag from his pocket. Using a pen, he slid the hair tie into it. Examining the scrap of material, he wondered if it was related to Ken Dwyer's death or nothing more than a forgotten piece left behind days or even weeks ago.

His eyes narrowed as he studied it. Well, if it did belong to Lara they could know soon enough. The long blondish-brown hair wrapped in the band should give them DNA. She'd submitted samples to get her job, so a match, if there was one, would be easy to make.

Until the lab got back to him, he'd focus his attention elsewhere. First thing tomorrow—Martin Coughlin.

Chapter Nine

By the time Pax's car pulled into a driveway in the historic section of Annapolis, exhaustion had whipped through Lara, leaving her weary to her bones. None of them had spoken and the radio had stayed off on the short drive. Wrapped in a blanket and cuddled up against Davis's side, her muscles had released all of their tension. Despite being wet and smelling like a sewer, she could barely keep her eyes open long enough to take in her surroundings.

They pulled around a three-story redbrick house and to the garage that sat separate behind it. She didn't need to see the plaque by the front door to know it was a historic property. It was in the Federal style with a top floor only two thirds the size of the two below. Trees outlined the gravel drive. A bright light burned on the back porch and another attached to the garage clicked on from the motion of the car pulling in.

The place was so bright there was no way anyone could sneak up. She guessed that was the point.

Gravel crunched under the tires, and the car came to a stop. Pax and Davis jumped out a second later. The slamming doors revived her, but not enough that she wanted to race anywhere. She was too busy hoping her legs would hold her when she finally got up. The only way she'd even made it through the past half hour was to block the details of the day out of her mind.

Dead bodies. Explosions. Knives at her throat. She'd left the law firm on the hunt for something a *little* more interesting. But this was way over the top.

Davis opened the door and stared at her. That dark gaze swept over her body and an eyebrow lifted. Even soaking wet and half bent over, he was the toughest, sexiest man she'd ever met.

Somehow he had steered them through tonight's disaster. And to think one of her main complaints was the emotionless way he dealt with danger. Now she wondered if she'd been wrong. Maybe he needed the distance to survive.

She could accept that. Even apologize for being wrong. It was the rest, the secrets and messed-up priorities, she couldn't understand and had trouble forgiving.

But none of that mattered now. Not when he was looking at her as if he was two seconds away from dragging her to a hospital.

She knew exactly what he was contemplating in that whacked-out alpha-male brain of his. "Don't even think about picking me up. I'm not an invalid. I can walk."

A rare breeze rustled the leaves but disappeared as fast as it had come. Humidity thumped around them and her body grew sticky from the combination of wet clothes and hot air. None of that meant she wanted to be thrown over his shoulder and lifted off the ground.

His lips twitched. "You need rest."

"So do you. Rest and a doctor."

He winked at her. "Don't believe in either of those."

Pax peeked around his brother's shoulder. "Don't worry. I'll take care of the ribs and check him out. But we need to get you both inside and showered first."

"Where are we exactly?" She put out her hand and accepted Davis's assist out of the backseat.

"The Corcoran Team headquarters."

Clearly Davis thought that explained everything. "Your new office?"

"Offices are on the bottom." Pax pointed as he gave a verbal tour. "It's a residence on the top."

The last thing they needed was to destroy more of Pax's property. "Do you live here?"

He laughed. "No. Not really my style."

Davis scowled at his brother. "We can run through all of this tomorrow. Right now she needs sleep."

Davis ushered her toward the back door with Pax

trailing behind. He whistled, acting as if his boat hadn't just exploded into a million fiery pieces. His loss put hers in perspective. At least she had a home to go to…eventually.

When they got to the door, Davis stopped and glared at his brother. "You done with the noise?"

"Didn't like the song?"

Davis shook his head as he pressed his right hand against an oddly out-of-place dark square next to the back door. Then he leaned down and stared into it.

So much for the not-a-spy thing. "What the—"

"Security." With a hand at her back and a no-nonsense tone to his voice, he pushed her through the doorway and inside.

The room whizzed by her, but she thought she saw a country kitchen with a farmhouse sink and blue cabinets. The six-burner stove had that made-to-look-old style about it. The place was homey and warm, complete with a bowl of fruit on the scarred wood table.

No way did the Weeks brothers live here. They went for straightforward and simple. This place had a woman's touch, a realization that had Lara's brain blinking back to life.

Pushing through the kitchen door, they stepped into a large open room filled with desks and computers; large cabinets lined the far wall and a conference-room table sat in the middle. No one needed to explain this part. It was work central.

"Rough night?" The voice came from the far corner.

Lara followed it and saw two men stationed in front of a huge screen watching the scene at the marina. She checked the corners for news-channel markings. Nothing. The picture was clear and aimed from slightly above. Lara was pretty sure she was seeing a private inside camera loop.

"Impressive," she said under her breath. All eyes turned to her.

She immediately regretted the whispered word. By the stunned expressions she guessed she looked like the wrong end of a zombie apocalypse. She ran a hand through her hair and gave up when she snagged knot after wet knot. Add in the blanket and what she feared was a pound of mud caked to her face and you got one scary-looking woman.

A terrific first impression.

The man who had spoken used a remote to turn down the volume. He stood like they all did, feet slightly apart and hands deceptively hanging by his sides but more likely just within inches of a weapon. It was as if all these guys had taken a class in appearing formidable and in charge.

Davis waved the concern off. "We're fine."

She thought he should speak for himself. She was not fine.

Pax scoffed. "I'm not."

"You have insurance," Davis said.

With all respect to the discussion about "things,"

she had something bigger in mind. "Then there's the part where we almost died. Again."

Pax smacked his lips together. "Sorry."

The man with the remote stepped up. All six foot three or so of him. The dark hair and blue eyes combination worked for this one. A smile opened his handsome face and the scruffy beard gave him a bit of an edge.

Something about the way he held his body, shoulders back and sure of his place in the room, made her think he filled the leadership role of the group. He was muscular but not as filled out as Davis. Still, it was as if these Corcoran men all came off the same shelf. They had the lethal look down.

"I'm Connor Bowen." He pointed to the fourth guy in the room. "The tired one with his head in the pot of coffee is Joel Kidd."

Yep, a matching set. The last one looked younger than the rest of them, probably in his twenties. And he took the scruff thing a little more seriously. The grungy look matched the black hair and near-black eyes.

Then he nodded to her, and she saw a touch of scoundrel in him. "Ma'am."

Because Davis didn't bother introducing her, she took over. "I'm Lara Bart and, honestly, I've had better days."

Connor nodded. "We know."

"What?"

"Your name. We know who you are." His smile grew even wider. "What can we do to help? Tell us what you need."

A bed and something to make me sleep for about a month. She was tired enough to drop but feared what she'd see when she closed her eyes.

She'd experienced horrifying trauma before. It had taken months for the memory of the pain and terror to dull. This time she wanted to race through it and put all the death behind her.

"In addition to the promise that I can get through the next twelve hours without being shot at?" Because, really, she'd pay good money for that promise at this point.

Joel shrugged. "That's asking a lot."

Connor talked right over him. "We'll certainly try."

She glanced at Davis but he just stood there. His shoulders were stiff and the strain showed across his cheekbones. He likely wanted to launch into work mode and she was messing up his schedule.

She was more than happy to duck out. "Then I'll settle for a shower and a change of clothes."

"I can run out and get you something." Pax's keys jangled as he grabbed them out of his pocket.

"Don't bother," Connor said. "Jana has something Lara can wear until we can get her something else."

That explained the look of the kitchen. Lara wondered if the upstairs had the high-tech industrial look of this space or if it more mirrored the kitchen's feminine style. She was hoping for the latter. "Jana is?"

Connor's smile turned a little sad. "My wife. She's out of town."

It didn't take years of training to know there was something else at work there, but Lara was too tired to ask. Besides that, she refused to judge relationships. Some of her friends had done that to her with Davis, questioning if his work trips were really about work, and she'd hated it. "You sure your wife won't mind?"

"If I didn't offer she'd kick my…" Connor cleared his throat. "Yeah, it's fine."

Davis nodded to her. "Go ahead and shower."

He'd suggested exactly what she had in mind but it was the way he'd said it. Like an order. With an edge of dismissal.

Those days were over. "No."

"Excuse me?" The words carried a menacing thread. Davis was not a man accustomed to being questioned.

She was convinced that summed up what went wrong in their relationship. She never rolled over, but she'd let him get away with too much. Asked too few questions. Now that they weren't even dating, her tolerance for the tone was gone.

Ignoring their audience and her usual need to make a good first impression, because she'd blown that with the hair-wrapped-in-seaweed thing, she launched into the tirade that had been building since she'd hit that first guy with a lamp this morning. "This is not going to be one of those situations where the little lady leaves the room so the men can talk. I'm in this. Don't want to be, but I am. If you talk about the case, I'm here."

"I like her."

Davis practically growled at Joel over the comment before turning back to Lara with his full angry-man persona in place. The tick in his cheek was new and drove home his tenuous hold on his control. "You're going to get sick."

"Hardly," she said, even though she feared he was right. To prove her nonexistent point she let the blanket fall to the floor. "It's still over ninety degrees outside and it's two in the morning."

Pax whistled as he slipped into one of the conference-room chairs. "She got you there."

Davis's gaze dropped down her body. The heated stare had her squirming in her skin. But she refused to check and see what he was seeing. If her shirt was plastered to her or a piece of garbage from the water hung off her shirt, she didn't want to know. She didn't want anything to ruin her stand.

Davis held up a hand. "You'll get mad over this—"

"Then don't say it."

"—but the truth is there are things you can't hear." The whirling in her head sped up then popped. "A man got gutted in front of me. We can pretend this is about your job, but I still think it's about mine."

Connor cleared his throat. "I tend to agree with her. She was conducting an emergency interview for a pretty important NCIS position. A lot is at stake here for Martin Coughlin. We don't know what Wasserman planned to say but he sure was hot to say it."

"Makes me wonder what this guy Coughlin is trying to hide." Joel grabbed a file from the desk behind him and threw it on the conference table. It slid to a stop in front of Pax. "And I think we should find out."

"You all know about my interview?" She regretted the question as soon as she said it.

Never mind the confidential nature of her job—of course they knew. She'd filled Davis in out of necessity and he'd told Pax. It was like a covert-operative gossip circle. The news and theories likely spread among this group within minutes.

Pax winked at her. "We're on it."

There was a low rumble of laughter in the room. They shifted and filed into seats around the table. It was as if the tension had snapped and they felt safe to move again.

All but Davis. He stood stiff and still a few feet away from the conference table. "You're all forgetting the most important point."

Pax glanced up from the file. "Which is?"

"No one but the people in this room and a very few in the Department of Defense with the right clearance and a need-to-know have any idea about Pax's boat."

"May she rest in peace," Pax mumbled. Added a few profane words, too.

"Our financials are not available to just anyone." Davis folded his arms in front of him. The simple move, along with the monotone quality to his voice, had everyone snapping to attention and looking at him. "Our list of assets is confidential and buried deep. If the attacker found it, and it looks like he did because I know I wasn't tailed on the drive to the marina, someone handed it to him."

The theory made sense, but Lara wasn't convinced. When she closed her eyes she felt the storm brewing around her, not him. She truly believed whatever guilt he had about dragging her into this was misplaced. "You're still certain the attacks are about your work?"

"I think someone leaked the boat information and my house address to your attacker. The same someone who knew that you had ties to me and suspected you would come to me for help. My fear is someone came for me and decided the best way to get to me was through you."

The comment sat there for a second. Joel and Connor stared at her, probably realizing for the first time she was the ex. And wasn't that just great? She could only assume she didn't come out well in Davis's version of their breakup.

"We haven't been together for eleven months," she said because they were likely all thinking it.

Joel rolled his eyes. "Oh, please."

The air shifted again and she wasn't sure why. "What?"

"The last job…" Joel choked on the last word when Davis sent him the death glare. "What did I say?"

Oh, something was definitely going on. Something about her that they all knew. She hated that. "Someone explain."

Pax glanced at Davis and then back to her. "Joel's just talking out of his—"

"Davis." Yeah, that was where she would have to get the information. "Now."

Joel looked over at Connor. "Why did he break up with her again?"

"You think he left her?" Connor frowned. "Come on."

Davis turned the death ray of a look on them all, clearly not happy with whatever this was being played out in front of them. He should try being in her position.

He finally spoke up. "I was on an off-the-books job."

And that told her absolutely nothing. Well, except that whatever he was hiding was going to be bad.

She grabbed on to the back of the conference chair and dug her dirty fingernails into the soft leather. "Skip the covert-operative speak and tell me."

"Someone from an old job made a threat. It got back to me and I neutralized the guy."

Her stomach clenched. He made it all sound so mundane, but she knew better. "Neutralized?"

He shot her one of his famous you-can't-be-this-naive glares but stayed quiet.

Joel filled in the blank. "Killed."

Davis exhaled loud enough to drown out all the other noise in the room. "Yeah, Joel, I think she figured that out."

She blocked them all out except for Davis. She could see figures moving on the screen behind Connor and hear the buzz of the lights over her head. The only thing, only person, who mattered was the man trying so hard not to answer a straight question.

Davis's careful wording finally penetrated her brain. "What kind of threat?"

"Against you." Joel slid his chair back when Davis took a step in his direction.

"Wait, your rib injuries are because of me." She didn't phrase it as a question because suddenly she knew the right answer.

"Technically, they're because a guy hit him with a car," Pax said.

Davis never broke eye contact with her. "Don't help."

It all made sense. A sick kind of sense. "Someone was following me and you stopped them?"

Davis didn't even blink. "Yes."

She'd had more attackers following her and he'd never warned her. People she didn't know wanted her dead and he stepped in front of her and suffered in quiet on her behalf. "Who was it?"

"You don't know him."

"I can stand here all night, dripping on this floor, until you spill more facts."

Davis's gaze bounced down to her feet, then back up again. "We work with the Department of Defense and other agencies and private companies to conduct kidnap rescue missions."

He stopped there, acting as if that told her anything. "And?"

"We helped out recently when an off-duty service member got caught in the wrong place in the Philippines. A drug runner was killed and his brother didn't like it. He decided to make an example of me. Someone from my DIA days sold the information about your identity and our relationship, and the news got back to me. Simple."

Her life had turned into an action movie. "I think you're unclear on the definition of *simple*."

"The point is—anyone who investigates Davis's background will eventually find you." Connor shot her a sympathetic smile. "If they look deeper, they'll see he still watches over you and realize the bond isn't broken."

Davis closed his eyes and let out a small groan. "I meant to tell you to leave that last part out."

It was all too much. She'd given back the ring because he'd picked helping someone over being with her. She'd needed him as her stomach had cramped and she'd felt the blood rush out of her.

She'd lost their baby, miscarried, and he'd been so busy and gone so often that he hadn't even known what had happened. He thought they'd failed to get married and that was the biggest issue, but that was just the start.

The sudden rush of anger raced up and swamped everything. She was furious over his cluelessness and mad at herself for not confronting him all those months ago.

She'd accidentally left a door open and he'd found it and pushed his way through. Instead of moving on and forgetting about her, he still waged battles on her behalf. The last thing she wanted was for him to wade into even more danger because of her.

She pointed at him. "You stink at breaking up."

"I believe I warned you about that when you left," Davis shot back.

He'd actually warned her they weren't over but she hadn't listened. Now she didn't know what to think.

Inhaling as big a breath as she could gulp down, she turned and looked at Connor. "Where is this shower?"

He pressed his lips together as if he was trying

to suppress a smile. "There's a crash pad on the top floor."

"I don't know what that means."

"An apartment," Connor said. "You and Davis can stay up there until we work this out."

The guy seemed nice and all, and definitely comfortable in his leader role, but no way was she following that suggestion. "What's on the second floor?"

His gaze shot around the room before settling on her again. "My home."

"Good. Davis can stay there." When Davis opened his mouth, likely to say something to make her temples pound, she held up her hand and sent him her best we're-done-here scowl. "I took out two attackers with a lamp. Don't tempt me to practice my furniture-throwing skills on your head."

This time Connor did laugh, but he tried to hide it with the worst fake cough ever. "I'll be right up."

Chapter Ten

Ronald Worth headed toward his front door. The usual headache-producing yelling that went along with having two teen daughters fighting over clothes had ended tonight with banging bedroom doors and his wife playing intermediary. Normally he didn't tolerate such nonsense for long, but he had other things on his mind.

He opened the front door to his assistant, Wayne, and motioned for him to follow into the study. The visit broke his usual rule of separating work and family. He wasn't a fan of after-hours meetings, but Wayne didn't exaggerate. If he took the risk of bothering his boss at home, an actual emergency did exist. Something that might be better handled outside of the office.

"What is it?" Ronald asked in a tone he hoped would signal a need to get to the point quickly.

Wayne stood with his hands behind his back, never leaving the safety of the door. Even though it was closed, Wayne looked as if he could bolt right through it.

As far as Ronald could tell, that was the norm for his assistant. Between the sweating and the heavy swallowing, the guy always looked ready to run.

After one of those throat-moving swallows, Wayne started talking. "Ben Tanner."

Ronald sat in his red leather chair. It was either that or give in to the frustration building inside him and whip something across the room at Wayne. Not that it was his fault. No, this was Steve Wasserman's fault. The man had stayed silent, observed the pact, for years. One day he grew a conscience and everything went to hell.

But Ben was supposed to contain this mess. He was the guy who understood that rules often didn't fit a situation and had to be…manipulated. Or that was what his record had said, the personality Ronald had counted on when he'd maneuvered the case to be dumped in Ben's lap. "What did he do?"

"It's more like where he is."

"I am not in the mood for cryptic word games."

"There was a fire at one of the marinas in Annapolis tonight." Wayne stepped forward and slipped a sheaf of folded papers out of the inside pocket of his blazer.

Ronald didn't see the logical leap from fire to Ben. "Did one of the academy midshipman do something?"

"Someone blew up Paxton Weeks's boat. He's—"

"I know who he is." Pulling every string and using every back channel to make sure the trail didn't lead back to him, Ronald had read the Weeks brothers' confidential files. He'd given Ben just enough information to connect the players and keep his focus on the Bart woman. Or he thought he had. "Why is Tanner there?"

"I don't know but he got onto the scene by flashing his NCIS badge. After a few calls, a detective got rerouted to me to confirm Tanner's legitimacy."

After only a day Ben Tanner was proving to be a liability. "Injuries?"

"One dead. A male, but it appears to be unrelated to the fire."

So, no Lara Bart, the woman at the very heart of everything. "This is getting too messy."

"Sir?"

Maybe this was a good thing. The more focus on the Lara-Bart-as-scorned-lover angle, the less attention on Steve Wasserman's accusations. "It looks like we have another link to Lara Bart. That woman does seem to turn up everywhere, doesn't she?"

"I'm not sure if anyone has made that connection."

This part Ronald could handle without using Ben. "Call your detective back and make sure they do."

SILENCE THUMPED THROUGH the room as Lara stormed up the steps. Davis had seen her hurt, seen her ticked off. Tonight was a whole new level of anger. She looked as though she could follow through with that lamp threat.

He just wished she'd saved that for a private conversation. He hadn't wanted to tell her about the car accident just yet. And having it unspool in front of these guys guaranteed he'd be hearing about it forever. The men had gone in together after their DIA team leader had got married and traded his job for a private-security company.

Pax and Davis had decided they preferred Annapolis over San Diego and came back home. Connor had convinced Pax and Davis to join Corcoran and then lured Joel from the government job that had him disillusioned.

Connor broke through the quiet. "That's an angry woman right there."

"I'm kind of in love." Joel took a long drink out of his coffee mug. "In fact, forget the 'kind of' part."

"She's had a rough day." Davis grumbled the words because that was all he could manage at this point. Lara wasn't the only one who'd had enough for one evening.

"Yeah, the *day* was the problem," Pax joked.

Davis was ready to declare this conversation over. He glanced around at the empty desks on the opposite side of the room, noticing clean tabletops and knowing that meant one thing. "Where's the rest of the crew?"

"Doing post-job cleanup in Mexico."

The idea of a new assignment and the chance to legitimately change the subject appealed to him. "What is it? Who's missing?"

"A diplomat's kid. It was an easy run and grab for us. The boy is still stunningly spoiled but he's home now." Connor shook his head. "But you don't get to spend even one minute thinking about that job. You have enough to worry about with your woman and figuring this mess out."

Davis liked the sound of Lara being his. Well, he usually did. Right now he wasn't sure.

The fighting wasn't his favorite. He could never understand why every minute couldn't run smoothly. You fell in love, lived together and—boom—things should straighten out.

Boy, had he been wrong on that score. "You might want to explain to her how she's mine."

"I'm not ticking her off by bringing your name up." Connor handed the remote to Joel, who immediately turned the volume up and flipped back around to rewind the tape. "But I will go get her some clothes."

As much as Davis wanted to ignore this, he couldn't. Letting things fester had helped to land them their messed-up relationship in this spot.

Still, he let out a long-suffering poor-males sigh. "Show me the way. I'll take care of getting her what she needs."

Pax whistled; this time it sounded like a warning. "Uh, are you sure that's a good idea?"

"Whether she likes it or not, we're in this to-gether." Davis's only worry was that she really didn't like it.

Pax didn't back down. "Are you talking about this operation or the sleeping arrangements?"

"Both."

It actually took Davis longer than expected to get upstairs. Connor got the clothes and helped Lara settle in. Because every step hurt, Davis let Pax check his injuries and wrap his ribs. The pain pills Davis took had his eyelids drooping.

All he wanted was to climb into bed…with Lara. No sex because, really, he'd never stay awake long enough to enjoy it now that he had the painkillers in his system. But he could hold her.

When he opened the door to the crash pad, the room was dark. He didn't need a light. He'd stayed there for a few weeks at the beginning of his employment when he couldn't bring himself to actually move into the house he'd planned to share with her. For almost a month he'd debated selling it without ever putting so much as a shirt in the closet.

Now he saw the Lara-size lump in the bed and thought about lifting his T-shirt off. He gave up when he decided shifting around would only make his ribs ache more. The boxer briefs only stayed on as a concession to her. Sliding into the cool sheets, he lay back and nearly groaned in relief as his head hit the pillow.

She was up and twisting a second later. The light flipped on, highlighting the room in yellow.

"Hey." He threw his arm over his eyes to block the light.

She shoved it down and stared at him. "What are you doing?"

"Sleeping."

"Not here."

"I'm not going to touch you." Though he was tempted. Her oversize V-neck T-shirt hinted at the amazing body underneath. It had been a long time but he could still remember how soft her skin was and how perfectly her breasts fit his palm.

"Davis."

For a second he was worried he'd said that last part out loud. "Lara, look. I'm exhausted and in more pain than I want to admit." He added that last part in the hope the guilt might sway her. "Pax took care of the new injuries and gave me some pills. I could barely stand up in the shower."

"I'm happy you took one."

The smell of his shirt would have kept him awake. "I don't want to fight."

"I don't either."

Could have fooled him. "Are you sure? Because you're kind of good at it."

The flat line of her mouth went even straighter. "How much pain are you in?"

He guessed she was debating if she should add more. "Some. What about you and that knee?"

"It's no big deal. Not like your injuries." She nibbled on her bottom lip. "So, you're skipping the doctor?"

He was done talking about his ribs. That conversation could only lead to trouble. If she asked too many questions, they'd circle right back to what had ticked her off so much downstairs—the reason behind him getting run over by a car.

"Does this hurt?" He traced his finger over the small nick on her throat. The ends of her hair, damp from a shower, brushed against his hand. "I wanted to kill him for hurting you."

Her eyes did that thing where they got all soft. He had no idea how women did that. It was one of those secrets perfected over time and handed down through the generations. Women's eyes got big and sweet and men turned stupid. He was no exception.

She rubbed the back of her hand over his beard stubble. "You rescued me."

"Eventually." Almost too late, and that ate at him. He'd see her face, the pleading as the terror threatened to swamp her, every time he closed his eyes.

She tilted her head and her hair slid over her shoulder. "Don't do that. You're not superhuman."

"But you are." Strong and sexy and so damn

determined that his heart swelled just from watching her.

He still loved her. A piece of him had always known it, sensed the deep feelings had never gone away. He piled anger and regret on top of the love, but it thumped as strong as ever. Seeing her convinced him of that. Touching her, kissing her brought home the reality that he always would love her.

He had no idea what to do about his feelings or how to win her back. Then there was the very real part where he wanted her to explain and admit that leaving him had at least been a little difficult for her. She'd broken him and he didn't even know if she cared.

But now wasn't the time. His words were starting to slur and his brain skipped and stammered over making simple connections. Still, he needed her to know one thing. "You made me proud today."

Her smile was instantaneous. "Really?"

"Yeah, honey."

She dropped a kiss on his nose then scooted back to her side of the queen-size bed before he could respond. She glanced back at him over her shoulder. "Okay, you get to sleep here, but keep your hands to yourself."

"Oh, I can't promise that."

"You need your sleep."

He could hear the smile in her voice. "Then you're safe."

But for tonight only. As soon as the pain subsided he planned to remind her just how good they were together. If it took a battle to get her back he'd come armed for war.

Chapter Eleven

Ben rang the doorbell at Martin Coughlin's house the next morning. The one-story rancher in Virginia sat on a large lot with a leafy green front yard that defied the burning of the beating sun. Rows of perfectly trimmed bushes and bright red flowers highlighted the white bricks. The place was right out of a "work hard and you get this" public service announcement.

That fit Martin. He had graduated with honors from the U.S. Naval Academy, went on to serve with distinction and retired in time to get offered an impressive position with NCIS. He had plenty of experience, even worked in a joint command with NCIS, but another man had been the lead contender for the senior-intelligence-officer position. Then the deputy director had put his old friend's name at the top of the list.

Ben knew the details because there were no fewer than ten men in the special-agent field who had lined up to talk to him off the record. Martin was a favorite among the politically connected set, but men on the ground weren't impressed.

There was talk of an ego and outrageous sense of entitlement. More than one person commented on his heiress wife and the family's carefully crafted public persona, complete with two beautiful, blond private-school kids.

Although the gossip held a certain fascination, whatever Wasserman knew that might have got him killed interested Ben more.

After the second ring of the bell, the door opened. Ronald Worth stood there. "Good to see you again, Ben."

Ben couldn't really agree. "Sir? Why are you here?"

"To supervise your interview with Martin." The deputy swept his arm across the foyer and in the direction of the mumble of voices to the right.

Because Ben hadn't told anyone except Martin about the meeting, that could only mean Martin had run to his old buddy Ronald. The inbred information of this case made Ben's head spin. There was nothing neutral about this case review.

When the case had landed on Ben's desk, he had wanted to dig in. Now he wished someone else had pulled the assignment. Of course, someone else might be willing to go along with the deputy's vision of the case, but Ben wasn't that guy.

He glanced around. Everything was in a shade of blue or yellow. Not a stick of furniture looked out of place. The no-dirt, no-clutter thing made Ben wonder where these people hid their kids.

He turned the corner and stepped into the doorway of the formal living room. The dark wood and small, shiny collection behind a glass-front cabinet didn't leave much room for question when it came to these folks' financial status. The place had an old-money feel to it.

So did Mrs. Coughlin. She sat perfectly straight in her chair with her legs crossed under her dress, and she sipped tea out of a tiny cup.

Ben shook his head. It was as if he'd walked into a Rockefeller family photo.

A man rushed forward. Fortysomething, fit and wearing dress pants and a tie while presumably relaxing on his day off at home. Yeah, that was normal.

"I'm Martin Coughlin. This is my wife, Nancy." She stood up with a smile seemingly frozen in place and came over to shake hands. "And this is John Gallagher."

Gallagher had a rich, useless look to him. Fancy watch and a smirk where a smile should have been. He, too, belonged to the business-suits-on-Sunday group. Made Ben grateful he lived in Georgetown because he preferred jeans on his days off.

No one bothered to define the man's role, so Ben guessed he should recognize the name. He didn't.

He filed it away in case he didn't figure it out in the next few minutes.

He also made a mental note to polish his résumé because it was now clear the deputy had a telegraphed ending in mind to this so-called investigation, and finding out the truth didn't appear to be a priority.

"Am I interrupting something?" Which struck Ben as impossible because he had called the meeting.

"We're all here for your talk with Martin." Something in the deputy's tone suggested he expected to be made aware of all private meetings in the future.

Martin motioned toward the end of the couch. "Have a seat."

Ben obliged even though the seat put him right in the deputy's line of sight. Worth leaned against the wall right next to the baby grand piano. The bench had a cover that looked as if it had been brushed with a comb. Also, it didn't have an indentation that would suggest someone actually sat down and played the instrument now and then.

"You are in a difficult position." Martin sat perpendicular to Ben in a separate chair and assumed a serious man-to-man look. "We understand you need to go through the checklist, but the reality is the murderer's identity is known."

Ben tried to figure out if he agreed with any of that. "And that person is?"

"Lara Bart." John jumped to take this one. "Looks like a lover's spat gone wrong."

"It's terrible, but Steve always did struggle when it came to women," Nancy said, complete with a sympathetic head shake.

The entire conversation was too choreographed for Ben's liking. They each played a role, and none of them did so convincingly. He stared at the grandfather clock in the corner, watched it tick a steady beat and decided to play along. For now.

"Meaning?"

"He liked the type inclined to passion, and by that I mean fighting and screaming." Martin glanced at his wife and waited for her to give him a pursed-lip nod before continuing. "He'd twice had the police called when fights with a previous girlfriend escalated."

So the game was blame-the-victim. No surprise there. Ben decided to impart a little reality into the conversation. "Ms. Bart is a security-clearance investigator."

John waved him off. "And the last one was a stripper. The career choice doesn't matter. We're talking about the personality type."

Ben heard the dismissive tone and watched the fake smile slip. This guy, whoever he was, didn't like playing this game. "Refresh my memory. You are involved in this how?"

"John is a friend of the family and handles all of

our personal legal matters plus those of my business." Nancy made the pronouncement as she took a seat in the only other chair in the room.

Ben didn't get her at all. In fact, many of the facts didn't fit. For all the fancy clothes and knickknacks, they lacked many of the trappings of obsessive wealth. The sprawling house, with its separate wings and three-car garage, was impressive by Washington, D.C., standards, where a square of property in a neighborhood with good schools cost a mint. But by all accounts this lady was so-much-money-no-one-bothered-to-count-it rich. Plenty of streets and parts of the metro area were filled with mansions. This wasn't one.

Ben made a mental note to take a closer look at the company she'd inherited. He remembered it starting as a financial-investment firm with its tentacles in everything from pharmaceuticals to government contracts training militia operations overseas. Before the financial markets collapsed, Nancy and her board had diversified, removing them from the commercial real-estate market that had built the firm originally. She'd earned praise for having foresight and gratitude for hiring while every other business fought not to go under.

Where John fit in, Ben had no clue.

He really hated having his time wasted. "While this show of support is impressive, and I think it says a lot about who Mr. Coughlin is—"

"Please call me Martin."

"I do have a few things we need to talk about. Maybe we could take a few minutes in private. We'll run through the preliminaries, answer some open questions and move on."

"Not necessary." Martin's wide smile faltered, taking on a more plastic cast. "You can ask me anything in front of them."

Because that would be productive. "That's not really the protocol for these types of things."

Ronald shifted at his place against the wall. "You can make an exception."

Which Ben took to mean he *would* make one or the deputy would end this pretend discussion prematurely. Ben balanced the pros and cons. No way would he get an honest answer. All he could hope for now was an honest reaction.

"It's a difficult question and I apologize in advance," he said.

"Just get to it." Martin's comment came out like an order. Adding the smile to the end didn't soften the impatience.

Ben steepled his fingertips together. Why bother taking notes? This was all about impressions anyway. "What information did Steve Wasserman have on you?"

Martin's eyes widened. "Excuse me?"

Nancy went with dropped-mouth indignation. "What are you saying?"

Before Ben could respond, the defensive shields snapped shut around the room. The air went from uncomfortable to choking with tension.

He told them what they clearly already knew as he watched for the smallest flinch or eye twitch. "Steve volunteered to be interviewed. He went to Hampton Enterprises' owner, Greg Parker, and because of the confidentiality issues Parker called NCIS. When Wasserman refused to speak with anyone in government, Parker sent Ms. Bart out there."

John reached into his pocket and came out empty-handed. It was the act of a former smoker, and the way he kept wiping his mouth suggested he needed a cigarette right now. "It sounds as if this Greg Parker got conned. Clearly Ms. Bart knew Steve. I'm thinking the entire interview was a front for something else, something going on between this couple."

Martin nodded. "Her personal items were found in the house. I told them." Martin leaned in. For the first time in this meeting he wasn't watching from the sidelines. "Figured they had a right to know."

Not under any investigative strategy Ben had ever heard of. He circled back to the question pounding his brain. "Do you have any idea what Steve intended to tell Ms. Bart or what he did tell her?"

"There's nothing to tell." Martin didn't offer more or try to convince them. He said his line then sat back in his chair. Other than a quick glance to his wife, he looked disinterested in what was happening around him and not one ounce threatened by the questions coming at him.

The clock chimed with a deep, heavy bong. Ben wondered if that was an omen. Maybe a signal of the impending death of his NCIS career.

"You can't think of anything that happened, maybe something you didn't think mattered but Steve could have let fester? It could be something minor that he spun into something bigger in his head." Ben tried to give them every out and shift the responsibility to the poor dead guy.

"Nothing," Martin said, ignoring the potential out sitting right in front of him. He looked to Ronald. "What about you? We were both there. If Steve was upset about something, it would likely affect both of us."

Ben stilled. The comment sounded suspiciously like a warning.

Ronald's intense glare never left Ben's face. "This line of questioning will not lead anywhere positive. Find another."

Ben was starting to get that. If he wanted answers, he'd have to go around his boss. "It's just for background. We ask these things to rule them out."

"Focus on Ms. Bart, Ben." The deputy's voice had a deadly ring to it.

"I plan to do just that."

The deputy glanced in the direction of the front door. "Then I will walk you out."

Ben took the hint. There was no information to be found here. Whatever they knew, and they clearly knew something, was buried under layers of loyalty and years of cover-up. That led Ben directly back to their days at the Naval Academy. The school bound them together.

He knew from only a few minutes of digging that Martin and Nancy had married at the academy's chapel right after graduation. The rich girl and the newly commissioned military officer. An odd match and a perfect place to start investigating.

Ben had almost made it to the front door when the deputy's furious voice smacked into the back of his head. "You are on a thin line."

Ben turned around. "I'm not doing anything any special agent wouldn't do."

Ronald's face was a deep flushing red. Anger radiated off of him and crashed into everything around him. "You're looking to ruin the reputation of a good man. You'll need to go through me to do it."

Because he'd already blown it, Ben took one more step in the direction of his firing. "Don't you think it's odd the wife and her partner insisted on being here?"

"No one insisted on anything." Ronald crowded them closer to the front porch and put his hand on the door as if to block anyone from getting inside.

"I just think it's interesting that the wife needed her assistant, but you didn't bother to bring yours."

The deputy's face fell. A thrumming tension pulled it down until the frown took over his entire face. "Are you trying to ask me something, Ben?"

"No." Ben grabbed his keys. "I think I have what I need here."

CLIVE SAT AT the window of the Thai restaurant across the street from the coffeehouse where he usually exchanged information with his boss. They passed everything in the middle of a newspaper left on the table for only a split second. One of them would get up and the other would swoop in.

Today he had put a buffer between them. He wore a baseball cap pulled low and sunglasses. In this neighborhood in the middle of summer, he fit in. No one outside of the usual trendy college, stare-at-their-laptops crowd was there.

Neither was his boss.

He waved the waitress away as he concentrated on the people passing on the sidewalk and all he had to accomplish. Time ticked by and the loose ends kept getting longer.

Because Clive had destroyed his main work cell in the marina, he was at a disadvantage. Sure, his boss had other numbers to reach him, but he hadn't tried any. The man followed the news closely, so by now he had to know about the marina explosion. Unless he'd totally fallen asleep, he should be able to move the pieces around and realize the marina fire had everything to do with this operation.

Clive turned his glass on the table, careful not to let it clank against the wooden top. His boss had wanted Wasserman out of the way. Clive had made that happen but hadn't been paid. The note inside Davis Weeks's file explained that the remainder of the transfer would occur when Lara Bart was neutralized. A task that turned out to be harder than expected.

In the meantime Clive had another problem. He knew many of the boss's deepest secrets, the kind that could not get out. Clive had done a lot of dirty jobs for him. His boss was a man dedicated to his own public image. Clive could destroy all that, but it also made him a target.

Lara Bart's boss had talked with Wasserman and set up her initial interview. She was supposed to have arrived later that afternoon and found Wasserman's body and the obvious burglary scene. She was to play the role of unwitting witness. One call to the police and all the work would have been done. Unfortunately for her, Wasserman had changed the meeting time, and the word had never got back to Clive to double-time his work. Everything had spun out of control from there.

She may not have had time to learn anything, but her boss at Hampton Enterprises did. That was Clive's in. The man, Clive thought his name was something Parker, had talked with Wasserman. He had to provide Parker with a reason for wanting to be part of the clearance investigation. There had to be a kernel of something important in there. Knowing the reason Wasserman needed to die would provide Clive with much-needed leverage in case his boss decided termination was necessary.

All Clive had to do was convince Parker to talk. Every man had a breaking point. Most could only take a touch of pain before spilling their bladders and their supposedly top secret information.

Clive smiled at the idea of crushing the guy who made his living investigating the backgrounds of others. Yes, Parker would talk.

Then the real fun would come. After a bit of practice, Clive would wield his cutting skills on Lara Bart and her annoying boyfriend. There would be a blood trail all over town, and Clive would make sure it led back to his boss. Let's see how he liked to be set up for a murder rap. Being the decent guy he was, Clive decided to not even charge for taking out Weeks. That would be pure pleasure.

Clive raised his hand to get the waitress's attention. Because there were only four occupied tables, she scurried right over.

"Yes?"

"I need a menu." Suddenly he was very hungry.

Chapter Twelve

Davis leaned back in his chair and rubbed his eyes. Between the restless night sleeping next to Lara but not touching her and the morning of searching through files for an angle on the attack, Davis's vision blurred. The coffee helped, but after three cups the impact had worn off.

Connor had called in some favors and found out an NCIS special agent had been assigned to the Wasserman case. The police were crawling all over the marina trying to link the dead man near the parking lot to the exploding boat. Eventually someone would try to wrap a bow around it and package it all as Lara's fault.

The Corcoran Team had to beat them all to the evidence.

He glanced at the doorway to the main hall and listened for Lara's footsteps. She was up there showering, which had his lower body twitchy and the self-destructive part of his brain arguing that he should join her.

The chair across the conference table from him squeaked. Connor tapped a pen against the side of his head while he read the file in his hands. The chair rocked back and forth, probably without him even knowing he was doing all that bouncing.

It was a quintessential Connor pose. Deep in thought but his hand an inch away from a weapon if he had to use it.

"You okay over there?" Davis asked. "I'm the one someone is trying to kill."

"You do have an interesting effect on people." Connor smiled as he glanced up.

"What has you so engrossed?"

"I'm double-checking the law-enforcement professionals assigned to investigate Lara to make sure we don't have an inside man. Someone is trying to implicate her. It would be easy for a person close to the case to do it."

"They all need to back off. We don't need help with this." The automatic reaction kicked up before Davis could stop it.

"You were never good at sharing."

Davis guessed Connor referred to their time together years ago serving on a Joint Terrorism Task Force. It predated Connor buying into and then taking over the Corcoran Team and reached back to his time in the FBI.

The work had solidified their friendship and made Davis's post-DIA return to nongovernment work an easy transition. He hadn't gone a single day without pay or a place to report to in the morning.

But Davis's thoughts ran even deeper. His patterns had been set long ago. Trust didn't come easily for him—and with good reason. For most of his life he could depend only on Pax. His mother had taken off after the car accident that had killed the father Davis had never known. It all had happened before a distinct memory could be formed of either of them.

Davis hadn't been saddled with a naive version of family. He lived the real thing. An endless parade of distant cousins with their hands out to the state for guardianship checks. Davis had broken away from his so-called relatives as soon as he could and grabbed Pax on the way out.

Pax, and now the team, held Davis's trust. But branching out and bringing in police, instead of wrestling with the case on his own, started a spinning in his gut that wouldn't stop.

He'd let Lara in because he couldn't build a wall against her fast enough. He'd interviewed her on a DIA assignment that crept into her office building, and they'd started dating three days after the case ended.

From the beginning he'd believed in her. She had lost both her parents young, too, so they were matched lost souls when it came to family. And then she had packed her bags and left him to wallow all alone. Thinking about the past, turning the rock over and looking underneath, made him feel as if a weight had dropped straight down on his skull.

Time to get back to the work topic. "Where are Joel and Pax?"

"Lara's apartment."

"You thinking someone has already been there?"

"Pax reported back that the neighbor complained about all the people coming and going lately." Connor picked up the remote and turned on the largest screen. A shot of Lara's family room filled the screen. "They're inside now seeing what all those people were determined to find."

Davis focused on the furniture. "It's not tossed."

"No, the person or people erased their tracks. Joel thinks it looks too perfect. Not even an indent for a footprint on the carpet."

It was a common mistake. Davis had seen it a hundred times, and it usually fooled the police. "They erased signs of her along with signs of them."

"Exactly."

Davis watched the scene on the screen. He could see Pax's back, which meant Joel was either holding or wearing the camera. The lens focused on a basket of laundry and the underwear stacked on top. Davis preferred them on her.

He sure didn't like other men seeing them. "That should make Lara happy."

"Are her worries a concern for you these days?"

Davis dragged his gaze away from the monitor

and to the man across from him with entirely too much amusement in his voice. "It's not like you to fish around in my personal life."

"I've known you for a long time and have been working with you exclusively for almost a year. It's not like you to fall all over a woman." Connor threw the folder on the table. "This one's special."

More than that. She was *the* one. The only one who would ever matter. "I thought so at one time."

"Whatever you have together looks alive and kicking to me." Connor reached across for the coffeepot and shook it. The inch of dark brown liquid sloshed in the glass.

"I'm not the problem."

"Are you sure?"

Davis gave up trying to read the words on the page. They'd mashed together into a long black smear. "Care to explain that?"

"You don't give away a lot. I can see where a woman might not like that."

"You talking from experience?"

"Yeah." Connor poured the last of the coffee into his mug then took off to the kitchen with the empty pot.

"Any chance you want to tell me where Jana really is?" Davis raised his voice just in case Connor tried to pretend he couldn't hear.

The guys had been talking about this issue for days. Without warning, Jana had packed up and left. Davis had missed it because he'd been too busy being hit by a car at the time, but according to Pax, they were more than two weeks into the sick-relative excuse and no sign of Jana.

Connor walked back in holding a replacement pot of coffee. They'd learned long ago one pot didn't work. "Visiting relatives."

"If you say so."

"I do." Connor slid back into his seat. "I've also heard your breakup story. I'm just saying you might want to go back over everything again and see what fact you missed."

To Davis it wasn't that complicated. He'd walked in the door and she'd left. He had called and she had ignored him.

"She was pretty clear when she gave the ring back." A fact that still killed him.

"That woman strikes me as a fighter. There has to be a reason she gave up on you."

The words bulldozed into him. "Yeah, you'd think."

A screen on the desk flickered to life. It focused on the front door to the Corcoran Team house and a guy standing there. He looked out at the street, then back to the door.

Connor leaned forward in his seat. "Who is that?"

"Someone who's not too comfortable about being out there and exposed."

"Smart man." Connor stood and pressed his

thumb to the reader on the desk drawer. It popped open, displaying a choice of weapons. He picked a gun for his hand and a knife for his pocket. "You don't recognize the guy?"

Davis struggled to get a clear picture of the attacker in his mind. Between his details and Lara's they'd put together a sketch. He had to rely on her for most of the pieces.

He'd spotted the guy in flashes, and they landed punches. The attacker had worn dark clothes and kept his face out of the light. He had instinctively known where the cameras were and avoided them. The guy at the door was not him.

"No." Davis dug the cell out of his pocket and typed in the emergency code. Now he had to hope Lara had listened to the earlier instructions and kept her phone close.

Her job now consisted of staying tucked safely up there and heading for the safe room hidden by a door in Connor's closet. They'd practiced twice before she'd rolled her eyes and declared she needed a shower. He hoped two had been enough to get the point across.

He then sent the panic code to Pax and Joel. Davis knew they'd received it when the movements on the screen stopped and the picture switched to static.

Connor nodded. "Always good when a plan works."

Connor slipped into the main hallway and approached the door. Davis watched from his position just inside the conference-room doorway. His attention went from the live action in front of him to the screen showing him what was happening outside. No visible weapon.

He whispered the go. "You're clear."

Connor opened the inside door, leaving the outer reinforced one closed. His gun stayed just out of sight behind the door. "May I help you?"

"Ben Tanner, NCIS." The guy flashed a badge.

"I think you wandered into the wrong neighborhood. The Naval Academy is three streets over." Connor pointed as he spoke.

"We both know that's not why I'm here."

"I don't know what you're talking about."

"Really?"

"So, are we done here?"

The guy looked straight into the security camera. It would take an expert to recognize it in the strip above the door. He did. "I'd love to play this game, but we don't have time. I need Davis Weeks and Lara Bart."

That familiar churning of energy started in Davis's gut. He inhaled, letting the adrenaline flow through him. The oxygen fueled his blood and readied him for action. The meds from last night had long worn off, and the dull thump in his ribs gave way to the blood pumping through him at super speed.

He closed the double doors to the conference room and stepped forward, hovering just over Connor's shoulder. "You've got one of us. As for Lara, we broke up eleven months ago."

"Look, I get that you're protecting her, and you're right to do it, but she is in bigger trouble than you think." Ben glanced behind him, a move he'd been making since he'd hit the front steps. "Let me in."

Davis had read the NCIS file and recognized the name. Inviting the enemy to have coffee was not anywhere on his afternoon agenda. "We can't help you."

"How about this?" Ben opened his hand and a bag unrolled. "Look familiar?"

Lara's pink hairband, or one that looked just like it. Profanity filled Davis's brain, but he forced his expression not to change. "What is it?"

"In a pretty short period of time I'm going to get the lab results back and hear about the DNA. I'm betting the hair from that band matches your girlfriend. She gave samples to get her job, so I have a comparison sample."

"Aren't you enterprising?"

"The DNA will put her at the scene of two murders in less than forty-eight hours." Ben shoved the bag into his pocket. "I want to prevent that from happening."

The stare down continued for a full minute. None of them moved. To his credit, Ben didn't let two guys with guns scare him off. And he clearly knew they were armed because his gaze went more than once to the space behind the door where they aimed at him.

Davis ran through the options. He settled on collecting more information over sending the guy away. With the potential hairband evidence he didn't think he had much of a choice. "Fine."

Without saying a word, Connor unlocked the door and stepped back. Ben slipped inside and Davis slammed a hand against his chest while Connor conducted a pat down and scanned him. Once he got the nod the guy was clear, Davis stepped back again.

"Was that necessary?" Ben asked.

"Only if you want in."

They walked him into the sitting room across from the conference room. Connor lingered in the doorway until Ben sat down on one of the couches. Davis took the seat on the couch directly across from him. When he looked up again, Connor was gone.

That was fine. Davis knew the drill and kept the guy talking. "You've got the wrong woman. She's not the type."

Ben moved to the front of the cushion. "Can we not do this?"

"I'm answering your questions." Davis glanced out the front window. He saw the same scene that had been reflected in the monitor—one car and no one else. Connor was probably even now scanning the grounds. Because it would take Pax and Joel time to get back to Annapolis from Virginia, they had to buy time.

As if he sensed the walls closing in, Ben braced his feet against the floor and shifted so his back was covered by the couch. "You already know I left my weapon in the car."

Not a move Davis would ever make but good to know. "Sounds dangerous."

Ben exhaled. "She's being set up."

No kidding. "By whom?"

"I'm not sure yet."

"You're trying to tell me you're on her side?"

"I'm telling you exactly one special agent has been assigned to this case and he's being told to keep things quiet, and the hints about what the findings should be are anything but subtle."

When Ben stopped and stared, Davis decided he needed more information. "I'm listening."

"Those preferred findings center on an unfounded theory about Lara having a secret relationship with Steve Wasserman."

Davis was impressed Ben didn't try to proclaim he'd solved everything. He stuck to the facts no one could dispute and added just enough information to keep the interest alive.

It was the idea of Lara with another guy that had Davis slamming his back teeth together until he heard a distinctive crunch. "That's garbage."

"I agree. I think this is about Steve having some

information about some very powerful people, information they don't want known. Your girlfriend was in the wrong place at the wrong time and now she is going to have all of this hung around her neck." All of a sudden, Connor appeared in the doorway and Ben glanced at him. "Can I have it back?"

"What?"

Ben held out his hand. "The badge. Did I check out?"

"Yes." Connor slapped the NCIS badge in Ben's palm. "I didn't think you knew I lifted it."

Connor didn't smile, but something about his expression showed he was impressed. Davis reluctantly agreed.

"It's what I would have done." Ben pointed to the lights hanging on the wall on either side of the fireplace. "Just like those aren't cameras. Right?"

Under different circumstance Davis decided he might like this guy. He was smart and pretty ballsy. He clearly had some information on Corcoran and the people who worked there. Knowing that, walking into this house showed more guts than Davis had found in most government agents. "How do you know about us?"

"I looked at the information on the laptop someone planted at Steve's murder scene. Lara's laptop. You figure prominently. After getting the name, I did a trace. If it's any consolation, you're not an easy man to find, but I happened to have a key."

"Explain."

"My boss at NCIS, the deputy director, handed me your file. The boat reference was in there."

"Interesting." Connor shot Davis a furious glance.

"Connecting you to the marina was a leap, but I guarantee you I won't be the only one who makes it." Ben tapped his pocket. "The hairband helps, but for now that's safe with me. If the police aren't inclined to share with me, then I'll return the favor."

"That thing could belong to anyone," Davis pointed out.

Ben smiled. "But it doesn't."

It was a lot of information to take in. The guy across from him scanning the room every time he shifted his head or body had some skills. He possessed an ego, which worked on this job, but not too much, which made him tolerable.

He said the right things, but that didn't mean he was clean. He had information he shouldn't have and Davis couldn't figure out if that made him a friend or an enemy.

His file on the agent didn't provide many clues. Ben appeared to play by the rules. But he could easily be the one who'd started this mess and wanted a piece of Lara.

Connor came around the couch to face Ben head-on. "What's in this for you?"

"If I'm leaving this job, and that seems pretty clear right now, either on my own or by being fired—"

Ben blew out a breath as if the words were hard for him "—then I'm making sure an innocent woman isn't framed."

"Hypothetically, if we knew where she was, what would your plan be?"

Davis tried not to flinch at Connor's question. Letting Ben in was a mistake. The fewer people who knew, the safer Lara would be.

"I need to ask her what Wasserman said, if anything, and then talk to her about her boss."

Davis had expected that. Hell, he'd already been through all of that with her and there was nothing to find. "Why?"

"I think he could be the next target."

Clive had not moved in almost an hour. He'd perfected the art of perfect stillness over the years and had trained his muscles to endure the aches and stiffness.

He stood now, watching the security guard walk the same pattern around the top two floors of the Gimmel Office Building. Tapping into the closed-circuit feed had been easy. Just slip into the building and down the emergency stairs to the server room.

He clicked a button on the black box in his hands and the view switched to the glass-front double doors of Hampton Enterprises. He scoffed. Glass, as if the aesthetics should ever overwhelm an office's security needs. It was an amateur move by a man who'd spent his life in business rather than security.

No one moved in the area by the reception desk. Only the guard in the hall.

Five-nine with a stomach stretched and hanging low thanks to too few salads. Clive didn't fight off the smile. This would be too easy.

He leaned down and grabbed his backup gun from his ankle holster. No reason to waste his favorite weapon. This one would end up in the garbage. After, he'd blend into the Georgetown tourist crowds filling the streets and walking along the water's edge, then slip away.

By his count, he had two minutes to get upstairs. He unclipped the listening equipment and smashed it under his heel. Nothing would trace back to him. It never did.

After a quick check in the hall to monitor for any surprises, he opened the door and slid out. A few feet more and he stood at the emergency stairs.

Minute-thirty.

Taking the steps two at a time, and careful to land his feet with as little noise as possible, he vaulted up the three flights to Hampton's floor. He reached his destination in record time, not even out of breath from the effort. With his hand on the lever, he pressed his shoulder against the door to the third floor.

A check of his watch told him he had thirty seconds.

He tightened his fingers and lifted his gun. The footsteps should sound at any minute. As soon as he thought it, he heard them. A sense of satisfaction pumped through his veins. It was about time something on this job went as planned.

He counted down. At ten seconds, he threw open the door and stepped into the hallway. The guard didn't even have time to blink before the bullet hit him.

Chapter Thirteen

"Greg is in danger?"

Lara had stayed upstairs as long as she could tolerate it. With a gun in her hand and a cell with 9-1-1 typed and ready to hit Send in the other, she headed down the stairs. She heard the low rumble of male voices, including one she didn't recognize. Rounding the corner she caught the comment about the threat to her boss.

Davis saw her and a mask of fury fell over his face. He pointed as he yelled, "Stay upstairs!"

"It's a bit late for that, don't you think?" Connor asked.

She saw the gun in Connor's hand and tried to make an educated guess about how many were in the room at that moment. She hoped at least one pointed at the guy she didn't know.

"I'm Ben Tanner." He stood up and held out a hand.

"I heard." She glanced at his outstretched hand

but didn't shake it until Davis gave her a nod. "And, no, I didn't kill anyone."

"I'm looking into the Wasserman matter and any ties it may have to the Dwyer murder at the marina."

The guy didn't even know what he was dealing with. He was talking about two deaths and missing one that she couldn't forget. "For the record, the number of deaths is at three," she said.

Ben leaned forward. "Excuse me?"

"An attacker came for me in my home right after Lara's encounter at Wasserman's. He failed." Davis delivered the sequence with all the emotion of a guy being asked to clean the house.

"My people took care of the body," Connor said as he sat down on the arm of the couch. The gun rested on his lap, making exactly the kind of statement these guys did best.

Ben shot him a look. "I'd love to know how you did that."

Connor shrugged. "It's easy to make people disappear, especially when no one cares about them."

And that was just about enough of that conversation. Last thing she wanted to talk about were more bodies. She'd seen too many at her feet to last a lifetime.

"Had you seen the guy at your house before?" Ben sat back down as he asked.

"No." Davis blew out a long breath. "The one who

killed Wasserman also killed Dwyer. Also blew up my brother's boat. He's the one still on the loose."

"Which is the only reason you're standing here," Connor said to Ben. "Someone tipped off the attacker about the boat. Someone with access to confidential information."

Ben's eyes narrowed. "Only a few people fit that description."

"Like the deputy director."

"Exactly."

Lara had lost the thread of the conversation. Somewhere along the line Davis and Connor had filled this guy in, which was a surprise. They kept the circle closed. Opening to a stranger struck her as a huge risk. If they were talking, things were more desperate than she'd thought. And that was hard to imagine because she'd painted a pretty horrible picture in her mind.

If it hadn't been for Davis crawling into bed with her last night, she probably wouldn't have slept ten minutes. Not that she wanted to examine the comfort he gave her. That was confusion for another day. She had to live that long and stay out of jail first.

Best way to avoid the death and prison thing was to end all of this. She started talking before Davis could hustle her out of there. "Steve Wasserman didn't say anything. He offered me a glass of ice water and then got a call. He was in the kitchen so long that I went in and found him dead on the floor. That's when the fun started."

"How was he acting?"

She took the seat next to Davis and sighed inside with relief when his hand slid over her knee. The warmth of his palm gave her the energy she needed to keep going. "Nervous."

These were all questions Davis had already asked her. Whatever training this guy Ben had felt familiar. He kept the inquiries short and clear. He didn't let up or waver from giving her eye contact. Davis had used all those techniques on her one time or another, though she doubted he knew he did it.

One of the constant complaints of the relationship stemmed from his insistence on treating her like someone he needed to interrogate. He never noticed. She always did.

"Were there papers or anything in the apartment?" Ben asked, as if working through his mental list.

"Just my…" Her voice hiccuped in her throat.

Davis's fingers curled around her leg as he leaned in with eyes filled with concern. "What is it?"

The blood drained from her face. She felt it whoosh out and leave her head. The dizziness smacked her a second later. "I left my file. My work file. It had Wasserman's information and some of mine."

The breach was significant. With every other

horrible thing happening it likely didn't matter, but it was so out of character for her that it hammered home how desperate she'd been to run from that house.

But the news did help a missing piece of the puzzle fall into place. For someone to attack her on Capitol Hill and launch a second attack about forty-five minutes later in Annapolis required significant planning. It shook her firm belief that the attackers traced back to her job and not Davis's. But this would explain it. If someone knew about her life, there could be another party somewhere overseeing and moving the people where he needed them.

Davis must have been thinking the same thing. "That explains how he tracked your name down and then got to me so fast."

Ben leaned forward with his elbows on his knees. His voice stayed calm but the air around him shimmered from the force of his will. "Wasserman didn't try to hand you anything or show you anything?"

"Really, we had just started when the call came."

Ben looked down, then his head shot up again. "You have the cell? There wasn't one in the house."

"There was when I left with the attacker on the floor." She tried to deliver it with a half chuckle but couldn't sell it.

Ben glanced at Davis before he continued. "Well, a lot of you is still at the house."

The way he put the words together tipped her off. She was not going to like this part. "What?"

"Personal things. Someone wants it to look like the two of you had a personal relationship."

"That's a lie." Shock punched into her. She didn't realize she'd jumped up until her feet hit the carpet. Her gaze bounced down to Davis. "It is!"

"We know, honey." He grabbed her hand and pulled her back to the couch. Once there he didn't let go. His fingers slipped through hers. "Why is her boss in danger?"

"Steve found out about the clearance investigation and contacted her boss, Greg Parker, directly. It's possible Steve said something." Ben made a hissing sound through his teeth. "Even if not, someone else might think Steve talked."

Connor got to his feet. He still held the weapon, but it seemed to have a different target now. "Let's head over."

Ben's mouth dropped open. "Me?"

"You came here asking for help," Davis said. "You're stuck with us now, especially since I'm not convinced you aren't at the bottom of all of it."

Ben swallowed hard enough that Davis could see his throat move. "That's comforting."

Davis's smile was almost feral. "So long as we all understand where we stand."

Lara had no idea what was going on. The room buzzed with energy. It was as if all the testosterone funneled into that small space and imploded. If anyone stormed the house right now, they'd run straight into a wall of male fury, including Ben. Somewhere along the line he'd been added to the Corcoran equation. His eyes hadn't stopped blinking since Davis had included him in the trip.

That left one person. Her. "I'm coming."

"No," Davis stated before she finished her comment.

He could yell all he wanted. This was happening. "This isn't a debate."

"Damn right." He dropped her hand and stood up. He'd probably have locked her in the closet if he got half a chance. "This could be dangerous."

She tried the one thing she thought would work—logic. To be safe she aimed it at Connor instead of Davis. "It's not during regular business hours. You won't get in without my key card."

Davis gave her a nice-try smile. "We're going to his house."

The man never learned. "Steve will be at work. He practically lives there. You should appreciate that since you're the same way. Work first always."

Davis frowned but didn't say anything to that.

But Connor was already moving. He stood in front of Ben. "So the deal is you stay quiet about Davis, and certainly about Lara, and in turn we look into this together."

"Yes, but if I find out I'm wrong and she did it, I'll deliver her to the police myself."

She wasn't worried about that because she hadn't done anything wrong. She had broken work protocol, but she doubted anyone would blame her seeing as she was being attacked by a trained killer at the time. A forgotten file couldn't matter that much.

Davis shook his head. "Connor, we should—"

"We need to drive to D.C. We should leave." She tried to telegraph a sense of urgency because the ball of anxiety bouncing around in her belly told her they didn't have time to waste.

Connor spared her a glance but kept his focus on Ben. It was clear Connor had downshifted into leader mode. "You could get into a lot of trouble for this."

"We'll all be in danger if I don't. You think whoever killed a navy lieutenant is going to just let this drop?" Ben shrugged. "Besides that, I don't think Lara should pay for something someone else did."

The man uttered the words that appeared to save his skin. Connor nodded. "Integrity. I like it."

"It's not exactly a novel concept."

"Right. That's why you plan to leave your government job after all of this is over." Connor looked as if he wanted to slap Ben on the shoulder but settled for a firm nod instead. Then he turned to Davis. "Lara goes. She'll be safer with us than here alone waiting for Pax and Joel to return."

Davis's eyes closed for an exaggerated second. "We could wait."

Both Ben and Connor shook their heads, but Connor got the words out. "Not smart."

She smiled at Connor. "Thank you."

He frowned back at her. "Don't make me regret it."

Davis scowled at all of them. "Let's get going. We have a drive ahead of us and I plan to break every law getting there fast."

CLIVE WALKED TO the window of Greg Parker's office. Towering glass panes provided an open view of the Potomac and Virginia on the other side. Off to the left sat the famous Kennedy Center. Boats sailed on this sunny day and people scattered in every direction on the streets and paths below.

Real estate in the waterfront section of Georgetown cost a small fortune each month. Renting an entire floor only increased the tab. Apparently, there was a good deal of money to be made digging into the personal lives of others.

Nosiness paid well—but not well enough to guarantee the supposedly "uncrackable" security would work as planned. Kill the guard, use his handprint and key card, and the door magically opened.

Clive tensed his hands against the windowsill. The view did nothing for him. He preferred the mountains to the water. Trees and as few people as possible. That was how he'd grown up, away from others, learning to shoot and live off the land. Lessons taught by a father who saw government as the enemy and an uprising of the people inevitable.

Put Clive in an enclosed space and the hypocrisy and general human waste choked him. Moving and living where he knew every leaf and stone appealed to him. He'd travel back to his cabin in West Virginia as soon as this job finished. No one knew him there. No one bothered him.

First, he had to dispose of Greg Parker.

He turned around and glanced at the type of man who disgusted him the most. He didn't produce anything or add to society. He made calls and held meetings. A well-trained animal could do those things.

But Greg's crimes surpassed laziness. He sat in an office and got paid to judge others.

Now it was Clive's turn to judge.

He stood on the opposite side of the oversize desk and watched Greg shift his hands, thinking he hid his movements as he tried to break free. That was not going to happen. Clive had bound the older man to the leather desk chair. Even now blood dripped from the slashing cut across his chest that slit his dress and had it gaping. The puncture wound on his upper arm didn't look any better.

Clive's only real concern was that Greg would have a heart attack before he coughed up any information. That was the problem with torturing men in their sixties. You tended to scare the life right out of them.

With his fists on the edge of the desk, Clive leaned in and saw Greg's eyes open on a bolt of fear. "It would be easier if you told me what I wanted to know."

Not that he could say anything with the gag pulled tightly across his mouth. The bloody knife sitting on the empty desk between them was there to make a point. One move and the blade would pin him to the chair.

Clive picked up the knife and touched the sharp end to his fingertip. Greg shook his head and mumbled into the gag.

"A quick admission would have meant a quick death. But you reached for that emergency button." Clive made a tsk-tsk sound. "I bet you're sorry you wasted my time now."

Greg strained his arms against the bindings. Sweat stained his armpits and dotted his forehead. His gaze shot around the room, and small thuds sounded as he shifted in his chair.

Clearly Greg thought there was a way out of this.

Clive found that notion amusing.

"Here's what's going to happen." Clive walked to Greg's side of the desk and grabbed him by the neck when he tried to shrink away. "I'm going to search this office inch by inch. For every drawer I go through and don't find something on Wasserman, you'll get cut."

Greg was whimpering now.

"After a few rounds I might give you a chance to talk again. Depends on how well you behave while I'm working."

The whimpering turned to actual sobs.

The pathetic sound only fueled Clive's need to keep going with the game. He crouched down so his face was even with the sniveling man. "For your sake, I hope there's something here worth finding or this is going to be a long and painful day."

Chapter Fourteen

A security guard lay in a sprawl in the middle of the third-floor hallway. Connor crouched to check his pulse. He shook his head but Davis didn't need the confirmation. A bullet hole through the forehead and blood pooled under the guard. Those clues said it all.

Davis heard Lara's soft cry and rough intake of breath, felt her body shake as she leaned into him. Once again he'd dropped her into danger. This was one more death and a desperate reminder of just how perilous it was for her to be at the Hampton offices.

He glanced around at the team and tried to think of a way to protect her, watch over Ben and shield Connor's back all at the same time. Dumping Ben on the sidewalk and leaving Lara in the car had been his vote. Connor had overruled him. For a man who trusted only after much hesitation, he seemed to want Ben's help.

Davis wasn't inclined to be that welcoming. If the special agent so much as twitched in a way Davis didn't like, he'd put a bullet in him and deal with the questions later.

Davis signaled for the rest of them to wait as he turned the corner and glanced down the hall. Seeing it empty, he motioned for the others to follow. He led and Ben shielded Lara. Connor brought up the back end, just as they'd discussed on the drive to D.C. Davis had verbally walked them through the plans several times and hadn't stopped until everyone could repeat them back without hesitating.

"This is bad," Lara whispered.

Davis stopped twenty feet from the main office door. "What?"

She touched her hands against his back and whispered into his ear. "Look at the bottom. The door is actually open and unlocked. It shouldn't be either after hours."

The situation was getting worse with every passing second. It was bad enough Pax and Joel had almost arrived in Annapolis when the rest of them had left for D.C., meaning they literally had passed on the highway at some point. This attacker had them running in circles. One more reason to want the guy dead.

Davis needed more data. He remembered the floor plan Lara had drawn in the car and mentally walked through it. "The only thing on the left is the conference room. Parker's office is on the right."

"At the end of the hall." Her killer grip on the back

of Davis's shirt didn't unclench even though they stood next to each other now. "But there are many places in between here and there to hide. Rows of offices, the kitchen, closets—"

"I remember." She'd picked up his repetition issue but he didn't mind. More information always increased the odds of success.

Connor eased his surveillance behind them. Taking a break, he turned sideways and glanced at Davis. "Thoughts?"

He could see only one option, and he didn't even like that one because it separated him from Lara. "You take Ben and Lara out of here and I check it out. I'll signal for backup if I need it."

"No," Ben said, his voice not lifting above a scant whisper.

Lara tightened her grip until the edge of Davis's shirt dug into his neck. "Absolutely not."

Davis responded to her before Connor could jump in. "You've been attacked enough."

With all that had happened and the threats that still lingered, Davis couldn't believe he had to explain. The narrow-eyed looks he was getting suggested he did.

"Greg didn't do anything wrong," she said. "He needs our help."

Ben leaned in and glared at them all. "And we're wasting time."

The man had a point. Davis weighed the odds

and couldn't come up with a way to make them work to his favor. He didn't trust Ben, but the man had done everything right so far. His file hinted at a bone-deep willingness to do what was necessary to finish a job. He could have turned on them, shot them or steered them into an ambush many times since he had shown up at Corcoran's door, but his resolve had never wavered.

Still… "If it turns out I shouldn't have trusted you—"

Ben nodded. "You'll put a bullet in me. You've made that clear."

Just in case, Davis drove the point home. "There won't be anywhere you can hide."

"Understood."

Davis pushed ahead before his doubts took over. If he hesitated, common sense might kick in, and then he'd have to get Lara out of there. If he tried, he'd likely have a mutiny on his hands.

"Connor and I go left. Ben stays in reception." Davis's gaze shot back to Ben again. "If anyone goes for her, you sacrifice yourself to keep her alive, got it?"

Lara tugged on his shirt. "Davis, that's enough."

"Got it," Ben answered at the same time, returning Davis's stare, head-on, man-to-man.

Davis took that as the vow it sounded as if it was. With a nod, he finished the orders. "Let's go."

With silent steps, they moved toward the door.

Before Davis could open it, Connor held up a fist. They all stopped while he dropped down on one knee and investigated the bottom of the door.

He glanced up and delivered his opinion in a near-silent voice. "No wires or explosives."

Davis let out a long breath of relief. At least the attacker hadn't stopped to booby-trap the door. One thing fell their way.

Lara gently pushed on the door and it opened with a swish. The noise barely registered, but in the thudding quiet, it was as loud as a blaring radio.

Waiting to see if an unwanted visitor turned the corner, Davis held up his fist. When no one appeared, he motioned for Connor to move. He sent Ben a final warning glare and winked at Lara.

They would all live through this day. They would go back to the crash pad and he'd tell her he loved her. That he had always loved and forever would. Getting to that moment was his motivation to survive the next hour. Saving her was his only mandate.

Davis and Connor slipped by the reception desk, first checking the conference room. They swept in, ducking under the table and opening the closets lining the one wall while Ben covered them from his vantage point in the reception area.

Next came the office on the right. Their gazes scanned and guns shifted to cover each hidden corner where someone could hide as they walked down the long corridor. They passed open office doors and a supply closet. Nothing in those, but the door at the end of the hall with the big plaque on it was closed and a light shone through the strip underneath.

Davis glanced at Connor and he nodded. Faster now they jogged to the end of the hall. Their feet scratched against the carpet but they didn't stop. Davis tested the knob and found the door locked. Looked as if they were going in the hard way. Not a surprise.

As Davis angled his body for the best leverage, Connor lifted his leg and kicked the door in. It bounced off the inside wall with a crash as Davis stormed by, with his knees bent, ready to fire at anything that moved. They rotated going high and low, their guns moving the entire time.

Something crunched under his foot and Davis looked down to see papers…everywhere. The room was in shambles—drawers dumped, files ripped and documents lining every inch of the floor until the carpet underneath was almost invisible.

Connor checked the closet and private bathroom while Davis ripped back the curtains blocking out the natural light. The rings screeched along the rod as the two men stopped, shoulders touching, in front of the desk. Blood seeped out of what had to be twenty cuts on Greg Parker's body. But it was the deep slice across his throat that had killed him.

"We're too late," Connor said, the vibrating anger

in his voice matching the fury thrumming through Davis's blood.

"Think the attacker found anything?"

"That is an angry death. I'm guessing Parker held out." Connor tore his gaze away from the macabre scene. "Good man."

"But still dead." Davis decided he'd seen enough death. This one and Dwyer hit the hardest. They weren't trained killers. They were men in the wrong place at the wrong time.

Davis lowered his gun and whispered an apology under his breath for being too late. His fingers shook from the force of the adrenaline pounding him.

"Let's go get Lara," Connor said as he turned around.

Davis grabbed his friend's arm before he could exit. "No matter what, she doesn't come in here. I can take papers out to her, but she stays out. It's too much."

"Agreed."

They'd almost made it to the door when they heard her scream.

LARA STOOD IN the reception area with her back wedged in the corner and the NCIS special agent plastered to the front of her. She strained to see over his shoulder, even a peek to make sure Davis was safe, but she mostly got an eyeful of black jacket and formidable shoulders.

Her thigh hit the edge of the table and the lamp bobbled. Ben's free hand shot out to catch it before it slammed to the ground and potentially broke. After using lamps as a weapon in her past two rounds against attackers, she figured it would serve her right to have her location exposed by one.

The catch didn't solve her problem. Her legs cramped and she shifted to get into a more comfortable position, but being penned in stopped all movement. When that didn't work she tried a request. "Any chance you could move forward an inch?"

The only thing keeping her from running down the hall after Davis was the knowledge that she'd be in the way. If he worried about protecting he'd become an even bigger target. Bulletproof vest or no, even with all his training, he was human and she would not watch him bleed out in front of her. Just the thought of him being injured made her stomach ache from all the violent clenching.

"No." Ben continued scanning the area in an arc that started in the general direction of the conference room and continued around reception and out through the glass doors.

He stayed still, didn't make any noise and kept his gun at the ready. Seemed he took Davis's threat pretty seriously.

She still wasn't taking any chances. She had the gun in her hand and hours of practice sessions from Davis just in case. It had been almost a year since she'd shot a gun. She hoped it was like that bike thing and you never forgot. She also hoped she could hit an attacker as well as she hit a paper target. Davis had warned her about the human factor and how it changed everything.

"The moving thing was more of a statement than a question," she said in a low whisper.

"I'd rather your boyfriend didn't kill me."

"He's not my boyfriend." The response was automatic. Someone mentioned Davis and the line floated through her head.

Ben shot her a quick frown over his shoulder. "Does Davis know that?"

Fair question. They'd been shooting mixed signals at each other ever since she had run into his arms at his house. The kiss had been a green light that suggested their breakup was more of a rest period than a true ending. But neither of them tried to push forward. Physically, yes, but not emotionally.

They had so much baggage piled between them. The baby he didn't know about, how his work was more important than her and the letter from his long-lost mother that he hid and to this day hadn't mentioned.

He was a man who thrived on secrets and kept his duffel packed by the door for escape. She craved stability, but right now she'd trade it all to know Davis was okay back there. Waiting for the horrible sound of gunfire to ring out or for Connor to report that Davis was in trouble was enough to buckle her knees in terror.

Because she needed all of her energy to stay focused and not let her mind wander to worst-case scenarios, she went with a response that said everything and nothing at the same time. "Our relationship is complicated."

Those shoulders in front of her shrugged, pushing her even deeper into the wall. "What relationship isn't?"

"No, really."

This time Ben's quick look suggested she was a little slow. "And I say again, no, really, they're all complicated."

She put her head back, rested it against the wall and fought back the urge to scream. There was just something about the way males like Ben and Davis and everyone she'd met at Corcoran downplayed important issues and lived in the moment that made her head feel as if it were being crushed until it might cave in.

But maybe that was good, because anger at their macho behavior gave her somewhere to channel all of the anxiety flipping around inside her. Between being squished from the front and suffocated from the fear clogging her throat, she needed all of this to be over. The attacker had escaped twice. He could not be so lucky a third time.

As Ben glanced to the left, Lara looked to the

right. She blinked when a pair of boots dropped out of a ceiling tile. She screamed when a man slipped out, jumping to the hallway floor and straight into a shooting position. Ben's head whipped around but the crack of the weapon beat him.

Something whistled right near her hand. As she watched, one of the glass doors in front of them shattered into a giant spiderweb pattern but didn't break. A small hole formed but the glass didn't crumble into a million pieces as she'd feared.

Ben shot as she felt his body buck against hers. His shooting arm dropped to his side and just hung there. When he grabbed for his arm, his hand came back smeared with blood. She tried to reach around to help him but he shifted their bodies, shoving her behind him and facing the attacker head-on.

Not *an* attacker. *The* attacker.

Her gaze locked on the man now a few feet away and aiming again. She swore she saw a sick smile form on his lips the second before he aimed again.

They were open targets. Nothing hid their position from the hall. The only thing standing between her and a bullet was Ben. If anything, he stood up straighter, making his body even more of a shield.

She refused to be a victim. She turned to look for anything to duck behind and saw Davis come flying around the corner with Connor right behind.

The attacker's attention wavered at the streak of motion and Davis got off a shot. Ben fired, too.

Through the thunder of booms the glass door broke apart, sending shards raining into the reception area.

"Lara, get down!" Davis commanded.

She was already ducking. With her hands over her face and body bent in half, she tried to avoid the glass shower. She almost fell over when Ben knocked into her. His footsteps wobbled and he started to slide.

Her only thought was to get him to the ground and out of the main shooting area. With her arms locked around his waist, she dragged him against her and dropped. His body fell hard against her, pinning her half against the wall.

Hard cubes dug into her skin through her jeans. She glanced down and saw the glass had broken into what looked like a million perfectly smooth squares. It must have been safety glass of some sort. Whatever it was, she loved it.

Everything else had her heart hammering. She looked around, catching the last glimpse of the attacker's shoes as he disappeared down the hall and around the corner with Connor a few steps behind. She struggled to find Davis, desperate to see him safe and hidden behind something.

He stood over her. "You okay?"

Her relief at seeing him turned all of her muscles to liquid. She had no idea how or when he'd got to her and she didn't care. "Fine, but Ben is—"

"Fine." Davis's glance dropped to the man in her arms. "Stay here. Shoot anything that isn't me."

UNABLE TO WASTE even a second holding Lara and checking to make sure she was fine or checking on Ben's injuries, Davis took off after Connor and the attacker. Glass crunched under Davis's feet and his shoe slipped on the desk chips and flurry of magazines and papers that had been kicked up during the shoot-out.

He blocked Lara's face and the blood all over her hands. *Not hers.* He repeated that five times as he pivoted to turn the corner and grab the door to the emergency stairs before it slammed shut. Momentum sent him shooting across the landing and right to the railing.

Leaning over, he looked down the spiraling steps.

He saw flashes of black one floor below him and another splotch the floor below that. Footsteps thudded on the metal stairs and harsh breathing thundered all around him.

Connor yelled twice for the attacker to stop. The guy answered by firing over his shoulder and into the air. The crack echoed through the confined space as the bullet pinged and ricocheted, chipping into the wall a few feet from Davis's head.

He took off. Ignoring the tug from his sore ribs, he jogged, taking two steps at a time and gaining space on Connor. They were still more than a floor behind each other and the attacker when the door clicked on the main floor. Picking up speed, Davis hit the main floor a few seconds after Connor. They both slammed into the door but Connor yanked it open.

The door led to a small hallway, then to an emergency exit. Davis pushed against the bar and winced when a shrill siren split the air. The sun nearly blinded Davis and the humidity smacked him in the face.

"Where did he go?"

Connor slid his gun into his vest. "Maybe another door. He didn't sound the alarm."

The noise in question wailed as a light next to the door flashed.

Davis's mind wouldn't accept that answer. Frantic, his heart racing with the need to finish this, he turned his head back and forth, looking for the retreating attacker. When Davis decided to try left, Connor grabbed his arm and held him back.

"Look around you." Connor panted as he said the words.

Davis noticed for the first time the groups of people walking the streets. Moms with kids in strollers. Couples with dogs. Many people using their cells and one guy frantically waving at a security guard a few doors down and yelling about the police.

Several people stared at them and a few pointed.

Probably more than one had taken their photo and Davis had no idea how to fix that.

Yeah, the attacker had dumped them in a busy Georgetown area. People used this path to get from M Street, the main shopping area, to the water. And there they stood wearing their vests and holding guns.

Not good.

Connor's mouth turned to a grimace. "Let's get out of here before we have a PR disaster."

"The attacker is—"

"Gone." Connor finally looked at Davis. "Lara needs you."

Guilt smacked him as he remembered the blood. "She's trying to save Ben."

Chapter Fifteen

The men crowded around Ben as he sat on the Corcoran conference table, his shirt balled up beside him. Discarded bulletproof vests had been piled right behind him, and they all watched as Joel cleaned and dressed the injury.

He'd been hit just under his vest, almost in his armpit. A few more inches and the attacker could have caused unbelievable damage. Joel said something about hitting a lung.

Ben took the ad hoc medical attention and accompanying chorus of questions well. He jerked when Joel hit the wrong spot and swore through most of the treatment, but he never showed any other sign of weakness. Never demanded an ambulance or trip to the hospital.

Lara thought about rolling her eyes but barely had the energy to stand. Even now she held on to the back of a conference chair to keep from sliding to the floor in a less-than-graceful exhausted faint. Keeping her eyes open proved harder.

But just once she wanted one of these guys to suggest calling in the police, the fire department—heck, even the coast guard—when something went wrong. They functioned as an independent unit and ignored the rules the rest of society followed for this sort of thing. To her, dialing 9-1-1 was a no-brainer.

Maybe clunking their heads together would help. They'd spent the first ten minutes, as Ben stripped down and Joel collected supplies, trading stories about their battle wounds. It was sick and deranged and so macho it had hair all over it.

Joel dropped the last bloody cloth in the small bowl Ben held. Joel eyed the bandage. "It's a through and through. You lost some blood but will be fine in a few days."

"Are you a doctor now?" Ben asked.

Joel's smile looked less than wholesome. "Nervous?"

She shook her head. Here she was ready to fall over and possibly sleep for six or seven solid years, and they were joking. Gunfire, chases—nothing slowed these guys down.

Davis was the worst. He stood to the side, by the doorway to the kitchen, and watched over the medical activities. With arms crossed over his chest, he'd shift now and then and bite down on a wince. His ribs hurt but heaven forbid he admit that or ask for treatment.

Stubborn idiot.

As if he read her mind, Davis pushed off from the wall and came over to stand in front of her. The other men continued their one-upmanship on scars as Davis stared at her with his gaze wandering over her face and down her neck.

This was the calmer version of Davis, not to be confused with the Davis that had nearly squeezed the life out of her when he'd got back upstairs after the office chase. He had asked her repeatedly if she had been hit. Even though she'd answered no, he'd brushed his hands all over. She'd half expected him to strip her down right there on the broken glass. He'd refrained, but she guessed the control cost him.

"How are you?" he asked.

His husky voice washed over her and she had to fight off the shiver at the back of her neck. "Still fine."

"What—never seen a guy get shot before?"

She didn't realize the male conversation had stopped and all eyes had turned to the couple in the middle of the room until Pax shot his sarcastic question her way.

Fine, she'd shoot right back. "Not before the past few days."

Ben slid off the table, half bent over, and with a loud groan turned to face Davis. "You going to make good on your threat?"

Davis held out his hand. "Thank you."

Ben's eyes narrowed as he stared at the out-stretched arm. "I let the guy get shots off."

Her head still was reeling from Davis's uncharacteristic gratitude when the reality of Ben's comment hit her. So, that was what this was about. A case of rescuer's guilt. They all seemed to be suffering from it.

Never mind that she was fine except for a few cuts from the safety glass. "The attacker was hiding in the ceiling. Who could prepare for that?"

Davis didn't drop his arm. "And you blocked Lara. You could have run or done anything, but you protected her. I saw it and appreciate it."

Ben blew out a long breath as he shook Davis's hand. "Anytime."

"I'd prefer if the attacks didn't become a habit," she mumbled.

Connor brought out the omnipresent coffeepot and a handful of mugs. The fact it was almost ten at night didn't appear to faze him. "Look at us all getting along."

"So, now what?" Pax sat down and looked at the stack of files in front of him. A second later he distributed them around the table to the other guys.

For some reason the move, so normal and out of touch with the danger pulsing around them, ticked her off. "Maybe we could take a second and feel bad for Greg."

"That goes without saying, honey," Davis said without looking up from the file in his hand.

He still didn't get it. She'd seen flashes, moments when his fear for her or anger of a situation would take over, but mostly he was a blank emotional slate. It was so unhealthy and so intimidating. She hated that side of him.

She also despised this thing where they compartmentalized human beings into body counts. "We should say it. He deserves that much while whomever Connor called goes over the murder scene and does whatever he does to separate it from Corcoran."

Davis dropped his arm and the file dangled from his fingers. "What's wrong with you?"

Even Ben winced over Davis's tone.

"Oh, I don't know, Davis. My boss was massacred, likely because of something I saw, Ben got shot—"

He waved her off. "I'm fine."

"—and I got trapped in the middle of a shoot-out that should have killed me. If you hadn't turned that corner when you did…" Her voice cracked and she wanted the floor to split open so she could sink right into it.

Something hard moved in Davis's eyes and he looked away for a second before turning back to her. The file crumpled in his hands. "I'm sorry I didn't get there sooner."

No one made a sound. It was as if they held their

collective breaths, waiting for her response. "Are you even listening to me?"

His mouth flattened into a straight line. "I thought I was."

"I was worried for you." She stepped up and poked him in the chest before sweeping her gaze across the room. "For all of you, and in light of the ongoing attacks, I would like you to admit, just once, that a man being killed is a big deal."

Davis's head snapped back as if she'd slapped him. "What are you talking about?"

When Joel and Connor started shifting and looking at the floor then the ceiling and Ben shot her a sympathetic smile, she gave up. "Forget it."

She shifted to circle around Davis and leave. She needed a few minutes to think. A few more to regain her game face and figure out how to go along with the crowd on this, to pretend she was as hard as they were. She didn't want them dropping her out of this because she was too emotional. But she needed some air before her head exploded.

Davis stopped her with a hand on her arm. "Of course it's a big deal. People are dying."

"Then why act like you don't care?"

"To survive." The answer came from Connor but they all nodded.

Davis's hold turned to caressing fingertips against her elbow. "That's exactly it."

"Explain it to me."

Davis looked around the room with an icy glare. When none of the other men even pretended to have something better to do, Davis let out a long-suffering sigh. "Let's take this somewhere private."

Pax folded his arms behind his head and leaned back in his chair. "We're all good with hearing this conversation."

"I won't feel bad about punching you."

The room whirled until Lara wasn't sure what she should say. Now that she remembered her audience, the idea of privacy sounded good. Problem was privacy likely meant a bedroom, and the bed could prove to be a distraction.

She'd promised herself she'd tell him the truth once she got him alone, to explain everything that had happened eleven months ago and everything that bothered her now. She'd tried before and he wouldn't listen; then she was too hurt and devastated to give it a second try.

But she wanted his comfort and his strong arms wrapped around her. If the heat in his eyes and desire pulsing off of him were any indication, he wanted more than that. One step upstairs and they'd probably be all over each other. She couldn't figure out if that was a good thing or a bad one.

Connor took the decision away from her. He pointed toward the staircase. "Head up and we'll regroup tomorrow."

Ben reached for his shirt. "I'll head home."

That fast, Davis's attention snapped from her to Ben. "You're not going anywhere."

"Excuse me?"

"The second you walked into this office you made yourself a target. The safest place for you to be is with us," Davis said.

Connor nodded. "I agree."

The I-don't-think-I-do expression on Ben's face suggested he fell into a different camp on this issue. "Well, I don't need a babysitter."

Joel put his hand over the bandage. "And we don't need a dead NCIS agent, so listen to the boss or we will knock you out."

Ben's mouth dropped open as Joel's hand pressed harder.

Ben's eyes actually watered. "You'll have to do better than that. This isn't my first interrogation."

Connor nodded. "You heard the man."

"The guy's been in the field. Press harder. He can take it, though it would be smarter if he broke sooner rather than later," Davis said.

Before she could speak up and stop the testosterone-fueled nonsense, Joel obeyed, even holding Ben still when he started to squirm. "Do you agree now, Special Agent?"

"I can't…" Ben's voice died on a sharp intake of breath.

Connor shook his head. "Ben, don't be dumb. Think of it as an opportunity to study us."

Much more of this and they'd accidentally send him to the hospital, so she tried to step in and offer a spark of common sense. "Pretend it's part of your assignment."

Joel shifted his weight. "This has to hurt."

"I'm fine," Ben said with a strained voice.

Men. It was all she could do not to roll her eyes. "You're about to pass out."

Ben tried to shove Joel away. When that failed, Ben treated them all to a small nod then slumped in a panting heap when Joel finally let go.

"See, it's always easiest if you just concede," Davis said to Ben, but looked at her.

She wondered if he realized that theory ran both ways.

RONALD PACED MARTIN'S gourmet kitchen. Nancy had dragged their lifeless but impeccably dressed children off to the symphony or some nonsense that young kids would dread. Glancing out over the acre of backyard, Ronald wondered if those poor kids ever got to play out there. No swing set or toys. There hadn't even been a bike in the driveway when he'd pulled up.

But that was Nancy, always more concerned with appearances than anything else. Ronald knew from talking with Martin that she only agreed to live here, in a house she found inferior and a neighborhood she described as pedestrian, until Martin secured his NCIS position. He didn't want her wealth to be an issue and insisted they maintain the pretense he paid most of the bills.

Ronald didn't know if it was an ego thing or spite. It was hard to tell when dealing with a marriage based on lies and deceit.

Waiting until she left the house had tested Ronald's patience. He'd never liked her and that opinion hadn't changed one bit over time. If anything, he liked her even less now.

"This situation is exploding," he said, jumping right to the point.

Martin wandered around the kitchen, picking up stray cups and wiping off counters. "Meaning?"

"Lara Bart's employer is dead."

Martin stopped while brushing some crumbs only he could see off the marble island. "I don't know anything about that."

That was Martin's party line. He professed to never know about anything that could harm his reputation. "This all traces back to Steve. Who else could he have told?"

"I still don't believe he intended to tell anyone."

"He asked to be included in your security clearance. He contacted this Hampton company to add his name to the list. Who does that?"

"His loyalty never wavered."

Ronald looked at his friend of over twenty years

and wondered what life he was living. "When was the last time you talked to him before he was killed?"

"It had been more than a year. He tried after, but we didn't connect."

"What does that mean?"

"A few weeks ago he called here to talk to me, but I was out. He may have called back." Martin waved the thought away. "Doesn't matter. The point is Nancy and I talked about it and decided I should ignore the call. We agreed nothing good could come from renewing that friendship."

Nancy—of course. Ronald figured she'd be at the center of any Martin screwup. Nothing had changed over the years on that score. "You didn't think to tell me that piece of information? It explains everything. Steve didn't just blurt something out. He tried to talk with you."

"No. Steve wasn't agitated or making threats. It was a routine check-in and nothing more."

No, Ronald thought. It was the beginning of the end and Martin had missed the signs.

Chapter Sixteen

"Are you okay?" Davis waited until they'd reached the third-floor landing and stood at her bedroom door before asking again. He'd been tempted to carry her up there but figured she'd put up a pretty big fuss. She seemed to be spoiling for a fight.

He was in the mood for other things.

Instead of giving him the usual strained answer, she threw open the door and walked inside, each step stiff and her head held high. She'd made it all the way to the chest of drawers before she whipped around to face him. "Do I look okay?"

Yeah, definitely wanting a fight.

That shade of angry red was not normal for her face. Neither was the way she stood there with her hands balled into fists, ready to punch if he said one wrong word, which he feared was inevitable.

Although he was starting to wonder if he knew anything about women, he did know this much. "This sounds like one of those questions women ask and men can't answer without wandering into jerk territory."

She leaned back against the chest hard enough to shake the sturdy wood. With arms folded across her stomach she assumed the we-need-to-talk stance.

He despised that pose.

Her eyes narrowed and her head tilted to the side. She'd pulled out every furious-woman gesture. "Is it that you hide your feelings or that you do not have any?"

This was worse than he'd thought. Whatever fury had been brewing at her office after finding Greg had been murdered boiled over now. He'd try to find a neutral topic, but he had no idea what one would be.

"What exactly is going on here?" he asked like the lost guy he was.

"Don't act like you don't know. We've been over this a million times." She dismissed him by turning around and searching through the top drawer.

The woman had exactly three shirts and three pair of underwear in this house, but she acted as if she needed to search through her extensive wardrobe for just the right thing to wear. As if he cared about that. As far as he was concerned, they worked best without clothes.

He opened his mouth to point that out, but he stopped when he saw her expression reflected in the mirror in front of her. Lines of strain around her mouth, and eyes almost dead of emotion. Seeing her wrung out drained the coiling anger from his body.

He'd spent the past hour desperate to hold her. Watching her protective instincts kick in as she wrestled Ben out of the line of fire, all while maintaining her aim at the attacker, hit Davis with a dual punch of pride and terror. He thought having her threatened was the worst. But, no, repeatedly seeing her at the wrong end of a gun was the nightmare scenario. Even the memory had the power to grip his heart with a pressure so strong it could burst.

He stood there feeling oversize and uncomfortable. He wasn't one to suffer from bouts of insecurity. In his line of work that meant death, but she had him shifting his arms and shuffling his feet like an embarrassed schoolboy. The bed was right there, yet well out of his grasp at the moment.

One more glance at her face and her strange sudden fixation on whatever was in that drawer had him rethinking his usual strategy. He could play the angry male or he could try one more time to make her understand he was more than an automaton with a gun.

"You want to know that truth? I have feelings for you I can't control and can't shake no matter how hard I try."

She frowned up at him through the mirror then turned around to treat him to the direct version. "We're not talking about us."

"I am."

"I'm referring to how you act on the job and how you deal with death and danger."

He wasn't. Not now. Not after all this time. "I'm talking about being so driven under with my love for you, so desperate to have something real and lasting with you that I can't get my vision to clear. That's how I feel about you."

Her frown eased. "Davis—"

He gave in to the need to touch her as he slipped into the space between her open arms and wrapped his arms loosely around her trim waist. "You have to know how much I love you. I never hesitated to say it and I always meant it."

Those eyes so sad a second ago went soft and a little cloudy. "I do know."

"But you don't fully believe it." A wild mix of love and attraction zapped between them. This close he could feel her breaths grow short and the frantic beat of her heart. "You think I don't feel, like I'm immune or something, but with you it never stops. It flips me over and rips me apart."

She sighed as her hand brushed across his chin. "I love you. That's never been an issue. The question is whether it's enough."

It had to be. "For tonight, let it be. We can figure out the rest in the morning."

He watched as emotions raced across her face. Doubt, excitement, maybe a touch of hope. He read it in the way she nibbled on her lip to the way her fingers tightened against his skin. When she leaned in and placed a short, almost sweet, kiss on his lips, a heart-stopping need rushed through him.

"Lara?"

Her hand went into his hair and she tugged his face down closer to hers. "Yes."

The simple word set fire to something inside him that had been smoldering for months. His heart jumped and his hands moved all over her. Touching, kissing, mouths linked and pressing deep. He could not get close enough to her or break away even for a second.

His palms slipped under the hem of her T-shirt and fingertips hit bare skin. Warm and soft just like he remembered. As the kiss crescendoed to a fever, his blood scalded his veins. He couldn't get their clothes off fast enough.

With a sweep, he lifted her shirt up and off. Before he could lower his arms, she had tugged his shirt out of his waistband and stripped it up his chest. Her lips went to his exposed shoulders and her fingers fumbled at the snap to his jeans.

They were lost in a frenzy of hands and mouths. The heat that had always flamed between them exploded into a roaring wall of need. Turning as he kissed her, he pushed her toward the bed and followed her down when her knees buckled.

The bra came next. With a slip he had it off and

on the floor. Nearly shaking with want, he looked down at her, at all that creamy skin that drove him wild. His mouth covered her breast and her back lurched off the bed as he rolled his tongue over the tip. He closed his eyes, enjoying the friction of their bare chests rubbing against each other.

He opened them again when her hand slipped inside his boxer briefs. She touched him as she trailed a line of kisses straight down his stomach. Her hand closed as it slid over him and his breath stuttered to a halt in his lungs.

Another minute of that and his body would explode. Shifting his weight, he reached for the condom he'd thrown on the nightstand earlier in a burst of optimism. The position put her head near his erection and she took advantage. She peeled his pants down and her mouth slid over him. The delicious mix of her hands and tongue put a wrecking ball to the last of his control.

Careful not to hurt her but with more force than he'd intended, he pushed her back against the mattress. He was about to apologize when she pressed the backs of her hands against the bed next to her head and smiled up at him.

On this they were always connected. She was as ready as he was.

A few tugs and he pulled her jeans and panties off. He wanted to spend time kissing her thighs and exploring every amazing inch of her. The screaming in his head wouldn't let him. It had been so long, so many lonely months, that he couldn't tolerate another second of not being inside her. He ripped the condom packet open and touched her to make sure she was ready for him.

She shifted, opening her legs wider. "Now."

That was all he needed and more than he ever thought he'd have again. He didn't wait another second. He slid inside her. One deep, long push before he could breathe again.

With a final burning kiss, he started to move. His body pressed and her mouth dropped open. The sounds and scents, the feel of her around him all came rushing back. It felt right and perfect and he cursed himself for ever letting her get away.

Her fingers trailed down the deep groove between his shoulders and she whispered his name. When her body tightened around him, he couldn't find the air to speak. When she told him to move, he did.

THE COFFEEHOUSE CLOSED in ten minutes. Clive stood on the sidewalk, just out of sight from the big front window, and watched his boss take his usual seat at one of the small tables. He glanced around, eyeing up the blonde at the cash register then returning his focus to the table.

No wonder the guy depended on other people to do his dirty work. His idea of blending in included an expensive business suit and wiping his hand through his hair to hide his face.

Amateur.

His stern frown was in place as always, but something was different. He played with the lid of his to-go cup and kept glancing at his watch. His usual controlled affect had given way to jerky moves and an air of desperate panic.

Clive found his first smile since killing Greg Parker. Looked as if his boss had got the message. Clive was no longer taking orders. He was more in the mood to give them.

He stepped inside. Instead of indulging the boss and playing their practiced newspaper-switching game, Clive sat down right across from the man who had yet to transfer the full payment for Steve Wasserman's extinction. That was a mistake the boss would pay dearly for.

His eyes widened and he glanced around at the few other occupied tables in the place. "What are you—"

"Right now I'm enjoying the look on your face." It almost made having to deal with the Lara-and-Davis duo tolerable. Almost.

The man's face flushed to a deep, angry red. "How dare—"

"Relax." Clive had had just about enough of the sideshow. What had started out amusing was now wasting his time. "You're a smart man. You know jumping around like that calls attention. Sitting and talking is normal in a place like this."

The boss's hand slashed out and his coffee cup tipped. He grabbed it, causing the lid to pop off and sending the liquid spilling down the sides. "There is nothing normal about what's happening."

"You do look like you've had a hard day." Clive hoped the man hadn't slept. That would make some of this annoyance worth it. Not the race through the office building or the clip he'd taken in the shoulder and nick in the thigh, but he planned on exacting revenge for that later.

His boss flicked the coffee off his hand and made a show of wiping his suit blazer off with a napkin. He completed the move by crumpling the wet napkin in a ball and letting it drop to the floor. "This isn't how we do things."

"It is now." Clive leaned back, making sure his gun still pointed at the entitled idiot in front of him. It was almost a shame littering wasn't a capital crime. "You didn't give me all the information I needed to complete this."

"Such as?"

"How do I get into Davis Weeks's house? I've been there and seen the security. I figure your contacts know a trick or two."

"You don't need to do that."

"Oh, I do if I intend to lure Davis there for a chat."

"Why touch him?"

That should have seemed obvious, but Clive spelled it out anyway. "Where he is, Lara is."

"This job is over."

Maybe technically but not in Clive's mind. He liked the title *rogue agent*.

The idea of not answering to this guy appealed to him. The thought of him bleeding out all over the coffeehouse floor sounded even better. "I'm afraid not. See, I always finish the work before I move on. You should know that from our past dealings overseas."

"Keep your voice down."

The harsh whisper did more to draw attention than anything Clive had done. The man had no idea how close he was to getting shot. "Right now I have a few very annoying loose ends to tie up. Or maybe I should say *cut up*."

"You had your chance."

"You're not hearing me." Clive leaned in when a college-age student sat at the table two down from them, just in case her earphones proved an insufficient buffer. "I am going to continue my work and you are going to pay me."

"Why should I?"

That one was easy. "Because I *do* know where you live."

LARA TRIED TO roll over but her leg was trapped under Davis's heavier one. Instead of breaking free, she slid her arm across his chest and snuggled in closer. He mumbled something as she tucked her head against his neck.

Even though his love of danger made her skittish and confused, she'd welcomed it the past few days. He'd stepped in and taken charge. He'd protected but never slipped into self-destructive mode. He'd even listened when she'd begged to go along to Hampton and then praised her when she hadn't got herself killed.

Truth was she loved him more now than she ever had. Deep to her soul where it wiped out the echoing darkness that had settled in at losing him and the child they'd created. She wasn't even sure how she had lived a life with so few connections and now craved one with him to the point where she doubted she could ever be complete without him by her side.

He rubbed his hand over her arm. Even in his sleep, he had to touch her, comfort her. Maybe the thought should scare her a bit, but all she experienced was a bubbling of something deep in her belly that she suspected was hope.

So much of the man she knew hadn't changed. He had exchanged one terrifying job for another and chased after someone who he thought might hurt her, never bothering to warn her about the danger. Always the lone wolf.

But she'd seen glimpses of his other side. The sweet side, like in the way he handled Mrs. Winston, shielding her and giving her a touch of excitement and the attention she desperately craved. And his quick acceptance of Ben never would have happened a year ago.

She guessed Davis was angry and confused about the way they'd left things all those months before. He'd said as much and so had Pax. Sure, she'd explained her fears at the time and begged Davis to understand. She'd tried to communicate and even suggested they talk to someone to help them, which he immediately rejected, but she'd never told him the one thing he deserved to know.

In that way, she was as guilty as he was. But his tendency to hold back went so much deeper.

Still, she needed to tell him the awful truth. Keeping it from him hadn't been from spite or even anger. It just happened. When he returned she was home from the hospital and determined to make him understand how staying in San Diego had crushed her. He blew off her concerns and left her no choice but to reach for her packed bags and get out.

The time to tell him had never been right after that, and she'd been so lost in her mourning of the baby she'd already loved and the man whom she'd love forever, that she couldn't see a way out of the pain that blanketed her.

She'd switched jobs and tried to start over. By the time she'd emerged from the crushing despair she couldn't see what telling him would do other than shift part of her burden to him. If she did that and he shrugged it off as he did every other moment of emotional discomfort, she didn't know if she'd recover.

He stirred under her gentle caresses of his bare chest. "Why are you awake?"

"I love you." She said it because she wanted to and because she thought he needed to hear it.

His eyes popped open. "A man could get used to waking up to that sort of declaration."

"It matters?"

"It means everything." Those big eyes brightened. "I love you, too."

The words washed over her, smoothing out the rough parts. "I think we should—"

"Oh, wait. I have an idea." With his hand over hers, he slid her fingers lower. His erection pressed against her palm and his body thrummed with a sudden awareness.

They'd made love twice already that night and he was still ready to go. Now, that was the Davis she remembered.

He rolled over, pushing her to her back as his head dipped to that ticklish place right behind her ear. He made this appealing little moaning sound as his mouth moved over her and he whispered her name.

The explosive combination zipped through her senses, pushing out the exhaustion. Her hand slipped into his hair before she could stop, but she made one last grasp for common sense. "Davis, we—"

His lips hovered over her eyes, placing nibbling kisses on her nose and cheeks. "Can talk later."

And then his mouth covered hers and all she wanted was more.

Chapter Seventeen

The next morning Davis finally felt as if his life had adjusted and slipped back on track. He'd gone from being on edge about Lara's safety to feeling calm and relaxed. It was about more than good sex, which was spectacular. Though he hated the idea and they wouldn't mean anything or feel as good as being with Lara, he could find other women. This was about a deeper connection with that person who brought the right mix of comfort and shocking heat. With Lara he got it all—sexy, smart, giving and loving.

The only casualty to restarting their relationship might be sleep. He yawned for the fourth time and looked across the conference table to find Pax glaring at him.

"Now you're just showing off," he grumbled.

Davis refused to feel guilty. He'd spent some of the worst months of his life replaying every minute of his time with Lara, desperate to figure out where it all went wrong.

He couldn't wrap his head around her complaints about the danger. She knew about his life and work going into the relationship. He'd been honest and disclosed more than was safe earlier than he should have to prevent a claim of bait and switch.

He pushed the details out of his mind and just enjoyed the morning after. "I took your advice. Well, yours and Connor's."

Pax closed the file in front of him and put it on the checked stack. "I'm happy for you."

"I can tell by how ticked off you sound."

Joel spun his chair around and used his feet and the rollers to drag it from the bank of computers to the conference table. "If you two don't stop talking about sex I'll get my gun."

Davis picked up on the load of male grumpiness in the house this morning. For some reason the angrier they got, the more he wanted just to laugh. "No one said *sex*."

Footsteps creaked on the hardwood floors. They all looked up to find Lara, fresh from a shower and in white jeans and one of those slim-fitting tops women wore to torture the males of the species.

He sometimes feared a heart attack from just looking at her. She shot him that megawatt smile and his chest ached from the power of it. From across the room he could smell her, read every gesture and watch as her skin flushed remembering last night.

She put the tray with the new pot of coffee and

pile of toast in the center of the table. Joel and Pax dived for the food. Davis grabbed the coffee before they knocked it over.

"It sounds like a locker room in here." She rolled her eyes. "Kind of looks like one, too."

Pax pulled out the seat next to him, the one that put her right across from Davis. "Technically, that's your fault."

"Pax, shut up before I let Joel shoot you." No woman wanted to be a punch line. Just because Joel and Pax were too stupid to know, that didn't mean Davis had to suffer.

"I can take it." She winked at him. "Where's Connor?"

Off breaking the law, but Davis decided not to phrase it that way because Ben was lurking around somewhere and the guy still had an oath to adhere to. "Taking one last run at some FBI files he's not supposed to have access to."

Joel held up a finger. "Hypothetically taking a run."

"Got it." She ran her hand over the side of the tall pile of files next to Pax. "Where are we in here? Looks like you've done a lot of gathering and reading while I was doing lazy things like sleeping and showering."

And other things, but Davis kept that quiet. The heated look he shared with Lara let him know she was thinking about those things, too.

"That's the bad news." Joel leaned back in his chair and talked while he munched on the toast. "I've been through the Naval Academy records and newspaper articles over a span of a few years. No school scandals and nothing in the background of Martin Coughlin, Steve Wasserman or the NCIS deputy director. They're linked by school, but not by anything that got the attention of the police, school board or media."

"And it gets worse. I used Connor's FBI contacts to dig deeper. Looked at juvenile-court records and academic files and transcripts, even went back to high school on those three, combing through all the stuff I shouldn't have access to. There's nothing." Pax tapped his hand against the top of his stack. "I even pulled the twenty years since college and, while I still have more to look at, so far I don't see anything."

Joel picked up the bad-news trail. "Their security-clearance records don't show issues either."

Lara's eyes narrowed. "How did you get ahold of those?"

Joel smiled. "I'm resourceful."

Like that, Davis's good mood slipped away. The lighthearted calm gave way to something dark and furious that was much harder to control. It took all of his concentration to stop his jaw from tightening, all his focus to keep his mind on track and not be derailed into what-if territory.

His future actually depended on it.

Giving in to some of that brewing frustration, he tossed the notepad in his hands harder than he'd intended and watched it slide across the table. "We're missing something."

Pax shook his head. "I can't see where."

The men started throwing out ideas. Each possibility Davis put forward, Joel or Pax shot down and vice versa. They discussed other databases and the unlikely possibility that this tied to something that happened overseas during military service. That should be in the files they had, but Ronald had a lot of power. He could bury pieces, but it was hard to imagine him being able to make a big issue completely disappear.

Lara paged through the notepad, rarely glancing up or getting sucked into the adrenaline flow surging around the room. If the argument and raised voices bothered her, she sure didn't show it. She didn't even flinch when Pax slapped a hand against the tabletop to make a point.

After a few minutes she put the pad down and stared at them. Her lips curled in the start of a smile as she glanced around the table. Ben jogged down the stairs and into the room, and she shot him a conspiratorial look.

Many of the questions died before they got to an answer. One discussion trailed off entirely. One by one all eyes turned to her.

She waited until silence fell and only the low rumble of the police scanner on Joel's desk filled the room. "The nonschool records."

Davis knew she had more than just the confusing phrase. The look of pure female satisfaction told him that.

Joel frowned at her. "I said—"

"You're searching school records and criminal records. What about the other stuff?"

Pax grabbed another piece of toast. "You lost me."

It was as close to an *aha* moment as Davis had ever experienced. The light clicked on and he heard the snap in his brain. He'd missed the hole and shouldn't have. They were running around searching but skipping crucial steps. He swore at his unusual lack of finesse on this one. They were all guilty and it took a nonexpert to see it.

Rushing right behind the temptation to kick his butt came a surge of pride. Most people would have been rocking in a corner after being attacked and seeing dead body after dead body. She didn't run or panic or even burst into tears, though she was entitled to do all of those. No, she dug in and didn't hold back even when it meant challenging them all.

No wonder he loved her. It was a miracle no other man had swooped in while he was stumbling around waiting to figure this all out. And he knew that was true because he'd watched over her from afar, dreading that day. He said a silent thank-you to the universe that that had never happened.

He winked at her. "The beautiful and equally brilliant Lara is right. We're going about this the wrong way by searching for an incident and trying to work from there. We need to look for a missing piece. Forget what's there. Find the hole."

That smile of hers turned up even brighter and she aimed it right at him.

He had to swallow twice before he could continue. The urge to drag her upstairs was that strong. Talk about bad timing. "Whatever this is won't be in an obvious record because it has never been found out. It's hidden. It looks innocent or at the very least not problematic."

"Interesting." Pax put down the toast and grabbed the files again. "We need to spread out over Annapolis and all of their hometowns in case whatever this is happened on vacation. Go through their families, expand to parents and siblings."

"Add Martin's wife." They were the first words Ben said since he'd walked in the room.

"Why?" Lara asked.

He leaned over and grabbed an empty mug and the full coffeepot. "She's a socialite from a wealthy family who plays the role like a pro, yet she married a blue-collar guy and agreed to travel around from base to base with him? I don't think so."

Lara shook her head. "Maybe it's true love."

Davis was inclined to go with Ben's gut feeling on this. Davis believed in love, but he also knew other emotions drove a lot of weddings these days.

Washington, D.C., being a purely political town made marriages-of-power-convenience all too common. If power could drive people together, maybe a scandal could, too.

"*Disdain* was more like it." Ben took the seat next to Davis, but not before he grabbed a few of the files from Pax's pile. "Something doesn't check out. She is a stereotypical all-for-show type but lives in a nice house but not a mansion, even though she could afford one and that life better fits her personality. I can't get a handle on her."

Lara's head fell to the side as she glanced at Davis. "Do you ever wonder what people say about us as a couple?"

"That he is one lucky bastard," Pax said.

Joel didn't even look up from his papers. "Pretty much."

Ben shrugged. "I didn't say it out loud because we just met, but I definitely thought it."

RONALD DISCONNECTED THE line on his regular Monday-morning videoconference with the field offices' heads. A knock sounded at the door before the images blinked from the screens. That could only mean his assistant had hovered at the door waiting for the two-hour meeting to end and decided a one-second break was sufficient. Because he wanted in and didn't use the intercom, the interruption could also mean bad news.

"Come in." Ronald got up from the couch and walked over to his desk. He didn't bother to sit down because he had back-to-back meetings all morning. "What is it, Wayne?"

"There is an issue."

"There always is. Be more specific."

Wayne glanced at the paper in his hand. As usual, he hung by the door and raised his voice to talk across the room. "We've had a security alert."

"Sit." Ronald mentally watched as his schedule disintegrated. He pointed at the chair right in front of his desk and sat down in the big one behind it. "Be more specific."

"It would appear someone is looking into your background."

Not the news he expected. His mind still focused on the work discussion he had just had about Naples. He forced a topic switch.

"A security-clearance update?" Although that didn't make much sense because his update wasn't due for another year.

"This is off the books." Wayne tucked the note into his pocket as a trickle of sweat broke out on his forehead. "The flag you put on your academy files tripped the warning."

Ronald's stomach dropped, which was a good

thing because he needed room for the fury boiling in his blood. "When?"

"Over the past twenty-four hours."

"Trace it back." Ronald knew where it would go, or he assumed he did. Somehow this would trace back to Martin and the killings and that damn Lara Bart and her boyfriend.

Ronald balanced his chin on his fingertips and blew out a shaky breath. He'd served his country with distinction. He'd made sacrifices and paid his dues. The idea that a twenty-year-old decision, one that wasn't even his, could rise up and slap him in the face refused to compute in his mind. He should be above this, his behavior unquestioned.

Martin had done this. Martin and Nancy. They'd left the girl that night and sent them all careening down this road.

Wayne cleared his throat. "That's the thing, sir. We can't."

It took an extra second for the words to settle in. "That is an unacceptable answer and you know it."

"I already talked with the tech experts—"

"You did what?"

Wayne was moving around and swallowing, his face blanching a scary white. Much more and the guy might pass out.

Not that Ronald cared. He wanted work done correctly and all signs pointed to a disaster from the beginning of this Steve Wasserman mess. Ronald never liked that guy and could not mourn his death, no matter how violent it had been.

"I didn't reference your situation specifically or give any clues that could lead back to you," Wayne said.

"You're my assistant. It's a logical leap."

"I took precautions to prevent anything like that from happening."

If he had, he was the first one associated with any part of this disaster to have done so. Even Davis's oldest friends failed on that score. "Continue to talk to whatever experts you need, keeping my name out of the picture, and find another avenue to track this down."

"We're going to get the same answer. The person breaking in is an expert. Like, can-beat-the-Pentagon's-security type of expert. This isn't just about a firewall."

"Wayne." For some reason his assistant was not understanding the import of this assignment. Ronald decided to make his position clearer. "Just do it. You have until the end of the day or be prepared for a new assignment in the worst detail you can imagine."

Chapter Eighteen

Lara worked around the Corcoran conference table with the men for two more hours, meticulously dissecting every detail, going line by line. Previously she'd viewed them as weapons experts and nothing more. They were the guys you called in when you needed muscle and a way out of an impossible situation. Necessary but limited in their role.

She'd forgotten, or maybe she'd never realized, that for their work to be successful, it required research, planning and strategy. The job dealt with puzzles, human and otherwise.

They sifted and analyzed data and none of those skills had to do with shooting a gun. Somewhere along the line she'd sold them all short. She vowed not to do that again.

The process continued without deviation. Each of them looked at a file. They checked, double-checked, then checked again. When they passed it around and all took a look, they passed the file to her for a final look from fresh eyes. Untrained eyes that might see something they'd skimmed over.

Being included, working side by side with Davis instead of being left behind, thrilled her. She never lost sight of the fact they were dealing in human lives, but she could move that to the side and focus on the piece in front of her.

Her head shot up.

That was it. All Davis's talk about facts over bodies, all his arguments about the job consisting of more than chasing and shooting—she'd never got it until now. She wasn't sure it was possible to mentally sort it all out unless you lived through it. Now she had.

Davis slid his fingers over to hers. "Are you okay?" Concern lit his eyes and his concentration suddenly centered on her.

This wasn't the right time or place. The reality was that she needed more time to work reality out in her mind. But for the first time in a long while, something flickered in the distance. A tiny dancing flame of hope she thought had been snuffed out months ago.

Last night she'd felt love and passion. In this minute she saw a possible future. So many land mines lay buried in the path, but the breath of understanding gave them a place to start.

She smiled at him, caressing every inch of his face with her gaze. "I'm fine."

His eyes narrowed and he looked ready to say something when Ben thumped his fist against the table.

"I think I got it." He turned the document around for all of them to see. "A dead girl miles away from Annapolis on the last weekend of summer before junior year."

Lara read the headline. "College Girl Found at Beach." It actually hurt to say the words because the meaning was so horrible.

She didn't see the direct connection, but she noticed how Davis smiled as he scanned the lines. The black-and-white photo attached to the article on the front page showed a girl, pretty and young. The first paragraph pointed to her background— rich and privileged. Her father was the head of some company and she'd attended a private high school before going to the University of Virginia.

Lara didn't understand why any of that mattered. None of the people in the case went to that school. And why was the young woman's school even relevant? The article should focus on who she was as a final sign of respect. She'd had dreams and a future and it all had died with her.

She glanced up to see Ben's nod of satisfaction, but she still didn't get it. "Okay, so…"

Davis pointed to paragraphs farther down as he read an edited version out loud. "'She overdosed at the beach and was left to die. Evidence at the scene suggested multiple footprints and a parked car gone by the time the police arrived.'"

The poor girl made Lara take back all those complaints she'd had as a teen about not having many friends. She'd pick alive over popular any day. "That's terrible."

Davis kept going. "'The police believed other kids were there for the party but they left.'"

Joel flipped his chair around to face his computer. "That might be a stretch but it's worth looking into."

"Especially because there's a woman named Colleen Bradford referenced in the article." At Ben's words, spoken in a clear, booming voice, all eyes focused on him. "The reporter caught up with Colleen at the memorial service. She says she didn't know the young woman who died but talks about how she saw the story in the newspaper and had to come out of respect."

Since no one else asked, Lara jumped in. "Who is Colleen?"

Davis shuffled papers. "The name is vaguely familiar."

Ben smacked the back of his hand against the file. "Because for one semester, she was one of Nancy's roommates."

The light popped on in Lara's head and refused to blink out again. "They were all there."

"Nancy, Martin, Steve and Ronald, the deeply screwed deputy director. I'm betting we dig and we'll find some ties between them and the dead woman. Or, more likely, we'll see a profound absence of ties—even things that would be natural coincidence will be missing because someone scrubbed the records clean," Pax added.

Davis rubbed his thumb over the back of Lara's hand. "Well, that kind of secret certainly could be an interesting basis for the shaky Coughlin marriage."

The idea made Lara's stomach flip. Tying your life to someone out of guilt was bad enough. Having a pact revolving around some poor girl's death was the ultimate marriage made in hell. "If it's true, they deserve each other."

Davis must have sensed her anxiety or heard the anger in her voice. Without looking at her or saying a word, his hand tightened around hers. The touch, so basic and freely offered, was about comfort, not sex, and the fact he knew the difference confirmed she'd picked the right man for the right reasons.

"I wonder why Steve started talking after all these years." Ben tapped his pen against the table. "There were numerous times when it would have mattered. I'd think Ronald getting the NCIS deputy position would have rung a bigger bell in Steve's mind."

"Guilt, or maybe he got sick of everything working for Martin and not for him. Martin and Ronald remained friends. Steve could have resented their bond." Pax threw up his hands. "Really, it could be anything."

Lara glanced at Joel's monitors and the big screen with the names and photos of all the suspects. The screen showed normal people who had kids and the usual worries about traffic and other mundane things. The kind of people she passed in the grocery store all the time.

The evil lurking underneath was what scared Lara. "So, which one of these folks is the actual bad guy here?"

Davis barely spared the monitor a glance. His face screwed up in an expression that spoke to his disdain. "If they left that girl to die, all of them."

Lara didn't disagree but her concern was more immediate. "I mean, who's writing the checks to the hit man?"

Joel shook his head. "I don't see anything in their personal finances to reflect big payments."

The smile that spread across Davis's mouth was slow and satisfied. "Then check the business one." He looked over at Ben. "You did say Nancy ran a company, right?"

"Why, yes, she does."

BY LATE AFTERNOON, Davis had checked in with Connor, who was on his way back from D.C. They were on a half-hour break. When Lara disappeared up the stairs, shooting him a sexy wink over her shoulder, he'd planned to race up after her. Connor's call had stalled that.

Sitting now at the computer with all of Joel's fancy programs and password-detection software in front of him made Davis think about the things he didn't know. Not about Martin and those other clowns, but about Lara. There were months unaccounted for, that time while he was away and running for his life and the month or so after she'd left when he'd pretended he didn't care about her.

He'd been an idiot. It took only a minute of honesty for him to realize she'd never leave his head.

After a quick look around to make sure he was alone, he started typing. It took only a minute for data to fill the small screen on the left.

"What are you doing?" Pax's voice came from behind Davis's shoulder, but the disappointment lingered.

Davis hit a button and the screen went blank again. "When did you start sneaking around?"

"That indignation would be more convincing if you weren't stalling by answering a question with a question." Pax put his mug next to Davis's keyboard. "You use that trick a lot."

"I'm checking something."

Pax's mouth formed a thin, disapproving line. "I got that part already."

"Something Connor said." Davis wiped a hand through his hair and tried to explain something he didn't really understand. "He suggested I go back to the breakup and figure out what else was happening. It's been bugging me since he said it. I've watched over her since we've been apart but I don't know what happened in those three weeks."

"We were away and she got sick of it. That's what you told me."

Pax wasn't giving an inch and that didn't surprise Davis. Pax and Lara had always been close and Pax had a soft spot for women. When Davis was slow to trust, Pax jumped in.

"There's something else, Pax. Has to be." Davis was honest enough to admit that he didn't know what he was doing.

Guilt crashed over him and his mind raced with excuses, but the bottom line was this check felt more invasive than anything he had done before. The rest of the investigation had been about keeping her safe and making sure the danger of his life hadn't seeped into hers. This was about picking her privacy apart.

Pax balanced a hand against the desk and leaned in. "What happens when you find it?"

"Meaning?"

The muscles in Pax's face dropped. "I'm going to let the answer-with-a-question thing go this time, but know that tactic isn't helping your case. Think this through. You're back together with Lara."

Davis wanted that to be true. Even as the guilt ate away at his insides, he justified his behavior by saying he needed the information for them to finally, once and for all, put the sordid parts of their relationship behind them. "Maybe…I'm hoping. I don't know."

That wasn't quite true. He knew what he wanted. He knew they loved each other. He didn't know where all of that put them.

Pax shook his head. "Wow, she has you chasing your tail."

"Get to your point."

"If things are back on track and you have a shot of convincing her to give you guys a second try, whatever you find—hell, the fact you're even digging around in her life—might mess your chance up."

It was all so logical but carried such a huge risk. The real issue was the way Pax said the words. They seemed to be carefully chosen and placed.

"What do you know?" Davis asked, dreading the answer he might get.

"Nothing about what happened then, but I do know you love her and should be with her." Pax dropped to his haunches with his hand across the back of Davis's chair. "Look, we haven't exactly been lucky in the women department, but somewhere along the line she broke that cycle. She's the one. Don't lose her."

That qualified as the most impassioned speech Davis had ever heard his brother give. The words came alive under the force of his voice. It was as if he wanted to bend Davis to his will.

He wanted to shrug it off. More than that, he

wanted to stand up and not research. But at that moment he couldn't choose. "I'll think about it."

Pax's chest fell. "You mean you'll ignore it."

"If you were in my place—"

He glanced down to the floor. "I'd be on my knees begging her to come back."

"That seems extreme."

Pax stood up again. "I'll remind you of that if she leaves when this case is over."

After Pax skulked from the room, Davis put his hands on the chair arms to get up. In midpush he glanced at the blank screen. Then to the keyboard.

He balanced there trying to decide what to do.

A second later he slid back into the chair and hit the space bar.

THE INFORMATION CLIVE received about the security codes and hidden cameras at Davis's house made him nervous. Not that Clive thought he would get caught or that he couldn't break the system. He was too good for that.

No, the worry was that his boss had put together a competent double cross. Hard to imagine, but the man sat in a position of power and that didn't happen without some skills, even if those skills amounted to nothing more than having an impressive address book.

It was entirely possible his boss fed wrong information in the hopes of landing a new person to blame for the Wasserman murder and all the fall-out that came after. Clive had no intention of going to jail, regardless of whether he actually committed the crime.

To prevent that possibility, Clive took the direct approach. He'd staked out the neighbor, a Mrs. Winston. She was the older, nosy type. No real family and few visitors. She collected government benefits and somehow survived on that pittance. But the character trait that interested him the most was the nosy one.

Perfect.

Clive lingered near Davis's front door. Even ventured around the side, making a big show of trying to see if anyone was home. The goal was to look as if he belonged there. Last thing he needed was for her to call the police.

"May I help you?" Mrs. Winston's shaky voice came to him only a few minutes later.

Clive smiled. There was nothing better than when a plan fell together. He turned around and lowered his gaze. The lady stood all of five foot nothing, wearing what looked like a robe and a heavy dose of blush.

He shot her his most genuine smile. He practiced often enough. "I was looking for Davis."

Her eyes narrowed as the grip on her cell phone tightened. "He's out of town."

"I talked to him a few days ago."

The older woman waved the comment off. "He comes in and out."

She also looked around, hesitating when her gaze fell on the camera hooked to the wall on the side of the house facing hers. She could stare all she wanted because he already had taken over that video feed and was even now running an endless loop to make it look as if nothing was happening in the yard.

He took his hat off and twisted it in his hands, hoping for the concerned look. It was foreign to him but he'd seen it in others often enough. "Normally I would not ask you something like this, but is there any chance you have a number or address?"

The last of her friendliness came down with a crash. "We're not close."

He could almost hear the wheels turning in her head. He glanced at the cell again and decided that was the answer. If she didn't play along with the plan in his head and invite Davis here, Clive would kill her and come up with another way to make the meeting happen.

He took another shot at the role of worried friend. "I understand. Really, he's not the one I need. I have to get in touch with Lara."

"You know Lara?" The older woman's frown disappeared. "She's lovely."

Now Clive had his way in. He would have bet Davis was the woman's weakness. Turned out Lara was the answer. Again.

"A very interesting woman." Clive had to force his mind to even come up with that. He had a lot of words to describe Lara, and none of them worked in this scenario. "But I don't want to bother you."

Clive played the last card. He turned as if he was ready to move on.

Mrs. Winston bought it. "Why do you need her?"

Clive turned around with that same friendly expression plastered on his face. He was going to need a shower after this.

"I can't really say." He leaned in as if sharing a big secret. "See, it's a family matter. The kind you can't talk about over the phone."

The woman's hand went to her chest. "An illness?"

Worked for Clive. "I'm afraid so."

"Oh, no. The poor thing." Mrs. Winston lifted the phone, even gave it a look then let her hand drop again.

"I thought if she was with Davis, he could help her through it. He's very protective of her." Which was why Clive planned to kill him last. Imagining the guilt and shame on that moron's face while the knife sliced into his woman's perfect skin had kept Clive going all day. It would play like dinner theater. "Maybe I can check back. I just worry it could be too late."

He dropped the comment but didn't leave. The woman was near tears with worry over Lara. After a few seconds of hesitation, she said the words he'd been waiting for.

"You know, I could call him and see if he's nearby."

Clive tried to look confused, although he wasn't exactly sure what that one would look like. "I thought you didn't have a number."

"I can't guarantee it will work." She gestured toward her house. "Have a seat on my porch while you wait. I can see if he's close enough to stop by and bring Lara with him. There's no need to upset Lara in the car."

Yes, Clive certainly wouldn't want to upset Lara. He smiled at the older woman as he debated the pros and cons of letting her live. "You've been very helpful. Thank you."

Chapter Nineteen

They didn't have time for a side trip but Lara insisted. When the call had come from Mrs. Winston fifteen minutes ago, Davis had picked up. She talked about making him a pie and leaving it on his table. It all sounded innocent, but the comment sent a fissure of panic through Lara. The last time anyone was in that house someone had died. She had no idea what state the place was in, but she knew Mrs. Winston was too old and too fragile healthwise to take that sort of shock.

Figuring out what had Pax and Davis sniping at each other before they'd left Corcoran was the bigger mystery. The argument had ended when Davis told Pax to wait at the house for Connor then ordered Joel to keep digging into the financial aspects of the killings. That left her and Ben riding along while Davis drove in silence.

The pulse of discomfort had her tugging on her seat belt. Because she didn't know what had happened or what had Davis staring at the road with a practiced blank expression, she tried for neutral conversation. "Do you usually see Mrs. Winston every day?"

"When I'm home."

So much for conversation. Clearly something had happened. As usual, she was the last to know. "Okay, then."

"This is an in and out, right?" Ben scanned the area as they pulled onto the far end of Davis's street. "I'm not comfortable with any of us hanging around town until we finish driving this thing to ground."

Lara had to chuckle at that one. "Not to scare you, but you already sound like one of them."

"Who?" Ben asked.

"The Corcoran Team."

"She's a nice old lady who is probably lonely." Davis's flat voice cut through the amusement and weighed the air back down again. "Really, I think she took a liking to Lara and wants to see her again. She was clear about bringing you along."

"That's sweet." Would have been sweeter if Davis bothered to look at her when he'd said it.

He tightened his grip on the steering wheel. "She told me to pull up in the back…"

Ben leaned forward between the seats. "What is it?"

Davis slowed the car and pulled it to a stop on the side of the street. Gone was the blank demeanor. Now he shifted around and looked over the area with the watchful eye she'd come to know. "How could I miss this?" he asked.

Lara knew the tone, too. Dreaded it, recoiled from it and hoped she'd never hear it again. It signaled something scary and dangerous, and just hearing it made the bile rush up the back of her throat.

She didn't want to know but she asked the question anyway. "What are we talking about?"

Davis thumped the heel of his hand against the steering wheel. "The back. Mrs. Winston is telling me someone is at the back of her house."

"Maybe it's just—"

He finally looked at her with dead eyes and a face drawn tight with worry. "She thinks I'm a spy and that this is some sort of helpful game."

Ben watched the street, his gaze hesitating on two men standing near the stop sign up ahead. "You think our killer is there?"

"It was someone who didn't feel right to her." Davis was talking out loud but the words sounded as though the conversation was playing in his head. "Someone who made her want to warn us."

Ben gave a humph. "Way to go, Mrs. Winston."

Davis glanced into his rearview window and put the car back in gear. "I'm taking you back."

Lara slapped her hand over his and held the car in Park. He'd break the hold soon, so she rushed to get her point out. "No. She could be hurt…or worse. You're good at plans, so come up with one."

"You've been through enough." His voice wavered on a thin line between concern and frustration.

She'd heard it before but this time it wasn't going to work. They could call in reinforcements and shoot the place down so long as Mrs. Winston got out of there alive.

Lara could not live with one more death on her hands and certainly not that of an old woman with a cute crush on Davis. "We're going in."

They all sat there. Davis didn't drive away but he didn't turn the car off either.

"Wasting time." Ben's head popped up between them. When Davis let out a noise that sounded oddly like a growl, Ben shot back. "You know I'm right."

Davis swore. "We do what I say and how I say. Got it?"

Before they agreed he'd started the car moving again.

THIS WAS A death wish. Davis couldn't help but think that as he and Lara walked up to Mrs. Winston's front door. Lara wore the one protective vest he had in the trunk with his long-sleeve shirt over it. It was large enough to hide the bulk but it dwarfed her. In this heat, it would likely have her sweating any second.

She'd put up a token protest about being the only one with the added protection, but he wasn't in the mood for an argument. Ben ended any discussion when he told her to hurry up. Davis liked that guy's style.

In the tense second before he knocked on the door, he thought about asking her the question kicking around in his mind and messing him up. Hell, he'd been so messed up over Lara that he almost missed the clue from Mrs. Winston, the clue he gave to her never thinking this situation could happen.

He'd found Lara's hospital record and it had him reeling. Well, the bill and admittance information. He was still waiting for a copy of the medical records to show up on his cell. With all the privacy restrictions, that information was buried and hard to access. Being able to tell Joel and put him on the task would have cut through the trouble. But because Davis was going it alone, everything took longer.

"Are you okay?" she whispered without moving her head.

He decided to answer the one he expected her to ask. "We're going to be fine."

He reached out and rang the doorbell. He had a key but he didn't know where anyone stood inside and didn't want to put Mrs. Winston in additional danger.

The door opened and her worried face peeked out. "Davis?"

Clearly she thought he'd messed up the signal. She couldn't know Ben had circled around the house and would come through the back as their element of surprise. "You said you had cake for me. Coconut, I believe."

Some of the tension left her face when he mentioned the one thing in this world she was allergic to. A wobbly smile came next.

To make sure she understood he got it, he nodded to her and motioned with his head for her to step to the side. "May we come in?"

"Both of you?"

Davis had asked the same question a dozen times while walking up the porch steps. "Lara would like to say hello."

The smell of mothballs hit him like a pan to the face the second they stepped inside. He knew from experience Mrs. Winston was a fan. The harsh scent mixed with a hint of Earl Grey tea as she walked them through the family room.

Collections of glass figurines and other knick-knacks filled cabinet after cabinet lining the dining room. The only thing Mrs. Winston had more of was detective novels. They were stacked around every room, making the place more of a maze than a livable space.

With each step Davis scanned the area, his gaze moving over every corner as he waited for their unwanted and very violent guest to appear. Clearly the guy had something special planned and was drawing out the moment.

The emergency call had gone out to the rest of

the team right before they stepped inside, but Davis hoped they wouldn't be needed…and wouldn't find dead bodies when they got there.

Davis kept his hand on Lara's back and more than once had to propel her forward when her steps faltered. He didn't blame her. Walking into a guaranteed shoot-out was dumb. If the attacker was smart he'd lie in wait and hit them with a sniper shot.

But this didn't feel professional to Davis. This had turned personal and that might be their only chance. If the guy wanted a final moment, he'd have to show himself.

No sooner had Davis thought it than he heard the soft press of a shoe behind him. He would have missed the sound if he hadn't been waiting for it. He shifted just as the guy leaped forward. Instead of landing on Davis's back, his momentum carried him forward and into Mrs. Winston.

The small woman went flying. Lara reached out to keep the older woman from crashing into a cabinet in the corner between the dining room and kitchen. The catch gave the attacker the extra second he needed to smash into Lara's path.

Before Davis could get a clean shot off, the attacker had his hand wrapped around Lara's upper arm and Mrs. Winston at the other end of his gun. He stood behind their bodies like the weasel he was. "It looks like I have your women."

Davis kept his gun aimed while his second

weapon burned through his shirt and into the skin at the small of his back. "Let them go."

"I don't think so." The attacker tugged Lara closer until her back pressed against his front. "It's not as if this was an easy plan to set up."

"You want me, then take me."

"If only it were that simple." He treated them all to a tsk-tsk sound. "No, see, your girlfriend here caused the problem."

"How?" she asked as she tried to shift and put a bit more space between her body and that of her attacker.

"You showed up at Wasserman's place early. The entire scene had been planned for you to arrive and find a break-in and dead body, but someone switched the meeting and I had to improvise."

Lara swallowed as her pleading gaze fell on Davis. "Steve."

"Ah, yes. He was very excited about turning in his friends."

Davis tried not to look at Lara. He needed to stay focused, and seeing her crumble or her eyes fill with fear could snap his control. With Ben nearby as backup, the goal was to collect as much information as possible.

This guy in front of him was a hired gun, which meant someone paid his bill. Davis wanted to know who.

"The people you work for wanted to remove Steve from the scene."

"I work for one person. One powerful person." The attacker shot Davis a smile so full of evil venom it was good the women couldn't see it. "But he is not your problem. I am."

This guy had gone full tilt. Davis would bet he was working on his own now. No way would his boss have wanted this kind of bloodbath, not on top of the dead bodies piling up all over town.

Even knowing it wouldn't work, Davis tried. From the way the women were listing and shifting around he knew he was running out of time. "Tell me the name and walk away. I'll go after your boss and you can leave with whatever he paid you."

"I'm still waiting for part of that, and Ms. Bart needs to die in order for me to collect."

That was a very bad piece of news. The attacker still had a reason other than revenge or anger to come after Lara.

Davis rushed to take away the incentive. "If she dies, you can't frame her for murder."

"You are a smart one."

Smart enough to have a contingency plan. Even now Ben slipped in the back door with his gun ready and slid into a small alcove, out of sight from this guy.

Davis switched the grip on his gun, holding his fingers up in a form of mock surrender. "We can think this through and come up with a solution."

"I've got it covered." The attacker began backing the women up, right into the kitchen doorway where Davis wanted him. "As I told you, I'm not working alone."

A bolt of panic shot through Davis. That suggested another player. Someone else on the property. With the gun odds evened, Davis no longer had the same confidence in his plan. He could throw his body over one woman and shield her, but not both. Not realistically.

"You first." The attacker motioned with the gun to Davis.

No way was he putting his back to this guy. Instead, Davis shuffled, keeping his gun steady and one slip from shooting. As he stepped into the kitchen, Ben came fully into view. He stood with narrowed eyes and a serious expression. As long as he could rapid fire, Davis didn't care what the other man looked like.

Just as the attacker turned into the kitchen, Ben stepped out with his gun raised.

The attacker just smiled. "It's about time you got here. I thought I would have to fight Mr. Weeks on my own."

"Ben?"

Davis felt as confused as Lara sounded. His head spun as he conducted a fast rewind on every conversation and action from the past day. The guy showed up and things fell together. He was too good to be true.

"Interesting." Davis shifted from confused to ticked off in a second. Whipping out his second gun, he aimed one at each of the other men in the room.

He thought he heard Mrs. Winston whimper, and the stunned looked on Lara's face, all wide-eyed and pale, made Davis hate Ben even more.

Ben didn't even flinch. He kept his gun on the attacker. "You're lying."

"You said you'd get him here, convince him his neighbor's call was legitimate then do the 'I'll be your backup' thing. It worked."

The attacker's words were convincing, delivered in a sure tone and without hesitation. Either he was a perfect liar or Ben was a plant. Davis went back and forth between the two possibilities. Until he decided, he planned on keeping a gun trained on each of them.

Ben shook his head. "He's playing you, Davis. Don't buy it."

"He sounds pretty clear to me." Davis waited for some sign. Any sign.

"What's his name?" Lara asked.

The attacker tightened his hold on her arm until she hissed out a breath and her knees gave way. He ended with a little shake. "I didn't tell you that you could talk."

Davis jumped in before the guy could really hurt her. Yelling, he brought the attention back to him. "If he's who you say he is—"

"I don't have to prove myself to you." The attacker glanced at Ben. "You want the young one or the old woman?"

"I'll take the loser between them."

Something about the way Ben had said it sounded genuine. If he was in on this, he should be moving. He had the element of surprise and could have ended this.

Davis wasn't good at trust, but he was desperate enough to believe in Ben.

"Fine. I'll decide." The attacker pulled both women in closer and let them go. He stepped back as a second gun appeared out of nowhere.

The room moved in slow motion as he raised both weapons, aiming for the dead center on the backs of each woman.

Ben's mouth dropped open and he started moving a second later. One arm wrapped around Mrs. Winston, tucking her head against his chest as he dived into a roll. The other arm came up to get off a shot.

The timing was wrong. Ben couldn't grab both women and that left Lara without protection.

But Davis was already moving. He motioned for her to drop as the room exploded in a rash of yelling and booming gunfire.

Lara screamed as Davis crashed into her from the side and sent her spinning toward the cabinets. They slid across the linoleum floor and landed with a bang as they flew into the oven door.

Glass shattered and plates crashed. More than one book stack toppled over. It all happened as Ben slammed a bullet into the attacker's side and Davis hit him in the forehead. The attacker's eyes flew open as his body lifted up and back. He bounced against the wall then slid down, leaving a blood trail along the white paint.

Davis pulled Lara against him, trying to block her view of the gruesome scene. She let out a soft cry into his neck and held on to his waist. Not even a breath of air separated them and his hands were shaking so hard from the relief that she was okay that it took him an extra second to tour them over her, looking for wounds.

When the echo of the shots stopped and the smoke cleared, Davis watched Ben lift away from Mrs. Winston. The small woman lay in a ball under his chest. Ben touched his fingers to her neck and her eyes flew open.

She stared up at him. "Are you one of the good guys, then?"

Davis answered. "Yes, he is."

THEY'D BEEN BACK for less than an hour and had just washed up and settled down when Deputy Director Ronald Worth showed up at the front door of the Corcoran property and leaned on the doorbell. No guards and no other people. Just him standing outside as if that were the most normal thing in the world.

But the team had expected him. Connor had got word before he'd arrived home from D.C. that Ronald had traced the breach of his privacy records to them. He likely jumped in the car and was close on Connor's tail to get here, which was exactly what they'd wanted when they'd opened the virtual door just long enough to let him peek in.

"You sure you're okay with this?" Connor stopped looking at the monitor long enough to stare at Ben.

He shrugged because there was really nothing else he could say. His life had been whipped into a frenzy over the past few days. This was the only play they had left.

They knew who'd done the actual killings. Now they had to figure out which one, or if all three, had ordered the deaths. This was imperfect but the best way.

Joel wasn't finding a money trail, which meant it was likely buried deep in Nancy's company and would take more time to unravel. But that was a race where someone could cover the tracks before Joel could get in.

"I was just in a shoot-out. Talking to my boss will be easy," Ben said, not quite believing that to be true.

"Yeah, you'd think so." Davis leaned against the conference table with an arm wrapped around Lara.

She hadn't moved since they had come back, and all of the men were starting to send her worried glances.

"You have one shot at this." Connor repeated the words he'd said twice already.

All this concern was starting to make Ben nervous. He'd been fine with the plan until the big push. He knew this was about the risk he was taking—not physical but with his career. He appreciated the thoughts but they had to get this done, uncover the conspiracy, before any other innocent people stepped into the middle.

"I get it." And he did.

Davis nodded. "Then go get him."

Before he stepped in there, Ben had to do one more thing. He stopped at the double doors to the foyer and ignored the third ring of the bell. "Davis? Thanks for believing me."

"I was just happy I didn't shoot you before I figured it out."

Ben nodded and slipped out into the lonely hallway. He didn't realize Connor had followed until he reached around him to open the door.

The deputy's shoulders fell as his voice dipped low. "Ben. I should have known you'd be behind this."

"Come in." Ben motioned toward the room across from the conference room. "This is Connor—"

"I don't care who any of you are." Ronald stopped walking. He stood in the middle of the hall and made his stand. "I want an explanation before I call the authorities and have you all arrested."

"We're not guilty of anything," Connor said.

"You looked at confidential records."

"Did we?" Connor pretended to think about the allegation. "I think if you check again you'll find a decided lack of evidence."

Ben didn't care about any of this. The idea this man would stand in front of him complaining about records after what he'd done was enough to make Ben want to punch the smug look right off his face. "Your hit man is dead."

Ronald's eyebrows fell into a thin line. "What are you talking about?"

"The one who killed Steve Wasserman, Greg Parker and Ken Dwyer." Ben refused to buy into the act. He'd watched an absolute pro try to convince Davis and almost succeed. Davis denied it now, but Ben had seen the look that had washed over the other man's face and the pain in Lara's. Ben would remember that moment of panic forever. "The same guy hired to cover up a twenty-year-old terrible decision that resulted in the death of a young woman."

"Andrea McClintock," Connor said.

Ronald's face went slack. It was as if gravity had taken hold and wiped the emotions clear. "I don't—"

"Don't." Ben could take a lot but not that. "The only question we have is how deep you're into the current conspiracy."

"I'm not involved in any of it."

Ben felt his temper spiral. He glanced outside at the sunny day and thought about how lucky he was to have survived the morning, but even that couldn't bring his thudding heartbeat back under control. "The girl died."

"I drove a car." When no one said anything, Ronald continued. "I picked Martin, Steve and Nancy up from the beach."

"And started a lie that would go on for decades, but someone doesn't want it out now, and Steve threatened to expose you, so, again, who is making the payments?"

Ronald shook his head. "I don't know anything about a hit man."

"But you suspected." Ben held out a cell phone. "Call Martin and tell him you're coming to see him."

Ronald looked appalled by the idea. "Why would I do that?"

Connor stepped forward and grabbed the phone. Shoved it right into the dead center of Ronald's chest. "Because your career is over. What you're playing for now is a chance to stay out of prison."

A charged silence followed Connor's threat. Neither man moved. When Ronald finally shifted, he took the cell and started dialing.

Chapter Twenty

Lara turned her hands over, rubbing them together until they turned red. They wouldn't stop shaking. Yeah, she'd been cool and sure when she'd gone over to Mrs. Winston's house, but she had come out a tangled mass of nerves. She had no idea how Davis handled this stress on a daily basis.

And it wasn't over.

Mrs. Winston was safe in the conference room with Joel. When Lara sneaked away to come up to the bedroom, Joel had been showing the elderly woman the different monitors and the camera angles on Davis's house. Mrs. Winston was like a schoolgirl, flirting with Joel with an expertise that made Lara think the older woman should give lessons.

Fearing her knees would be the next to go, Lara sat down hard on the edge of the bed. She decided to rest for a second, bring her body back under control, before the crowd left for Virginia and the showdown with Martin. Davis would balk about her going, but she had to see it through.

This mess, accident or not, poor timing or not, started with her and she had to finish it. She owed that much to all the people who'd lost their lives during the charade, including poor Andrea McClintock. She'd have her revenge; it was just a shame it took twenty years for her to get it.

After a sharp knock, Davis stepped inside. Between the scruffy and disheveled hair, the dark circles under his eyes and the exhaustion tugging at his mouth, he had a rough look that said his adrenaline was running thin.

"You okay?" he asked as he shut the door.

"I'm ready for a bout of boredom."

He let out a harsh laugh as he sat down next to her. "I'm with you on that."

The sheepish look and way he avoided eye contact worried her. She'd known this was coming and steeled her body for the fight. "I'm going."

He finally looked at her. "What?"

"Aren't you coming up here to tell me I'm not going to Virginia?"

"You're not going, but that's not what I want to ask." He balanced his elbows against his knees and stared at the floor.

She thought she'd seen him in every state—sure, demanding, controlling. But this one, all bent over, struck her as…vulnerable. But that couldn't be right. That wasn't who he was or how he acted.

"Oh," she said because she didn't know what else to say.

He took a big inhalation and let it go. "Why were you in the hospital?"

The question came out of nowhere and slammed into her with the force of a body blow. It didn't follow what they'd been talking about before and it stopped her heart when he said it. "When?"

"When I was in San Diego."

Shock knocked her breathless. She gasped as she tried to find breath. When she finally pushed the words out they sounded breathy and jumbled. "How did you—"

He reached into his jeans pocket and pulled out a folded piece of paper. "Here."

She opened it a bit and looked at the top. That was enough. She'd been in the hospital exactly twice in her life and she knew to her toes he wasn't asking about her broken arm at age nine.

This time, the one on this page, almost killed her. Certainly turned her into a cracked shell for months.

But that didn't explain why he'd gone digging or how he'd found it after all these months. He could have asked her. They could have talked. She tried to do just that, but he skipped into investigator mode and made her one of his suspects.

She shook the paper at him. "Where did you get this?"

The mattress squeaked under his weight as he sat up. "Just answer the question."

She unfolded the paper then refolded it. She looked at it but only saw black streaks where the lines should be.

All the anger at his sneakiness drained out of her. This was so much bigger. So much more devastating, and she ached for him and what he was about to hear. Just saying it would rip away a part of her she'd never be able to get back.

Regret choked her until she gagged on it. "This isn't the way I wanted to tell you."

He shifted until he faced her. "It can't be worse than what I'm thinking."

Then she saw it. Not anger but guilt. A huge mass of it that crushed in on him from every direction, pushing down his shoulders and stomping on his heart. His face was painted with it. It radiated out of every pore.

"Tell me what you think." She whispered the words because it hurt to say them.

"That you were really sick. That's why you begged me to come home and I didn't get it." The grim line of his mouth barely gave him room to spit out the words. "I can't figure out how I missed the clue. Was it cancer or something?"

The words were pure torture. "I lost a baby. Our baby."

He blinked a few times. "What?"

"I was pregnant. I found out right before you left but was waiting until you got back to tell you. Then you stayed all those extra weeks." The surprise in his eyes gave way to something else. A deep sadness that broke her heart, actually shredded it right in two. "I woke up one morning to these cramps and there was blood all over the bed.... I lost the baby."

"Why didn't you tell me?" Shock robbed his words of any punch.

She felt the thuds all the same. Blame and guilt—she'd wallowed in it for so long. "You made your choice."

He stood up and glared down at her. "That's not fair. You didn't give me the information."

He was right and she knew it, but she couldn't stop fighting. She needed him to understand how crushed she had been, how her mind had been foggy and that she'd stumbled around in a grief-stricken haze back then. "I pleaded with you."

Anger flushed through his face. Gone was the concern. This Davis she knew. Furious and hovering, determined to get his way.

"Do you really think if I knew about the baby I would have stayed away?"

She didn't know how to answer that, so she asked a question of her own. "Would you have gone if you knew I was pregnant?"

His mouth opened and closed a few times before answering. "I don't know."

She had to give him credit for honesty even as the words sliced through her. She looked down and expected to find blood on the floor. "You would have because your list of priorities had me at, maybe, number three."

"That's not true."

She stood up because she didn't like him looming over her. "You picked helping someone else's fiancée over helping your own."

"I didn't know!" The whole house shook from the force of his scream.

Her fury exploded to match his. He threw around concepts about trust, but he failed to show her any. "And I didn't know your mother contacted you."

His face went blank. "What?"

He had the nerve to pretend he didn't know what she was talking about. "That's right. I found her letter to you right after you left. I wasn't snooping, just looking through the desk for something and I found it stuffed in the back."

"I didn't write back to her. It meant nothing."

"Which is why you kept it and never told me, right?" Even now he refused to understand. He saw his life as his own and didn't let her in. Yeah, he'd open the door for sex and a few other things, but he stayed closed up and alone no matter how many times she pounded and begged him to open up again. "This huge emotional thing and you cut me out."

His eyes widened. "So you got back at me by not telling me about the baby."

She was stunned by that conclusion. No, she couldn't let him think something so horrible. "It wasn't like that."

"Are you sure? Because it feels like it."

Pain shot through her. "I would never use our baby as a weapon."

"Lara, you—" He exhaled as he brought his hands to his face, and then he dropped them again. "Were you ever going to tell me?"

"I tried the other night."

He stared at her with a face ravaged by a mix of rage and pain. "You should have tried harder."

Then he walked out the door, slamming it behind him.

Her legs held her for another second then her knees buckled. She was sobbing, her chest heaving from the force of her tears, before she hit the floor.

PAX CAUGHT DAVIS'S arm as he got out of the car in Virginia. They were down the street from Martin's house, ready to spring Ronald on them and end this thing. Joel was back at the office with Ben and Mrs. Winston handling the tech and comm stuff. Connor was guarding outside the house.

Davis just wanted this over.

"You going to tell me what's going on?" Pax asked as he secured his vest.

"Nothing." That wasn't a lie. Davis couldn't even feel anything.

The world was this odd shade of brown and his body had gone numb. They rode the entire drive from Annapolis in silence. Lara stared out the window, her chest hiccuping from spent tears and her cheeks stained with the tracks of her pain.

He wanted to comfort her. Thought more than once about leaning over and reaching for her hand. But he couldn't. She'd shaken his world.

A baby. His baby and he never knew.

Guilt pummeled him, but so did the pain. He'd lost so much and hadn't even known. She hadn't trusted him enough to tell him.

He wanted to blame her but he knew part of this was his fault. He hadn't told her about the letter because he hated that it mattered. He'd wanted to hear from the woman who'd given birth to him and not care, but that was not what had happened. The letter had shaken every part of his world, and maybe he did close off and hide his emotions. But he didn't deserve this.

Connor left Lara sitting in the car and came over. "Last chance to switch places."

"It won't work." The plan was for Ronald to take Davis and Lara in, presenting them to his friends.

The goal was to figure out who was behind this before the friends figured out Ronald had turned.

Connor nodded then left again to drag Ronald out of the car.

Pax watched him go. "That was the most uncomfortable car ride in the history of man. And you two weren't exactly quiet upstairs."

Davis couldn't do this now. It was all too raw and his emotions shot in every direction. "She shouldn't be here."

"Neither of you should. Not like this."

"I'm fine."

"Get your head in the game." Pax handed Davis his vest. "We're confronting people who—"

"I know what we're doing, Pax." Davis forced his mind to focus. He had to get through these next few minutes, then he could go off somewhere and think this through.

"Look, I don't get it and I won't pretend to, but when this is over, get into a room and talk with her. You love her. She loves you. Whatever is screwed up, fix it."

The advice fit Pax's life philosophy. He was a black-and-white guy. Davis was starting to think the whole world was gray. "It's not that easy."

"Yeah, it is."

Lara walked over, leaning into Connor as she stepped. "I'm ready."

She looked ready to throw up. If her skin grew any paler she'd be transparent. Davis wanted not to care.

Ronald came around the car. "Let's get this over with."

It was the first time Davis had agreed with something Ronald had said. "You have a mic on."

"I am aware of that."

Even after everything, the sense of entitlement still hung on this guy. "Just wanted to be clear who was in charge."

"Fine." Ronald took off walking.

Lara followed without looking up. Davis fought off the urge to touch her. It didn't matter that she was upset. She *should* be upset, but still…

They walked fifty feet and he couldn't take one more step. He slipped his hand under her elbow and spun her around to face him again. Now that she was looking up at him with those red and puffy eyes, he couldn't think of anything to say.

Before she could turn away again, he leaned down and kissed her. Soft and sweet and with a touch of hope that they could somehow work their way through this. By the end she was holding on to his shirt.

"It will be okay." He didn't know if he believed it, but he wanted it to be true.

By the time they reached the door, adrenaline

had started pumping through his body. His energy soared and his shoulders straightened.

He *could* do this. He walked into danger all the time and there was nothing more dangerous than being in love.

He would finish this job and the next day would come and he would figure out a way to make everything right. He believed it. This was not the end of his life or their relationship.

Martin opened the door and escorted them inside as Pax disappeared around the side of the house. They walked through the foyer and into the fussy living room filled with even fussier people.

From the photos in the conference room Davis identified Martin and Nancy. The hit man, whom they now knew to be Clive, had referred to the person who paid him as a he. That left Martin, likely funded by his wife's money.

"What's going on, Ronald?" Nancy asked, clearly upset that people she didn't know were traipsing through her house.

Davis answered for Ronald. "This is Lara Bart. I thought you might want to meet the woman you keep trying to kill."

Martin's nose wrinkled in a perfectly executed frown. "That's nonsense. What are you talking about?"

Davis knew he could toy with them and draw this out, but he wanted it over. Needed it over. "We know about Steve and about Andrea and about the lifetime attempt to hide it all."

Two sets of eyes went to Ronald but no one said anything, so Davis jumped in again. "The deputy, or should I say soon-to-be former deputy director, here confirmed the information surrounding Andrea's death."

Nancy put a hand to her chest as she gasped. "We don't know what you're talking about."

"Lady, you are playing with the wrong guy."

"No, Mr. Weeks, you are."

The guy Ben had identified as John turned the corner and stepped between Martin and Nancy. So much for the theory of him being a useless sideman to Nancy.

The problem wasn't in him showing up. The issue was the gun in his hand. Davis hadn't been ready for that, but he had people listening in and Pax loomed around here somewhere.

This time Lara stood by his side and Davis was going to make sure no one grabbed her. If someone wanted to shoot through him, fine. But Lara was walking out of here.

Martin looked at the gun and did a double take. "What are you doing with that?"

Davis didn't think that one was fake. Everyone looked surprised to see John's toy except John.

"Cleaning up."

Davis wasn't impressed. "Did they teach you to shoot that in law school?"

"Since my employee failed—several times, in fact—to finish this job, I see it's up to me. I believe your luck has finally run out, Ms. Bart."

That answered that question. Connor should have it on tape so that whatever happened now, they would be able to prove his guilt.

"John, stop." Nancy put her hand over the gun and tried to lower it. "This isn't—"

He shoved her aside. "What—necessary? Of course it is. I've been cleaning up your mess for years. Marrying this one." He pointed at Martin. "Covering the trail for this McClintock woman."

"Why?" Ronald asked.

"You think this is the first time someone crawled out from under a rock to dig into that case? Dear Steve was just the latest to try to capitalize on the situation." John aimed the gun at Davis. "But you will be the last."

That explained part of the plan but not all of it. Davis wanted every last piece. "You weren't involved back then. Why step up now?"

"Because I own a percentage of the business and it's grown every year. I have a significant financial interest in this family and they owe me." John waved his hand in Nancy's general direction. "Oh, she'll claim she grew the fortune, but it was all me."

In her fancy dress and high heels, she launched at her business partner. "That's not true."

Her husband caught her before Davis could rush in.

"If they go under, so do I and, frankly, I can't allow that to happen." John shook his head. "Not after all this time and effort."

"Nancy wasn't involved in Steve's death?" Lara asked.

Davis understood the question. He'd thought this would trace back to Nancy, too. And it still might, but the true genius behind the plan to quiet everything down was pretty obvious. He had the gun in his hand.

"Me?" Nancy screeched, all signs of the regal woman gone now.

"The hit-man money came from your company." John laughed. "Brilliant, wasn't it?"

Davis watched Pax slip into the doorway behind John. Davis returned the smile with one just as sick and deadly. "Up until now."

John shrugged, clearly not seeing that there could be an end here that didn't wrap up in a positive way for him. "What happens now?"

Pax stepped up. "Me."

John was turning when Davis got off his shot. He clipped the man in his side and watched him fall against the chair as blood spread over his white dress shirt. He hit the floor with a thud as a second crack vibrated through the room.

Davis looked around, ready to take on a second attacker, but everyone was frozen in shock at the sight of John sprawled across the floor. Nancy dropped to the carpet, her expensive dress forgotten as she threw her body over John's still form and cried what looked like actual tears.

Not wasting any time or allowing for another surprise, Davis took a few long steps to bridge the gap and used his shoe to trap John's gun against the floor.

When Davis stared back down at Nancy, he saw her weeping over the man who was supposed to be nothing more than a business partner. Martin watched, too, as the force of his new reality crashed over his face.

Connor rushed in the front door and started issuing orders. Sirens wailed in the distance as reinforcements and medical help stormed up the quiet street.

It had all worked out. Just as Davis had promised and insisted to Lara. He looked over at her and smiled, grateful when she smiled back.

Davis glanced over to congratulate Pax on his excellent timing.

It took Davis a second to realize his brother had fallen to the floor. The blood didn't register until Lara screamed.

Chapter Twenty-One

Lara sat in the chair next to Pax's hospital bed. Machines beeped and the heart-rate monitor took off every few minutes for a new test. Pax slept through it all.

John had got off a shot as he fell and it had gone straight into Pax's thigh. The bullet had lodged there and the bleeding had taken some time to stop, but he was going to be okay. Davis hadn't left his brother's side for hours, and now would only venture as far as the cafeteria for a cup of terrible coffee.

"You can go home." Pax's eyes stayed closed and his words slurred together from the medicine.

She jumped at the sound of his voice, relief flooding through her as she squeezed his hand. "I'm fine here."

"I was hoping you'd go sleep with my brother." Pax fell right back to sleep after making the comment.

That was okay because she kind of hoped for the same thing.

When the tears had dried and the pain had stopped thumping in her head, she thought about that moment in the bedroom. Davis's devastation was understandable. She'd dropped a terrible piece of information on him. She'd fired back about the letter from his mother. Actually, she was just the woman who'd given birth to him. Lara didn't think she deserved to be called a mother.

After all the death, after watching Nancy weep over a man who didn't seem to care if she lived or died, Lara viewed things differently.

Davis wasn't perfect. He was shaped by a tough upbringing but so desperate for her love that he didn't hesitate to tell her. He didn't hide behind a fear of commitment or some other nonsense. He loved her for her and she returned the favor by insisting he be someone else.

He still played a part in their rugged past that he needed to own, but seeing one more person hold a gun on him today had shifted her world into perspective. Somehow they would get through this. He would forgive her and she would forgive him. They'd work on trust and build a life together.

"He loves you." Pax's head fell to the side but his eyes stayed closed. "He's stupid with it."

She patted Pax's arm, trying to calm him back down. "I know. Save your strength."

"I don't know what happened…"

She watched the monitors to make sure his heart rate didn't kick up to danger levels. "It doesn't matter."

"But he—"

"This won't break us." For the first time in a year she believed the words as she said them. "We'll make it through."

"Will we?" Davis stood in the doorway with a cup of coffee in each hand.

Her heart hammered so hard she was surprised all these machines didn't pick up the beat. "Yes."

Waiting for him to say something, anything, ate away at her. She wanted a restart with him. But he had to want it, too.

She swallowed back her pride and dropped all of her instincts and every last breath of self-preservation. "Or am I going to fight alone?"

He took his time setting the cups down on the tray and walking around the room to stand in front of her. He didn't touch her but his presence reached out to her. "I never stopped fighting."

Her heart soared as she realized that was true. "I walked away. I had to because…well, I'm not even sure it matters."

The backs of his fingers trailed down her cheek. "It does."

She closed her eyes on a wave of unexpected pain. "Please, Davis. I don't want to fight."

When he lifted her chin and pressed his lips against hers, her eyes opened again.

"It matters because I need you to know there is no one more important in the world to me than you. Nothing ranks above you." With a gentle touch he slipped her arms around his neck and brought her in close. "I haven't done a good job of showing you that, but if you give me another chance I will."

Her breath hiccuped in her chest and tears clogged her throat. This deliciously strong, incredibly loving man stood in front of her offering everything she'd ever wanted. "Yes."

"The idea of you going through the hospital alone…" His voice cracked on the last word.

"I should have told you, let you in." She pressed a finger against his lips and closed her eyes when he lowered his forehead to hers. His body shook with a slight tremor.

He rubbed his head against hers. "You'll never be without me again."

"And we'll have more babies. Big, fat, healthy babies."

He pulled back and stared at her. "Are you sure?"

"I want to experience everything with you. The families we never had, the loving homes we always wanted."

"About my mom—" He swallowed. "I couldn't deal with it."

"I know." Lara kissed him. "We'll figure that out, too."

"I love you."

"And I love you."

Then his mouth closed over hers and all those months apart fell away. She felt love and commitment, promises and devotion.

His lips pressed against hers, deep and rich. It was a kiss that filled in those empty days and gave hope for the ones before them.

"Are you two done?"

They broke apart at the sound of Pax's voice and his words running together.

"How are you feeling?" Davis asked with laughter in his voice.

"Fine." Pax opened one eye. "Are you back together?"

She didn't know that she could feel so happy, be so free. She tried to nod but was pressed too close to Davis's chest to move her head. "Yes."

He kissed her forehead. "Definitely."

"Then get out of my room and let an injured man rest." Pax's eyes closed as he ended the sentence.

Lara started laughing at the outburst.

Davis looked at her with eyes filled with amusement. "You heard the man."

"He suggested I take you to bed."

"Excellent idea. But first we go get your engagement ring. I want to see it on your finger again."

When a tear rolled down her cheek, he kissed it away. "And it will never come off again."

She nodded. "Never."

CONNOR WALKED INTO the conference room and set down two beers before slipping into the seat across from Ben. "Pax is going to be fine."

Ben had already heard the news from Joel but was happy to hear it again. "He knows how to get attention."

"You have no idea." Connor tapped his fingers against the table in the same sort of frantic rhythm young boys used on new drum sets. "You did good work here."

Satisfaction flowed through him. Ben wondered if that was the last he'd have of that feeling for a while. "Maybe that will help in my administrative hearing at NCIS."

Connor shrugged as he took a long draw from one of the bottles. "I'm thinking you'll be fine."

"You going to pull strings for me?" Ben said it as a joke.

Connor took it very seriously. "I know some people."

Ben was humbled and grateful and a whole bunch of things he hadn't felt in a long time. This was a good team. An honest team. He thought he'd found that at NCIS, but those days were gone. Even if they did take him back, he might not want to return the favor. "That's not necessary."

"Yeah, it is." Connor stopped peeling the label and spinning the bottle and looked up. "You could have played this a bunch of ways and you picked one that showed integrity. I told you before that's not as popular a choice as you might think."

"And not a characteristic I find at NCIS right now." Ben grabbed the other bottle and leaned back in the soft leather chair. "I know that's not fair but it's hard to be excited about returning to a desk there."

"Then don't." The ripping tear of the label cut through the room.

"You going to pay my rent?"

For the second time Ben joked and Connor gave a serious response. "Actually, yes. I'm offering you a job."

The idea worked its way into Ben's brain and settled there. "Here?"

"It's the only business I own, so yes." Connor put his hands on the table and leaned in. "You know the work. You've met part of the team. I can't promise every case will end well, but I can promise you we'll try to make it happen."

"I don't—"

"And we have dental."

Ben lifted his hands in the air. "Oh, well, then."

"Think about it." With a knock against the table, Connor stood up.

Ben stopped him before he made it to the kitchen. "When can I start?"

* * * * *

LARGER-PRINT BOOKS!
GET 2 FREE LARGER-PRINT NOVELS PLUS
2 FREE GIFTS!

Ⓗ HARLEQUIN®

super romance®

More Story...More Romance

LARGER-PRINT BOOKS!
GET 2 FREE LARGER-PRINT NOVELS PLUS
2 FREE GIFTS!

HARLEQUIN®

Romance

From the Heart, For the Heart

YES! Please send me 2 FREE LARGER-PRINT Harlequin® Romance novels and my 2 FREE gifts (gifts are worth about $10). After receiving them, if I don't wish to receive any more books, I can return the shipping statement marked "cancel." If I don't cancel, I will receive 4 brand-new novels every month and be billed just $4.84 per book in the U.S. or $5.24 per book in Canada. That's a savings of at least 19% off the cover price! It's quite a bargain! Shipping and handling is just 50¢ per book in the U.S. and 75¢ per book in Canada.* I understand that accepting the 2 free books and gifts places me under no obligation to buy anything. I can always return a shipment and cancel at any time. Even if I never buy another book, the two free books and gifts are mine to keep forever.

119/319 HDN F43Y

Name	(PLEASE PRINT)	

Address		Apt. #

City	State/Prov.	Zip/Postal Code

Signature (if under 18, a parent or guardian must sign)

Mail to the Harlequin® Reader Service:
IN U.S.A.: P.O. Box 1867, Buffalo, NY 14240-1867
IN CANADA: P.O. Box 609, Fort Erie, Ontario L2A 5X3
Want to try two free books from another line?
Call 1-800-873-8635 or visit www.ReaderService.com.

* Terms and prices subject to change without notice. Prices do not include applicable taxes. Sales tax applicable in N.Y. Canadian residents will be charged applicable taxes. Offer not valid in Quebec. This offer is limited to one order per household. Not valid for current subscribers to Harlequin Romance Larger-Print books. All orders subject to credit approval. Credit or debit balances in a customer's account(s) may be offset by any other outstanding balance owed by or to the customer. Please allow 4 to 6 weeks for delivery. Offer available while quantities last.

Your Privacy—The Harlequin® Reader Service is committed to protecting your privacy. Our Privacy Policy is available online at www.ReaderService.com or upon request from the Harlequin Reader Service.

We make a portion of our mailing list available to reputable third parties that offer products we believe may interest you. If you prefer that we not exchange your name with third parties, or if you wish to clarify or modify your communication preferences, please visit us at www.ReaderService.com/consumerchoice or write to us at Harlequin Reader Service Preference Service, P.O. Box 9062, Buffalo, NY 14269. Include your complete name and address.

HRLP13R

LARGER-PRINT BOOKS!

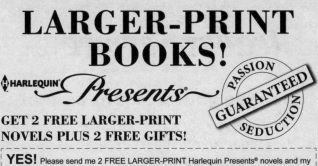

HARLEQUIN *Presents*

PASSION GUARANTEED SEDUCTION

GET 2 FREE LARGER-PRINT NOVELS PLUS 2 FREE GIFTS!

YES! Please send me 2 FREE LARGER-PRINT Harlequin Presents® novels and my 2 FREE gifts (gifts are worth about $10). After receiving them, if I don't wish to receive any more books, I can return the shipping statement marked "cancel." If I don't cancel, I will receive 6 brand-new novels every month and be billed just $5.05 per book in the U.S. or $5.49 per book in Canada. That's a saving of at least 16% off the cover price! It's quite a bargain! Shipping and handling is just 50¢ per book in the U.S. and 75¢ per book in Canada.* I understand that accepting the 2 free books and gifts places me under no obligation to buy anything. I can always return a shipment and cancel at any time. Even if I never buy another book, the two free books and gifts are mine to keep forever.

176/376 HDN F43N

Name	(PLEASE PRINT)	
Address		Apt. #
City	State/Prov.	Zip/Postal Code

Signature (if under 18, a parent or guardian must sign)

Mail to the Harlequin® Reader Service:
IN U.S.A.: P.O. Box 1867, Buffalo, NY 14240-1867
IN CANADA: P.O. Box 609, Fort Erie, Ontario L2A 5X3

Are you a subscriber to Harlequin Presents books and want to receive the larger-print edition?
Call 1-800-873-8635 today or visit us at www.ReaderService.com.

* Terms and prices subject to change without notice. Prices do not include applicable taxes. Sales tax applicable in N.Y. Canadian residents will be charged applicable taxes. Offer not valid in Quebec. This offer is limited to one order per household. Not valid for current subscribers to Harlequin Presents Larger-Print books. All orders subject to credit approval. Credit or debit balances in a customer's account(s) may be offset by any other outstanding balance owed by or to the customer. Please allow 4 to 6 weeks for delivery. Offer available while quantities last.

Your Privacy—The Harlequin® Reader Service is committed to protecting your privacy. Our Privacy Policy is available online at www.ReaderService.com or upon request from the Harlequin Reader Service.

We make a portion of our mailing list available to reputable third parties that offer products we believe may interest you. If you prefer that we not exchange your name with third parties, or if you wish to clarify or modify your communication preferences, please visit us at www.ReaderService.com/consumerschoice or write to us at Harlequin Reader Service Preference Service, P.O. Box 9062, Buffalo, NY 14269. Include your complete name and address.

HPLP13R

ReaderService.com

Manage your account online!

- Review your order history
- Manage your payments
- Update your address

> **We've designed
> the Harlequin® Reader Service
> website just for you.**

Enjoy all the features!

- Reader excerpts from any series
- Respond to mailings and special monthly offers
- Discover new series available to you
- Browse the Bonus Bucks catalog
- Share your feedback

Visit us at:
ReaderService.com

A
GLIMPSE
INTO
GLORY

A
GLIMPSE
INTO
GLORY

Kathryn Kuhlman
with
Jamie Buckingham

BRIDGE PUBLISHING, INC. • SOUTH PLAINFIELD, NEW JERSEY

Offset Paperback
PO #38030

A GLIMPSE INTO GLORY
Library of Congress Catalog Card Number: 79-90558
Bridge Publishing, Inc., 2500 Hamilton Boulevard
South Plainfield, New Jersey 07080, USA

ISBN 0-88270-393-5

Contents

Foreword

Everyone had an opinion about Kathryn Kuhlman. Especially those who had seen or heard her. And many, many had. Even these years after her death, people are still talking about her.

Some of them are saying her "mantle" is upon them—or upon someone they know.

That's not so. Kathryn had no mantle to pass on. She was far more kin to John the Baptist than to Elijah. Her task, among others, was to introduce the Holy Spirit to a generation—to a double millennium—who knew Him not. Not since Pentecost had the Holy Spirit evidenced himself with such power and freedom—and yet with such decency and order—as He did in her life.

Dan Malachuk introduced me to her in 1968—just about the time her ministry was being launched on a worldwide scale. Her first book, *I*

Believe in Miracles, had been out for a number of years. Wisely, she had refused to glut the market with more books until her ministry was firmly established. Now she was ready.

We went out to eat in a small, stylish steak house high on a cliff overlooking the Ohio River near Pittsburgh. After dinner—which she just picked at—we talked. She wanted me to write a second book for her—a book of testimonies. I was intrigued, for despite her theatrical voice and mannerisms, and the fact she insisted on paying for our steaks with a one hundred dollar bill ("These people are so nice to me. I try to give them a little something now and then"), I sensed there was something genuinely spiritual about her. From my Southern Baptist perspective, she was all the things I was not. A woman preacher. Involved in a healing ministry. Divorced. Domineering. Demonstrative. Yet she was also genuinely honest. Transparent. And so filled with the power of God that even the waiters in the restaurant stood back in a kind of awe. I took the assignment and wrote *God Can Do It Again*.

There followed several other smaller books. I attended a number of her miracle services, but deliberately chose not to get too close to her. She was too strong. Too intimidating. We both seemed to realize it would be better if I stayed at arm's length. Looking back, I realized this was one of the better decisions I made in my life. She totally consumed most of the people working close to her. By staying apart, I kept the objectivity which would be necessary when the time came to write her biography—and was able to live my own life as well.

One night I was visiting with my secretary and her husband in Melbourne, Florida, when the phone rang.

"Jamie, we've just got to write one more big book. These healing stories must be told. They are just pouring in from all over the world."

I had written her saying I would not be available to write any more books. I was filled with questions—not about her, but about me. Was I writing just for the money? Had I become some kind of a "kept man"? (Somehow, the idea of taking money from a woman to write her books cut across the grain of my Southern masculinity.) On more than one occasion she had walked me from her Pittsburgh office on the 6th floor of the Carlton House to the elevator. As I would step on the elevator to return to my hotel before flying back to Florida, she would press money into my hand. "Now, go on out and buy yourself a good steak. You deserve it." When the elevator door closed I would look down and discover two or three one hundred dollar bills.

She was just like that.

I loved it. And I hated it.

So, I had written her and said, "No more books."

She had tried several other writers. None

pleased her. She kept coming back. And I kept resisting.

Then she called me that night while I was eating dinner at the Watsons'. "Please, just one more. We must get this word out to the world. God is still performing miracles."

Nothing Is Impossible With God was a fun book. As before, she gave me the names of people who had been healed and I began traveling around the country. Interviewing. Talking to doctors. Checking out facts. Attending her miracle services. Then coming home to put the incredible stories on paper. God was, indeed, still healing people.

Not only that, but I began to develop a new respect for this woman upon whom the anointing of God seemed to rest in full power. The more I was with her, the more I realized she was not "buying me"—she was just like that. Her use of money, the way she dressed, these things were not a showman's trick to attract attention; she was one of the few persons I have ever met who had actually gone beyond the barrier of materialism. She saw money (and she had lots of it) as God's gift. She used it as she did the rest of God's gifts—wisely but generously.

I wrote other small books—published by Bethany Fellowship. This allowed me to keep in touch with her, as well as to have face-to-face encounters with God's miraculous power.

Several times I urged her to let me put some of

her teachings on paper. While most people knew her only as a woman of miracles, I felt her most lasting contribution to the Kingdom (other than opening the door for the Holy Spirit to enter the churches) was her teaching. For years she had conducted a weekly Bible study at the First Presbyterian Church in Pittsburgh. Her daily radio broadcasts were gems of truth and wit. I was eager to capture her spoken wisdom on paper—as well as tell the stories of those who had been healed under her ministry.

She finally consented. Her secretary sent me a big box of tapes—samples of her radio programs. I transcribed them, edited the material, then digested several of them into short teaching chapters.

Several months later I was in Pittsburgh and handed her one of the short manuscripts. She sat on the big, flowered sofa at the far end of her outer office—a sofa constantly covered with papers and flanked by two end tables covered with gifts which poured in from grateful followers.

I sat beside her as she read the short manuscript, watching her face for signs. She couldn't hide a thing. It was impossible for her to tell a lie—or pretend. The only way she could tell a lie was to believe a lie—which she sometimes did. But this morning she was totally transparent.

Throwing the manuscript on the sofa she

uncrossed her long legs and stood to her feet. "Nope," she said. "We'll not do it."

I waited. She looked down at me. "Tell me, is that the way I really sound? As you have it on paper."

I couldn't help but grin. "Not really," I said, standing up to face her. "I've edited your Missouri twang."

She laughed. A great big throaty laugh. "I thought so," she said, looking at one of her secretaries. "I'm still Missouri cornbread. I talked that way when I was a girl in Concordia, and I'll talk that way when I meet St. Peter at the pearly gates."

Turning back to her office, she said, "Nope, let's stick to writing stories about people God has touched. I don't see how anyone could be interested in me—or what I have to say."

But she was wrong. People were interested in her. They still are. That's the reason hundreds of thousands bought her biography, *Daughter of Destiny.* They wanted to know what she was really like. But more than what she did, what she said is even more important.

Before she died in 1976, she asked me to "tell it all." I thought I had when I wrote *Daughter of Destiny.* In fact, I told so much a lot of folks were upset. But I knew that was the way Kathryn wanted it. And I knew it was the only way I could write it. Honestly. To have done anything less would have given the glory to Kathryn—rather than to the God she loved and adored.

But now I realize that "tell it all" means more than telling the story about her life. It also means sharing with you what she said.

These little chapters have been carefully transcribed—and edited—from a number of her radio teachings. They also represent the best of some of the messages she preached around the nation. Several of them are from unpublished statements she gave various magazines and newspapers—taken verbatim from interview tapes.

I do not apologize that they sound, in places, like Missouri cornbread. That's the way she was. "Just like that," she would say. A small-town girl who became not only a citizen of the world but a prophetic leader in the Kingdom of God. What she had—and has—to say will give us not only insight into the real Kathryn Kuhlman but also provide something far more important: glimpses into glory.

Jamie Buckingham
Melbourne, Florida

A
GLIMPSE
INTO
GLORY

1

A Glimpse Into Glory

For years I have made it a practice to disassociate myself from anything written about me or said about me. If I listened to my critics—or my fans—I would quickly be destroyed. I have never considered myself to be the best known woman preacher in the world. In fact, I never think of myself in the terms of "preacher." That's the reason I never use the word "Reverend." I really do not consider myself a woman preacher. Believe me. I'm just somebody who loves souls. I love people. I want to help them. It's just that simple.

Helping people is the most rewarding thing in the whole world. You do not have to be a Kathryn Kuhlman to help people. The goal of every Christian, every born-again man and woman, should be helping people. God's children are born to serve. That's what Jesus did. Jesus lived to serve. And if you are a born-again man or woman, you, too, will feel your responsibility in serving and helping people. It's the most rewarding thing in the world.

Last Christmas among the cards and gifts I received there was a little card with a great big Santa Claus on it. It came from a twelve-year-old girl. The doctors had said that perhaps she would not be living by Christmas. They had wanted to amputate her leg because of cancer. But she sent me this card, and in the card she had written these words: "I am living to see this Christmas. I still have two good legs, because God answered prayer, and you helped." I cannot begin to tell you the tears I shed over that Christmas card. It was the greatest gift I received. Some people put angels on the top of their Christmas trees. Others beautiful ornaments. But I had the most beautiful gift of all, for I put that little girl's card at the very top of my tree.

Rewarding? There's no way to buy what I felt.

When I walk out on the stage at the great miracle services, I realize that sitting there in the audience are men and women who have made great sacrifices to be there. For many of them it is their last hope. The doctors have given up. Medical science says no hope. But I see beyond physical healing. I know that spiritual healing is far greater than the physical. So even though I believe in miracles, I know that far more important is the call for a spiritual healing—for it may be their last chance.

The physical healing is so very secondary, believe me. You can well afford to live and die with a sick body, not having been healed physically. But when those last moments come and the Holy Spirit is speaking at the close of a service, I always remember the spiritual healing is far greater than the greatest physical healing. It's wonderful to see a body healed from cancer. It's glorious to see a man or woman come out of a wheelchair, and see that wheelchair pushed down the aisle—empty. But there is something that's far greater—that new birth experience. I stand there in those last moments of a great service and give an altar call and realize there may be those who are receiving their last call from God, spiritually. And the destiny of that soul is at stake. That, my friends, is the most awesome feeling. That is when the great responsibility is really felt. And when the lights have been turned out in the great auditorium, my only concern is whether I gave every ounce of strength I had, whether I could have done a better job than what I did—not performing miracles, for I am no miracle worker, but in calling men and women to Jesus Christ.

Oh, sure, there is a responsibility when it comes to those who come for physical healing. And I'm just human enough to say the responsibility is so great that sometimes I wish I had never been called to this type of ministry. Sometimes that responsibility is almost overwhelming. It isn't hard work. I can stand on a platform, the stage of some auditorium, for four and a half hours and never feel the weariness because I am completely yielded to the Holy Spirit. But the burden of the responsibility drains the physical body.

I know better than anyone else that Kathryn Kuhlman has no healing virtue. I'm not a faith healer, please understand that. I have no healing power. I have never healed anyone. Know that. I'm absolutely dependent on the power of the Holy Spirit, on the power of God. I have stood before sick people and cried, wishing I could give them the strength from my own body. But without the Holy Spirit I have nothing to give. Nothing.

I remember something that my papa, who worked so very hard, said to me when I was a little girl. I remember him as he extended his open hands, and he said, "You know, baby, you can have anything in the world you want if you'll work hard enough with your hands."

That made a very great impression on me, because my papa was a hard worker. I've learned to work, and to work very hard. But papa didn't quite understand the work of the Holy Spirit. I've stood before people thinking if it was only hard work that was needed, I'd work the flesh off my bones. When I see a daddy standing there with a little child who has cancer, or perhaps a deformity, and I see those great big tears rolling down the cheeks of that big strong man, I would gladly give my life if that child could live. But I have no power. Hard work won't impart healing. And in those moments, I know better than anyone else how dependent I am on the power of God.

It's just like that.

People ask, "Is this not a thrilling experience? Being chosen by God for such a responsibility?" No, not thrilling, but awesome. Sometimes so awesome I wish I had never been called.

But with the responsibility come the rewards—like that child's card at Christmas. And even though I'll probably burn myself out and die in the ministry, I'll die happy—and satisfied. For the great God who called me has given me, also, a glimpse of His glory.

2

I Believe in Miracles

To tell you the truth, I answer every question that's asked me. I do not believe there is anyone in the religious field today who is more honest in answering questions than I am. And it's just like that. I want to be perfectly honest with you. I bare my soul to you. When it comes to answering critics and skeptics, I want to be like Jesus who said to them in substance, "If you do not believe that I am all that I say that I am, then believe me for the very work's sake."

That is His only answer. And that is mine. But to honest people, who want honest answers, I bare my soul.

I believe that if the Lord himself would return in person, and do the same works today that He did when He walked this earth in person, He'd have more skeptics than He had when He was here the first time. Back then people did not have as much "worldly knowledge" as they do now. But with the advancement of technology, we have far more tendency to believe in ourselves as the source of all strength, rather than in a God of miracles.

You see, Jesus said, "Flesh and blood have not revealed this unto you, but my Father which is in heaven." Spiritual things are only spiritually revealed. You cannot force a human being to believe something he does not want to believe. If you do not want to believe in the absolute power of almighty God, if you do not want to believe that God has the power to heal, if you refuse to believe that divine healing is for today, then even if one were to be raised from the dead before your very eyes you would still not believe. People are looking for some excuse not to believe. For to believe in miracles means we have to believe in God. And if He is a God of miracles, then we have to obey Him. And we'd rather obey our own sinful instincts than the God who created heaven and earth. So, when faced with a miracle, we prefer to say, "It probably was psychosomatic." Or, "The person was hypnotized." Or, "There's a catch in it somewhere."

So, when it comes to skeptics and critics, I leave them with God. But when it comes to answering questions, I answer the questions of the believer and the unbeliever the best that I know how.

Sometimes it is a very difficult thing for me to

talk to some inquirer about miracles. He knows nothing about the power of the Holy Spirit, he knows nothing whatsoever about spiritual things. He may be a very wise person and intelligent. But when it comes to spiritual things, he has no idea whatsoever of the working of the Holy Ghost. I try to give answers that I think he will understand, but so often it is like casting pearls before swine. He not only does not understand, but he twists that which is true to fit his own concepts. So I leave them also in the hands of God.

But one day a reporter from St. Petersburg, Florida, who had attended the miracle service in Curtis Hixon Hall in Tampa, came back to my dressing room following the benediction. "I came a skeptic," she said with tears in her eyes, "but I leave a believer."

That's the reason for miracles. Not miracles for miracles' sake, but to lead nonbelievers to faith in—and commitment to—the Lord Jesus Christ.

3

My High Calling

Recently I returned to that little Methodist church in Concordia, Missouri, where I was converted. I was in Kansas City holding services in the opera house. I took members of my staff along with me, and we drove over to Concordia.

"Oh, you must see where I first accepted Jesus," I told them. I tell you the truth, I was so shocked when I found out how small that little Methodist church had gotten through the years. There was a time when it looked so big to me, it looked almost like a cathedral. Then I realized that perhaps it doesn't seat any more than 75 or 100 people. I walked into the little vestibule. There was the same rope that rang the bell—the first bell, the second bell, you know, announcing the time of the services. It was the same bell they always tolled when someone died in town. One ringing meant a child had died, two rings meant a middle-aged person had passed away.

When an elderly person died, they rang it three times. This would cause everyone to rush to the telephone and ask the operator, "Who died?" That's Concordia, Missouri.

That afternoon I walked into the church. The same pews were still there, the same railing, the same pulpit. Nothing had really changed in that little church. But, oh, how I had changed.

I thought back to that Sunday morning so many years before. Standing there, holding the Methodist hymnal in my hands, I was standing next to mama. Everybody in mama's family was Methodist. Grandpa Walkenhorst always attended that church and sat in the same pew until the day before he died. He lived and died believing sincerely that only Methodists would make it to heaven. Since that time I've often thought what a shock it must have been for Grandpa Walkenhorst—if he got to heaven himself—to find out there were Baptists, Presbyterians, Lutherans, and Catholics in heaven! I'm not quite sure whether he could have adjusted to all that.

Anyway, that Sunday morning was my first introduction to the Holy Spirit. I knew nothing about the third person of the Trinity, but He came with great conviction upon me. And standing there, holding that Methodist hymnal in my hands, I began to shake with great conviction. I was only fourteen years old—so I did the only thing I knew to do. I stepped out from where I was standing and went to the front pew, sat down in the corner, and wept. Not out of sorrow, but because of the great feeling that came upon me. Something had happened to me.

One cannot really describe spiritual experiences, because they *are* spiritual. There are no words in the human vocabulary to describe spiritual things. But I knew, in that exact moment, I had been born again. I never doubted my new birth experience from that moment until this very hour. I knew something had happened to me. I knew my sins had been forgiven. I knew my sins were covered with the blood. In that moment, Jesus Christ became very real to my heart.

My call to the ministry was just as definite as my conversion. You can say anything you want about me, as a woman, having no right to stand in the pulpit and preach the gospel. Yet even if everybody in the world told me that, it would have no effect on me whatsoever. Why? Because my call to the ministry was just as definite as my conversion. And it's just like that.

I preached my very first sermon in Idaho. I preached to those farmers. Name any little town in Idaho, and you'll discover that one time, years ago, Kathryn Kuhlman came through trying to evangelize it. I would find a little country church that was closed because they couldn't afford a preacher. I would go to the deacons, or the board, or the members and ask to preach.

I remember going to the head of the board of a Baptist church and saying, "Your church is closed anyway. You haven't anything to lose, and maybe a little to gain." And he let me open the church for meetings. Twin Falls, Emmett, Payette, Boise—those were the days when I got my early spiritual training.

All I knew how to preach was salvation, the new-birth experience. No one can give any more than what one has experienced himself. All I knew was what I had experienced in that little Methodist church in Concordia. The very first sermon I preached was Zacchaeus up a tree. And God knows if anybody was up a tree, I certainly was when I preached that sermon. I remember well that after the sixth sermon I honestly felt I had exhausted the Bible. I'm telling you the truth. I felt there was nothing more to preach about. Six sermons! I had preached on Zacchaeus, I had preached on heaven, I had preached on hell, I had preached on the love of God—you know—and what more was there to preach about? But years have come and years have gone, and I have found out that you can never exhaust the deep truths in God's Word.

I know so well what the Apostle Paul meant when he declared that he was called of God to preach. Why He called me, I do not know. I haven't the slightest idea why I was chosen to preach the gospel. There are millions who could do a better job, I am sure. Millions better equipped than I.

The only reason I can give you is the fact that I knew I had nothing, and I never forgot from whence I came. When you have nothing, and you admit you have nothing, then it's so easy to look up and say, "Lord Jesus, if you can take nothing, use it. Take my hands, take my voice, take my mind, take my body, take my love—it's all I have. If you can use it, I give it to you." And He has taken my nothing and used it to His glory.

It isn't golden vessels He asks for. It isn't silver vessels. It's yielded vessels. The secret is yieldedness to the Lord.

One day I will have preached my last sermon, I will have prayed my last prayer, and I will stand in His glorious presence. Oh, I have thought of this many, many times. I have often wondered what would be my first words to Him, the One whom I have loved so long yet have never seen. What will I say when I stand in His glorious presence? Somehow I know the first words I shall say when I look in His wonderful face.

"Dear Jesus, I tried. I didn't do a perfect job, because I was human and made mistakes. There were failures. I am sorry. But I tried."

But—He knows that already.

4

Methods

One day, if the Lord tarries His return, there will be advanced technology which God's people can use to spread the gospel. Until that happens, we use what we have. And the most effective measures I have found are radio and television. I base this on the response we receive to our ministry.

Yet when it comes to the number of letters I receive, it's sort of like the number of folk who come forward when I give an altar call. You have never heard Kathryn Kuhlman say there were 500 who were converted in the service Sunday. I can say to you that there were 500 who came forward, but when it comes to those who were really born again, only God knows that. The same is true when it comes to the response in the number of letters received. People will respond to anything that's on television. I don't care what it is. Yet I cannot help but be impressed with the great number who write saying, "I have never in my life written a letter like this. I want to be born again. I watched your telecast. I'm hungry for spiritual experience. I want that more than anything else in the whole world."

You see, our telecasts are probably different from most telecasts. We do not offer any giveaways. No free books, jewelry, pictures, or prayer cloths. We offer no premiums trying to get people to write us. People write in only because they are hungry for the Lord. They need spiritual help. Our telecasts are supported entirely by the freewill contributions of those who have been so blessed, who have been so helped, those who see the great results from these telecasts. They see it as an investment in the preaching of the gospel of the Lord Jesus Christ. They know I am not building my own empire. I have all I need or want. Believe me, my only desire is to win souls.

How effective is the TV ministry? I can only tell you that the most unlikely people stop me on the street and say, "I wouldn't miss one of your telecasts for anything in the world."

I've just returned from one of the most remote parts of the United States. I was shocked to find that everywhere I went, people said, "Oh, you are Kathryn Kuhlman. We watch your telecasts." I respond at first by saying, "But we're not on television around here. How do you get it?" Then I discovered it is on cable TV, channeled all over the nation. People I've never met, who have never contacted me, have paid to have the program run on their stations.

Seldom do I ever get into a cab but what in hearing my voice the cab driver will say, "Oh, oh, I know that voice, you're Kathryn Kuhlman. My wife and I watch you on television all the time." There's seldom a time I go into a restaurant to eat but what the waitress or the waiter, when I give my order, will say, "That voice—you'll never know what my family has gotten from your telecasts."

Financially, the telecasts do not pay for themselves. Sometimes we have to pray like a house afire, as we used to say in Missouri, for the money. But I'm still depending on the Lord to come through. And He's never failed us yet.

The greatest combination is television and radio. Through means of the radio, we teach. Through television, we testify and inspire. God uses both, and we have an outreach ministry that's unbeatable.

Speaking in Tongues

When it comes to speaking about speaking in tongues, I like just to lay it on the line. That's the kind of person I am. Do I believe in speaking in tongues? The answer is yes! I have to believe there is such a thing as speaking in an unknown tongue because I believe the Bible. One cannot just take the Word of God and believe only that which is agreeable to them. If you did that, you'd cut out everything you wished was not there. It wouldn't be long before we'd no longer have a Bible. Thomas Jefferson did that, you know. He published the "Jefferson Bible" from which he had clipped out all he didn't like. Very few people bought it because it was powerless.

People still want to do that. They keep Psalm 23. They keep everything the Word says regarding heaven. That's glorious. But either we accept the whole Word of God or we don't accept any of it. And I'm a firm believer that one needs to stay with the Word of God. If it isn't in the Word of God, don't do it. If it is—do it.

We're in an hour of great deception, and the Lord himself warned us regarding the day in which we are living. If it were possible, He said, the very elect would be deceived. I believe that's one reason this ministry, through the years, has stood the test of time and the test of the critics. We have no fanaticism. None whatsoever. No one can ever accuse me of being fanatical. Nothing is unseemly in our services. It is done according to God's Word. It's scriptural. And it should be so, because the foundation of this ministry is God's Word.

For so long I was afraid of the word "Pentecostal." Oh, it was easy to accept everything that was done on the Day of Pentecost. Millions still observe Pentecost Sunday. But what millions have not accepted is the fact that we are still living in the Day of Pentecost. Everything that happened on the Day of Pentecost should be happening in every church in the world at this very hour. The coldness, the deadness, the lack of power in many of our churches today is unnatural, not natural. For wherever you find the Holy Spirit, you'll find action, you'll find supernatural manifestations of the mighty Third Person of the Trinity— including speaking in tongues. The word "Pentecostal" is a word one used to whisper. Now, though, and very boldly, you will find

Catholic priests saying, "I am a Catholic Pentecostal priest." You'll find a Baptist minister saying, "I am a Baptist Pentecostal minister." And all those wonderful Lutheran Pentecostals. It's glorious. Thousands around the world are enjoying the Pentecostal experience.

But remember something. Speaking in an unknown tongue has nothing to do whatsoever with one's experience of justification. It is the blood that makes the atonement for the soul. I want to repeat it: it is the shed blood of Jesus Christ, God's Son, that makes us heirs of God and joint heirs with Jesus Christ. If your sins are covered with the blood, if you have accepted Christ and the forgiveness of those sins, accepting Him as absolute deity and divinity, whether you have ever spoken in unknown tongues or not, when the old heart takes its last beat and your soul goes all the way from earth to glory, you will stand in the wonderful presence of the great High Priest, your Christ, your Redeemer.

The Holy Spirit was not given for our justification. Jesus is the one who effected our justification. But this wonderful experience that the Bible calls the baptism in the Holy Spirit is given for one purpose and one purpose only, and that's for power for service. Just before Jesus went away, He left a message for the church—the church then, the church now. He said, "But ye shall receive power, after that the Holy Ghost is come upon you. . ." (Acts 1:8). The greatest evidence of having been filled with the Holy Ghost, the greatest evidence there is, is not speaking in tongues (as wonderful as that is), but power in an individual's life. You may speak in tongues every hour on the hour, but, my friend, if your life isn't measuring up with the power of the Holy Ghost, then I wouldn't give you much for your experience of speaking in an unknown tongue. And it's just like that.

No one has ever heard Kathryn Kuhlman say that she had one, or more than one, of the gifts of the Spirit. I'm always afraid of the folk who boast of having received special gifts. I've come in contact with those who have very boldly stood before me and said, "You know, I have all the gifts of the Spirit." They say it as though they think they have arrived, and there is nothing more for them. I'm always a little skeptical of those folk. When one has been filled with the Holy Spirit, when one is controlled by the Holy Spirit, he will never be boastful. Never.

That's the reason I never say I have a particular gift. There is but one gift. The gift given is by Jesus—the person of the Holy Spirit himself. Everything else—tongues, faith, healing, even wisdom—are manifestations the Holy Spirit brings with Him.

All I know is that I have yielded my body to Jesus to be filled with the Holy Spirit. I have surrendered myself to Him. My life is no longer my own. He possesses me: body, soul, and spirit. Anything the Holy Spirit has given me, anything, anything that He does through me, any results that there might be through this life of mine, is not Kathryn Kuhlman, it's the Holy Spirit. If He has given me something very special, it is still not Kathryn Kuhlman; it is only the working of the Holy Spirit through a yielded vessel. That's the reason we must be so very careful to give Him the praise and the glory for everything the Holy Spirit does.

The one thing I am so afraid of is grieving the Holy Spirit by trying to share the glory. When the Holy Spirit is lifted from me, I am the most ordinary person who ever lived. There is no woman living today who is more ordinary than Kathryn Kuhlman. I know that better than anyone else. For that reason I cannot boast of something special. All I can do is tell you what the Holy Spirit does—and vow to be very careful to give God all the praise and all the glory for everything.

6

God and the Institutional Church

Every Friday for years I have conducted a miracle service in the First Presbyterian Church here in Pittsburgh, Pennsylvania. It is one of the finest and most influential churches in the nation. The services begin around 9:30 A.M. and continue to about 1:30 P.M. Every week we see great manifestations of the power of God. They come—Roman Catholic, Greek Orthodox, Lutheran, every denomination, people from around the world—gathering in the sanctuary of the First Presbyterian Church. Everybody forgets their denominational ties. We worship together on the common ground of Calvary.

What is happening in those meetings in the First Presbyterian Church in Pittsburgh ought to be happening in every church in the United States.

I have a very close tie when it comes to the institutional church. As long as I can remember, mama was Methodist. Thus I've always had a high regard for the Methodist church. Papa was Baptist. And I am still a member of a Baptist church. But if our institutional churches are to be the kind of churches God wants them to be, if they are to carry out the work, the purpose of the church, they must open their eyes and realize the day and the hour in which we are living.

We've come to the place where the world is literally challenging the church. The youth of this generation have every right to challenge the institutional church. Yet this could well be the finest hour of the institutional church. If only they could realize it. But the church must do something about the Holy Spirit. The institutional church must realize we are still living in the Day of Pentecost. The institutional church must not close its eyes and say, "We will accept only a portion of God's Word, and forget the rest." This comes from the highest authority in heaven and earth. For to this glorious body of believers that we call the church (both Catholic and Protestant), Jesus gave the gift of the Holy Spirit. Jesus had been talking to the Father, referring to this body of believers saying, "These that Thou hast given to me." And before Jesus went away, He gave to the church the greatest gift it was possible for Him to give: the mighty Third Person of the Trinity. The same gift the Father gave to the Son, the Son in turn gave to His own. Long before God gave His only begotten Son, long before Jesus came in the form of flesh to carry out redemption's plan, the Word of God says He first offered himself through the Holy Spirit to be given. He knew the Holy Spirit better than you, better than I, will ever know the Holy Spirit. He knew the Holy Spirit. He knew the power. He knew He could not go in His own strength, for He was coming to earth in the form of flesh. He would soon become as much man as though He were not God. In perfect knowledge and perfect wisdom, He knew that the hour would come when He would have to stand face to face with Satan. He knew that unless He had the glorious power of the Holy Spirit as He walked the earth, He would be powerless in the face of the enemy. He knew it. He recognized it. That's the reason I say to every minister who stands behind the sacred desk, if Jesus the very Son of the living God needed the Holy Spirit, surely you and I need Him also.

Don't be afraid of the Holy Spirit. Don't be afraid of the power of the Holy Ghost in your ministry. Jesus trusted Him. Jesus had confidence in Him, and He did not fail Jesus. That is the reason before Jesus went away, the very last thing He did was to give this gift to His church, this great body of believers. And He said, "Ye shall receive power." To whom was He speaking? Not the unbeliever, but to His own. "And *ye* shall receive power, after that the Holy Ghost is come upon you." What power? The same power that was manifested in His ministry. There was no greater gift ever given to the church than the gift that Jesus gave—the Holy Spirit, this mighty Third Person of the Trinity.

The hour has now come for every minister to come face-to-face with the Holy Spirit. That's the reason I say this could be the finest hour of the institutional church. But if the institutional church will not accept the Holy Ghost, will not accept the manifestations of the Spirit, then, my friends, the Holy Spirit will continue His work in spite of the institutional church. He will carry out God's plan outside of the institutional church. But it should not be that way. The institutional church should be so powerful that when the world challenges it, when unregenerated man challenges it—it can reply with God's miracles. God grant that the ministers of the gospel seek God's best and give the members of their churches the deep truths of the Spirit. We are living in a great hour. God is literally pouring out His Spirit upon all flesh. We are on the threshold of the greatest spiritual awakening, the greatest revival, in the history of the world. But only those who have spiritual ears will hear.

Miracles

"Miracles" may mean one thing to one person and quite something else to another. Webster says that a miracle is an event or an action that apparently contradicts known scientific laws, and so it is thought to be due to supernatural causes, especially to an act of God.

I remember one day coming out of Bullock's Wilshire Boulevard store in Los Angeles. I had gone in there to get a little something, and I was rushing out of the store when I saw two little boys (I found out later they were brothers), about eight and ten years of age. They were standing outside the store selling candy bars. One came rushing up to me and said, "Miss, would you like to buy a candy bar?" When he looked up into my face, his eyes got big as saucers and he shouted: "Willie! Willie! Here is the miracle lady! Here is the miracle lady!"

I just stood there and smiled.

He was so excited, he was stuttering. "You know, I had a miracle happen to me once. I had a wonderful miracle happen to me."

"What was it?" I asked.

"Well," he said, "one day I needed a quarter. I needed it awful bad. I asked God for a quarter. And you know what? I was walking down the street, and there on the street was a quarter! God had made a miracle for me!"

To the little boy, *that* was a miracle. To a man who needs to be healed of cancer, finding a quarter would not be much of a miracle. The medical profession has told him there is no cure. Then suddenly, in His tender mercy, God reaches down and the supernatural happens. Contradictory to all known scientific laws, the supernatural power of God brings healing. And that is as great a miracle as the little boy's finding a quarter on the street.

There are two questions I want to ask the Master when I get home to glory. The first one is, "Jesus, why wasn't everyone healed?" I'd like to know. I don't have the answer to that question. My second question has to do with the manifestation of the power of God—the slaying power of the Holy Spirit. I have nothing to do with it whatsoever. I don't understand that either. Why it is some people fall to the floor when I pray for them. I do know the experience is scriptural. But why it happens in my meetings I do not know.

I have read of the conversion of Saul on the road to Damascus. Something suddenly happened to him. He found himself physically knocked to the ground. Flat on his back. I'm just sorry I wasn't there. He didn't have someone to catch him when he fell either. But the Lord spoke and said, "Come on, get up." What happened? Me thinks his face shone with the glory and he could not answer the question any more than I can answer it. Literally thousands have experienced the slaying power of the Holy Spirit—and they cannot explain it either. All those thousands can tell us today is that it was a supernatural power.

Like all the other miracles, it defies description—defies definition. But, oh, so peaceful. So wonderful. And who needs a definition when they have an experience? Only the skeptics. But there are no skeptics left after God touches. Just amazed believers.

Perhaps it is best expressed in a letter I received from the late Dr. Paul Fryling, pastor of the First Covenant Church in Minneapolis, Minnesota.

We had been in the large arena in Minneapolis. Dr. Fryling was on the front row where several other preachers were seated. When the power of God was falling and people were being slain by the power of the Holy Spirit, Dr. Fryling, too, was slain by the power. Now remember, he was the very conservative pastor of a very conservative church.

After I returned to Pittsburgh, Dr. Fryling's letter arrived. It said, in part:

People from my congregation and fellow pastors have asked me about the experience of coming under the power of the Holy Spirit, who touched me. To which I can say that it was a very simple and beautiful experience. It was, in fact, the most normal, unsensational spiritual feeling. Far from being, as some might imagine, extremely different from other proper spiritual manifestations, it seemed rather to bring together and harmonize in that moment all the beauty, the charms, which the Holy Spirit had previously given. To be under the Spirit's anointing is the truly normal state. All else is abnormal.

8

Women in the Ministry

I sometimes wonder what it would have been like had I been a man. I really don't know. For I am very much a woman.

A lot of people seem to think that being a woman in the ministry means I have two strikes against me. I've never felt that way. I just lift my chin a little higher and act like I don't hear the insults. I didn't ask for this ministry. God knows I'd much rather be doing something else. But He put me in the ministry and those who don't like having a woman preach should complain to God—not me. It's just like that.

I'll tell you something very confidentially—the true conviction of my heart. I do not believe I was God's first choice in this ministry, in the ministry He has chosen for these last days. It's my firm conviction. You'll never argue me out of this conviction, never. I'm not quite sure whether I was God's second choice, or even His third choice. Because I really believe the job I am doing is a man's job. I work hard. Few people know how hard I really work—sixteen, seventeen hours a day. I can outwork five men put together, and I'll challenge you on this. Only those who know me best know how little sleep I get, the hours I put into the ministry. Those who attend our services know I am on the stage, behind the pulpit, three and a half to four and a half hours. I never sit down.

I believe God's first choice for this ministry was a man. His second choice, too. But no man was willing to pay the price. I was just naive enough to say, "Take nothing, and use it." And He has been doing that ever since.

That is why I say to you, I know the power of the Holy Spirit is real. You can't give without receiving. After all those hours, I can still leave the stage as strong as when I walked on. I have given myself completely to the Holy Spirit. I have given my body as an empty vessel to be used by the Holy Spirit, but as I give, I receive. Even more than I give.

One day in Los Angeles a representative of women's lib called to ask if I would appear on a television program for women's lib. I laughed. "You won't want to hear what I have to say!"

You see, I'd give anything if I could just be a good housewife, a good cook. Oh, I'd like to be a good cook. I'd like to have about twelve children. Sometimes I feel like the mother of the world now. I've got so many spiritual children I don't know what to do. I worry about them. I mother them. I love them. I care for them. It would be so nice to have a man bring in the paycheck. I would just love to have a man boss me. It might not last long, but for a little while it would just be great!

So when it comes to women's lib, I'm still as old-fashioned as the Word of God. I still think that the husband should be the head of the family. I know how it was at our house. Papa was always the head of the family, and if papa said it, it was just as though God had said it. We never had any women's lib at our house, but we had a mighty happy family. Papa did the work, and mama ran papa without papa knowing it. It was a beautiful situation.

A woman's place is where God puts her. For the housewife and mother, it is with her husband and children. For me it is in this ministry. This is my place, because God put me here.

In 1 Timothy 2:11-12, Paul says, "Let the woman learn in silence with all subjection." It looks like Paul didn't believe in women's lib either. Verse 12: "But I suffer not a woman to teach, nor to usurp authority over the man, but to be in silence."

Let me give you something very simply. I am quite certain that if it was contrary to the will of God to let women preach, Paul certainly would have reprimanded Philip, in whose home he visited. Philip, you remember, had four daughters who were preachers (Acts 21:9). Now that's a houseful of preachers, I'll tell you! Paul visited Philip and all four daughters were there. They wouldn't have missed seeing Paul for anything in the world. But I cannot find a single Scripture that says that Paul forbade these four daughters to preach. Peter quotes Joel in Acts 2:17, saying in the closing hours of this dispensation, not only will your sons prophesy and preach, but your daughters shall also prophesy and preach. Powerful words.

So what do we do about Paul's command for women to keep silent in the church? Look at the situation. In the synagogues of that day, women would sit in the balcony. This is still done in some parts of the world today, such as India, where the women are on one side and the men on the other. The women would talk so loudly from their places in the balcony that the rest of the people could not hear the speaker. Women are just the same today as they were then. I can just hear John's wife calling down and saying, "John, do you remember? Did I turn the stove off?" Or maybe they were doing a little voting and Elizabeth would call down and say, "Abe, say no, say no, you know I don't like him, don't put him in office." They talked so loudly no one else could hear. They just couldn't keep their mouths shut. So Paul said, "Let the women be quiet." That did not mean that women were inferior. The Bible teaches that men and women each have their proper places. Each has God-given responsibilities. The man, for example, is the head of the woman. That doesn't mean he is a tyrant, that he goes around with a big stick. Thank God there is a difference between men and women. But that does not mean that women are somehow lesser—just different. Some of the greatest leaders in Hebrew history were women. I admire Golda Meir very much. She's a strong personality, a strong leader. What Golda wants, Golda gets. I admire Deborah, a judge of early Israel. I admire Queen Esther. I admire Sarah. I admire Mary, the mother of Jesus. All strong women.

Down through the centuries, in every society, there have been some things men have naturally done and other things women have done. But it was Christianity that freed the woman from her subservient role. I have never understood how any woman could reject Christ, for it was Christ who gave dignity to women. Christians may have problems with women in ministry—but Christ never did. He elevated us. He set us free. I am glad I am a woman.

What About Those Who Are Not Healed?

Whether one is healed or not is in the hands of God. At no time is it my responsibility. I am not perfect wisdom, I am not perfect knowledge. I have no healing virtue. I have never healed anyone. I have no power to heal. The whole responsibility rests in the hands of God and the individual. And it's just like that.

But of course I'm human. No one really knows how I hurt inside when a service is over, and I see those who have come in wheelchairs leaving in the same wheelchairs in which they came. You'll never know the ache on the inside—the suffering that I feel. But the answer I must leave with God. And one of these days, when I get home to glory, I'm going to ask Him to give me the answer from His own lips, as to why everyone is not healed.

Something happened while I was in Kansas City. The *Kansas City Star* sent a reporter to the services. I became acquainted with her, a lovely young woman with a keen journalistic mind. She attended all the services, and the last night, following the meeting, she came back to my dressing room. One of my helpers let her in, and she found me crying. She was embarrassed, but I went ahead and just sort of bared my soul to her, forgetting she was a reporter.

I said, "You know, people would think that after a miracle service like this, when scores and scores have been healed, that I would be the happiest person in the whole world. I am grateful I have seen the manifestation of God's power. But no one knows the hurt and grief I feel for those who were not healed. I wonder if perhaps I had known better how to cooperate with the Holy Spirit, more might have been accomplished for God." I could not hold back the flood of tears, and the reporter finally slipped out.

About three weeks later, I received a letter from this reporter. She said, "I am not writing as a reporter for the *Kansas City Star*, but as someone who had a friend in that last service. He was an attorney. He was dying of cancer. They brought him in on a stretcher. About a week after you left Kansas City, I went to his home and was greeted at the front door by his wife. She told me Tom had died. I started to leave, but she insisted I come in. Her face was radiant. She said, 'That service in the auditorium was the greatest thing that happened to Tom. Obviously he was not healed. We took him back home on the same stretcher on which he was carried in. But it was during that service that Tom prepared for death. Lying on that stretcher, while the power of God was falling, my husband accepted Christ and received forgiveness for his sins. Before then, he was struggling. Afterwards, he was peaceful. Death was easy—victorious. It was glorious to hear him thanking Jesus for the forgiveness of his sins.' "

The reporter finished her letter: "Kathryn Kuhlman, don't weep after a service any more. When you think there should have been greater results than the healing of sick bodies, always remember my friend Tom. The greatest miracle that could have happened to him was the salvation of his soul."

No, I don't understand why everyone is not healed physically. But all can be healed spiritually. That's the greatest miracle any human being can know.

10

Healing and the Atonement

Man is a trinity, even as God is a trinity. Jesus died for the whole man: body, soul, and spirit. God would be an unjust God if He permitted His Son to come and die for just a part of man. When Jesus cried on the cross, "It is finished," the price was paid through the atonement for the whole man, every part of man—his body, his soul, his spirit. The whole debt was paid in full.

I am often asked: "Is there healing in the atonement? Did Christ die to relieve us of our physical as well as spiritual infirmities?" Let's go back to the first Passover, as recorded in Exodus 12:3-6. "Speak ye unto all the congregation of Israel, saying, In the tenth day of this month they shall take to them every man a lamb, according to the house of their fathers, a lamb for an house: And if the household be too little for the lamb, let him and his neighbour next unto his house take it according to the number of the souls; every man according to his eating shall make your count for the lamb. Your lamb shall be without blemish, a male of the first year: ye shall take it out from the sheep, or from the goats: And ye shall keep it up until the fourteenth day of the same month: and the whole assembly of the congregation of Israel shall kill it in the evening."

In verses seven and eight, it says: "And they shall take of the blood and strike it on the two side posts and on the upper door post of the houses, wherein they shall eat it. And they shall eat the flesh in that night, roast with fire, and unleavened bread: and with bitter herbs they shall eat it."

It was the first Passover. The blood was to be sprinkled on the lintel of the doorposts of the house, but the flesh of the lamb was to be eaten. We forget the true meaning of the flesh of the lamb. In the Holy Communion—which is the Passover feast of the New Covenant—the meaning of the wine is quite clear to most. Nearly all Christians realize as they hold the cup in their hand, or drink of the wine at the altar, that the shed blood of Jesus Christ makes atonement for the soul. But what about the bread? Every time the bread is served, it should be taken for the healing of the body. The whole man was included in that atonement. That's the reason Isaiah cried out: "He was wounded for our transgressions, he was bruised for our iniquities . . . and with his stripes we are healed" (53:5). Yes, there is healing in the atonement. Christ died to give us healing—not only in the spiritual areas, but also for our physical infirmities.

Yet I do not believe anyone can receive a physical healing without also receiving a spiritual healing. The two go hand-in-hand. In every one of my miracle services—sometimes right in the middle of the service while bodies are being healed—sinners will come walking down the aisle, weeping, and saying, "I want to be born again." Yet I have said nothing about salvation or repentance. I have given no altar call. Yet they come. It is the moving of the Holy Spirit. You see, wherever you find a great moving of the Holy Spirit in healing, you will also find Him moving in deep spiritual things. The spiritual healing, which is the greatest of all healings, always accompanies healing miracles. In fact, that is the very reason for miracles—to glorify God and to draw men and women to Christ.

11

Prescription for Healing

The greatest enemy a human being can take into his life is fear. If you are able to conquer the enemy of fear, you have come a long way toward bringing health to a physical body.

Life is not built for negative achievement. It's built for positive contribution, outgoing love.

You can never get rid of your own troubles unless you take upon yourself the troubles of others. When you find yourself oppressed by melancholy, the best way out is to find something you can do for somebody else. When you dig a man out of trouble, the hole which is left is the grave where you bury your own sorrows. Go out each day and do something that nobody but a Christian would do. It won't be long before you'll forget about your own troubles.

That, of course, is where the mind enters the picture. I really believe you can talk yourself into being sick. Dwell on the fact you have a little pain, and how that pain increases.

I can always remember papa saying something. It wasn't scientific. You won't find it in the doctors' manual. It's just good common sense. He used to say, "Oh, just go out and work it off." The best medicine in the world is hard work. They've got pills for everything today. We're almost pilled to death. But no one has come up with a capsule which makes people want to work.

Hard work is the best medicine I know anything about. The right mental attitude is glorious. Those who sit around waiting for a miracle will seldom find it. You help God from within by giving to others. When you do, miraculously, your fears, doubts, and self-centeredness will vanish.

Miracles start from within, not from without. Throw your will on the side of outgoing love, and all the healing resources of the universe will be behind you. Try it. It's the best medicine I know anything about.

12

Faith

Volumes have been written, more volumes have been spoken regarding that indefinable something called "faith." Yet in the final analysis, we actually know so little of the subject.

Faith is that quality or power by which the things desired become the things possessed. That is the nearest to a definition of faith attempted by the inspired Word of God. You cannot weigh faith, or confine it to a container. It is not something you can take out, look at, and analyze. You cannot definitely put your finger on it and positively say, "Now, this is faith." You can no more explain faith than you can describe time or define energy.

In the realm of physics we are told the atom is a world within itself. The potential energy contained within this tiny world bewilders the mind of the average person. If you attempt to define it, you run into difficulties. And so it is with things in the realm of the Spirit—especially faith.

We do know, however, what it is not. One of the most common errors is to confuse faith with presumption. We must be constantly alert to the danger of mistaking one for the other, for there is a vast difference between the two.

For example, there is a pebble on the beach. But the beach is more than one pebble. It is millions of pebbles. And billions of grains of sand. When the pebble asserts that it is the beach, we say to it, "You are assuming too much." There are many who mix the ingredients of their own mental attitude with a little confidence, a little pinch of trust, a generous handful of religious egotism, quote some Scripture, add some desire—then mix it all together and label it "faith."

Not so.

Faith is more than belief. It is more than confidence. It is more than trust. It is more than the sum total of all these things—and none of them in particular. Above all, it is never boastful. If it is pure, Holy Ghost faith, it will never work contrary to the will of God.

One of the chief difficulties is our failure to see that faith can be received only as it is imparted to the heart by God himself. You ask me a personal question: "Kathryn, do you have faith for the healing of that physical body, that one who comes to you wanting a healing for cancer?"

(When the prayer requests come through the mail, by the way, the majority are for the healing of cancer.) Do I have faith for the healing? Only if God gives it to me. If I stand praying for someone to be healed of cancer, and if there is faith accompanying that prayer, that faith is definitely a gift from God.

The Word of God teaches that faith is a gift. And Jesus is the author and the finisher of our faith. One of the chief difficulties is the failure to see that faith can be received only as it is imparted to our hearts by God himself. You cannot manufacture it. You cannot work it up. You can believe a promise and at the same time not have the faith to appropriate that promise. But we have formed the habit of trying to appropriate by belief, forgetting that belief is a mental quality. Trying to conjure up faith through belief puts us into the metaphysical realm.

I repeat: We have formed the habit of trying to appropriate by belief, forgetting that belief is mental—while faith is from God.

Faith, as God himself imparts to the heart, is spiritual. It's warm. It's vital. It lives. It throbs. Its power is absolutely irresistible when it is imparted to the heart by the Lord. It is with the heart that man believes unto righteousness. Heart belief is faith. Mind belief is nothing more than deep desire combined with mental assent.

That's the reason faith is a struggle with most

of us. It is merely an attempt to believe. It may be that with all our struggling we come at last to the place where we do believe. Then we have been bewildered by the fact that we do not receive the thing for which we pray. We must discern that such belief is not necessarily what the inspired Word calls faith.

Matthew 17 is a chapter of contrasts. It climbs to the heights and then goes down to the depths. It talks of mustard seed and mountains. Of despair and transfiguration. What a lesson the Holy Ghost would bring to you on this great subject of faith through the priceless Word of God. Down from the mountaintop came our blessed Lord, down from the gates of heaven where the glory breezes kissed His cheek, where the angels wrapped His shoulders with robes that had been woven on the looms of light. Down from the place of holy communion and encouragement to the place of human defeat and of despair. At the foot of the glory mountain was a gloom valley, and through it ran the trail of human bewilderment. There was sickness there, a crushed and bleeding heart was there, a father who had met an obstacle which had crushed him in spirit and heart was there.

Sure, the preachers were there, too. They had gone through the formulas—they had rebuked the devil, they had shouted and groaned. Yet the thing for which they had prayed had never happened.

Then Jesus spoke. Oh, matchless words of authority. With Him there was no struggle. There was no groaning, no battle that was fierce and long, to bring the answer to a broken father's prayer. Jesus spoke. The devil fled. A happy boy cuddled in his father's arms. A grateful father embraced his boy and looked with tear-stained eyes of love and adoration at the face of the man before whom devils fled. Then Jesus spoke. He said, in answer to the bewildered disciples who had tried but failed: "[It was] because of your unbelief: for verily I say unto you, If ye have faith as a grain of mustard seed, ye shall say unto this mountain, Remove hence to yonder place; and it shall remove; and nothing shall be impossible unto you" (v. 20).

What a statement from the lips of Jesus himself. "And nothing shall be impossible into you." All we need is faith as big as a grain of mustard seed, and mountains will tremble in fear as we approach.

Do we realize what Jesus was saying? He declared that the least amount of faith that He could give was greater and mightier than the largest amount of the power of the devil. Here was the David of faith combating the Goliath of unbelief. A mustard seed doing battle against a mountain. And faith always wins. But such faith is only given by God—never acquired by works, never bestowed because you gave an offering or even gave your body to be burned. It comes from on high. And it's just like that.

Did those disciples believe? Yes, they did. They believed in Jesus. They believed His promises. They believed in divine healing, or never would they have held that healing meeting that day. They believed just exactly like you and I have believed in healing services. They prayed, but nothing happened.

What they needed, according to Jesus, was faith. Not a carload of it, but just a little bit, as big as a grain of mustard seed. That would be enough. That would be all that was necessary, if it was really faith.

Let us face the issue squarely. Let us with open, surrendered hearts ask the Holy Spirit to send forth His light and His truth and lead us to that holy hill. Is it not evident that when we pray what we thought was the prayer of faith, and nothing happens, it must be that what we thought was faith was not faith at all. Do you understand what I'm trying to say? It's so simple. So simple.

When we see the truth, we shall no longer be standing around hour after hour, rebuking commanding, struggling. With faith there is no struggle. There will be a place for intercession. Know that. But when God's faith is imparted, the storm dies down and there's a great calm and a deep settled peace in the soul. The only noise will be the murmured voices of thanksgiving and praise. For then the full realization will steal, like morning daybreak, over the soul; it was not our ability to believe that made the sickness go, but rather the faith which God imparted to us through His mercy.

We can believe in healing. We can believe in our blessed Redeemer and His power to heal. But only Jesus can work the works that will lift us to the mountain of victory. Always remember, faith is a gift—given to us by the Giver.

The Gift of Healing

Now concerning spiritual gifts, brethren. . . .

Paul is writing to the Christians, to those who are spiritual.

Now concerning spiritual gifts, brethren, I would not have you ignorant (1 Cor. 12:1).

The gifts of the Holy Spirit are absolutely, vitally important. They are essential to the functioning of the church. Without them, the church lacks its spiritual equipment that is outlined in the first epistle to the Corinthians. This twelfth chapter is so necessary for an aggressive conflict with the powers of darkness. Without it the church is deprived of that edifying enrichment which comes from the manifestation of the Holy Spirit's presence and power in her midst.

The Bible is full of God's supernatural dealings with His people. The experience of regeneration, whereby we become new creatures in Christ, is supernatural. Christians readily admit that the devil is supernatural in his person, in his powers and activities. Yet those same Christians often shrink from the thought of the supernatural baptism in the Holy Spirit, with supernatural signs attending it and ensuing supernatural gifts. I don't know why it is that the average minister is so afraid of the supernatural power of God, supernatural manifestations, supernatural gifts. The early church was founded on the supernatural, and we need to get it back again—or die. Wherever we find the presence of the Holy Spirit, we will always find the supernatural.

The Lord Jesus said, "He that believeth on me, the works that I do shall he do also." He also promised that "Ye shall receive power, after that the Holy Ghost is come upon *you*."

But if we ignore the gifts of the Holy Spirit, we despise the heritage which is granted to us in Christ. That is why the Apostle Paul exhorted his friends in Corinth: "Now concerning spiritual gifts, brethren, I would not have you ignorant."

Should any man advance the argument that the gifts were bestowed just to usher in the present dispensation, and that they are not for today, we should quote the Apostle Peter on the Day of Pentecost. "The promise is unto you, and to your children, and to all that are afar off, even as many as the Lord our God shall call" (Acts 2:39). Looking down through the telescope of time, he saw the day, the hour, in which we are living. That's the reason the promise of the Holy Spirit, the promise of the supernatural manifestations of the Holy Spirit, is not limited to the early church. The promise is unto you (those to whom He was speaking) and to your children (the next generation), and to all that are afar off, even as many as the Lord our God shall call (and that's us today). When we speak of the power of the Holy Spirit, when we speak of the gifts of the Spirit, we need to remember it is the heritage of the church today. Every Christian should be enjoying the supernatural.

If a person is called to be a son of God, through faith in Jesus Christ, that person is also in consequence a prospective recipient of the gifts of the Holy Spirit. It's that simple. It's just like that.

What do the Scriptures say? "There are diversities of gifts, but the same Spirit." The apostle is pointing out that though the gifts are different one from the other, their origin—or their source—is the same. Gifts of the Spirit are really various manifestations of the Spirit. The Holy Spirit manifests himself in different and distinctive ways. The gifts function differently in each individual. Take, for example, the working of miracles. In Elijah, it was associated with the mantle he wore. In Moses, it was with the rod that had been changed into a serpent. In Samson, the miraculous power was inseparable from his hair, which was his sign of submission, so he remained supernaturally strong when the Spirit was upon him. However, in each instance, it was the manifestation of the same gift, although the operations were so different.

The selfsame Spirit divides to every man severally as He wills. It is the prerogative of the Spirit to give us what gifts He sees most suitable for the individual.

At the end of 1 Corinthians 12, we read that while we are to covet earnestly the best gifts, the apostle will show us a more excellent way. What is the more excellent way? It is to seek the love of God first, and to desire the gifts of the Spirit in order that we may serve God better. The answer is given in 1 Corinthians 14: "Follow after charity [or love], and desire spiritual gifts."

If we put spiritual gifts before the love of God, we shall make a very serious mistake. For the first and the most important thing is love.

Those who love God will normally desire spiritual gifts, since they are manifestations of His Spirit, given for His glory and for the enrichment of His church.

Why do so few people have the gift of healing? That is not a legitimate question. For to one is given by the Spirit, the word of wisdom. Why not ask: "Why are there so few who have been given the word of wisdom?" To another the word of knowledge. Why are there so few to whom has been given the gift of knowledge? To another faith by the same Spirit. Then comes the gift of healing, the working of miracles, prophecy, the discerning of spirits, tongues, the interpretation of tongues. There are far more gifts than those that Paul named here. Don't limit the Holy Spirit, whatever you do. Don't limit Him to just nine gifts. There are more. Many more.

I have come to the conclusion that He who is perfect wisdom, and perfect knowledge, who knows the individual better than that individual knows himself, knows whom He can trust with certain gifts.

It's something like the man who asked: "Why doesn't God bless me with riches?" Yet the same man who asks that question has not been obedient to God with that which he has. He doesn't even give his tithe, that part which is rightfully God's. If he is not obedient with that with which he has, God will not trust him with more.

Why, bless you, if God were to give certain people a gift, they would misuse that gift within the first twenty-four hours. God knows exactly what He is doing. And that is the reason, you see, I do not brag and say I possess any spiritual gift. No one has ever heard Kathryn Kuhlman say she possessed a certain gift. Do you want to know why? Because I know that along with every special gift is also a great responsibility. And that responsibility calls for us to give *all* the glory to God, and not even talk about the gift—but always the Giver. It is He whom we praise, not the gift.

I think sometimes people become weary of hearing me say, "Kathryn Kuhlman has nothing to do with it. Kathryn Kuhlman has never healed anyone." Yet I know the truth of that statement better than anyone else. I know, better than anyone, it is all the supernatural power of God. My responsibility is to be very careful to give God the praise, to give God the honor, to give God all the glory. I must guard that which He has given me very carefully. For one day, when I stand in His glorious presence, I am going to have to give an account of that with which He has entrusted me today.

Look up just now, and remember you are His child, and these things that I have been talking about are a part of your inheritance. Do you want to be filled with the Holy Spirit? He'll fill all that you yield to Him. Do you want to be given a gift of the Spirit? Search your own heart. See whether you're being faithful and true to Him with that which He has entrusted to you now. And above all, remember the gifts of the Holy Spirit are given for one reason alone—to glorify the Son of God. Anything less is an abuse of that which is most precious to the Father.

14

Ultimate Victory

I have come to the conclusion that this age
knows almost everything about life—except how
to live it. It's not enough to know about life, we
must know how to live life.

We've handed over our bodies to the doctors,
our minds to the psychiatrists, and our souls to
the ministers. But we are not three separate
entities. Man is a trinity: body, soul, and spirit.
Life is a whole. You cannot affect one part
without affecting all three.

Doctors vary in their estimate as to the
percentage of people who pass on mental and
spiritual sicknesses to their bodies. Such illnesses
are called psychosomatic: physical illness whose
origin is mental or spiritual. It's easy to pass on a
mental or spiritual sickness to your body. A
doctor in Pittsburgh, Pennsylvania, has
contacted me very often. On several occasions he
has come up to the office to see me. He said, "You

know, Kathryn, I am deeply interested in that which you teach. I have been listening very closely and watching your ministry very closely. I would like to bring into my practice as a doctor that which you give as a minister. For," he said, "the combination of both would make for a perfect practice."

They tell me that in a group of Johns Hopkins doctors, one psychiatrist said 40 percent of the cases that come to their clinic are mental and spiritual in origin. Many doctors estimate the cases as high as 80 percent.

Man was made to give himself to a higher power than himself. In other words, man is going to be mastered by something. If you are not mastered by God, then you are going to be mastered by things. Or by circumstances. That's the reason a Christian need never go down in defeat. Never. No man, no woman, if his confidence is in God, need ever go down in defeat. A Christian knows where to go and what to do in his hour of disappointment. "I'm not going to be mastered by things or circumstances!" is one of the greatest declarations a Christian can utter. The man who is completely mastered by the will of God will never be mastered by anything else.

If you are completely mastered by the will of God, you will not be defeated in the hour of sickness, in the hour of mental strain, in the hour of disappointment, in the hour of temptation.

You and I are not only conquerors, we are *more* than conquerors through Christ who loved us. Even sorrow, disappointment, and death cannot master us. But when we take our eyes off Jesus, when we refuse to submit to His lordship, His ownership, we gradually turn the control of our lives over to circumstances. Sickness takes over. And we are mastered by things.

That's the reason I say the greatest healings are not of the body, but of the spirit. If, with the gospel of the Lord Jesus Christ, I can get through to the mind of an individual and allow him to see that God is still God Almighty, bigger than his sorrow, greater than his heartbreak, more powerful than his circumstances, then he can finally understand he does not have to go down in defeat. Jesus has given to each of us all the necessary resources for health and abundant life. All things are at our disposal, and we can live an abundant and victorious life through Christ. "As a man thinketh, so is he." If you think defeat, you will be defeated. If you think discouragement, you will be a discouraged person. You can't think pain without feeling pain. You can't think sickness without being sick. It all goes together.

Oh, don't go down in defeat. Don't be a person who is beaten. God is still God Almighty. The God of Abraham is still our God, the God of Elijah is still our God. The God who made the iron to swim is still God Almighty. The God who sent the water from the rock, the manna from heaven, is still alive. The God who supplied the little widow with her meal and her oil is still God Almighty. There is no uncertainty about that.

Don't be mastered by things. Be mastered by God. Then when afflictions do come (and no human being is immune when it comes to disease and affliction), you will be victorious. No human body is immune from cancer. I believe in divine healing. I preach divine healing. I believe in the power of God to heal bodies. But in spite of all this, my own physical body is not immune to cancer. I think of that so very often. My own physical body. I'm still in the flesh. The mortal has not yet put on immortality. This which is corruption has not yet put on incorruption. I'm still a part of humanity. I'm still living in the flesh. Sickness may come to my body. But when it does, there is a heavenly Father, there is a God to whom I can go. I may die, but I will not go down in defeat. A million times I've wondered what people do in an hour of tragedy who do not have a simple confidence in God Almighty. They are defeated. They are beaten. Many give themselves to self-pity. But for those who are "in Christ," there is no defeat. Death? Yes! For all of us. But we are not only conquerors, we are more than conquerors in the face of tragedy, seeming defeat, affliction, even death. Cancer, heart disease—these may be the agents which snuff out our lives. But God is still God. And in the end—when all else is past and only the issues of life and death remain—God is in control.

15

Faith and Gumption

Every person has a problem on his hands. That problem is life. I never hold a tiny baby in my arms but what I think, "You dear little thing, you precious little baby, if only you knew what you are up against: just being a part of humanity." Yes sir, everybody has the problem of life on his hands. And I'll promise you something. If you do not know what to do with life, life will find something to do with you.

Almighty God knew what He was doing when He created you. He had a purpose for you, a purpose for your life. In order for you to carry out that purpose, He gave you the marvelous capacity to develop faith. Thus, the man who has no faith is defeated before he begins.

Dr. Wernher von Braun, the man who developed our space industry, said, "Today, more than ever before, our survival (yours and mine and our children's) depends on our adherence to ethical principles." Then he continued to say, "Belief in God gives us the moral strength and the guidance we need for virtually every action in our daily lives." Now we would expect words like that coming from a preacher, a priest, or a minister of the gospel. But these words came from the pen of one of the world's greatest scientists.

Faith is so great, so powerful a force, that when taken in the soul and lived by, it can see you through anything. I do not speak these words lightly, for I am fully aware of the fact that there are those who this very moment are filled with grief, trouble, doubt, and conflict. Yet it is to you I speak—you who have feelings of complete defeat and despair.

But I want you to know something. Against these feelings, against your utter defeat, against your grief, your trouble, your doubt, I offer you the power of God's tremendous Word. If you have faith, nothing shall be impossible to you. Faith is such a powerful force that when taken into the soul and lived by, it can see you through anything in life.

Millions of words have been written about success. But if these millions of words could be squeezed out in just three short, meaningful words, I believe the formula for success would read: faith and gumption.

Of course the Bible speaks of this in just a little different terms. The Bible says, in James 2:26,

"For as the body without the spirit is dead, so faith without works is dead also." There is nothing quite as dead as the physical body when the spirit has left—unless it is faith without works.

This gets right down to where we live. Anyone can wish for success, but it takes gumption to make things happen. Faith and wishing are not enough. You can have all the faith in the world, but if all you do is sit there claiming faith, and wishing that something would happen, you will sit from now to doomsday and nothing will happen. Works without faith is dead. But faith without works will leave you in the state of accomplishing nothing. You must put forth effort to achieve. It takes gumption.

There is a certain man in Missouri who has a keen, marvelous mind. When he was seventeen years of age, the head of Sweeney School for Mechanics in Kansas City, Missouri, said the lad was a mechanical genius. He was a natural to succeed in the field of aviation. He was such a marvelous genius that the government sought his services at the air base in Wichita, Kansas. All his associates described him as a mechanical genius.

But you know how he spent his life? I'll tell you. Sitting in a comfortable chair resting. Just resting. That man is my brother. He never has had anything. He never will have anything. Do you want to know why? Oh, sure, he has the mentality. He has the brains. But no gumption.

One day I got so exasperated. I sat down beside mama and I said, "You know something, mama? That son of yours is the laziest man God ever let live." Mama just smiled. I can see it just as well as if it had happened only fifteen minutes ago. She said very sweetly, "Now, Kathryn, you know Boy hasn't been very well physically since his last operation." Since his last operation? The only operation he ever had was an appendectomy when he was fifteen years old. And he never had a sick day since.

I said, "Mama, what operation?"

"Oh," she said, "that operation he had when he was fifteen years of age and had appendicitis. It took a lot out of him."

That's mother's love.

But I'll tell you something, no mother's tender love will ever make a success out of any precious boy. It still takes gumption. If you don't make an effort, you'll never succeed.

Now I'm going to say something that a lot of people are going to resent. Sickness can come to anyone. So can disaster and misfortune. But in most instances they are only temporary. Yet there are hundreds of thousands of people on relief today, drawing monthly relief checks from our government, all because they lacked gumption. They let the temporary misfortunes become permanent. Many, many people could once again become productive and creative if they would just get up and do something about their condition.

From exactly the same materials, one man builds palaces while another builds hovels. And often the one who builds his hovel is jealous and critical of the one who has worked like a dog and built his mansion.

I know plenty of people who have failed, who have more brains and stronger physical bodies than the ones who have been successful. But they lacked the gumption to succeed.

There are no limitations to what faith and gumption can accomplish. Absolutely none. As long as your faith in God is intact, all the reservoirs of power are at your disposal.

"I can do all things through Christ which strengtheneth me" (Phil. 4:13). There is no exception. That's the Word of God, and you can stake your very life on it.

But hear me. God won't do a thing to help you bring it to pass until you get up and out of that chair and start doing something about it. Faith without works, faith without gumption, is dead. But with God's power, and your gumption, the opportunities are unlimited.

Hard Work:
The Secret of Success

Let's start with the revealing words of a man who rose from humble beginnings to amass one of the great fortunes of our time. Says he, "I have succeeded not because I have any more ability than people who have not succeeded. But because I applied myself harder and stuck to it longer."

I know plenty of people who have failed to succeed in anything, who have more brains than I have. No. It's not brains. It's simply because they lacked application and determination.

I know an executive who started from scratch and had to hurdle many obstacles and disappointments on the way. The man who reaches the top is the one who is not content with doing just what is required of him. He does more. He makes up his mind that if he expects to succeed, he must give an honest return for the other man's dollar. You absolutely cannot get around it, that is the basic law of success. When you've got a job to do, do it with enthusiasm and do it well.

A friend of mine told me about a famed captain of industry who once said, "Give me the choice between a man of tremendous brains without tenacity, and one of ordinary brains but with a great deal of tenacity, and I will select the tenacious one every time. A determined man can do more with a rusty wrench than a loafer can do with all the tools in the machine shop."

Isn't that a knockout? That's great.

You need to have confidence that if you've done a little thing well, you can do a bigger thing well too. A man who emerged from obscurity at the age of forty, to become one of the great wizards of mass production, reminds us that nothing is especially hard if divided into small jobs. An executive who made an outstanding success of his life candidly admits that his chief starting assets were nothing more than a friendly smile, a cooperative spirit, an enthusiastic earnestness to pitch in and get things done. There are no limitations to what you can do, except the limitations in your own mind. Don't think that you can't do it. Think you can, and you will.

"Concentrate on the business in which you are engaged," advised a mighty tycoon. "Resolve to lead in it. Adopt every improvement. Know the most about it, and do not be impatient. The man who informs himself about his firm, its methods, and its products, who does his work so well that there is no need to follow him to patch up the ragged edges, is on the safest, surest, and sharpest road to achievement."

You see, the surest way to qualify for the job ahead is to work a little harder than anyone else on the job. Employers are constantly seeking men who do the unusual. Men who think. Men who attract attention by performing more than is expected of them. These men have no difficulty making their worth felt. They stand out above their fellows. There is plenty of room for all, and plenty for all in this abundant land. So start working.

17

Determination

By all means, start now. For this business of making a success of oneself boils down to these simple but oh, so important steps.

First, if you seriously want success, you must go after it with all your heart and soul. With all the energy, all the enthusiasm you possess. You must work, act, live for the goal you seek.

Second, you must not be jarred or discouraged by disappointments and snags. You must take them in stride with a smile. And do not let the pricks of friends, or would-be friends, turn you for a single moment from your aims.

Third, it's the man who goes about his work with unruffled calm, who is not afraid to cooperate, who welcomes suggestions and criticism, who is always willing to learn, who keeps an open mind and an attentive ear and an observing eye. Who gives the very best that is in him, day in and day out. He's the one who is sure to get ahead, to be a success.

It takes gumption, but the rewards are great. The opportunities are unlimited.

The same principles that are used in the making of a successful business apply to the Christian life.

If you want to be a successful Christian, you must set your mind to it and never look back. Do you really want to be a Christian? Do you really want the joy of salvation? Do you really want the peace of God in your heart and your mind? You can have it if you want it. But "want" is the key word.

If you've made up your mind you want to be a successful Christian, Jesus will come into your heart and into your life in a glorious born-again experience. Then you must work, act, live for the goal you seek. Not just on Sunday. It's your life. Make up your mind it will be your life. Go in for it with everything you've got. You can give no less of yourself in being a successful Christian than you can give in being a successful businessman, or a success in anything you do in life.

That's why we have some backsliders today. They never went into this thing of being a Christian with everything they had. But it takes exactly that to live a daily, successful Christian life.

"As thy day, so shall thy strength be," the Bible says. It's a day-to-day proposition.

Sure, there will be obstacles. There will be

trials. There will be heartbreak. There will be temptations. But if you live your Christian life one day at a time, you will meet that temptation. The Holy Spirit will be your holy strengthener. You must not be daunted or discouraged by disappointment or snags. Take them in stride, with a smile. No man, no woman need ever be defeated in this thing of being a successful Christian, unless he or she allows himself to be defeated.

Sure, it will cost you something. Success doesn't just happen. But I promise you something. The rewards are great, the opportunity unlimited.

Missouri Cornbread

If other folks should open my mail, not knowing anything about my ministry, they wouldn't know what to think when they began reading a letter saying, "Oh, Kathryn Kuhlman, we just love your Missouri cornbread." But you see, I can't help it if I'm simply—and sometimes—corny. I'm just like that. Sometimes I spread a little butter on my cornbread, sometimes it's Missouri 'lasses, but most times it's just plain cornbread.

One lady wrote and said, "Honestly, I'd give anything in the world if I really could see the kind of cornbread your mother made." Well, maybe nobody else thought it was tops, or the world's greatest, but I sure did enjoy it.

And that's the way I feel about being a Christian. About preaching. About the Word of God. How often I've walked off the stage or the platform after a service and said to myself, "Well, if nobody else enjoyed the sermon, I sure did!" Nobody enjoys being a Christian more than I do. That's right. I enjoy it. I enjoy my salvation. I enjoy being born again. I enjoy this Christian life and Christian living. I wouldn't exchange it for anything I know anything about.

If I thought there were something better, I'd go after it. But Christianity is the best thing I know. Oh, I enjoy preaching. I'd rather preach than eat, sleep, or do anything else I know anything about. There's not a person in the whole world who enjoys preaching any more than I do. The same thing is true of reading my Bible. I can't read the Word of God without getting blessed. It just does something to me. But most of all, I enjoy my relationship with my heavenly Father. That's what being a Christian is all about.

There are certain laws which if followed will bring success. There's no need for failure—not among Christians. If you follow these spiritual laws, you will be a success, not only in God's eyes, but in your own, too.

The defeated life has never been part of God's plan. He has given us every implement, every tool that is needed to live a daily successful Christian life.

Do you think that it's ever in the plan of God, in the mind of Jesus, for any person to be defeated in their Christian life? Do you think Jesus ever had such a thought? Of course not. If you are defeated in your Christian experience, it's because you have yielded to defeat—not because He was not there to give you everything that would take you through to certain victory.

Paul said, "I can do all things—not in myself, not because I will to do all things, not because of mental attitudes, not because of positive thinking—through Christ." He is saying there is no need for defeat in your life. All the days of your life you are His child. For each child of God, there is a daily rate of strength, a daily giving of courage, a daily impartation of His faith to you.

If I am ever defeated, I can blame only myself. If you are ever defeated, you have only one person to blame. How easy it is to blame someone else. Everybody else. That's one of the weaknesses of human nature. It all goes back, you know, to Adam and Eve. Oh, sure, "He tempted me." "They did this." "I'm not to blame, it's all him." Uh-huh. That's the weakness in human nature.

But when it comes right down to it, when we look ourselves directly in the face, we can put the blame only on ourselves. We can't put it on the neighbors, or even the in-laws. The only person left to put it on is God, and since we feel He can't talk back to us, we blame Him.

Others, fearing God, blame the devil. Oh, I tell you, that is the one thing that gets me. These people who blame the devil for everything that happens. "I tell you, Kathryn Kuhlman, the devil did this to me. Everything would have come out all right, but the devil did this, and the devil did that. . . ."

Go to the nearest mirror. Stand before that mirror. And you will see right where you should put the blame. Be big enough to lay the blame exactly where it belongs.

I believe in Satan. I believe in the power of the evil one. But he will never be able to defeat you any more than he was able to defeat the One whom you love—the Lord Jesus Christ. Jesus did not yield to defeat, He did not yield to temptation. Neither do you have to be defeated by Satan, neither do you have to yield to temptation, or defeat, or failure.

Somebody says, "Was that the kind of cornbread your mother made in Missouri?" Well, she said it was good for me, and it must have been, because I grew up to be a mighty healthy Missourian, and a healthy Christian as well.

It's one thing to have that experience of being born again, that experience where you know that you have passed from death unto life. It is the greatest transaction in the life of any human being. Yet there are literally thousands who have had this wonderful experience, who wipe away the tears from their cheeks, and then get up from their knees and believe that is all there is to the Christian life.

But my friend, that's just the beginning. You have only started. You need to go on to improve your knowledge regarding the things of God. You have not used everything you can to know the most about that which you've taken into your heart, into your life.

Here we are, living in the closing moments of this dispensation. What a thrilling hour to be alive. This is the day of great adventure for God's children. He is pouring out His Spirit upon thousands throughout the world.

But do you realize how few people who are filled with the Spirit know what to do with this experience after they've been filled? Few are those who know the real scriptural purpose of being filled with the Holy Spirit. That's right. That's the reason so many are bringing a reproach on this beautiful experience. They are bringing a reproach on the person of the Holy Spirit. Because they have been filled without the knowledge of the Word.

The worst ignorance in the world is spiritual ignorance. There is nothing worse than an overdose of zeal without spiritual knowledge, without the knowledge of the Word. Christians need to go deep into God's Word. You must not be satisfied just to know your sins are forgiven. The Bible must become, literally, a part of your flesh, a part of your life, a part of your living, a part of your breathing.

So here we are, my friends, in this hour so full of adventure, in this day that is the greatest day in human history. We are God's children. The Holy Spirit is being poured out on all flesh. The best of the wine has been saved for the last. There is so much that is ours, yet we know not what to do with it.

One of the secrets I learned early in life is this: "Study to show thyself approved unto God, a workman that needeth not to be ashamed, rightly dividing the word of truth" (2 Tim. 2:15).

That's just plain old Missouri cornbread. It's up to you. God will do the rest.

19

Nerves

As he thinketh in his heart, so is he. (Prov. 23:7)

Nervous diseases are not diseases at all, but are varied degrees of emotional outbreaks. No condition or set of circumstances is in itself a calamity to be feared. Always remember that. It is our little reaction to it that makes it a Waterloo or a field of triumph. It's just like that.

The brain can be likened to the central office of a telephone or telegraph system. Each brain cell appears to be a minute telephone apparatus through which messages are sent to different parts of the body, or through which calls are received from different parts of the body: stomach, liver, fingers, toes, skin, and so on.

The "wires" that connect the brain to the parts of the body are called nerves. They are threads of living tissue consisting of a central core surrounded by membrane, resembling the wire in its insulated covering.

If we follow a nerve from its beginning (perhaps in a cell in the skin), we find it ends up in a brain cell. Bear in mind one thing, however, that the nerves are only a *means* of communication. They do not govern anything.

Thus in most cases when a person complains of his "nerves," he doesn't know what he is talking about. In most of these so-called nervous conditions, the nervous system (the machinery) is found to be in perfect order. Therefore, the trouble must be deeper than that. It is here we come to that unseen worker within who presides over the central office and uses this wonderful mechanism to control the body. We call that worker the "mind."

We must realize that any of these so-called nervous conditions (from the simplest case of fidgets to the most pronounced hysteria) is caused by some state of mind which interferes with the orderly control of the affairs of the body.

If we understand this point, we are in a position to deal with these conditions.

Let's take, for instance, the hand. I sometimes find my hand is trembling. I say, "My hand trembles. It must be my nerves. Something is upsetting me terribly."

Your hand trembles and you say you are nervous. For some reason you are not able to exercise the normal control over the muscles. This is caused by a state of mind. In other words, what we call nervousness is a partial loss of control in the central office. When this becomes acute, we have a condition called hysteria. (All of us know people, some maybe in our own families, who become hysterical at the slightest provocation.) When you let your feelings take charge and give up all self-control, hysteria (or some form of it) is the natural result.

Years ago I was in a Baptist church holding a two-week revival meeting. I was young then—inexperienced. I was staying in the home of one of the church members, a nice little old maid in her seventies. I slept in the guest bedroom. I remember it so vividly because it was election week the year the late Mr. Roosevelt was running for the third term as president.

Miss Anna (my hostess) had a close friend who was probably seven or eight years older than herself. She was a large, portly woman who was absolutely dead set against Mr. Roosevelt's election to a third term. She was so determined that she had embarked on a one-woman campaign to stop him. Her husband was very wealthy, and she had spent literally thousands of dollars on her campaign.

Well, election night rolled around and she was absolutely exhausted from the mental strain and physical effort. About 7:00 P.M. her husband said, "You go to bed. You must get some rest. When the last returns come in, I'll call you. You won't miss anything."

She retired feeling confident she would awaken to a great celebration—a great personal victory.

Those of you who were living then know what the returns were like. Mr. Roosevelt was swept in for the third term. I shall never forget. The telephone rang at Miss Anna's house. It was the husband of the other woman who was still asleep. He said, "Anna. Come quickly. Mr. Roosevelt won, and it will kill my wife. When she awakens and I have to tell her, it will be the death of her. She'll suffer a heart attack. Come quickly and help me tell her."

Miss Anna said, "Kathryn, I'll be back in a little bit. I don't know how long it will be."

She told me later what happened. It was 2:00 A.M. and Miss Anna tiptoed into the room with the smelling salts. She had taken every precaution to keep the older woman from suffering a complete collapse.

She awoke and saw Miss Anna by her side. "Anna? What happened? Did we win?"

Miss Anna, with the smelling salts in her hand, came close to her old friend and said, "I'm sorry, but Mr. Roosevelt is in for the third term."

The portly woman sat up in bed. With her chins up in the air and her nose higher than ever, she said, "Anna! Anna! We'll just act like it never happened."

And to her dying day she never discussed it with anyone. She never acknowledged the fact that Mr. Roosevelt was in office. She just acted as though it never happened. Her heart kept right on beating and not a nerve in her body was affected.

This is one of the greatest lessons I have ever learned. Never a week goes by, believe me, without something happening that could upset me terribly. I could go into a thousand pieces. When you deal with human lives as I do, it is the hardest work in the world. Believe me! But over and over again I have done what that portly woman did. I have said to myself, "Kathryn, just act as though it never happened." It's one of the best ways in the world to accept hurt and disappointment.

Sure, it doesn't change the condition or the circumstances. But I become master over that thing rather than having it master me. It's just like that!

Do you want to know something? A healthy, wholesome mind is better than silver, better than gold, better than all the material blessings in the world. It's the truth. An undivided mind—a mind void of fear, anxiety, worry, pettiness—a mind free from jealousy, selfishness, envy—is one's greatest possession outside one's salvation.

As a man thinketh, so is he. Hold in mind that nothing you fear is as bad as the fear itself. If you keep that mind intact, if you keep the center of your life intact, then you can come back from anything. But if your mind is filled with worry, fear, jealousy, pettiness, littleness—you'll be knocked down and defeated by happenings whether they are real or imaginary.

What's the answer? How can you overcome this condition? The answer lies in fastening your attention not on the thing to be feared, not in the circumstances or the situation around you, not on individuals or personalities—but on Christ.

Remember, you are His. He will defend you. He will protect you. You are His and He claims you *now* against all adversaries. You are His and no one else can have power over you. You are His and therefore you should trust Him with complete confidence today, tomorrow, and until that last day when your redemption is perfected and you stand in His glorious presence.

Wonderful Jesus, give me a mind that is free from fear, free from worry, free from jealousy. Give me a healthy mind, for this is my greatest possession outside of my salvation. For Jesus' sake I ask it. Amen!

20

Success and Enthusiasm

I beseech you therefore, brethren, by the mercies of God, that ye present your bodies a living sacrifice, holy, acceptable unto God, which is your reasonable service. (Rom. 12:1)
I can do all things through Christ which strengtheneth me. (Phil. 4:13)

Nobody enjoys being a Christian more than I. That's right. I enjoy it. I enjoy my salvation. I enjoy being born again. I enjoy this Christian living. I wouldn't exchange it for anything in the world. That's the truth. If I thought there was something better I'd go after it. If I knew of anything better, I'd tell you about it. But there isn't anything better, believe me.

Yet sometimes I find God's children so lacking in enthusiasm. I honestly believe we have given the skeptics cause to make much of the idea that God is dead. An awful lot of Christians are going around as though they were at God's funeral . . . in mourning every day . . . black veils . . . long faces . . . all leaving the impression that perhaps God actually did die.

That always gets to me. Look at the crowds in the baseball stadium. Even when the Pirates are losing, the Pittsburgh fans yell and scream for their team. Talk about enthusiasm!

Why do God's children so often show less enthusiasm than sports fans? We've got something to get excited about. We're on the winning side. Our team will never be defeated. Beloved, we've got something to rejoice about and shout about. A Christian armed with the Word of God and the person and power of the Holy Spirit is fully equipped for victory. He can do far more than one who is not born again can do with all the tools, machinery, and organizations combined.

Can you see why I'm enthusiastic about this business of being a Christian?

A noted executive who started from scratch flatly asserts: "The man who reaches the top is the one who's not content with doing just what is required of him. He does more." This is one of the basic laws of success, and you cannot get around it.

The man who'll go that second mile, the man who'll give more than is expected of him—is the man who succeeds. Enthusiasm and success go hand in hand.

When you have a job to do—do it with enthusiasm and do it well.

I guess I am a perfectionist when it comes to doing things for God. I can't help it. I want things done as near perfect as possible. I want every letter that goes out of my office to be as near perfect as possible. When you get a letter from me, I promise you it's the best I can do, because that letter doesn't represent Kathryn Kuhlman, it represents the One whom I serve—Jesus Christ, the Son of the living God.

You know, if some of the folk who are doing such a sloppy job for the Lord were to do the same kind of sloppy job for their employer— they'd no longer be employed.

Many years ago I had a printing job that needed to be done. I sent it to a printer in Pittsburgh. When I saw the finished material, I was aghast. The imperfections were almost unforgivable. I called the printer and asked him to please come back and pick up his work. I couldn't accept it.

Do you know what he said? He said, "Well, Miss Kuhlman, I figured that since yours is a religious organization, the people wouldn't notice a few mistakes."

I said, "Sir, you wouldn't think of doing a poor job for Mr. Harris of the Ice Capades. You know he would have demanded perfection, and you would have given him a perfect job. I represent something that's greater than the Ice Capades. You may not look on it as such, but this workmanship as it's sent out represents the greatest company in the world—a corporation of three: the Father, the Son, and the Holy Spirit. And I want perfection for them."

I believe that. I don't think we should give Him anything less than our best. You and I have no right to give Him anything less than we would give our employer. That's right. When God gives you a job to do, do it with enthusiasm and do it well.

Jesus didn't give a part of himself on the cross. He gave it all. He didn't spare a thing. And if you want to be a successful Christian, if you want to be all that God wants you to be, then, beloved, it means you're going to have to give yourself completely and entirely to Him. "Present your bodies a living sacrifice," Paul says. This and this alone is a "reasonable service." Jesus asks our all, our best, because He gave His all—His best.

You see, there are certain laws that govern success. If you're living a defeated Christian life, you can be sure it's not part of God's plan for you. God wants you to succeed. He has given you everything you need to live daily a successful Christian life.

I would have been defeated. I would have been snowed under a long time ago if I'd had to live my whole Christian life in just one day. If I had known at the age of sixteen what I would have to go through before I reached this stage of my life, I would have said, "I can't do it. I'll never make it." But that's not the way one lives the Christian life.

A man who emerged from obscurity at the age of forty to become one of the great wizards of mass production reminds us that nothing is especially hard if divided into small jobs. That's the secret of living a successful Christian life, too. God has promised us strength, but only for one day at a time.

"As thy days, so shall thy strength be," Moses told Asher. Yes, no matter what the day holds: if it's sorrow, He'll be the glorious strengthener; if death comes, He'll give you grace; if you're faced with temptations, all you have to do in that moment is call on the name of the Lord. He'll give you the victory.

You and I can conquer anything. I don't care how big the job, if it's divided into small jobs, it can be done. All of us can live victoriously and gloriously through Christ who strengthens us.

Dear Jesus, thanks a million for your blessed promises of victory. Teach us your Word and fill us with your Holy Spirit so we might do all things through your strength. In your blessed name I pray. Amen!

21

Going Under the Power

I had just returned from lunch and was met by three men who were waiting for me in my office on the sixth floor of the Carlton House in Pittsburgh. I recognized two of them as prominent Presbyterian ministers in the city. They introduced the third man as a professor of theology from a well-known theological seminary in the East.

"My friend said he had heard of you and your miracle services," one of the ministers said. "He wanted to stop by and meet you before leaving town."

I welcomed him and showed him through our offices. We went back into our recording studio where we make the tapes for our radio programs, and then I gave him copies of some of our literature. As we walked back into the front offices, the professor got up enough courage to ask a question which obviously had been bothering him.

"Miss Kuhlman, even though I teach theology, there is still a great deal I don't know about the ministry of the Holy Spirit. In particular, there is one facet of your ministry which leaves me completely baffled."

"Well, ask me. Chances are I don't understand it either."

"Well, it's about all this fainting. I understand from my friends that in your meetings you often pray for people and they . . . they . . . sort of . . . well, faint."

"Oh, no," I laughed. "They don't faint. They simply fall under the power of God." I gave him a brief explanation. He smiled politely but was still obviously puzzled. It was time for them to go.

We were standing in the doorway that leads from my office into the hall on the sixth floor of the hotel. He looked at me and said, "I may never see you again. Would you say a word of prayer for me?"

You know, I still think God has a sense of humor, for as I took a step toward him and extended my hand to place on his shoulder to pray for him, his legs suddenly buckled under him and he fell backwards to the floor. I didn't even have a chance to begin my prayer with "Dear Jesus" when suddenly he was on his back on the carpet in my office. And it was as though the whole room were filled with the glory of God.

I shook my head and looked down as both Presbyterian ministers dropped to their knees beside him. The secretaries at their typewriters had stopped typing, and I glanced up and saw their faces bathed in tears. There was a heavenly light filling the entire office suite.

The ministers helped the professor to his feet. He was wobbly, and staggered back a couple of steps.

One said, "Are you all right?"

He stuttered for words, and all he could say was "Wheew!" and down he went again, flat on his back on the carpet.

His friends helped him to his feet and he started out the door, still shaking his head with a glow on his face that must have been like the glow that was on the face of Moses when he returned from Mt. Sinai. "Wheew!" he kept saying over and over again.

He was staggering, as if drunk, and he missed the door and walked into the side of the wall. The ministers grabbed him by the arms and pointed him toward the door as he wobbled out, his face still bathed in that heavenly light.

I contend these physical bodies are not wired for so much power. One of these days, mortal will put on immortality, but here in the flesh we can take only so much of God's dynamite—and we short-circuit.

These old bodies of ours are still carnal. They are made of flesh. They are not geared for heaven. These fleshly bodies literally *cannot* stand in the presence of almighty God.

The only thing I can tell you is the power of the Holy Spirit is so great that our minds and bodies cannot fathom the bigness of God.

Most people are simply playing religion. They talk about God much like they talk about George Washington. They know he is (or was), but they never expect to see him and if he should appear it would literally scare them speechless. So it is with God. We talk about God. We talk about the Holy Spirit. But we seldom have an encounter with Him because it's all talk. When a person does come face to face with Him, it is too much for his physical body. His nervous system short-circuits momentarily, and down he goes.

God is alive. He's real. He is the very essence of power. He's not just the author of power, He *is* all power. Man often tries to conjure up God in his own image, shape, size, and power. But God is more—far more. When we see Him or feel Him as He really is, we simply can't stand it.

The only way I can tell you about "going under the power" is to say that when the Holy Spirit literally comes upon a person, he cannot stand in His presence. His legs buckle. His body goes limp. Oftentimes his very soul is filled to overflowing with the Spirit himself. It's not fainting. A person seldom loses his faculties. Usually those who go under the power are right back on their feet and testify that it was like being caught up in a giant charge of painless electricity—that momentarily leaves one out of control.

When you consider the Holy Spirit can heal a sick body without anyone touching that body—that's power. Therefore, isn't it logical to believe this body can stand only so much of that power before it is short-circuited?

Don't you remember what happened when Saul fell under the power, traveling to Damascus and falling to the earth? He was still able to talk. He was still able to think. He was still able to ask questions and make decisions. But he was unable to stand in the presence of the power of the Holy Spirit.

On the Mount of Transfiguration, a bright cloud overshadowed the three disciples who were standing next to Jesus. Then God spoke. "And when the disciples heard it, they fell on their face, and were sore afraid" (Matt. 17:6).

Whenever the Holy Spirit comes in great power, things like this happen.

The Holy Spirit now lives in every follower of Jesus—if they have invited Him in. And when He does come in, He brings the same power Jesus had. What He has done for me is not unique. God is no respecter of persons. Every minister, every lay person, has the same power. When people are slain in the Spirit, it is not me—it is the Holy Spirit. And He resides in each of you. Step out. Do not be afraid. And you, too, will see evidence of His mighty power.

22

Ambition

You know, I think I must have gotten a double dose of ambition when I was born. I think when God made me, He just forgot to stop when He started to pour in the ambition.

I remember the time when I was a kid in Concordia, Missouri. Concordia, you know, never had a population of more than 1,200. The year I was five, a high-powered salesman came to town and offered a pony to any youngster who could get fifty thousand wrappers of a certain brand of soap.

Oh, I begged and pleaded with mama. "I know if you'll just let me, I could sell fifty thousand bars of soap. I know it. Please let me. I want that pony so badly. I want it."

Population of 1,200. Five years of age, and I knew I could sell 50,000 bars of soap to get a pony. Talk about ambition! I had it.

But it takes more than ambition. It takes determination. And plain hard work. Believe me.

You know, it's a funny thing about this kind of ambition. From exactly the same materials one man builds a palace while another builds a hovel. That's the thing that always has amazed me. There can be two children in the same family. They have the same mother, same father, same advantages, eat the same food. They get the same attention, the same training. Yet one can be a success and the other a failure.

I never cease to be amazed at the different ways people react to my sermons. One person can have his entire life changed by the power of God; another peson, hearing exactly the same words, can go out of the place not having experienced a thing.

The same holds true with life in America. We all have opportunities. There are those who will debate that with me, but beloved, anybody in America can be a success if he'll pay the price. I believe that. If you want to work, you can work, even if you have to create a job for yourself.

It's not easy. You get what you go after because you go after it to get it. And the same thing is true in the Christian life. The Christian life is not easy. I would be the greatest deceiver in the world if I told you it is. It's not a bed of roses. It costs you something. It has cost me everything. But I want you to know it has been worth the price. You never get something for nothing. I don't care who you are.

Even in the Christian life you'll never get God's

best, you'll never know the deep truths of His Word until you start digging down underneath the surface. There's where you're going to find the deep treasures. There's where you'll find the deep oil of the Holy Spirit.

The deeper you dig, the more you'll find. But you've got to *dig* to find it.

A man who rose from humble beginnings to amass one of the greatest fortunes of our times said, "I have succeeded, not because I had any more ability than people who have not succeeded, but because I applied myself harder. I stuck to it longer. I know plenty of people with more brains than I who have failed because they lacked application and determination."

Isn't that a dandy?

In our office hangs a little wooden plaque that the office employees gave me for Christmas. I like it. It says, "If it were easy, everybody would be doing it."

You'd be surprised if you walked into the offices of the Kathryn Kuhlman Foundation in the Carlton House in Pittsburgh. We took an apartment suite and converted it into office space. There's a little kitchen with a refrigerator and stove—all the comforts of home.

The other day I passed by the stove in that little kitchen. I was looking for something and happened to glance in the glass door of the oven. I thought I saw something. I opened the oven door and there was a pillow, a blanket, sheets, and towels. I couldn't believe it.

I said, "Girls, what in the world is this in the oven?" They finally told me. Sometimes the work load was so heavy, they stayed all night and slept in the office. Do you see what I mean? If it were easy, everybody would be doing it.

I'm not so foolish that I don't know there are those with far greater talent than I in the ministry. Many people are far more capable. I recognize it every day of my life. I do not profess to be a smart person, a brainy person, or even a talented person. I know myself better than you know me. But I'll tell you something. A long time ago, I determined that by the grace of God, if I was going to live a Christian life, it wasn't going to be halfheartedly.

I've never done anything in my life halfheartedly. I believe that had I not been a Christian, I would have been the worst sinner in the world. I would have tried everything. I don't believe something just because somebody says so. I have to try it for myself. I'm just like that.

I want you to know, though, when I decided to live for the Lord Jesus Christ, I made up my mind I was going to be the best Christian possible. I gave Him all there was of me. I closed my mind to everything else.

The Bible is everything to me. I eat it. I sleep it. I live it twenty-four hours a day. I confess I am not a very open-minded person. There are some things to which I refuse to open myself. I don't want to poison my mind with the things that are not spiritual or not of God. I don't want to be clogged up with things that are impure and displeasing to Him.

This thing of living a Christian life costs plenty. It has cost me everything. But it's worth the cost, and I would do it again ten thousand times. I don't mind reaching for the highest prize. I'll never settle for anything less than the best God has for me.

Precious Jesus, help us to remain dissatisfied with everything that falls short of perfection. May we always press toward the mark for the prize of the high calling of God in you. Amen.

23

Laziness

Today we are going to have one of the most practical heart-to-heart talks that I know anything about. Of course you understand, the Bible is practical. This thing of living a Christian life is the most practical thing in the world. The laws of God make sense. They are practical. It's just like that.

A former employee of the Peter Loftus Corporation happened to pass my desk one day and just threw a little booklet on my desk and said, "Here, Miss Kuhlman, read this." I picked it up. I enjoy reading small things. Big books sometimes overwhelm me.

The first thing I saw was the word "gumption." Well, I am all for that, believe me. I have believed in gumption even before I knew what gumption meant. I didn't know what it was, but I sure had a lot of it (and still do).

"Anyone can wish for success," it stated, "but it

takes gumption to do the things that make success possible."

I stopped right there and I thought, "If that isn't the truth!"

Not only is this true in a big corporation—it's true in the Christian life. There are literally thousands of God's precious children who have done nothing the past ten years but just sit and wish.

There is something I don't care for, and that's a rocking chair. You may like rocking chairs. But I don't like rocking chairs, for there is something about a rocking chair that I associate with laziness. I've seen Aunt Litty in Missouri (that was Grandpa Walkenhorst's second wife) sitting in that rocking chair. She was so big and fat, and she rocked, and she rocked. Mama always said Aunt Litty was the worst cook when she cooked. But she never got much time to cook because she rocked most of the time. Mama said Aunt Litty was the worst housekeeper she ever saw. But that's because she didn't take time to clean the house. She had to rock all the time. You came to Aunt Litty's house at ten o'clock in the morning, she was in her rocking chair. You came to Aunt Litty's house at three o'clock in the afternoon, she was still rocking. She'd just sit there by the hour, wishing. Wishing the work would get done. Wishing the washing was over with. Wishing that she didn't have to get grandpa's meal. Wishing she had what the neighbors had. Rocking and wishing.

I guess that's the reason that to this day I don't like rocking chairs. I've seen so many of God's precious children afflicted with this spirit of laziness. They wish God would do something for them. They wish God would heal their bodies. They wish God would meet their needs. They wish they could have, spiritually, what other people talk about. But they never receive because they are slothful.

You don't get things from God that way. You've got to get yourself out of that rocking chair. You've got to put feet to your wishes. You've got to have gumption. You've got to do something about your dreams—or they'll never come true.

That's what Jesus meant when He said, "Ask and ye shall receive." Some have never asked. "Knock and it shall be opened unto you." There are those who have never even knocked. "Seek and ye shall find." Some have never sought.

If you only knew the potentialities in your own life—the potential you have in Christ Jesus. If you only knew. If you this very moment, sitting there in defeat, despair, and despondency, could only see the great power plant to achieve that is sitting idle in your soul, waiting for you to throw the switch. If you only knew what you could be in Christ Jesus. But laziness robs you of success.

I'd still be in Missouri, my friend, I'd still be one of those 1,200 people that make up the population of Concordia, Missouri, if I'd let laziness possess me like it did Aunt Litty. I would have married one of those Missouri farmers. Can't you just see me out milking cows? Can't you just see me out there in the henhouse, gathering the eggs? Oh, dear me! But it's the truth. I would have still been in Missouri, married to a Missouri farmer, if as a teenaged girl I had not determined God had something for me to do. And I did something about it.

I still believe there is more for me as an individual. If only I knew how better to cooperate with the Holy Spirit. If only I knew how to connect with the power of God. If only I had the divine wisdom.

This very moment you may feel that you are rich in the things of God. And you are. You may feel as though you have gone places in Christ Jesus. And you have. But—every person has much more ability than he tries to get out of himself. You have greater potentiality for God than you ever dreamed possible. But you have not been willing to surrender yourself to that extent to Him, so that you might receive greater things from Him.

I believe that I shall live and either go up in the rapture, or die, not having received all that God has for me. I mean that. It's as I yield myself to Him, as I consecrate myself to Him, that He gets much more from me—and uses it for His glory.

I see people who are so unsteady. They are up one day, down the next. They'll never grow in

God that way. They'll never know heaven's best, never in a thousand years. This victory one hour, despondency the next hour. Oh, I know, you call it "temperament." But we use the word as a screen for our bad disposition, our moods, our laziness. We use it as a screen for our meanness. But when it comes right down to it, nothing really hides an ugly disposition.

You'll never grow spiritually if you are off-again-on-again with your consecration and your Christian living. Never. God can't use you. You'll never be a power. You'll never be the receiver of great blessings from the Lord. Oh, you say, Kathryn Kuhlman, go a little easy, a little slow.

All right. I'll give you the Scripture. The little book of James is loaded with wonderful jewels, priceless jewels.

But let him ask in faith, nothing wavering. (James 1:6)

Not up today and down tomorrow. Victory at ten o'clock in the morning, and by noon you have hit the bottom. No sir!

For he that wavereth is like a wave of the sea driven with the wind and tossed. For let not that man think that he shall receive any thing of the Lord. (James 1:6-7)

The off-again-on-again Christian never receives anything as long as he is wavering, as long as he stays on the fence, as long as he teeters one way or the other. Let not that man think that he shall receive anything from the Lord.

Just being ambitious is not enough. You must seriously and earnestly and enthusiastically back up your ambition with determination. I believe that. You know, I always will stop and listen to somebody who will say, "I know it's true, I can prove it. I can prove it with my own life." I stop and listen to that one.

I've seen some ambitious people who were never successful. They never got anyplace in life. Ambition must be backed with real, honest-to-goodness determination. The lazy man may make it into heaven, but he'll never amount to anything here on earth.

I never weary of talking about that room in Twin Falls, Idaho. I believe it was one of the most critical times in my life. I was no more than fifteen or sixteen years of age. I believe that was one of the greatest crises in my life. Young, inexperienced. But I had enough gumption to lick the whole world for God. Enthusiasm? Had I bottled up all the enthusiasm that was in my body and sold it in 5¢ capsules, I could have supplied every human being in the world. I mean that, oh, my goodness! Whew! You should have known me back then.

But beloved, it took more than gumption. It

took more than ambition. It took more than enthusiasm. It took determination—which is the opposite of laziness.

I remember that old blue bedspread in that rented room in Twin Falls. I remember that old worn-out carpet in that rented room. I remember those faded blue walls in that rented room. I didn't have the price of a meal. I remember it as though it were yesterday, when I walked the floor of that cheap rented room. Alone, yet literally clenching my fists with determination. I looked up beyond those faded blue walls, beyond that old ceiling where the plaster was coming down. I didn't close my eyes. I looked with my eyes wide open into the face of my wonderful Jesus, and I said, "I'll do it. I'll do it if I have to live on bread and water the rest of my life. I'll serve you. I'll preach the gospel. I'll win souls."

All laziness died that day—and was never resurrected. And that's why, with the grace of God, I am who I am today. It was not luck. Or influence. Or by being at the right place at the right time. It was just hard work—and God's providence.

A great combination!

24

Religion of Love

We live such false lives. Sometimes, when I think of it, I remember the spun sugar candy I used to get as a child when the fair came to Concordia. Oh, it was beautiful to look at. That wonderful, pink, cotton candy. "Oh, papa, I think it costs only a nickel. Please, papa, please!" The first thing I bought at the fair was cotton candy. But did you ever try to eat it? You get only a couple of grains of sugar. That's all there is to it. It looks so big and wonderful. You think, how in the world am I going to eat all this? But in five minutes it's all gone. And all you had was just a couple of grains of sugar.

You know, most living is like that. We live such cotton-candy lives, so empty, so useless, so meaningless. It's all such a big sham. It's hard to find people who are really genuine. Many people aren't sincere about anything—so unreliable, so untrustworthy. There are few people that you can say of them as papa used to say of some of his friends, "Their word is as good as their bond." Papa never signed a note in his life. When one of papa's friends came to borrow money he never asked them for anything. In those days, friends trusted each other. Today, though, we don't have a bond and we don't have a word. We don't have anything. It's like that.

You say, "Miss Kuhlman, are you a pessimistic person?" Oh, dear me, I don't have an ounce of pessimism in me. When God made me, He didn't put one ounce of pessimism in me. The clouds may be there, but I don't think about them. There may be things to be discouraged about, but so help me, I look beyond the discouragements. I was just born to be optimistic. But remember something, beloved— there are some things you have to face. We are a part of humanity. There are certain laws God has that govern success, and adherence to these laws spells success. Disobedience makes us a sham.

An awful lot depends on how you get up in the morning. A friend of mine once wrote:

Start out every morning with your mind firmly resolved to do your triple best—not just something that's good enough, not just your best, but your triple best. Without any let-up, without any excuse. And you'll zoom right past the dilly-dallier, the clock-watcher, the contented cow, the alibi artist, and the intended-to folks.

Every office has the alibi artist—the one who has an alibi for everything. I can think of a person right now who is ahead of his class when it comes to alibis. I don't care what it is. If I ask him, "Have you done it?" he'll answer, "I was going to, but. . . ." I've never quite figured out whether he can think that quickly on the spot, or whether he spends all his time thinking about what alibi he is going to use next.

Then there is the person who constantly watches the clock. "Oh, girls, thirty minutes more, then it will be time to go home." "Just fifteen minutes more, and we'll get out of here." Five minutes before time to leave, they are gone. You don't see hide nor hair of them again. The clock watchers. Rare is the person who is so involved in his work, enjoying it so much, that he forgets the clock. This is the person you have to touch on the shoulder and say, "Let's get out of here. It's past time." Yet that's the kind of fellow who is always promoted to the better position. That's the kind of person the world is looking for today. He's never without a job. I promise you that. He's the one who starts each day happy—living not for himself, but for others.

Mama had a little frame hanging in the dining room. When she died I brought it with me to Pittsburgh—the paper in the frame now yellowed with age. It's called "Guideposts to Success." It was mama's formula for life. This is what influenced me as a youngster. It stated, in part:

Go out of the way to please others. Be determined to be kind and helpful to everyone.

Be truthful.

Be optimistic, no matter what comes.

Make a great effort always to give somebody a lift whenever possible.

Radiate sunshine, hope, good will.

Scatter flowers as you go along.

Enjoy each day. Live the present to its utmost, and do not wait for tomorrow before you begin to enjoy these things. This is what opens wide the door to happiness.

We really make our own happiness when we come right down to it. If you want to really be happy, go out and do something nice for somebody else. If you do it with the right purpose in mind, if you do it without expecting anything in return, if you do it because you want to do it, you'll find happiness.

No doctor can prescribe a bigger better pep pill. You'll find yourself so glad, you'll find yourself so satisfied on the inside. Of course there are some folks who love being miserable. But if you want to be happy and feel good, do something kind for someone else.

There's a final item on mama's "Guideposts to Success" list.

You must believe in the religion of love. Love for everybody, everywhere, the rich and the poor, the learned and the unlearned, the well and the afflicted. That's the religion of love. It satisfies the heart. It's deep enough for the soul, and broad enough for the whole world and everybody.

Now that's exactly what the world needs today. A religion of love.

The religion of love is the religion of the Lord Jesus Christ. It's not a religion you can legislate. It's not something you can force upon men and women. There is only one true religion of love, and that's the religion of the Lord Jesus Christ. This kind of love is not a natural love, it is a love God has to impart. It's inside. It's His love. Remember:

You pass through this world but once. Any kindness you can show any human being, don't defer from it. Be thankful for each day. Get out of it all the good that you can, and give as much good as you can.

That's the religion of love.

25

Common Sense

What we need is some good old-fashioned common sense along with the Word of God. I can understand why God would put the anointing on a woman. Sometimes I think she has more courage than a carload of men.

In my case, I have a ministry that has stood the test of time. More than twenty-five years. I've given my life, literally, for what I believe. I've stayed with the Word of God. And that is the reason this ministry has the respect of all the denominational churches. Not long ago Charles Allen, who pastors the largest Methodist church in the United States, made an appointment with me in Houston, Texas. He said, "Kathryn Kuhlman, I want you to know you have a great responsibility. We Methodist men were not taught regarding the Holy Spirit in our seminaries. We're watching you very closely. You are one of our guides when it comes to the

Holy Spirit. We accept what you say regarding the Holy Spirit."

I have long recognized that responsibility. This ministry has the respect of the world. I expect to keep it that way. I cannot afford to go where there is fanaticism. I have too much at stake. I have a responsibility to God. I have a responsibility to the great High Priest. I have a responsibility to the Holy Spirit. I have a responsibility to men and women, and I'm going to keep that responsibility clean before God. I want Him to trust me.

You know, I think sometimes the world gets the idea the only people who believe in the power of God are senile women and men who are not too intelligent. We've brought this all on ourselves. Some of our actions, beloved, are not intelligent. All the screaming and carrying on. . . . Believe me, if I was being introduced to the Holy Spirit for the very first time in a meeting like that, I'd take for tall timbers and I'd never come back again. We need an old-fashioned baptism of good common sense.

The hour has come when we need some good old-fashioned teaching on the Holy Spirit. Spiritual ignorance is the worst kind of ignorance. I'm as Pentecostal as anybody who stands behind the pulpit. I've taken my stand before the whole world. I've taken my stand before millions. I've declared my position. I'm as Pentecostal as the Word of God. But I want nothing to do with fanaticism. I want nothing to do with the demonstrations of the flesh.

Much of our noise is a substitute for power. Noise isn't power. I once had an old Model T Ford. It was the noisiest thing on the road. I had it when I first started out in Idaho. If noise was power, that old Ford would have been the most powerful thing on the road. Some of the greatest manifestations of the Holy Spirit that I have ever seen in my life, some of the greatest miracles I have ever seen in my life, some of the greatest baptisms of the Holy Spirit I have ever witnessed in my life were so quiet and beautiful. When the Holy Spirit arrives, you want to take off your shoes in His holy presence. Some of the greatest baptisms of the Holy Spirit that I have ever witnessed in my life were so sacred and so beautiful that all you heard was the weeping of the ones witnessing that beautiful experience. When the Holy Spirit speaks, when the Holy Spirit gives utterance, it's sacred.

Again I say, don't be afraid of the Holy Spirit. I beg of you, if you're a minister, if you're a Catholic priest and you're just on the edges, don't be afraid of the Holy Spirit. Don't be afraid to trust Him. If Jesus could trust Him then surely you and I can trust the Holy Spirit.

Sometimes Christians get excited over newly discovered truth and get carried away in fanaticism. But I beg you to look beyond the noise and exuberance to the Holy God who still speaks in a quiet but all-powerful voice. Serve Him. Love Him. Follow Him. He will not let you down.

26

Eternal Security

This is the church's greatest hour. This is my greatest hour. This is your greatest hour. Believe me, I tell you the truth. This is our greatest hour. We're living in the hour of restoration.

There are many who admit to the baptism of the Holy Spirit, who've never been baptized in the Holy Spirit. Some think they have received the Holy Spirit because they speak in tongues. But that's all they have. Others think they have arrived because they've joined a charismatic organization or church. I've never joined any organization. Therefore nobody can kick me out. The only thing I've ever joined was the little Baptist church in Concordia, Missouri. But I'll tell you something, I've got the greatest board behind me that any person could possibly have. I have the Father, the Son, and the Holy Ghost.

We're living in the greatest hour of the church. For lack of a better word, we call it the charismatic movement. But it's more. He's about to rapture His church and the church is about to go up, and when it goes up, when it leaves this old world, it's going out as a perfect body. It's not going out in defeat. When His church, this beautiful gift that God, the Father, gave to His Son goes out, it is going out a perfect Bride.

Do you think for one moment that when the Bride of Christ goes up, do you think for one second that when the church goes up, that it's going to go as a defeated body? Not on your life. When the church goes up, it's going up with all the gifts, all the fruits of the Spirit restored in full. It's going out as a perfect Bride.

That's the reason in these last moments I refuse to let any reproach come upon His church. I refuse to let any reproach be brought upon the Holy Spirit. Not that He needs any defense, but He is so sacred to me. I've given my life for Him.

Most people don't understand, but I've given my whole life. That's all I know. That's all I've done. I've given my life for what I believe. And I'm not going to let a reproach be brought upon what we believe. There are some who profess to have been filled with the Holy Spirit. Oh, sure, you say, I've received the baptism of the Holy Spirit because I've spoken in tongues. And lest there be one who might misconstrue that statement, I've taken my stand before the whole world. Everybody knows where I stand when it comes to speaking in an unknown tongue. But beloved, I only believe in the speaking of an unknown tongue as the Holy Spirit gives utterance. And there are literally thousands and thousands in the great charismatic movement who have never become acquainted with the person of the Holy Spirit, only with His gifts. Their actions speak more loudly than their many testimonies.

The Word of God says, "For as many as are led by the Spirit of God . . . ." Do you really know what it means to be led by the Spirit of God? If one is being led, then that one follows. You ask how these miracles come to pass? They come to pass because I follow the Holy Spirit. He leads. I follow. I die a thousand deaths before I ever walk out on the platform or the stage, because I know how ordinary I am. I know that I have nothing. I'm completely dependent on the Holy Spirit. There is a place in Him, a death. But remember this: Kathryn Kuhlman does not have one thing that God won't give you if you'll pay the price. I don't care who you are. I don't care how ordinary you are. There's not one thing that I have received but what He'll give to you if you'll pay the price. It costs much, but it's worth the price. It'll cost you everything, absolutely everything.

There's a Scripture that few understand, and yet thousands of sermons have been preached on it: "Take up thy cross and follow me." Always remember the cross is a sign of death. And many a person has said, "My mother-in-law is my cross." Many a married woman feels her husband is her cross. But that cross on which Jesus died was His cross. It was not my cross, it was not your cross. That was His cross. Before He was ever nailed to it, however, something happened. In those hours before He dismissed His own spirit, He looked up and surrendered His will to the will of the Father.

When Jesus walked this earth, He was as much man as though He were not God. Sometimes we forget that. That's the reason He offered himself first of all through the Holy Spirit to be given. He knew He'd face Satan. He knew that. He knew He could not do it alone. He knew that by taking the form of flesh He would be as much man as though He were not God. He came in the flesh with a will separate and apart from the will of God. In exactly the same way that I have a will, a will of my own which is separate from the will of God, so Jesus had a will. And before He ever died on that cross, He looked up and surrendered His will to the will of the Father. The two wills became as one. "Not my will, but Thine be done," He prayed.

"If any man will follow me," He said, "let him take up his cross." There's a cross for you. There's a cross for me.

The greatest hour of my life was the moment Kathryn Kuhlman died. That was the greatest moment of my life. That's the reason you can talk about Kathryn Kuhlman, say anything you want to. I can read about Kathryn Kuhlman and as sure as God's on His throne, it's as though I'm reading about someone else. She died. And when she died, her will was yielded to the will of God.

So I wait for His leading, for His will. I fear no man. I fear not all the powers of hell. I fear only one thing, lest I be out of the will of God. But I'll never get out of His will as long as my own personal will remains surrendered to the will of God.

If, my friends, you've surrendered your will and two wills have become one, and you've taken up your cross to follow Him and you are following and He is leading and you've paid the price of death—beloved, you can't miss God's perfect will. For you have one constantly in position of great High Priest, ever living to make intercession for you and for me.

If you ever get to the place where you do not know God's perfect will, then don't do anything. Wait. Look up and say, "I don't know." Listen not to the voice of man. Be quiet. Some of you are never quiet enough so you could hear Him if He did speak. He was not in the thunder, He was not in much babbling. He was in the still small voice. The Holy Spirit, who knows the perfect will of the Son of the living God, makes intercession for us. Sometimes even praying through you.

The trouble is that ninety-nine percent of us want our will and not His will.

It's not that most Christians don't know the will of God. Rather, they come face to face with the will of God and shrink from it, saying, "It's too great a price to pay." Too many of us think of the will of God only in the sense of the ecstasy, the emotionalism that is connected with it. I believe in the ecstasy of it. I believe in the emotionalism of it. But when it comes to the real fundamentals of it, when it comes to the place where you love Him enough that you are willing to surrender your will to His will and you want His will, then it hurts. It isn't easy to die. Every person wants to live. And spiritual death is the hardest.

I believe in eternal security, but not in the same way that some may believe in it. I face the future unafraid. I have no fear of all hell and all the power of Satan. And I'll tell you exactly why. As long as I stay crucified, the Holy Spirit will defend me. I do not have to defend myself. When I hear one who stands behind the sacred desk defending himself, I smile and I know he's not dead. He's a very lively corpse. When the enemy shall come in like a flood, the Spirit of the Lord shall lift up a standard against him. As long as I stay crucified, as long as my will is yielded to the will of the Father and I am in His perfect will, I am safe. Secure. As long as I'm in His perfect will, I'm covered with the blood. I'm overshadowed with His love. He'll speak through my lips of clay. He'll take the yielded vessel and use it for His glory.

That's all He asks of you. Be a yielded vessel. He'll take your mind. He'll give the anointing. He will be your defense. Your security.

27

The Cost and the Love of God

There are four steps that lead up to a little landing where the door opens on the stage of Carnegie Auditorium, Northside, in Pittsburgh. There is a black doorknob on the door. I have walked up those four steps and have stood on that little landing with my hand on that black doorknob and Kathryn Kuhlman has died a thousand deaths on that one spot, because I knew that when I opened that door I would have to walk out on that stage, and I knew that sitting out there in that audience were people who had traveled hundreds of miles. People out there from every walk of life. People who had made sacrifices to be in that miracle service. There were people out there who had come because it was their last resort. The medical profession could do nothing more for them, and they had come saying, "This is the last resort. We'll go into one of those miracle services and we'll believe

God to answer prayer." I knew that sitting out there in that audience there would be a father who had taken off from work, who had come with his wife with a little child. They had tried everything. Perhaps it was cancer in the child's body, and that child was more precious to them than anything else in the world. They had come as a last resort bringing their child to God in prayer.

I knew as I stood on that last step with my hand on that black doorknob that there were people sitting out there in the audience who had come in great pain, making an almost insurmountable effort just to get there, and many, whether they had spoken it audibly or not, had said within themselves, "If I can just get there, I know I will be healed."

I have died a thousand deaths on that last step. Only God knows my thoughts and my feelings, and how often I have been tempted to turn and walk down those four steps. It would have been the easiest thing in the world to just run from it all, because Kathryn Kuhlman knows better than anyone else in the whole world that she of herself has no healing virtue—no healing power. And I know myself well. I, too, am human. I have my own weaknesses, my own failures. Standing on that top step I know that I have no power to heal. If my life depended on it, I could not heal a single person out there in that audience. Oh, the utter helplessness and the complete dependency on the power of the Holy Spirit! I wonder if any of you can really understand. I have died not once, not twice, not a half dozen times, but over and over and over again.

Each time the moment arrives, I compel myself to open that door and walk out on that platform. I go out smiling and walking very quickly. Many people have remarked about how rapidly I walk, whether it's from the wings of the great stage of the Shrine Auditorium or through that door of Carnegie Auditorium, or wherever else it may be. I am not aware of the fact that I am walking unusually quickly. I think I must do so spontaneously because I know that the very second I stand before that great audience, I am no longer Kathryn Kuhlman. The Holy Spirit takes that which I have totally relinquished to Him—myself. It is a yielded, pliable vessel of clay which I give to Him, through which He can work. It is just that simple. Nevertheless, I believe one of the most difficult of all lessons for any one of us to learn is how to yield one's self to the Holy Spirit. I know how difficult it has been for me, for I discovered a long time ago that the Holy Spirit is not a person or a power that I can *use*. This is the lesson which you, too, must learn. He requires the vessel and that is all I or any one of us can furnish.

In addressing you in this fashion, I am taking the lid off my heart and baring things to you that few people know and few will ever understand.

There is a place where one yields himself completely to God. When you give your entire being over to Him—your body, your mind, your lips, your voice, your consciousness—you become a completely yielded vessel and it is this that He uses to perform His mighty works.

The other day someone came into my office and said: "Kathryn Kuhlman, did you know that men of great influence in many of our leading denominational churches consider your ministry of the Holy Spirit one of the purest ministries today?" I responded automatically, "Oh, thank you. How nice of you to say that."

In a somewhat chagrined tone, this gentleman said, "Well, aren't you pleased, even thrilled? Don't you consider that a great compliment?"

I could only reply, "Oh, of course I am deeply appreciative. But you know, after one has gone through such sacrifice and stood entirely alone, after one has fought so long to remain completely yielded to the Holy Spirit, the trophy when it is finally given really doesn't mean very much. You have paid the price, and the price has been high. You have paid the cost, and the cost has been great, but you would do it again with joy were God to ask it of you."

There are those who say I have the gift of healing; there are those who say I have the gift of faith; however, I do not profess to have even one gift of the Spirit. I contend that if the Holy Spirit has so greatly honored an individual by entrusting to him a gift, if He has so willed to bestow any of His gifts upon a person, such a gift must be treated as a sacred thing. It must be treasured, not talked about, not boasted about, for it is a holy trust. It must be used carefully, wisely, discreetly, for along with the giving of that gift there comes an overwhelmingly great responsibility.

Many is the time I have stood on that top step with my hand on that black doorknob wishing He had called someone else instead of me. With the knowledge that He has given me of the Word, with the cognizance that He has given me of the powers that are, with that which He has endowed me there goes a responsibility so great that it almost overpowers me. It is so overwhelming that more than once I have envied the little woman on that Missouri farm who gathers the eggs from her little henhouse at the close of the day, who perhaps helps with the milking and takes care of her precious little family. I could so easily have been that farmer's wife in Missouri, had God not called me at the age of fourteen. The farmer's wife can go to bed at night, tired to be sure, but she rests well, and when the gray streak of dawn breaks she goes again about her daily duties. She has a responsibility to her family of course, but oh, beloved, the responsibility of one who has been called by God—the responsibility that goes with that with which He has entrusted such a one!

At the close of a miracle service when I walk off that platform, those who leave the service say almost enviously, "Miss Kuhlman must feel so well rewarded. Think of those who were healed today in that great miracle service."

But, beloved, I have walked off that platform seconds before thinking, "Did I yield myself completely to the Spirit today? Perhaps if I had known how better to cooperate with Him, another might have been healed. If only I had known how to better follow Him as He moved in that great audience, someone else might have been set free." That tremendous sense of responsibility is always with you. I am never from under it, never released from it.

The secret of those bodies healed in the miracle services is the power of the Holy Spirit and it is His power alone. The only part the servant plays, the only part that I play, is in yielding my body unto Him, and He works through that body in lifting up His only begotten Son. But the vessel must be wholly yielded if Jesus is to be lifted up, and herein lies the responsibility.

Thousands have marveled at the fact that I can go through a service which is at least four hours long and frequently six without stopping, continually on my feet, never once being seated. Yet at the end of four or five or six hours, I can walk off that stage just as refreshed as when I went on at the beginning of the service. Doctors have told me that from a medical standpoint it is impossible for any human body to take the punishment to which mine is subjected year in and year out. A medical man in Pittsburgh told me fifteen years ago that at the rate I was going then, my physical body could not last more than three years. Yet here I am, still going at the same pace seven days a week, twenty-four hours a day.

Not only do I walk off a platform fully refreshed after a very long service, but I feel as if I could turn around and do it all over again! The secret of it all is this: Kathryn Kuhlman has nothing to do with it: it is the power of the Holy Spirit. An hour under the anointing of the Spirit enables me to walk off that stage more rested in body and mind than when I first walked on the platform. There is infinite renewal for my own body as He fills this body with himself and His own Spirit.

There are those who inquire regarding the slaying power of the Holy Spirit. Quite honestly, I cannot answer these questions, for I neither yield or understand this power. I did not understand it, for example, when one Tuesday night some years ago a woman stood up and said, "Miss Kuhlman, last night I was healed when you were preaching."

I paused before I said to her, "You mean you were physically healed during the sermon?" She answered, "Yes." I questioned her closely from the platform and found that as I was preaching, a tumor had literally dissolved in her body. She said, "I was absolutely certain of my healing, and today my doctor confirmed it. He examined me and said, 'It's true. The tumor is no longer there.'"

So far as I can recollect, that was the first time in my ministry that anyone had ever been healed as he sat listening to me preach. Since that day, thousands have been healed just sitting in the auditorium. How can it be that someone just coming into a service, just sitting there, no one touching them, is healed? There is no healing line, there are no healing rites, but people just sitting there are suddenly completely healed of their afflictions or diseases. Explain it? All I can say by way of explanation is that the presence of the Holy Spirit is there to heal. He does not need me to lay hands on you or to touch you. I have no healing virtue in my hands or in my body. But the same Holy Spirit who performed those miracles through the body of Jesus as Jesus walked the earth is active today. Christ, as much man as though He were not God, knew that it was the Holy Spirit who doeth these works. Peter understood. He, too, acknowledged it was the Spirit of God who performeth miracles (Acts 10:38). And so today the Holy Spirit continues His healing work and it is He who heals those bodies out there in that great auditorium. Many of the sick are so far from me that I cannot even see them. They are strangers to me, but not to Him.

What God has done for me, He will do for you,

for He is no respecter of persons. There is not a minister called to preach the gospel but who can have the same power in his life and in his ministry. There is no lay person who cannot have what I have. It is my firm conviction that if God knows He can trust you, He will give you that which He feels you are sufficiently trustworthy to receive.

As for me, I still feel there is so much more yet to receive, and there is no one living today who is more hungry than I am for more. The greatest saint who ever lived failed to receive all that God had to give. I do not believe that anyone has ever learned how to surrender himself so absolutely that the Holy Spirit was able to do all He could do and was willing to do through that yielded vessel. There is more, and when we get home to glory and stand in His wonderful presence, we will be amazed to know how much more could have been ours if we had only learned more perfectly how to yield to Him.

There is something that I guard very carefully, because aside from my knowledge of being born again it is the greatest treasure I possess. It is something that cannot be adequately described in either spoken or printed word. It is something that is not of myself; but it is the most real thing I know anything about. It is my love for humanity.

This love is distinctly not of myself, but it is divine. "Hereby know we that we dwell in him,

128

and he in us, because he hath given us of his Spirit" (1 John 4:13). And by the power of the Spirit, His love is perfected in us as we yield ourselves to Him. To know His love in this way is a staggering experience which defies both description and imagination. I know that should I ever lose that love, I could no longer reach the souls of men and women, and I would never be effective in praying for sick bodies.

I only wish it were possible for me to really describe my feeling when I pray, let us say, for the father standing there with a child in his arms. I only wish I could tell you how I feel in the depths of my being. The father stands there with his baby in his arms, and at that moment I am completely unconscious of everyone else in that auditorium. There can be thousands in that vast audience, and yet for that moment, I am aware only of a strong man with a tiny child cradled in his arms. I know how gladly that young father would give his own life if only his baby girl or boy would be healed. I feel this with a flaming, consuming intensity—and at that moment I love completely. This is not human love, it is wholly divine. It is not natural love, it is entirely supernatural. It is not my love, for I am totally incapable of this all-encompassing, all-pervading compassion. This is the love of God.

At that moment, I would gladly give my own life to see that baby healed. For a second, there washes over me a feeling of complete helplessness. I, of myself, can do nothing, and how well I know it. I realize anew my utter dependence on the power of God, and then I begin to pray audibly, "Wonderful Jesus, please touch this child." But the prayer of my heart is one which no man can hear. Emanating from my innermost being, this silent prayer ascends to the Throne of Grace and only the Father and myself know the essence of my petition: "Father, please, if that child can live, I am willing and eager to pay the price with my own life." I have prayed that prayer not once, but a thousand times.

I stand there before a little woman, and what all the crowd sees is the small kerchief on her head. I cannot tell you how she is dressed. All I see are those tired, worn hands, very often twisted and distorted. I see the hard work, the sacrifice, and in that moment, although I may not see her face, I take those hands in mine and pray to God that she can feel the love that is in my heart. My audible prayer may be so simple; perhaps all I pray is, "Wonderful Jesus, forgive me for not knowing how to pray better," but while I am saying these words, there is that supernatural love—God's love—in my heart for that precious woman.

Just then I would gladly give my life if the heavenly Father in His great and tender mercy, if the wonderful compassion of our Savior, would just touch that body and relieve her of her suffering. Nobody except God knows what is inside of me when I pray that prayer of faith.

There is a man standing there, but I not only see him as one who is bound by alchoholism, I see more than that. I see the man that he could be when he is delivered from the power of sin.

People wonder why I sometimes ask certain questions before I pray. I ask this man, for example, "Do you have a family?" I do not ask merely to make conversation. I want to know who will be influenced when that man has been delivered from liquor, perhaps young boys, perhaps his own sons who think their dad is the greatest man in the world, yet are embarrassed and ashamed knowing that at any time he may come home under the influence of alcohol and the other kids will say sneeringly, "Is that your dad?"

I see perhaps a little wife who has prayed and prayed, only God knows how long. And many a time when a man has been delivered from liquor I know it is not *my* prayer that has been answered; it is the prayer of a wife who has prayed for years and years and at that precise moment during the service her prayers have been answered. Or it may be the prayers of a little girl for her father which are suddenly answered as that man is instantaneously set free.

No one knows my thoughts when I am praying my customary, simple prayer; no one knows that the one for whom I pray is surrounded not only by prayer but with an overwhelming love. I see him through the eyes of love. And my friend, if I should ever lose this love, my ministry will cease to be. A sinner may not understand what I am talking about. He may not understand the Bible. He may not understand God. He may not understand a miracle, but if he can feel my love for him and my love comes through, I can win him to the Lord Jesus Christ. For the love that he feels and what I am saying to him is actually the love of Jesus made manifest.

How often in a service there are those who do not understand English. They cannot understand what I am saying. They cannot understand a word of the sermon that was preached. But when the altar call is given, they accept Christ. They have recognized Him at last as their personal Savior. It wasn't what I said, it was what they felt—the presence and the power of the Holy Spirit, himself.

The other day a prominent businessman in Pittsburgh stopped me in the lobby of the Carlton House Hotel. "Miss Kuhlman," he said, "I have been wanting to tell you something for a long time, and now is my chance. I want you to know this: my mother is from the old country. She is Russian, and she can neither speak nor understand English. But," he went on, "my mother wouldn't miss one of your broadcasts for anything in the world. Every morning before I go to work I have to set our radio to the place on the dial where you will be coming on, and she waits for it. She knows the first strains of the music, and she knows this is Miss Kuhlman's broadcast. She hasn't missed one of your broadcasts for years, and yet, to this very day, she understands practically nothing that you say."

The gentleman speaking to me paused and then with a smile said, "But you know, she sits there for one full half hour and just weeps for thirty minutes. The tears of joy roll down her cheeks, and sometimes she will burst forth in the Russian language in praise and prayer. I say to her, 'Mom, you don't understand what Miss Kuhlman is saying. Why do you cry so?' And she replies to me in Russian, 'It is because I can feel the power of the Holy Spirit. It's all so wonderful. I couldn't live without her broadcasts.' "

Stretching out his hand to me, my friend in the hotel lobby grasped mine hard. "Frankly, Miss Kuhlman," he said in parting, "it has always been a mystery to the rest of us at home. However, thanks for what *we* don't understand, but mom does."

And now, beloved, I part with you praying that you may know the presence and the power of the Holy Spirit in your life. I leave you with these words: "Beloved, let us love one another: for love is of God; and every one that loveth is born of God, and knoweth God" (1 John 4:7). As for myself, when I no longer love as I do; when I can no longer love people into the kingdom; when my sermons are no longer backed by love; when I pray for the sick and no longer feel their heartache and their heartbreak and their suffering, then, my friend, I will never preach again.

28

Discipline and Desire

In one of our miracle services, at the altar call, I saw a precious gentleman come forward weeping like a child. I went over to him and I said, "Is this the very first time you have ever accepted Christ as your Savior?" He nodded his head.

"How old are you?"

"Seventy-eight."

"You have never, in all your life, ever done this? You have never accepted the Lord?"

"I knew nothing about it until a week ago when I came into a service."

Then, looking at me, the tears just streaming down his cheeks, he said, "Oh, I wish I had done this sooner."

It's wonderful when these older folks come to God, but how much more wonderful when the young, with a whole life before them, learn early.

The only way a child learns is through discipline. There is nothing worse than uncontrolled and undisciplined desires.

You know, there is a way of living that may be likened to a horse that lies down in a harness. He won't move. You can't get him to move. He refuses to move. He lies there. Then there is the other way which may be likened to the horse that runs free and breaks the harness and smashes everything. Papa had one of those. He never knew when that uncontrolled horse was going to break away from the harness and go down the road, thirty miles an hour. An uncontrolled and undisciplined horse.

But so also was the old Missouri mule papa had. When he didn't want to go, he wouldn't go. Sometimes he would be so balky he'd simply sit down in the harness. Papa had both extremes. One was just as bad as the other.

Abundant living has to find the poise between the two—between lying down and running away. It must find the constructive, but disciplined life. The disciplined life, the controlled life, is the life that goes in the middle of the road. It is neither the balky old Missouri mule that's lying down in a harness and won't go, nor the horse that's raring to go and will break away from his harness at any time and rush down the road, smashing everything that comes in its way.

Follow me a minute. Desires are the God-given forces of the personality. And as such, they are right. Without desires, life would stagnate. You cannot cure the ills of life by reducing life. You cannot get rid of your headache by getting rid of your head. The remedy of life is not less life, but more life. You must have enough inward life to master outer environment and circumstance. But if life is to be raised, it can only be raised through disciplined desire.

The desire itself is not a sin, is not wrong. But it must be disciplined. The only way to get rid of a desire is to replace it by a higher desire. Or to fasten the already existing desire upon higher ends and higher goals.

Desires are the driving forces. The driving forces cannot be taken out of life. If you take them out of a youngster's life, you defeat him before he ever gets started. But they must be redirected through discipline. They must be controlled. And there is nothing worse than uncontrolled and undisciplined desires.

That's exactly what's wrong with many of our teenagers today. They are running wild with undisciplined, uncontrolled desires. Yet how can one discipline and control the desires of teenagers, when their dads and mothers have never had their desires controlled and disciplined?

There you are. This is so serious, that literally one may be ruled and ruined by undisciplined desires.

A child, any child, will eat every piece of candy in that candy bag if he isn't stopped. He likes candy. You give a bag of candy to a youngster and he will eat every piece of candy in that bag, unless he's stopped. I would have eaten every cookie that ever came out of that oven when mama was baking cookies, unless she spanked my hands. The hotter they were, the better they tasted. I would have eaten those cookies until I got a stomach ache, had I not been disciplined.

One of the best things you can give your child is discipline when he is young.

I am not writing as a mother, for I have never been a mother. I can only share as one who has been a child.

As a child I was taught to wash dishes. I'm sure that mama would have far rather washed those dishes herself. It would have been much easier. I can remember that I had to wash dishes when I was so small that mama put the oven lid down off the range, put the dishpan on that lid, and I had to wash dishes. I had to set the table. There were just certain things I had to do in the kitchen as a child. I was never taught to cook. But I watched mama do it. As a child, I was given the laws of cooking. I was disciplined as a youngster. I had to work.

When my friend Eve died, the hardest battle I had to fight was walking into that kitchen. I had no part, no place, in that kitchen as long as Eve was with me. She took care of the kitchen. She was the queen in the kitchen. Why, bless you, since a child in those early days of my childhood, the kitchen played no part in my life. I was busy doing other things. I was preaching. I was on the public platform. I was in public life.

When I walked into the house for the very first time after Eve was gone, I never felt more defeated in my life than I did standing alone in that kitchen. The first thing I did—I'll admit something to you—I went to the refrigerator. I took every bit of food out of that refrigerator. I emptied it. I was so defeated. Every thing that even looked like food, I emptied out of that kitchen. And it remained that way for nearly a week. Then one day I looked myself directly in the face and I said, "Do you mean to tell me that you are so small that a little thing like that could defeat you?" I went out and bought groceries for the first time. I put food in that Frigidaire. I learned how to cook a good pot of coffee. I learned how to make good mashed potatoes. Then I conquered spareribs. I cooked my first ham. And do you know something? As I did it, my early training came back. It came back to me. It all came back to me. Bless you, I mastered the thing, and I tell you, I'm a pretty good cook today.

Why? "Train up a child in the way he should go, and when he is old he will not depart from it."

Desire and discipline had been matched.

29

Rich or Poor

Rich man, or poor man. You may be living in a little attic room, own not one stick of furniture, have not a copper cent in the bank; but if you can look up and know that the mighty God of this universe is your heavenly Father, then you have something all the money in the world cannot buy.

What could be more thrilling than learning that we had been remembered in a legacy? That riches beyond all our dreaming had been left at our disposal? Beloved, that is the believer's position exactly.

Jesus, in taking His departure, called His servants and delivered unto them His goods. That puts you in the center of the highest possible sphere of service. You are entrusted by the Lord with His most priceless possessions. You are charged with making the most of them during His absence on this earth. Ascending to the Father, victor over sin and death, He received a name which is above every name. It is His name which He has left us. "And whatsoever ye shall ask in my name, that will I do, that the Father may be glorified in the Son. If ye shall ask any thing in my name, I will do it" (John 14:13-14).

What a bequest! You are rich. You are His child. Perfect in life, triumphant in death, glorious in ascended splendor, coming again with great power and glory, occupying a position far above all the rule and authority and power and dominion—all that is given over to us. Think of it. "If ye shall ask any thing in my name, I *will* do it."

You talk about a family tree! Think of the spiritual family tree that is ours. The mighty God of the universe is our heavenly Father. Jesus Christ is joint heir with us. We are joint heirs with Him. We are rich. We are no longer poor.

There's more He left us in His legacy. "Peace I leave with you, my peace I give unto you: not as the world giveth, give I unto you. Let not your heart be troubled, neither let it be afraid" (John 14:27). Think of it. *His* peace is ours. That peace is as real as the air you breathe. It faded not under the shadow of the cross. It remained unaltered under the severest strain known to history. This tried and tested peace has been bequeathed to us—to you and to me. It's the peace that Paul spoke of which passes all understanding. It's ours.

Beloved, have you accepted this bequest? Are you living in the calm of its conscious possession? Is His peace your peace? If you have that peace, if you are enjoying that peace, you are rich. You are not poor. You may have a title deed to this whole world, and yet without that peace, you are poor. You may not have a copper cent, but with that peace of mind, you are rich. If you can lie down at night with that peace of mind, you are rich.

Then, He's left us His joy. "These things have I spoken unto you, that my joy might remain in you, and that your joy might be full" (John 15:11). Think of it. *My* joy, He says. The secret of the unfailing source of His joy in our hearts is His abiding presence in our lives. In His presence we enjoy this sweet sense of His love, we walk in obedience and in His perfect will, we bask in the smile of His approval and rejoice in the consciousness of His presence.

Do you want to know something? Happiness is outward, it is governed by circumstances. Happiness is ours only as our happenings warrant it. On the other hand, joy is personal. It is found deep down in the soul where circumstances and conditions and happenings cannot faze it.

Are you maintaining the relationship with Jesus, where in spite of persecutions, in spite of circumstances, in spite of trials, His joy is filling your cup to the fullest? Is it part of your inheritance? If you have that kind of joy, you are rich. Without that joy, you are poor. If all that you have is just happiness, then you are being controlled by circumstances, and you are poor. If you have joy, His joy, you are rich.

"In my Father's house are many mansions: if it were not so, I would have told you. I go to prepare a place for you. And if I go and prepare a place for you, I will come again, and receive you unto myself; that where I am, there ye may be also" (John 14:2-3).

Drawing His own closely about Him, with a depth of tenderness unsurpassed, the Master lay bare His heart. He revealed the provision that He had made for His own in His Father's house. His own heavenly home would be made over to them as their home. That is the height of His provision, the goal of His thought for His children. "That where I am, there ye may be also."

Do you have that hope in the future? If so, then you are rich. You may be living the finest home in America today, with servants and everything money can buy. Yet, without the glorious hope hope of the hereafter, you are poor.

On the other hand, even though you may live in one room, with threadbare furniture, if you have assurance of this glorious hope beyond the grave, then you are rich. Rich in the things that money cannot buy.

30

Luck

Last Saturday, sitting in my office, I had a few minutes to spare and casually picked up a newspaper. There was an interesting discussion regarding "luck." Do people make their own luck? Four people shared their opinions.

The first, a personnel officer, had this to say: "They influence their own luck by their attitude towards life. If a person is pessimistically inclined, bad fortune seems to follow."

The second was an ice cream vendor. "Up to a certain point, we do make our own luck, good or bad. Take me, for instance. I could be sitting back, brooding and doing absolutely nothing but complaining that luck is against me. But instead, I'm out selling ice cream on the streets, and I consider myself lucky to be able to do so."

The third person was a meat inspector. This was his idea: "First let me say there is no such thing as luck. Whatever success we attain we do it by our own ambition and efforts. People who say luck is against them are usually those who refuse to get off their seats."

The final opinion came from a retired postal employee. "Luck is something we are destined to have or not have. For example, one person with a lot of ability for reason of what we might call luck, cannot enhance his status, whereas someone else with less ability but lots of luck reaches the top."

This thing of luck has been discussed by practically everybody living. I have my own ideas. You have yours. Papa had his.

You see, mama was Swiss and papa was German. Papa used to say to me, "Baby, don't ever be jealous of anything anybody else has. No matter what it is. No matter what they have, never be jealous of that. Because if you work hard enough, you can have anything anybody else has." That was papa's philosophy. I was brought up on that.

"If you work hard enough. . . ." Believe me, my papa really worked. I was brought up as a little girl to work. I had to wash the dishes when I was so little that mama had to put the dishpan down on the oven door. I was brought up in an old-fashioned home where we worked. Everybody worked. That was papa's philosophy: work hard enough, and you can have anything in the world you want.

Since I have grown up, I have found out that

papa's philosophy doesn't really hold up. Work alone is not enough. I have seen some people work from five o'clock in the morning until the last ray of light. They work and work and work and yet they have never gotten ahead. They have no more at the end of the year than they had at the beginning. They will have no more at the end of next year than they had at the end of this year. It takes something more than just hard work to get ahead.

Consider with me for a few minutes. On the morning after the greatest fire in Chicago's history, the merchants were deciding what to do. A young man, whose store was still lying in smoldering ashes, turned to the men around him and said: "Gentlemen, on this spot I am going to build the world's greatest store." It seemed impossible. His whole world had crumbled and was now lying in smoldering ashes. All others could see was seeming defeat, but he had a vision. On that very spot today stands Marshall Fields, one of the greatest stores in the world.

Why? Because a young man's determination turned defeat and failure into victory. That was not luck. That did not just happen. It was a combination of work and determination.

Glenn Cunningham, the man who became the fastest human in a mile race, was so badly burned as a lad that the doctors said he would always be an invalid. They said he would never, never walk again. Bad luck, some said. The fire was in a little country schoolhouse in Elkhart, Kansas. The school had burned to the ground. Yet the young lad, horribly burned, gritted his teeth as he lay in the hospital bed, lips trembling and great tears brimming his eyes. He turned to his mother after the doctors had left the room and said, "But I *will* walk again! I tell you, I will walk again." Brushing away the tears, his little chin stuck out in determination, he continued: "I'll not only walk again, but I'll run. I'll not only run, but I'll be the world's fastest runner." That's what a little youngster said, lying there with third-degree burns over his entire body. It made no difference the doctors had just said he would never walk again, that he would spend the rest of his life in an invalid's chair. He had determination.

Ninety thousand people packed Madison Square Garden in New York City and screamed and applauded as Glenn Cunningham broke all records as the world's fastest human in a mile race. The boy who was destined to be an invalid turned that destiny into victory by sheer determination. Don't you tell me Glenn Cunningham's success was due to luck. He set about his own success by hard work, determination, and an undefeated spirit.

There, my friends, is a magic formula.

If you will turn to the Scriptures, you will find it outlined, described again and again, for the writers of the Holy Scriptures are the greatest writers who ever held a pen.

Here is a marvelous story I have always liked. I deals with Peter and John, a strangely assorted pair. One was always getting angry. He never had any control over himself. He is referred to as "a son of thunder." The other was an impetuous fisherman, a rough kind of fellow. Yet when the Holy Spirit invaded their lives, everything changed. One day, on their way to the temple to pray, they encountered a beggar with his dirty hands outstretched, begging for alms. He was lame from birth, with withered limbs. Every day friends carried him to the steps near the gate, coming back at night to carry him home. He sat there all day crying for alms. "Have mercy on me, give me some alms, alms." People dropped coins in his hands. But that did not solve his problem. His problem was not one of money, but of defeat.

Peter and John knew that giving him money would do him no good. They were not as enlightened as our government agencies. They did not believe that all you have to do is hand out something to everybody, and life will be sweet. No, they were just poor, simple fellows, watching the beggar. They noticed he did not even look up at the passing people. Peter, always first to speak, said to the beggar, "Look on us." But not being in the habit of looking up, he paid no attention. Again, Peter said to him, "Look on us." There was something of a command in his voice, an undefinable power that caused the beggar slowly and painfully to lift up his head. His weak, watery eyes met Peter's level gaze. He saw that Peter's weatherbeaten face was kindly yet strong. And there was a certain light—a light from within. In his eyes there was something the man had never seen before.

Then Peter spoke. "As you are now, so once was I. In the name of Jesus Christ of Nazareth, rise up and walk."

The beggar cried, "But I've been lame from my youth. I cannot walk." You know, sometimes people long in prison, though they think they hate their chains and pray for freedom, really do not want to be free.

Peter repeated his command, "In the name of Jesus of Nazareth, rise up and walk." Slowly the man reached out his hands. Peter took one hand, John the other. They pulled him to his feet, and the beggar rested his whole weight upon ankle bones that had never been used. A look of amazement, of joy and gladness, shone in his eyes. And the Word says, "He leaping up stood, and walked and entered with them into the temple, walking and leaping and praising God" (Acts 3:8).

Somebody, right now, reading this, has lived a life like that beggar—full of skepticism, refusing to believe that this thing can happen. You do not believe there is any such astonishing power in the universe, a power that can change defeat into victory. You say you are unlucky. You blame your own defeat on hard luck.

Beloved, there is a Christ who will turn your bad luck into victory. Right now, you can be healed. Rise and walk!

In Proverbs it says "Trust in the Lord with all thine heart; and lean not to thine own understanding. In all thy ways acknowledge him, and he shall direct thy paths" (Prov. 3:5-6).

Do you want a life of victory? There are three things to follow: hard work, determination, and wisdom. Not your wisdom. No. Lean not to your own understanding. It's *His* wisdom. In all thy ways acknowledge Him, and He shall direct thy path.

Are your life plans broken up? Then you can say, by God's grace, I'll make new and better ones.

Not by luck. By God's love.

31

Humility

When St. Augustine was asked the first of the Christian graces, he replied, "Humility."

When asked what he considered the second greatest Christian grace, he replied, "Humility."

He was then asked, "What do you consider the third greatest Christian grace?" he again replied, firmer than ever, "Humility!"

This thing of humility is grossly misunderstood. Yet I do not believe there is a harder lesson to learn than that of humility. It's the rarest of all the gifts, the hardest of all lessons.

We have gotten to the place where we feel that humility is a sign of weakness. My friend, humility is not a sign of weakness. It is not a weak and timid quality. It's a show of strength and maturity. Show me the virtue of humility, the greatest of all Christian graces in the life of a man or woman, and I will show you an individual who has great spiritual strength, and great spiritual security. Only the one who is spiritually secure can afford to be humble.

The first test of a truly great man or a truly great woman is humility. Humility is the solid foundation of all the other virtues.

Humility allows one to make a right estimate of oneself. Nothing is worse than the person who brags about his humility, the person who is always talking about his humility. So humble, yet so proud of it. Uh-huh.

Sometimes you feel like doing what the little girl did who took out her pin and punctured the toy balloon. Whoosh! You would just like to take a pin and puncture their spiritual pride. Only when all spiritual pride is out do you find a vessel yielded and flexible, and a vessel that God can use.

The Master himself said, "Learn of me, for I am meek and lowly in heart."

The more spiritual a person becomes, the more of Him he has in his life, the more he has of the Holy Spirit, the more yielded he is to the Spirit of the living God, the more consecrated he becomes, the closer to the Lord he gets, the more humble he becomes. It is not a sign of spiritual timidity; it's a sign of spiritual strength and spiritual security.

The day came when mighty Abraham said, "I have taken upon me to speak to the Lord, which am but dust and ashes." Abraham, seeing himself, had a right estimate of himself. He cried, "I am dust and ashes."

Today, if God spoke to one as He spoke to Abraham, giving mighty promises and covenants, such a man would become so puffed up, and so proud you couldn't get him inside of his coat jacket. The buttons would pop off, and he would go around saying, "Oh, look what God told me. Look what God promised me. Look what great covenants God has given to me and my seed." But not with Abraham. He said, "I am but dust and ashes."

Look at Moses. Look at the relationship Moses had with God. Look at the closeness Moses had, look at the favor Moses had with God. Yet Moses said to God, "Who am I, that I should go unto Pharaoh, and that I should bring forth an answer of peace?"

Look at Solomon. The wisest of all men, Solomon, still quoted even in today's courts. Yet Solomon said, "I am but a little child. I know not how to come out or come in."

That, my friend, is real wisdom. The more an individual knows, the more he realizes how little he knows. It's an ignorant person who feels he knows everything. It's an ignorant person who never takes advice. It's an ignorant person who cannot be told. The more one knows, the more he realizes how little he knows. That's the reason Solomon with all his knowledge said, "I am but a little child. I know not how to come out or to come in."

Look at David. In all the Psalms, one cannot find one place where David makes any mention whatsoever of killing Goliath. He left that for somebody else to tell. The spiritually secure individual, one with spiritual strength, doesn't have to go around blowing his own horn. No. He treads softly. He treads quietly. Knowing he is absolutely dependent on the power of God.

I still say this lesson of humility is the hardest of all lessons to learn, which is the reason it was the last lesson Jesus taught His disciples before going away.

You know the incident well. He had overheard the conversation of the disciples as to who would be the greatest in the kingdom. The Master very quietly girded himself with a towel—as a slave—and got down on His knees. He, as much God as though He were not man, the One who had all power in heaven and earth, washed the feet of His disciples. Then He said, "I have given you an example, that ye should do as I have done to you. Verily, verily, I say unto you, The servant is not greater than his lord; neither is he that is sent greater than he that sent him" (John 13:15-16).

Great men do not have to worry about monuments to leave behind. God never ordained that any one of His children should leave a great monument unto themselves after they were gone. The greatest monument a Christian can leave is having led some soul to the Lord Jesus Christ.

After Pentecost, Matthew took up a pen to write. But as he wrote, he kept Matthew out of sight completely. He called himself "the publican." Peter put himself down and lifted Jesus up. Luke would be "Dr. Luke" today, but you can't find Luke's name in the Gospel he wrote—much less his title. John kept undercover by saying, "the disciple whom Jesus loved." And Paul, the greatest of all saints, when speaking of himself said, "the least of the apostles, less than the least, the chiefest of sinners."

That, my friends, is humility.

32

Prejudice

Human weakness is as old as man, yet as current as today's newspaper. Man's intolerance of his fellows. Down through the ages this fault has darkened history's pages with hatred, feud, and war. Again today it threatens to wipe mankind off the the face of the earth. Our ignorance of others' aims or virtues, failure to discover them or refusal to tolerate them drive us to hate—and murder. Misunderstood long enough, people and nations become demons in our eyes, and we in theirs.

A faded clipping turned up the other day, pasted on a cue card. It was the theme of some speech, probably to a service club some forty or more years ago. Yet the message of an unknown writer is more timely today than it was before.

When you get to know a fellow, know his
joys and know his cares,
When you've come to understand the
burdens that he bears,
When you've learned the fight he's making
and the troubles in his way,
Then you'll find that he's different than you
thought him yesterday.
You find his faults are trivial, there's not so
much to blame
In the fellow that you jeered at when you
only knew his name.
You are quick to see the blemish in the
distant neighbor's style,
And you can point to all his errors, you may
even sneer at him awhile.
And your prejudices fatten and your hates
more violent grow,
As you talk about the failures of the man you
do not know.
But when drawn a little closer and your
hands and shoulders touch,
You find the traits you hated really don't
amount to much.
When you get to know a fellow, know his
every mood and whim,
You begin to find the texture of the splendid
side of him.
You begin to understand him, and you cease
to scoff and sneer,
For with understanding all these prejudices
disappear.

You begin to find his virtues, and his faults
you cease to tell,
For you seldom hate a fellow when you
know him very well.
When you get to know a fellow and you
understand his ways,
Then his faults won't really matter, for
you'll find a lot to praise.

I do not know who wrote those words, but
they are just as fresh as today's newspaper.

After I read those words the first time, I began
to think. Jesus uncovers our Father. He also
uncovers our brother. He lifts the veil from our
prejudiced eyes and lets us see the infinite
worthwhileness in every man of every race, of
every color, of every class. The Gentiles were not
problems to Jesus, they were possibilities.

All Christendom needs the baptism of the
Spirit of God. We need a fresh baptism of the love
of God in our hearts, to turn our religion into a
revelation of possibilities of people instead of into
something that bolsters our prejudices and
causes hatred in our hearts.

Christianity is a double revelation: of God, of
man. When Christianity does not show us man
the way God sees him, it is no longer
Christianity. We need a religious faith that
brings faith in people as well as in God. Every
Christian should pray and practice this prayer:

Dear God, help me this day to catch your vision of the infinite possibilities in all people. However overlaid by strange wrappings these possibilities may be, even though we do not understand, I pray that our love shall cover our misunderstandings. Help me to set out on the great adventure of bringing out those possibilities in all people. And perhaps as I do so, some of my own may be brought to light.

Dr. George W. Carver, the black saint and scientist, who has done more for the agriculture of the South than anyone living or dead, white or colored, wanted to be an artist until the teacher said, "George, your people need agriculture more than they need art." He put those brushes away in a trunk and did not look at them any more for a number of years. He lost himself in his people's need. Now he has unconsciously painted his image in the hearts of all of us. He forgot himself into greatness.

It's so easy to be small. Small in our ideas, small in our thinking, small in our religion, small in our attitude toward people, small in our love. I pray to God that we shall in this hour when it means so much, when so much is at stake, forget ourselves into greatness. We shall forget our prejudices into greatness. We shall forget, that we might be used of Him.

159

For me to live is Christ, and Christ is love.

Again this hour I am reminded of the words of Jesus, found in John 13:34-35: "A new commandment I give unto you, That ye love one another; as I have loved you, that ye also love one another. By this shall all men know that ye are my disciples, if ye have love one to another."

Did you give him a lift? He's a brother of man,
And bearing about all the burden he can.
Did you try to find out what he needed from you?
Or did you just leave him to baffle it through?
Do you know what it means to be losing the fight
When a lift just in time might set everything right?

Remember, you are God's child, and for you to live is Christ, and Christ is love.

33

Dungeons

This letter arrived in my morning mail:

Dear Miss Kuhlman,

All day I contemplated suicide because I cannot go on. I lost my dear mother who was 85 years old. I felt God had betrayed me. Now I have nothing to lean on.

She led a good life, the perfect example of a godly mother. Yet I wanted her for just a few years longer. My four sisters and myself lived with my mother. We sat with her constantly and kept her company, and now it is so hard having no part. I feel I cannot go on.

I am a business executive, but nothing matters now. Please pray that my faith may be restored. I need your help.

As I read that letter, I wanted very much to stand face to face with this man and tell him he was one of the most ungrateful persons I had ever heard from.

I too had a mother. No girl loved her mother more than I loved mine. Yet in that hospital in Kansas City, Missouri, when my mother took her last breath, I slipped to my knees by the side of her bed and I thanked my God for the years He had given mama to me. I thanked my God that in His tender mercy He so graciously took her without having her to suffer for years longer.

So I say to the letter writer, "Sir, thank God you had your mother those many years. You say she was eighty-five years old when she died. That's longer than most folk have their mothers. Be a man. Face the situation. Remember it's not what happens to you that's so important, it's what you do with that thing after it happens that determines the results."

Whether life grinds a man down or polishes him up depends on what he's made of. Any man, any woman can make any calamity in their life count for God and for good, if they will only use it.

Sure. We all have our sorrows. We all have our heartaches. We all have dungeons of various kinds. Sometimes it's hard to find grace in our dungeons. But God will give you that grace. God will give you that strength. All you have to do is ask for it.

Clifford Beers, once in an insane asylum, later wrote *A Mind That Found Itself*, and founded the National Commission for Mental Hygiene. The mentally upset today owe much to a man who himself was mentally upset.

Another man was set aside with a broken hip. While lying in bed day after day looking at the wallpaper, he conceived the idea of becoming a sketch artist. And he became a very successful one. He found grace in the dungeon.

A poet who failed on the very first night of a public reading felt the next day that everybody was pointing the finger of scorn at him. He went home, wrote his greatest inspirational poem on the ability to take it when you fail. That poem fell into the hands of a man in the hospital who had lost both his arms and feet. It so inspired him that he became a very successful public reader. All found grace in their dungeon.

Dr. Mary McCracken was totally crippled in her lower limbs from infantile paralysis. The medical colleges of America refused to allow her to take a medical course, saying she could never practice. What did she do? She went to China and took her medical training there. She stood at the top of her class at Peking Medical, then returned to the very city of Philadelphia where she had been refused a medical course, and began practicing medicine in an institution for crippled children.

Among the most beautiful of Paul's writings

are these lines: "This salutation is in my own hand. Remember, I am in prison. Grace be with you."

Oh, sure, you would have expected him to say, "I am in prison. God give me grace." But he didn't. He put it the other way. "I am in prison. Grace be with *you*. I have found grace in the dungeon. Not only grace, but enough and to spare. I pass it on to you."

No, it is not what happens to you that's so important. It's what you do with that thing after it happens that determines the result. And to the letter writer with the broken heart, I say, "Instead of contemplating suicide, you who have just lost your mother, go out and give comfort to another who needs that comfort."

For every hill I've had to climb,
For every stone that bruised my feet,
For all the blood and sweat and grime,
For blinding storms and burning heat,
My heart sings but a grateful song;
These were the things that made me strong.

For all the heartaches and the tears,
And all the anguish and the pain,
For gloomy days and fruitless years,
And for the hopes that I've lived in vain,
I do give thanks. For now I know
These were the things that helped me grow.

Tis not the softer things of life
Which stimulate man's will to strive,
But bleak adversity and strife
Do most to keep man's will alive.
O'er rose-strewn paths the weaklings creep,
But brave hearts dare to climb the steep.

34

What Money Won't Buy

A twelve-year-old boy enclosed a picture of his father with his letter. This is what he wrote:

Dear Miss Kuhlman,
Today is my dad's birthday. He said he would like a pair of bowling shoes. That's such an easy gift to give him. But instead of giving my dad what he asked for, I am praying that my heavenly Father will give my dad a birthday present—my dad's salvation. Because you see, Miss Kuhlman, I would rather have my dad give his heart to Jesus than anything else in the whole world. I am sending you a picture of my dad at work. One of these days, Miss Kuhlman, I hope soon, I can introduce him to you. He's great.
Danny.

A twelve-year-old boy. I looked at the picture of his father. His dad was a good looking man dressed in carpenter's coveralls. I can tell by looking at him he would be willing to work his fingers to the bone to earn some money to supply the needs for his young son. He thinks he's being a wonderful dad by paying for the food on the table, buying shoes for the lad's feet, clothes for his body, providing a good home for him, a good bed to sleep in—everything that money can buy.

But here is a dad who is missing the mark. He is only looking through eyes that have a dollar and cent value on them. His twelve-year-old son has far more wisdom: "My dad . . . would like a pair of bowling shoes. That's such an easy gift to give."

It's easy because it's something money can buy. But what this lad wants for his father is something that all the money in the world cannot buy.

Poor is the man who has only money. Poor is the man who can see only through eyes of money.

I'm not belittling the fact that money is essential. It is. But the day has come when even the church counts its blessings in materialistic things—dollars and cents.

Money is a good servant, but a mighty poor master. Money never made a man happy. Nor will it. There is nothing in its nature to produce happiness. The more a man has, the more he wants. Instead of filling a vacuum, it makes one. If it satisfies one want, it doubles and triples that want in other ways. Money has little value to its possessor, unless it also has value to others.

Consider something. Money and time are the heaviest burdens of life. The unhappiest of all mortals are those who have more of either than they know how to use.

Have you ever considered what money cannot buy? It can't buy the love of a twelve-year-old boy. It can buy popularity. It can buy attention. It can buy flattery. But it cannot buy a youngster's love.

It cannot buy the love of a good woman. The love of a good woman is not for sale.

Who can find a virtuous woman? For her price is far above rubies. (Prov. 31:10)

Money may buy you flattery of a younger woman. It may buy insincere affection. It may buy the attention of one who will feed your ego. But all the money in the world cannot buy the genuine, sincere, unselfish love of a good wife. And it's just like that.

Though you may be the richest person in the whole world, money cannot buy peace of mind. The older I grow, the more I value my peace of mind. To be able to come to the close of the day and have peace of mind is the greatest treasure in the world. It's priceless. To be able to lie down at night, close your eyes, and in those last moments before sleep overtakes you, have peace of mind, is life's greatest gift. To be able to awaken in the middle of the night and lie there in absolute stillness and have peace of mind is something money cannot buy.

But hear me. Most of all, the wealth of kings will not buy your way into heaven.

I have looked, as it were, in a dream, through the gates of heaven.
I stood, as it were, by an angel's side, who was there to guard the way.
And as I stood there, the spirit of a rich man came and tried to get admission with his money.
Money. It had bought him prestige. It had bought him political power.
It had bought him membership in the best clubs while on earth.
And he told the angel of his wealth, and the vast treasures he had gathered on earth.
But the angel only pointed to his gold and said, "Ha. We pave our streets with that stuff.
You have not enough to buy even a glimpse of heaven."
No, my friend, though you have the world's wealth, though you hold the title deed to this world,
It won't buy your way into heaven.

It takes the blood of Jesus Christ, God's Son. It's accessible to the poorest man, the poorest woman, who lives and breathes this hour.

35

Weakness Is No Excuse

I get so weary of hearing people say, over and over, "This is the way I was made. This is the way I was born. This is what I am. I am weak, and I can't help it. This is the way it's always going to be."

Hearing people's troubles is my life. I walk down the street, and I seldom get a half block before somebody has stopped me and begun to tell me their troubles. It's just like that. Invariably they place the blame for their difficulties, their failures, and their defeat on somebody else. How often they have made excuses for their sinning on their weakness. In conclusion they say, "This is my weak point. This is my weakness."

But why does it have to be your point of weakness? Why do you accept the idea you have to be weak at some point? God never built weakness into anybody. If weakness has developed, it is because we have developed it.

A man says "women" is his weakness. But God didn't put it there. His weakness for women was developed and encouraged by himself. Another says he has a weakness for liquor. Yet his weakness for liquor has developed because the man himself developed it.

A man sat in my office one day and actually said he had to steal. It was the greatest thrill of his life. He said he *had* to do it. Then he went on to excuse himself for this sin by saying that he was just weak along this line. God never built this weakness into this man. If this weakness for stealing has developed, it's because the man himself developed it since a young lad. Perhaps as the result of bad associations.

I want to tell you that there is a power, a power that is available whereby any man or woman can overcome their weaknesses. I have seen people whom I had written off as absolutely hopeless, who have become wonderful, efficient, reliable, and successful individuals. This is one's starting point: "If any man be in Christ, he is a new creature: old things are passed away; behold, all things are become new." It's there. Read it. In 2 Corinthians 5:17. And the authority comes from the most reliable Book ever written—it comes from God himself.

Without a doubt this is the greatest thought ever to occur in the human mind. Far greater than Descartes's "I think, therefore I am." It means that you and I can become new. All these old weaknesses, that have plagued us for years, can be done away with.

"Oh," somebody said, "she wants us to embrace religion." The strange thing is, that embracing religion isn't the solution. I mean that. Being a Presbyterian won't save you from sin. It may take the joy out of it, but it won't save you from sin. That is just the difficulty in many partly changed lives. The joy of the thing is gone. But the fact of sinning is not, it is still there.

To indulge in joyless sinning is no joy. You have just enough religion to make you miserable by your sinning, and not enough to make you masterful by our Savior. Then where is the snag? Is this the best that Christianity can bring? Some modern theologians frankly say yes. And they continue going around muttering "God have mercy upon us."

Suppose a child should go around the house and continually mutter, "Father, mother, have mercy on me. Please have mercy on me." Do you know something? That attitude would very effectively block the relationship between parent and child.

In exactly the same way, God doesn't want us to continually put the emphasis on our guilt, but rather upon His pardon, His goodness, His love, His forgiveness. Not upon me at all, but upon Him.

The definite transaction of conversion must take place. The attitude of repentance must come. It has to come, and come decisively. But it should lead us out of penance and into pardon, then that pardon leads us to fellowship, and that fellowship into joy. The joy of salvation. The gift of God has been accepted by the individual, and the one has become a new creature in Christ Jesus. Old things having passed away, and behold all things having become new. You are now reconciled to God. You have put off the old man. You may be conscious of your weakness, but you will be more conscious of the mighty power that is sustaining you. "I can do all things through Christ which strengtheneth me" (Phil. 4:13).

My friend, there is no defeat in those words. There is no place for weakness in that promise. "I can do all things." All. "Through Christ." And where does the strength come from? "Christ which strengtheneth me."

There are elements of strength behind the man, the woman, who accepts Christ as Savior, who overpowers, who overcomes all weaknesses all fears, and all defeat.

Remember to Whom you belong.

I am His, by Him created; I am His, by Him redeemed; I am twice His, by original right and by purchase; I am His, and He will defend me, He will correct me, He will make use of me, He will love me, He will delight in me. I am my beloved's, and no one else possesses either right or power over me, except according to His will. He is mine, and all that is mine is His. All my sin, all my weakness, all my condemnation, all my misery, all my fears, all my shortcomings, I give to Him. They are His. His strength is my strength, His righteousness my righteousness, His wisdom, His holiness, His salvation, and His God is my God. His Father is my Father. His brethren my brethren. And His heaven my home. For I belong to Him, and He is mine.

36

My First Healing

I had the most perfect father a girl ever had. In my eyes papa could do no wrong. He was my ideal.

He never spanked me. He never had to. All he had to do was get a certain look on his face. Mama wouldn't hesitate to punish me when I needed it. But papa punished by letting me know I had hurt him—and that hurt worse than any of my mother's spankings.

When I was a little girl I used to have terrible earaches. Mama would pour sweet oil in my ear and use all the home remedies she knew. But the thing that eased the pain best was for papa to stay home from work, take me on his lap in the rocking chair and let me lay my aching ear on his shoulder.

My father, Joe Kuhlman, was mayor of the little town of Concordia, Missouri. He had been a farmer, but later moved into town. And that's where I was born, the third of their four children.

When I was fourteen I was born again in the Methodist church (mama's church) and was baptized in water in the Baptist church (papa's church). Two years later I was called to preach.

My first preaching experiences were in Idaho. I went from community to community, sometimes having to hitchhike. I would find an empty building, advertise the services, set up benches, and the people would come—strictly out of curiosity to see a red-headed, teenage girl preacher. If I found an abandoned church building, I would ask around until I found out who owned it, then request permission to hold services.

Usually my congregation consisted of a handful of Idaho farmers whose only reason for letting me use the church was that they couldn't pay a regular preacher. I sometimes slept in somebody's guest room or perhaps a small rented room that I had found myself. And once when there was no other place to go, I slept in a turkey house while holding nightly meetings in a deserted church located at the crossroads of a little country community. But I was full of enthusiasm and felt I could lick the world for God.

My only regret was that my father had never heard me preach. I yearned for the day when papa could be in the audience and see his daughter behind the pulpit. That would be a great day.

It was a whole year before I managed a trip home; travel was expensive and I needed every penny to buy handbills and newspaper space. I spent a few wonderful summer days with my parents and my younger sister who was still at home.

Then I was off again. By December I had reached Colorado. It was my second Christmas away from the family, but invitations to speak had started coming and I couldn't stop now. My first services in Denver were in an empty store building on Champa Street and I had arranged with the lumber company to furnish the material for benches. Mrs. Holmquist, who owned the St. Francis Hotel, rented me room 416 for $4 a week.

It was there at 4:30 P.M. on the Tuesday after Christmas that the phone rang. I recognized the voice on the other end as an old friend from home. "Kathryn, your father has been hurt. He's been in an accident."

"Hurt—bad?"

"Yes," she said.

"Tell papa I'm leaving right now. I'm coming home."

I had bought an old V-8 Ford and I threw a few things into the back and started out. Only God knows how fast I drove on those icy roads, but all I could think about was my father. Papa was waiting for me. Papa knew I was coming.

The weather got worse as I drove out of Colorado into Kansas. The roads were covered with ice and drifting snow, but I didn't stop to eat or rest.

One hundred miles from Kansas City I stopped at a telephone station beside the deserted highway and called ahead. My Aunt Belle answered.

I said, "This is Kathryn. Tell papa I'm almost home."

"But, Kathryn," Aunt Belle said in a shocked voice, "didn't they tell you?"

"Tell me what?" I said, feeling my heart begin to pound madly in my chest.

"Your father was killed. He was hit by a car driven by a college student who was home for the holidays. He died almost instantly."

I was stunned. I tried to speak but no words came out. My teeth were chattering wildly and my hands shaking as I stood in that forlorn phone booth, surrounded by the swirling snow. I can only remember the biting wind freezing the tears on my cheeks as I stumbled back to my old car and resumed my trip homeward.

I've got to get there, I thought. *Maybe it isn't true.*

The next miles were like a nightmare. The highway was a glare of ice. Mine was the only car on the road. Night fell and my headlights shone back at me from a wall of blinding white. I was crying, trying to hold the car on the glassy road.

Papa can't be dead. It's just a bad dream. If I ignore it, it will go away.

But it didn't go away. When I arrived home, my

father's body was in an open casket in the front room of our big white frame house on Main Street. I sat in the bedroom upstairs alone, refusing to go in and look at him. I could hear the soft shuffle of feet on the front porch and the whispered talk around the house.

I was afraid that if I went in there and saw papa's body, I would suddenly have to face the reality of his death. I felt if I awakened from this bad dream and found it was all true, my whole world would come to an end.

And I was struggling with another feeling. Hate. It surged in me like a volcano and to everyone who came into the room I spewed out venom toward the young man who had taken the life of my father. I had always been such a happy person. Papa had made me happy. But now he was gone and in his place were these dark strangers of fear and hate.

Then there came the day of the funeral. Sitting there in the front row of the little Baptist church, I still refused to accept my father's death. It couldn't be. My papa, so full of love for his "baby," so tender and gentle, it couldn't be that he was gone.

After the sermon, the townspeople left their pews and solemnly walked down the aisle to gaze one last time into the casket. Then they were gone. The church was empty except for the family and attendants.

One by one my family rose from their seats

and filed by the coffin. Mama. My two sisters. My brother. Only I was left in the pew.

The funeral director walked over and said, "Kathryn, would you like to see your father before I close the casket?"

Suddenly I was standing at the front of the church, looking down—my eyes fixed not on papa's face, but on his shoulder, that shoulder on which I had so often leaned. I remembered the last conversation we had had. We were in the back yard, last summer. He was standing beside the clothes line, reaching up with his hand on the wire. "Baby," he said, "when you were a little girl, remember how you used to snuggle your head on my shoulder and say, 'Papa, give me a nickel'?"

I nodded. "And you always did."

"Because it was what you asked for. But, baby, you could have asked for my last dollar and I would have given you that too."

"I reached over and gently put my hand on that shoulder in the casket. And as I did, something happened. All that my fingers caressed was a suit of clothes. Not just the black wool coat, but everything that box contained was simply something discarded, loved once, laid aside now. Papa wasn't there.

Even though I had been preaching for a year and a half, that was the very first time the power of the risen, resurrected Christ had come through to me. Suddenly I was no longer afraid of death; and as my fear disappeared, so did my hate. It was my first real healing experience.

Papa wasn't dead. He was alive. There was no longer any need to fear or hate.

Numerous times I've been back to the little cemetery in Concordia where they buried the body of my father. There are no tears. This is no grief. There is no heartache, for that morning in church I knew the Apostle Paul's words to be true: "To be absent from the body is to be present with the Lord" (2 Cor. 5:8).

That was many years ago. Since then I have been able to stand at the open grave with countless others and share the hope that lives in me. There have been mountain tops across those years, opportunities for travel and ministry and preaching. But, you know, growth has come not on the mountain tops but in the valleys.

This was the first valley, the deepest, the one that meant most. When I walk offstage today, after hours of confronting sickness and need in every form, I go back to the dressing room. And often at that moment I have a strange feeling. I feel that papa is there. He never heard me preach, in earthly form, but I know he knows that his girl is trying to do a good job for the Lord. And he knows that now I constantly lay my head on the shoulder of the heavenly Father, knowing I can claim all the blessings of heaven through Jesus Christ.

(Editor's note: "My First Healing" is copied from *Guideposts* Magazine, June, 1971.)

37

After Death—What?

Man is a trinity consisting of body, soul, and spirit.

It's hard for us to understand this unique aspect of man. The trinity of man may be likened to the trinity of a peach. The flesh of a peach is the part we eat. Peaches are often thought of only in terms of the meat, or flesh, that part which we eat, can, and put on our cereal in the morning. But a peach is also the stone. And the peach is also the kernel. The peach is a trinity: flesh, stone, and kernel.

The kernel is not the stone, neither is the stone the flesh. What the flesh is to the peach, so is the human body to man. Each of us has a human body. But inside this body of flesh resides a soul. What the stone is to the peach, so is the soul to man. The Bible also teaches, however, that the soul is not the spirit. Each is separate and apart from the other. What the kernel is to the stone, so is the spirit to the soul.

Remove the flesh of the peach, and the kernel still has a body: the stone.

This soulish body of man can hear, speak, think, feel, and remember—therefore it must have a tangible form. Just as I am as much myself when I am stripped of my clothing as when I have my clothing on, so I am just as much myself as when I am stripped of my fleshly body. Even after the soul has left the body, and the body is placed in the earth, I remain myself forever. My flesh dies—my soul and spirit live on forever.

Let me make something so clear there will be no confusion in your mind whatsoever. At the time of physical death, the child of God goes right on living. If you know Jesus Christ and His saving power, then you are an heir of God and joint heir with Jesus. The greatest inheritance, the greatest possession, the greatest treasure any man can possess is eternal life with Christ. If death comes to that one this very moment, immediately the soul and the spirit of that one goes all the way from earth to be in the presence of the Lord. Two-thirds of that one leaves the body instantly. Only one-third is left here on earth. Just as the flesh of the peach is left, so the body of that one is left.

"To be absent from the body is to be present with the Lord," Paul said in 2 Corinthians 5:8. That happens instantly when the old heart takes its last beat.

Right now, while I'm talking to you, if my own

heart should cease to beat, and life goes out of my body, that second, even before my body slumps in the chair where I'm sitting, my soul and my spirit in that split second will be in the presence of the King whom I love and adore and serve, yet have not seen. When you hear Kathryn Kuhlman has died, don't believe it. Since I'm born again, I shall be in His presence. I shall see Him. Only one part shall remain on earth—my body. That which will be placed in the casket is only the flesh of the peach. And when they place my body in the grave, that will be all of me that will be placed there—the real me lives on.

No, beloved, the soul does not sleep. The spirit does not sleep. All on earth that's placed in that open grave is just the body. You can never place me, not the real me, that part of me which is eternal, that soul, that spirit, in a tomb. I will never be buried. Death cannot touch me. Fire cannot destroy me. Only my flesh will be placed in that grave. And even that part shall await the glorious resurrection morning when it shall be reunited with the real me.

As long as I'm still in this body of flesh I am susceptible to sickness, disease, sorrow, and heartbreak. It's a body of corruption. It is a mortal body. But one of these days it shall no longer be a vile body. It shall be changed from corruption to incorruption. It shall be changed from mortal to immortal. It shall be raised, not as a vile body, but as a body fashioned like unto His body, the body of our wonderful Jesus.

We thrill to the glorious fact that our sins are covered with the blood. But my redemption will never be perfected until that day when that which is now corruption, that which is now mortal, shall be raised in incorruption and immortality. One day I shall stand in His glorious presence, with a glorious new body. When the trump of the Lord shall sound and the dead in Christ shall rise first, and those which are still alive shall be caught up to meet Him in the air, so shall I ever be with Him.

Those who have gone before are not lost, not separated from us permanently. One of these days I'm going to see papa again. One of these days I'm going to see mama again. One of these days I'm going to be with my loved ones.

I won't exchange that glorious hope for a title deed to all the world. My place in heaven is prepared. My hope is secure. I'm ready to go—I'll see you on the other side.